AGENT BRIDE

BY
BEVERLY LONG

Published in Great Britain 2015
by Mills & Boon, an imprint of Harlequin (UK) Limited,
Eton House, 18-24 Paradise Road, Richmond, Surrey, TW9 1SR

© 2015 Beverly R. Long

ISBN: 978-0-263-25327-6

46-1215

Harlequin (UK) Limited's policy is to use papers that are natural, renewable and recyclable products and made from wood grown in sustainable forests. The logging and manufacturing processes conform to the legal environmental regulations of the country of origin.

Printed and bound in Spain
by CPI, Barcelona

Beverly Long enjoys the opportunity to write her own stories. She has both a bachelor's and a master's degree in business and more than twenty years of experience as a human resources director. She considers her books to be a great success if they compel the reader to stay up way past their bedtime. Beverly loves to hear from readers. Visit www.beverlylong.com, or like her at facebook.com/beverlylong.romance.

For Brynn and Eric, who both made the leap from
college kid to adult look easy.
Hope you're having fun in Missouri!

Chapter One

Cal Hollister rarely let anything stop him. And that included the weather. But when the freezing rain in the upper plains had turned to snow, then more snow, making the I-70 corridor a real mess, even he'd had to admit it was time to take a break.

Now, an hour east of Kansas City, Missouri, he'd filled up both his gas tank and his belly. He sat back in the tattered booth of Dawson's Diner and watched the television that was mounted in the corner of the truck stop. It was on mute and the words flashed across the screen. *Early winter storm paralyzes Midwest.*

Cal stopped reading, just as he'd turned off the radio in his rental car earlier. It was all they were talking about. The storm, the storm, the storm.

Missouri rarely got heavy snow and to get it in November was real news. He didn't care. He wasn't going to let a little ice and snow stop him.

He was going home. Back to Ravesville. The idea had taken root after Cal had talked to his brother last month and learned that Chase was getting the old house they'd inherited from their mother ready to sell.

Chase hadn't asked for help. He never did. Especially not from Cal. But it was time for that to change. Cal had finished his assignment and put plans in motion to get back to the States. It had taken a month but finally, he was a mere hundred miles northwest of his destination, more than three weeks early for Thanksgiving dinner.

"All finished?" the waitress asked as she passed the booth.

"That was amazing," Cal said. The woman had encouraged him to get the daily special, the roast pork, especially if he was pressed for time. He didn't have a schedule but he'd gone along with the suggestion.

She smiled. "I know. People are always surprised. They don't expect a place like this to have a chef. Pietro worked for years at Moldaire College in a high-end restaurant in their student union. He's always talking about how he used to cater all the important events at the college, even the private parties that the president of the college hosted." She picked up the dirty dishes. "Can I get you anything else? Maybe a piece of apple pie?"

"I'm stuffed but because I suspect it will be every bit as good as that roast pork, I'll take it to go."

"Good choice," she said. She walked over to the pie case, opened the door, slid a piece into a cardboard box, and brought it and a plastic fork back to the table.

Cal pulled out a twenty. "Keep the change, Lena," he said, looking at her name tag. She looked tired. Hell of a job slinging hash.

But at least she had a job.

Which was more than Cal had at the moment.

No job. No expectations to live up to. No one else's timetable to adhere to. It was a heady feeling for a man who'd spent eight years in Uncle Sam's employ as a Navy SEAL and the past six months as a contractor doing much the same kind of work at a considerably higher rate of pay.

"What are they saying about the roads?" he asked. He'd seen Lena chatting with two state police officers at the counter.

"It's bad and supposed to get a whole lot worse. Interstate is still open but there's lots of spinouts and cars in the ditch."

About what he'd expected. First bad storm always resulted in a bunch of fender benders as people relearned their winter math—that speed plus following too close equaled crap-on-a-stick.

He scooted to the end of the booth, stood up and stretched. "Well, wish me luck," he said.

She shook her head. "You're like all the other crazies around here today. There was a heck of a commotion in the parking lot right before you came in. People running around, slamming doors and carrying on. They cleared out fast when my friends at the counter, who never miss an opportunity for apple pie, pulled their squad cars into the lot. Probably couldn't wait to get out on the road and kill themselves."

That was a happy thought. He was grateful he'd missed the excitement. He'd had plenty recently. It had been less than two weeks ago that he'd barely missed getting up close and personal with enemy fire.

"Anyway, for what it's worth," she added, "there's a hotel about five miles east. They might still have a room."

He winked at her and smiled. Then he pulled his coat collar up and walked out the door. The cold wind hit him hard.

Crazy. Maybe. But Lena had no idea the number

of truly outrageous things he'd done. And usually in the name of protecting national security or preserving American interests.

The hotel might have been a good option if he was continuing on the Interstate. He would be turning off before that, for the final leg of his journey. The two-lane highway that would take him into Ravesville would likely be in worse shape than the Interstate but he had another hour of daylight left and he intended to make good use of that.

If everything went well, he'd be at the house in a couple hours. He thought about calling ahead but disregarded the idea. While Chase would intuitively know that the weather was a mere inconvenience to any former Navy SEAL, he still would worry.

Chase had always taken his big-brother role seriously. They were going to finally have a talk about that. The conversation Cal had been running from for years.

It took Cal ten minutes to brush the snow off his SUV. When he was finally back inside his rented Escalade, it was nice and warm. He pulled out of the parking lot.

The plows had gone through at some point but another couple inches had fallen after that. But he settled in, going a brisk thirty-five miles per hour. Two miles east, he took the exit, realized he'd been right that the secondary roads were in worse shape. It was somewhat reassuring to see wide tracks in the fresh snow. Somebody driving a big truck had made the same turn within the past ten minutes.

The wind was really whipping up the snow. It wasn't white-out conditions but damn close. Which was why he thought he was seeing things.

He checked his rearview mirror, didn't see any other cars and risked pulling over to the side. He got out, leaving his vehicle running.

Three feet off the road, something had hit the fresh snow, denting its whipped perfection. The object had rolled several more feet before stopping, forward progression halted by a study wooden fence that was likely there to keep cattle in.

He could hardly believe his eyes. There was a woman in a bridal gown and nothing else, no coat, no shoes, just a long veil, which was what had caught his attention. It was flapping in the breeze like a wayward flag.

She was on her side, turned away from him.

He figured she had to be dead.

SHE WAS SO COLD. Had never been so cold. And her head hurt. But she had to keep going. Had to get up. Get away.

She forced herself to move and heard a man swear. Suddenly there were hands on her. She had to fight.

No. No. She could not go back.

Felt a hand on her neck. She swung an arm, a leg. Knocked into something.

"Hey," he said. He pulled on her shoulder, flipping her to her back.

It hurt to open her eyes. The man was big and dark and he loomed over her.

She screamed and knew that no one was going to hear her. No one was going to help her. Just like before.

"How the hell did you get here?" he asked. But he didn't seem inclined to wait for an answer. She felt strong arms, one under her neck, the other under her knees, and she was swung up into the air.

He held her close, pulled tight against his coat.

And he started walking.

She tried to struggle, to force him to loosen his grip. But it was as if his arms were bands of iron. And her arms and legs felt heavy, useless.

She was dying. She knew it.

She closed her eyes and waited for it.

She felt him shift her weight. Suddenly, she was standing. She needed to run. Go. Now.

So tired.

Took one step. Saw the vehicle. Saw the door that he'd just opened.

"Get in," he said.

When she didn't move, he scooped her up again and deposited her into the warm, the heavenly warm, SUV. He shut the door. Within seconds he was climbing into the driver's side.

He was big and snow-covered and for one crazy minute, she could only think of the Abominable Snowman. But then he was moving, reaching a long arm into the backseat. She heard the sound of a zipper.

He had a big gray T-shirt in his hand. Suddenly, he was rubbing her face, her arms, brushing snow off. It was piling up on the floor, by her feet. He flipped the heater on high and more of the delicious heat poured from the vents.

His hands stilled suddenly. She looked down. He was staring at her left wrist. Saw his gaze move swiftly to her right arm. She looked, too. They matched. Both wrists sported a wide reddish band of skin.

And she remembered pulling, pulling with all her might. And being so angry.

"What happened here?" he asked, his words sharp.

She didn't answer. Just stared at him.

He hesitated, then reached into the backseat again. Pulled out another T-shirt, this one white and long-sleeved, and some gray sweatpants. "We've got to get you out of that wet dress," he said.

What?

She looked down. Saw what she was wearing and felt her heart start to race in her cold body.

How had this happened?

"Are you injured?" he asked.

Huh? He had evidently easily gotten past that she was wearing a wedding gown but she was having trouble moving on.

A wedding gown. She lifted her hand, touched the satin fabric, noting, rather dispassionately, that it was dirty in several places. Her hand started to tremble.

The man reached his own hand out, caught her fingers. "You're shaking," he said.

"Cold," she said. She had been. For sure. But that wasn't why she was shaking. Her body felt odd. As if she was on edge, just this close to spiraling out of control. At the same time, she felt nauseous, as if maybe she'd drunk too much and gotten too little sleep.

She turned her head to look at him. To try to offer up some sort of explanation.

"You're bleeding," he said, his cadence quick. "I didn't see that earlier." He leaned toward her and, with surprisingly gentle hands, prodded the right side of her head, just above her ear, with the tips of his fingers. She heard him hiss.

"You've got a hell of a knot here," he said. "But just a small slice in the skin. It's already stopped bleeding."

She reached up. Their hands connected and she

could feel his barely contained energy. His skin was warm. Vibrant.

He pulled his hand away. She continued to press and realized there was something on her head. A veil. Pinned tight into her hair.

She started yanking bobby pins and tossing them onto the floor. One bounced off the dash. She pulled and pulled. When the veil was loose, she ripped it off her head.

The man was staring at her, his hazel eyes assessing.

She reached up, pulled down the visor and stared into the mirror. Terror seized her, making her want to throw up.

Think. You need to think.

But it was as if all coherent thoughts had deserted her.

She started to shake. Badly. Not just her fingers or her hands. Her whole body.

And the man moved suddenly. Using both hands, he pulled the dry T-shirt over her head, stuffed both arms in. Pushed her forward in the seat, so that he could reach around her back. She felt him release the zipper of the dress. Felt him unclasp her bra.

Then he was pulling down her dress, her strapless bra, and lowering the T-shirt at the same time, preserving her modesty. His touch was quick, impersonal, but she felt the intimacy of it. She shook his hands off.

If she didn't do this, he would.

She pulled the T-shirt down. It came to her thighs. Then she yanked on the wet, heavy wedding dress. When she had it off, she handed it to him. He tossed it into the backseat. She pulled on the sweatpants, cinching the tie strings as tight as she could. When he handed her thick white socks, she put those on, too. She was drowning in his clothes but it felt absolutely wonderful to be warm and dry.

"I'm not sure where the nearest hospital is," he said, "but I think our safest bet is to head back to the Interstate."

Hospital? She grabbed his arm. "No."

He stared at her. "What the hell is going on here?"

She had no idea. All she knew was that she couldn't go to a hospital. Couldn't go anywhere.

They would find her.

"What's your name?" he asked.

She didn't answer. Couldn't trust this man with the truth.

He waited.

"What's your name?" he asked again.

"Mary. Mary Smith."

He narrowed his eyes at her. "I don't think so."

She said nothing.

"How about I just call you…" He paused. Then looked forward, into the blowing snow. "Stormy," he finished. "That'll do."

"What's your name?" she asked quickly, desperately trying to shift his focus.

He seemed to hesitate for just a moment. "Cal. Cal Hollister." He put the car in gear, pulled back onto the highway and started driving.

"Where are we going?"

He didn't answer her.

He was taking her to the hospital. She just knew it. She had to get away. She reached for the door latch.

He was faster, stretching his arm across her body, blocking her hand. "Please. I would like to help you.

I just came from a diner where there were two cops. I think they may be your best bet."

The police. Again, she could feel her heart start to race. Why? She searched her mind, her terrifyingly empty mind, and tried to reason it out. Was she in trouble with the police? Was she running from the police?

"I just need a place to stay. To get some sleep," she said. "Can you just drop me off at a hotel?"

He waved his hand in a semicircle. "We're sort of in the middle of nowhere."

She could see that. Everywhere she looked there was snow. And it was getting dark.

"Will you drive me as far as the nearest town?" she asked. "I'll pay you. I promise. I mean, I don't have any money with me, but I'll send it. Just give me your address."

He stared at her, his eyes showing absolutely nothing. Was he about to kick her out of his car, thinking that she was going to be more trouble than she was worth?

"I won't be any inconvenience," she promised.

"There have to be people looking for you, worried about you. At the risk of stating the obvious, I think today might have been a big day for you."

Had she gotten married today?

She didn't think so. She'd know that. Deep down she would know. Right?

"I'll contact people once I get to the hotel," she said.

He reached into his pocket and pulled out a cell phone. Handed it to her.

Her arm felt as if it weighed eighty pounds when she reached to take it. Her fingers brushed against his.

Warm skin.

So different.

And a flash of a memory, jagged at the edges, in grays and blacks, like an old movie, jumped into her empty head. Cold hands. Wrapped around her upper arms. Pushing her. Cold, cold hands.

She closed her eyes. Willed it to come. But that was it.

"Please just take me to the nearest hotel." She put his phone down on the gearshift console. Maybe rest would help.

If it didn't, she didn't know what she was going to do.

Chapter Two

Under normal conditions, having a beautiful woman beg him to take her to a hotel was not an invitation that he needed to give much consideration to.

Hell, yes.

And if all went well, a half hour after they'd checked in, neither one of them would even remember it was snowing.

But there was nothing normal about this. The woman had been lying in the snow in a wedding dress. As he'd approached, he'd seen a slight movement in her arms and legs and had reached out to check for a pulse. She'd responded like a mad dog, throwing a punch and kicking her leg. Her movements had been uncoordinated, as if hypothermia was setting in.

While he had no formal medical training, every SEAL had the basics. He'd quickly sorted through the options. Moving someone before a full assessment was always a risk. But her extremities all seemed to be in working order, maybe a little jerky, a little awkward. He'd identified the cold as his biggest challenge, decided there was no time to waste and flipped her over to her back.

Then, even though her arm and leg hadn't connected

with anything vital, he'd been knocked back and just a little breathless.

She had a stunningly beautiful face. Dark hair. Very dark eyes, almost black. Rich, almond skin that hinted at an ethnicity that was more exotic than his own common German-Irish mix. Maybe from one of the Pacific Islands.

When she'd screamed, he'd gathered his lust-spiked wits and moved into action. He didn't think she'd been there long. Dressed as she was, it would have taken less than twenty minutes in these conditions—twenty-degree temps with a thirty-mile-an-hour wind—for her to be in real serious trouble.

He hadn't been confident that she could walk, so he'd carried her to the car. Once inside the vehicle, he'd been processing what to do next when he'd seen the marks around her wrists that looked suspiciously as if she'd been tied up.

It was possible that it had been consensual. What people did behind bedroom doors was nobody's business. But he'd spent the better part of the past decade in countries where men routinely mistreated women and he couldn't get the idea out of his mind. But when he'd asked, she'd stared at her wrists, as if it was the first time that she'd seen them, seen the damage.

Then he'd seen the small trickle of blood on the side of her face. He'd been very concerned when he'd felt the lump on her head, which he suspected she'd gotten from connecting with the fence post, and had been relieved when he'd seen that the cut itself was just a slice that would heal quickly.

He'd pushed aside his concern over her possible

mistreatment and dealt with the immediate need of getting her out of her wet clothes.

When he'd pulled the T-shirt over her head and lowered her dress, he'd done a quick inspection of the rest of her to assess for injuries. Had caught a glimpse of pretty breasts and smooth skin but no other significant bruises or red marks.

The wedding dress had been wet and heavy and, quite frankly, had knocked him off his stride.

And oddly enough, it had seemed to have a similar effect on her. She'd ripped the pins out of her veil as if she was attacking a nest of snakes with a garden hoe. Her wet dark hair, free of constraints, had fallen around her shoulders.

How had a bride ended up in the snowdrift? Where the hell was her husband?

When he'd picked her up, he'd made a visual inspection of the surrounding area. No footprints besides the ones he'd left. No sign of a vehicle, with the exception of the wide tire tracks on the road, but he was fairly confident that the truck hadn't stopped. There was no sign of heavy exhaust in the fresh snow that would have been there if a big truck had idled for any amount of time.

Was it possible that she'd fallen out of the truck while it was moving? That someone had pushed her out?

None of it made sense and she wasn't helping. She'd lied about her name. He was pretty sure about that. Had tried to let her know that he knew in a nice way by calling her Stormy instead. When she'd asked his name, he could have reciprocated and lied. He had a half-dozen different aliases that he'd gone by in the past years. Instead, he'd offered up the truth.

It might have been a mistake but he'd felt the need

that one of them should be honest. Why it was important, he wasn't sure. They were ships passing in a storm. He was offering a helping hand until she could reach out to someone else.

Which she didn't seem inclined to do. He'd expected her to look upon his cell phone as an unexpected lifeline but there didn't seem to be anybody she was interested in calling.

Odd. To say the least.

There were probably a couple choices. He could keep driving toward Ravesville and take her to the old house. But given that he didn't know her story, he wasn't inclined to want to do that. It was too great of a risk that he might be bringing trouble to his family, to Chase especially, and he was done with that.

He had enough guilt already.

He could disregard her instructions that she didn't need either a hospital or the police and drop her off at whichever he encountered first.

Or he could turn around, take her back to the Interstate, find the hotel that the waitress had said was just miles down the road and send her on her way.

That was probably the best option. Now that he'd gotten a closer look at her, he could see the fatigue that shadowed her eyes. He supposed it was a busy time leading up to a wedding.

Had she gotten cold feet? Was there a groom pacing the aisle in some church, at a loss to understand where his bride might be?

But it was a Tuesday. Cal didn't know much about weddings but he was fairly confident that they were usually on a Saturday. Maybe she was simply unconventional. Maybe she and/or the groom worked on the weekends. Maybe they got a better price on the reception if the event was on a weekday. Could be a hundred explanations.

She did not, however, look interested in offering up any of them. She was staring straight ahead, her arms wrapped around herself.

In all likelihood, he'd saved her life. It would be nice to know her name but not necessary. He wasn't the type to brag or dwell on past accomplishments and this, quite frankly, wasn't the first time he'd saved an unknown person's life. That was what SEALs did best. Save the good guys. Kill the bad guys.

He was going with the assumption that she was on the side of right and that he wasn't assisting the wrong person. That was what his gut told him and he'd learned to listen to it.

"Buckle your seat belt," he said. He checked his mirrors, slowed down and then made a narrow U-turn on the snow-covered highway.

"Where are we going?" she asked, her voice small.

"Back to the Interstate. There's a hotel a couple miles east. I'll drop you off there."

He turned on the radio. Maybe he'd try to get some information on the weather after all. It seemed as if the storm was picking up in intensity. It dawned on him that he hadn't cared as much when he'd only had himself to worry about. Now he was responsible for her.

It should have felt suffocating to a man who'd recently deliberately shed all his formal responsibilities. At least irritating that he'd been sucked back in so quickly.

But oddly enough, it felt okay.

"Don't worry," he said.

She said nothing for a long minute. Over the sound of the radio, he could hear the tires working hard to grab pavement.

Finally she turned to him. "Thank you," she said. "I owe you."

IT WAS TRUE. She owed this man her life. But as soon as she could, she was getting away from him. He was young, maybe not even thirty, but his hazel eyes seemed to hold knowledge beyond that. He had short dark brown hair in a buzz cut and his skin was very tanned.

The only time he'd really pushed for information had been when he'd asked her name. She'd had to tell him something. And he'd called her on the fact that he didn't think it was legitimate. Yet he was still willing to help her.

She wished she could accept that it was as simple as one human being extending a kindness to another. But something told her that she should trust no one. *No one*.

He was a good driver. His hands were relaxed on the steering wheel. She'd have been a nervous wreck.

She didn't like to drive in bad weather.

Didn't know how she knew this. Just knew it.

In less than five minutes, they were on the Interstate that he'd mentioned. She saw a sign. St. Louis, 194 miles.

St. Louis. She let that dance around in her head for a minute. "Joe Medwick. Ducky Medwick," she corrected.

He turned to stare at her. "What?"

"St. Louis Cardinals. He holds the record for most runs batted in during a single season. Late 1930s."

"Thirty-seven," he said, "1937." He paused, then added, "How the hell did you know that?"

She'd surprised him. Oddly enough, that made her want to smile. Nothing else that had happened up to this point had seemed to faze him but he looked absolutely flabbergasted that she knew baseball. "Sports trivia is not reserved for the male species," she said.

"Right," he said. He was silent for a long minute. "Motel should be just up the road." He paused again. "Have you eaten lately?"

She didn't feel hungry. "A little while ago," she said.

He nodded and kept driving. The SUV churned through the snow on the road, its tires slipping occasionally as they encountered patches of ice. They stayed on the road, however, which was more than she could say for the three cars they passed that were in the ditch.

It took them fifteen minutes to get to the hotel. He pulled into the lot and she stared at the building, trying to catch some feel for whether she'd ever been here before. She didn't think so.

It was a two-story wood building, painted mostly red with some white trim, with each room having an exterior door. She counted them. Eight up, eight down, with a small office at the front of the building. The parking lot was full of cars and had already been plowed at least once. There was a big white sign with blue lettering and a red border. The Daly American Inn. There was a flagpole and a flag near the front door. She wondered if someone had braved the elements that morning or perhaps they simply never took it down.

She stared at the flag, watched it flap in the wind, partially obscured by the flying snow. Something fluttered in her chest. "Oh," she said, putting a hand to her heart.

"Problem?" he asked.

She shook her head. What could she say? *Yes, plural but none that I can talk about.*

He took the space in front of the office. She gripped the door handle tight. "Like I said, I don't have any money on me."

He shrugged. "We'll worry about that once we know if they have a room. I'll go check."

It sounded as if he was willing to pay for it. Thank goodness. She would send him a check. Right away. She paid her debts. At least she thought she did.

He got out of the vehicle and snow blew in. It was really getting cold.

She watched him walk into the office. His dark down jacket came only to his waist. He wore jeans and cowboy boots and with his narrow hips and nice long legs, he was totally rocking the look.

It felt a little ridiculous that given the circumstances she had even noticed. But it was also oddly comforting, as if her subconscious was letting her know that everyday pleasures, even those as basic as admiring a sexy stride and a fine rear end, were not beyond her grasp.

The office was well lit and she could see a young man behind the desk. He was staring down at his cell phone, punching buttons. He looked up, evidently listening to whatever Cal was saying, and shook his head.

Her heart sank. She hadn't realized how much hope she'd had pinned on getting a room, having a place to rest. If that wasn't possible, she had no idea what she was going to do. Maybe they would at least let her sit in the office until…

Until what?

That was the great unknown.

She saw Cal reach into his pocket. Push something across the counter. Take the plastic key that the young man offered.

Hallelujah, it looked as if it was going to be okay.

When Cal returned to the vehicle, he handed her the plastic key. "You got the last room," he said.

"I was worried. I saw the clerk shaking his head."

"Just didn't understand what I was asking for."

It was perfect. She could sleep. For as long as it took. Then wake up and be able to deal with everything.

"How much do I owe you?" she asked. "I want to keep track."

"Rooms are eighty-nine bucks a night. You're in number fourteen. Second floor, two doors from the end."

"Perfect."

"How's the head?" he asked.

"Still hurts," she said honestly.

"Nauseous?" he asked.

She actually felt better than she had a half hour earlier. "No."

"Your pupils look normal," he said. "Which hopefully means that you don't have a concussion. But I'm still worried about that. You're sure that you're going to be able to call someone to help you?"

"Absolutely," she lied.

He drove the SUV to the corner of the building where her room was located and put the car in Park. He reached into the backseat and pulled out another pair of thick white socks. "Your feet are going to get wet walking in. Take these so you have something dry to change into."

He was a really nice guy. "Can I have your address?" she asked. "To mail you a check. For the hotel, and these," she said, waving at the clothes he'd given her.

He shook his head. "Don't worry about it. Pay it forward someday."

That was a nice idea. "Well," she said. It was crazy but she didn't like the idea of getting out of the car. She felt as if something bad was about to happen. But this man had done enough for her. There was nothing to be gained from stalling.

"Thank you," she said. She extended her hand.

There was a slight pause before he reached out and very formally shook her hand. His index finger had a callus and she resisted the urge to rub the pad of her thumb against it. "Good luck," he said.

She swallowed hard. Some good luck would be nice. She opened the door and got out. She went to close the door.

"Hey," he said. He pointed to the backseat. "Don't forget this."

Her wedding dress. She grabbed it and the horrible veil that had hurt her head and wadded them under her arm. She ran up the exterior staircase and inserted her key into the door. It opened. She turned.

He was still there. Watching.

She waved.

He nodded and pulled out of the parking spot.

She went inside, feeling strangely sad. She should be happy to be free of the man. She needed time to figure out what to do next and she needed to be totally focused. That would have been difficult if Cal Hollister had stuck around.

She sat down on the ugly green-and-gold bedspread and stared at the tan carpet. What the hell was she going to do?

CAL'S FRONT FENDER was edging out of the lot when he decided that he might be a fool but he didn't intend to be a hungry one. He still had the pie that he'd tossed into his backseat but it wouldn't hurt to have a backup supply of candy bars, chips and red licorice, his favorite, if he did happen to get stuck. And the hotel vending machine was probably his best bet.

He backed up, parked his SUV and went inside. The desk clerk, phone still in hand, looked up. Cal waved at him and pointed his index finger at the vending machine in the alcove off to the side. The kid smiled back. When Cal saw the prices, he realized the kid was probably laughing *at* him, not with him. It was practically highway robbery. But he started feeding in his dollar bills.

Stormy had seemed a little reluctant to get out of the car. And he'd had the craziest urge to want to keep talking to her. Maybe they could have traded baseball trivia. She'd surprised him with that one. Her eyes had lit up and he'd gotten a glimpse of what her face would look like without fatigue and cold clouding it.

He'd felt an attraction to her. And that, ultimately, had been what had kept him from chatting it up in the car. She was either someone's fiancé or someone's wife. Off-limits.

Just two years ago, he'd had to pick up the pieces when his best friend on the team had gotten a Dear Leo letter. Leo's wife had met someone and had filed divorce papers. Leo had gone a little crazy and Cal had been seriously worried that the man was going to make a mistake that could take the whole team down.

He didn't ever want to be in the middle of something like that. So he'd said goodbye to Stormy and accepted that how she came to be in that snowdrift, in her wedding gown, was going to be one of life's unanswered mysteries. When he'd checked in, he'd verified that there were phones in the room. Hopefully, by now she'd made her calls and help was either on the way or, at the very least, relieved to hear that she was okay.

He had just pressed the last button when the door opened. Two men, both wearing long black coats and dark pants, came in. The taller man had an ugly scar, running from the corner of his eye to halfway down his cheek.

Both men gave Cal a cursory look but focused on the desk clerk. "We are looking for our cousin," the taller one said. His tone was low, almost guttural, and he'd turned his back to Cal. But Cal, who had always had excellent hearing, didn't have any trouble making out the words. The guy had a slight accent, clipping the end of his words, rolling his *r*'s just a little. Maybe Russian.

The man held out his smartphone so that the clerk could see something on the screen.

"Pretty bride," the clerk said.

"Yes, very beautiful," the tall man said. "Have you seen her?"

Cal casually reached into his pocket and fed in another dollar. Took his time considering his choices.

"Nope," said the clerk. "I'd have remembered her if she'd checked in," he added with the exuberance of a horny young male.

The two men looked at each other. They were frustrated. Trying to hide it but not doing a great job.

"It is very important that we find her," said the shorter one. "She would have arrived within the last hour."

The desk clerk nodded. "Sorry I can't help. I'm the only one here. If she'd have rented a room, I'd know it. There are a couple motels down the road another ten or fifteen miles. You may want to try there."

The two men nodded and walked out the door. The shorter one had a stiff left leg, swinging it from the hip, rather than bending it at the knee. Cal grabbed his purchases and stepped back into the main office. Glanced out the window. They were driving a black Mercedes. They pulled out, headed east.

Cal held up his bag of chips. "My favorite," he said. "Should get me through the night."

The clerk shrugged and picked up his phone.

Cal pulled up the collar of his coat, opened the door and walked back to his vehicle. Once inside, he started it and flipped on the wipers to clear the windshield of snow.

Pretty bride.

Very beautiful.

Arrived within the last hour.

One only had to be smarter than the average bear to figure out that they were talking about Stormy, or whatever her real name was. And they seemed pretty determined to find her. Cal figured they'd be back for a second check once they got up the road a ways and nobody had seen her.

Really wasn't his problem.

He glanced in his mirror and sedately pulled out of the lot.

Chapter Three

She took a shower and stood under the hot spray for a long time. She stared at her wrists, rubbed them with the washcloth, noting that they were tender. Bruised.

She shampooed her hair, carefully rubbing the bump and the open cut. It stung a little but she figured that was a good thing. Even though it was just a small cut, it was probably a good idea to get it cleaned out.

Not that getting an infection was her biggest problem.

She got out of the shower, dried off and used the small bottle of lotion provided by the hotel. She rubbed Mango Magic on her legs, her arms, her hands. She thought her knuckles were chapped from her time in the snow but realized that they were skinned up and several of her nails had broken off, leaving a jagged edge behind.

She had a very vague recollection of grasping something with her hands, slipping off, grasping again. Hanging on.

She could feel her anxiety mounting and she told herself to breathe deep, to not try to force it. She towel-dried her hair, wishing she had a comb. At least the hotel had provided a blow-dryer. She used it, running her fingers through her hair, jerking when one of her jagged nails caught a strand and pulled.

She used her finger along with some soap to *brush* her teeth. Then she rinsed and rinsed, feeling as if had been days since her teeth had been clean.

She opened the bathroom and was very grateful that she had a towel wrapped around her because Cal Hollister was sitting on her bed, back propped against the headboard, arms behind his head.

He was chewing on a stick of red licorice.

What the hell? "Get off my bed," she said, working hard to keep her tone even. She would not let him see that she was scared to death.

"No." He reached down to the end of the bed, where she'd left his T-shirt, sweatpants and her underwear. He scooped them up and tossed them in her direction.

She reached automatically and almost lost her towel in the process.

"Get dressed," he said.

She stepped back inside the bathroom and slammed the door. Looked for a lock but there wasn't one. Of all the nerve. He may have saved her life but who did he think he was coming here, surprising her, putting her at a disadvantage? She yanked on her clothes, grateful that she'd put the strapless bra in the pile, along with her panties. Once she was finished, she looked around the small room for a weapon. Saw the only thing that might work. A minute later, she walked out, her hands together, casually cupped at her belly button.

She crossed in front of him, sat in the chair near the door. His duffel bag was on the floor, near her feet. From this angle she could see that he had an assortment of candy bars and chips on the bed next to him. "Going for a sugar high?" she asked.

"Always." He tossed her a Hershey's candy bar. She let it fall in her lap.

"Got these from the vending machine in the office," he said.

She waited. Where was this going?

"While I was there, two men came in. Squirrelly-looking guys. Lots of black hair and gold jewelry. One guy has a big scar on his face. Other one had a bad knee."

He was watching her. "Okay," she said.

"They showed the desk clerk a picture of someone on their phone. Someone, according to the clerk, who was a pretty bride."

She could feel her stomach clench. "What did the clerk say?"

"Said he didn't have anybody here that resembled the woman."

She felt some of the pressure lift off her chest. "They left?"

He nodded. "I suspect they'll be back. Them and their friends."

"Friends?"

"The first two left in a black Mercedes but there was a matching vehicle parked toward the back of the lot. It stuck around. I suspect they were waiting to see if the clerk was lying. If he was, it would be a fairly safe assumption that he'd make a mad dash to the person's room or use his cell phone that appears attached to his hand to put out a warning call. They might have been expecting somebody to quickly exit from one of the rooms."

"But that didn't happen," she said.

"Nope."

"Did the two men see you?"

"Yes. So I suspect the guys in the second car were also told to watch me. So I drove off, in the opposite direction of the first car. I waited to see if they'd follow me. But they didn't. They went the same direction as the first car. Probably didn't want to get split up in this weather."

"But you came back?" Why? To warn her? Or maybe he'd decided that there might be a way to profit from this unexpected encounter. Maybe he'd considered whether the men might be willing to pay for information on her. "How did you get in?" she asked, feeling very vulnerable.

He held up a plastic key card. "When I first checked in, I asked for two rooms. I thought maybe I'd try to get some sleep before going on to my final destination. That's when the guy told me that he only had one room with one bed. I told him that I'd take it, that my brother and I would have to sleep together. I laughed it off, said we'd done it as kids, that we could probably do it for one more night. He gave me two keys, one for me and one for my brother."

She'd seen the hotel clerk shake his head. When she'd asked Cal about it, he'd dismissed it. *Just didn't understand what I was asking for.*

"You lied to me earlier," she said.

He shrugged. "I thought if you knew that I was interested in getting a room that you'd feel compelled to offer to share this one. I didn't think that would work out so well for you when your new husband showed up."

She did not have a new husband. At least she didn't think so.

"You might want to take your wedding gown and veil out of the garbage," he said, looking in the far corner. "That might not make him feel so great, either."

She'd stuffed the offensive items into the brown plastic wastebasket. They spilled over the edge.

"You know," he said, "that's how I found you. I saw your veil blowing in the wind."

It was a miracle that he'd been able to see it, especially in white-out conditions. Most people would have driven by, clueless that a woman was freezing to death.

She was getting a sense that Cal Hollister wasn't *most people*. "So the hotel clerk thinks there are two men in this room. He doesn't know about me," she said.

"Nope. I suppose it's possible that he saw you get out of the car but I don't think so. Angle was wrong, plus the guy is obsessed with whatever he has on his phone."

She was safe. For the meantime. But who were these men? Why would they be chasing after her? She lifted her chin. "I certainly appreciate you letting me know," she said.

He sat up and frowned at her. "Congrats on being so very civilized and proper. Here's the thing, though. I don't think they were here to invite you to tea. So, I don't think good manners are going to be all that helpful in this situation."

He wouldn't think she had a civilized bone in her body if he knew how close she was to losing it, to screaming and kicking the damn bed.

"Why are they looking for you?" he asked.

"I don't know."

"Come on, Stormy. You can do better than that."

"I. Don't. Know. And I don't know who the men are. In fact, how do I even know that you're telling the truth?" She tossed her hair and tried not to wince when it hurt her head. "How do I know that you didn't just want a reason to come back to my room? How do I know that you're not my biggest worry?"

He stood up. "If I was, you'd already know it for sure. Now, I suggest you start thinking about what you're going to do when those men come back. I know the type. They won't want to be bested by a woman. And whoever is paying for those expensive cars isn't going to be happy that his guys couldn't get the job done. When they don't find you up the road, they'll come back and start turning over rocks. The motel clerk will break in about ten seconds and he'll be opening every one of the rooms for them to inspect."

Something told her that he was right. Some past experience.

"How long do you think I have?" she asked.

He shrugged. "They told the desk clerk that you would have arrived within the last hour. So, I think their radius will be anywhere you could have gotten in an hour. On a normal day, that's seventy miles, give or take. Today, half that at most. Today, they'll be forced to stick to the main roads. But in a day or less, when this storm dies down, they'll be able to cover ground much more quickly."

"How long?" she repeated.

"I think you've got eighteen to twenty-four hours. After that, you better be on your game."

Was she on her game? Not hardly. Something flashed in her head. She shook it, trying to clear it.

"What?" he prodded, maybe thinking that she wasn't taking the threat seriously.

"You said I needed to be on my game. And all I can think of is Leon Durham."

"The baseball player?" he asked, as if he really couldn't believe it.

"Yeah. He played first base. Talented player but unfortunately, there was the time he let a ball roll through his legs."

"In 1984. Cubs versus Padres," he said. "Padres went on to win." He paused. "How the hell do you know these things?"

She had no idea. It was just there.

It was horribly frightening. She had men chasing after her and all she had a grasp on was useless baseball facts. "Well, Mr. Hollister, it appears that I continue to be in your debt." She looked toward the door, to give him the hint.

"You can start paying up right now," he said.

What? He couldn't be suggesting…that, could he? "It's time for you to leave," she said more sternly.

"Nope." He lay back on the pillow, stretched his long legs out and kicked off his boots. He folded his arms across his chest and closed his eyes.

"You can't stay here," she said, louder and with more of a shrill than she expected.

He opened one eye. "I'm tired. I've lost the better part of the evening helping you. Now, I don't care if you want to sit in that chair all night or if you decide to stretch out next to me, but I'm getting some sleep. I suggest you do the same."

"But…"

"Your virtue is safe with me. I don't date married women and I certainly don't sleep with them. And," he said, "don't get any ideas of rubbing that shampoo you've got cupped in your hands in my eyes. That would just piss me off."

She had never been so furious. Or so grateful. It was preposterous that he was bulldozing his way into her room but there was something about him that, quite frankly, made her feel safe.

She needed sleep and she didn't intend to do it in this chair. She got up, went into the bathroom to wash her hands and came back. "You don't happen to have a nail file, do you?"

He lowered his chin. "Do I look like I file my nails?" he asked, his tone low.

"Not really. I thought you were the Abominable Snowman earlier," she added. "And I guess he probably doesn't file his nails either," she finished weakly.

He laughed. It was the first time she'd heard him do that. It was nice.

He got off the bed, rummaged in the duffel bag that he'd tossed on the floor and came out with a small plastic box. He opened it and tossed a pair of clippers her direction. "Will these work?"

"Yes." She was so grateful to be able to fix her poor nails that she quickly started clipping. She put the discarded nails in a pile and, when she was finished, dumped them in the wastebasket in the corner of the room, on top of the horrible dress.

"You really messed up your hands," he said. "How did you do that?"

She was ready for the question. Had anticipated it while she was clipping. Felt good that she was functioning at a level where her brain was working again. "Bridal shower," she said. "Nasty boxes with too much tape."

"Uh-huh."

She pulled back the covers on her side and crawled in, ignoring the fact that six feet of handsome muscle was on the other side of the bed.

He reached up and turned off the light. The room was not totally dark, however, because she'd left the bathroom light on and the door halfway open.

She closed her eyes and concentrated on breathing deep. In her head, she counted. By the time she got to two hundred, he was breathing deep and she assumed he was asleep.

She thought about trying to sneak out. He'd tossed his keys on top of the chest of drawers. All she would need to do was grab them and get out without him hearing her.

She was good at that kind of thing.

Didn't know how she knew that but felt it.

But where would she go?

That was the truly terrifying part—to have no idea where her safe place was located. Where her family might be.

She didn't trust Cal Hollister but she trusted the outside world even less.

Chapter Four

Cal felt the candy bars and chips roll into him as she slid in under the covers. She smelled good. Very feminine. He had the craziest urge to reach out, to see if her skin was as soft as it looked.

But he kept his arms folded, his eyes closed, his breathing deep. She was scared. Of him. But more so of the men that he'd described. So for now, she'd filed him under the category of *lesser evil*, which was just fine with him.

When he'd seen the second Mercedes idling in the lot, hidden to the casual observer, he'd realized that she was in the middle of something big. There was some serious muscle trying to find her.

He'd considered his options. He could forget what he'd overheard and seen and be on his way. He could go to the cops. Or he could barge his way into this room and try to protect this woman.

Who was lying to him. Of that, he was confident.

But he was also pretty sure that she was scared. Really scared. And he couldn't forget those marks on her wrists.

When he'd walked in and seen her pile of clothes at the end of the bed, he'd known there was a good likelihood that she might walk out of the bathroom naked. And if he'd been a gentleman, he'd have knocked on the bathroom door, announced his presence and given her a chance to collect herself.

He'd considered that plan for about half a minute before he'd settled down on the bed, determined to let the cards fall where they may. She'd come out in her towel, which for some twisted reason was even more sexy than full nakedness. She had a compact little body. No taller than a couple inches past five feet, she had gentle curves and one set of really gorgeous legs.

When she'd walked past him, he'd seen immediately that she was holding something in her hands. But he had to admit, she was good. She'd seemed relaxed and her stride even, unhurried. Confident.

Perhaps too confident. An operative? It was possible. Since he'd heard the men's foreign accents, the thought had been nagging at him. Was she part of a foreign terrorist group intent on screwing the United States? If so, even more reason to stick close to her. Was she an innocent, caught up with the wrong people? Then she needed his help.

He listened to her breathe, knew the exact moment that she let loose and fell asleep. He waited another five minutes, then carefully propped himself up on one elbow. Examined her.

She slept daintily, with her mouth closed. Yet, she wasn't totally relaxed. Her jaw was set as if she might have her teeth together. And one hand grabbed the corner of the sheet, fingers clenched tight.

He was still worried about the lump on her head but she certainly wasn't showing any signs of concussion.

Her speech was clear, her pupils the same. Still, she should probably be checked in the night.

It was still blowing outside. That would slow the Mercedes Men down. But they would be back. He wasn't concerned for his own safety. One against four were reasonable odds for a SEAL. But his attention would be diverted by her. And that could prove fatal.

When she woke up, he was going to force her to come clean. Once he had the story, he'd know what to do.

He closed his eyes and drew in a deep breath, remembering that mango was one of his favorite fruits. A little tart. Juicy. Delicious.

Damn.

Two hours later, he gently rolled over and bumped into her, his knee to her hip. She shifted but didn't wake up. He reached up and turned on the light.

"Hey," she said. She turned to look at him. "What's going on?" she asked, her tone sleepy, yet coherent.

"Just had to use the head," he lied. He looked at her eyes. Pupils still looked good. Her color was fine. "Go back to sleep," he said, turning off the light.

She was quiet for several minutes but he could tell by her breathing that she was agitated. He wasn't surprised when she suddenly sat up in bed.

"You did not have to use the bathroom."

"I didn't?" he asked with deliberate surprise. "That's rather personal, isn't it?"

"You woke me up on purpose."

"Why would I do that? So I could have this lovely conversation?" He rolled over and gave her his back.

She waited a full minute before she shoved his shoulder. "You were worried about the bump on my head." She paused. "That was nice of you," she added somewhat grudgingly.

He smiled. "Good night, Stormy."

SHE LAY IN BED, covers up to her neck, relaxed for the first time. She knew it was because she'd finally let down her guard. Cal had had multiple opportunities to harm her and he'd taken none of them. Instead, he'd disturbed his own sleep to wake her up and make sure that she didn't have a concussion.

He was smart, cocky, a little brash. Sexy in his blue jeans and forest-green Henley shirt.

He reminded her a little of a lounging tiger. Relaxed yet ready to pounce. He moved with quiet confidence.

She envied that. She didn't have any confidence right now.

But maybe by morning. She closed her eyes and let the sleep come.

The next thing she knew, strong hands gripped her shoulders. Half-asleep, old instincts kicked in. She wrenched her body sideways, attempting to fight.

But she couldn't budge her attacker.

She opened her eyes, saw Cal on his knees, straddling her.

It was several more terror-filled seconds before she processed what was going on. She forced herself to breathe, to clear her head. He was holding her, not hurting her, simply trying to avoid getting hurt himself. She looked at the bedcovers. They were in a tangled heap, wrapped around her legs.

"What day is it?" she demanded.

That surprised him. "It's Wednesday. Why?"

She let out a breath. "I needed to know if it was Saturday."

"Because?"

She didn't answer. Couldn't. But she saw the determined look on his face, knew that he wanted answers. "I had a bad dream," she said.

"You think?" he asked, his tone tense. His big body hovered over her, his weight off her but his presence immense.

While bedcovers and layers of clothes separated them, their closeness was suddenly intensely intimate. And disconcerting as hell to go from something horrible, like her dream, to something that offered a promise of being good, very good.

Breathe, she told herself.

"I think you scared ten years off my life," he said, his tone a little easier now.

"Sorry," she murmured.

He moved fast, swinging one leg over so that he was kneeling beside her. His hazel eyes looked troubled. "Want to talk about it?"

Could she? Could she go back to that dark place? Could she pretend that it had just been an oddly disturbing dream?

Could she trust this man who had barged into her room and taken up more than his share of the bed?

He'd saved her life.

Had doubled back to let her know about the men looking for her. She looked at him closer. He had a red mark on his face. He hadn't had it the night before. "What happened there?" she asked, already suspecting the truth.

"You've got a strong right hook," he said nonchalantly. "Unfortunately, you popped me one at about the same time you started screaming. It was a bit disconcerting for a minute."

Someone with less control might have killed her by mistake in response.

"I was lying on a bed," she said. "It was narrow, more like a cot."

He nodded.

"I wanted to get up, knew I needed to get away. But my wrists were tied to the bed frame. I pulled and pulled but it was no use."

"Who tied you there?" he asked.

She shook her head. "I don't know. It…it looked like a ghost. All white."

He didn't say anything.

"I know, crazy, right?" she said.

"Nope. Did the ghost talk to you?"

She thought for a minute. He had. She knew that. Couldn't remember what he'd said. "I'm not sure."

"What else do you remember?"

She pointed to the garbage can in the corner. "That was hanging in the corner of the room."

"The wedding dress?" he asked.

"Yes." She'd been scared of the dress but she could hardly admit that. There was something else and she tried desperately to recall it but it was out of her reach.

"Do you remember anything else?"

"I was sick. The ghost made me so sick."

He seemed to consider that. "You were screaming when you woke up. Why?"

"The ghost had come in and something bad was going to happen."

"What?"

"I don't know. But it was bad. I started screaming. And then…I guess I woke up."

He seemed to consider his words. "You have marks on your wrists," he said. "Like you've been restrained."

He was pointing out the obvious. She could ignore it, dismiss it. Or she could take the risk, leave herself absolutely exposed. If she didn't, she'd be all alone. "So you're saying that maybe it wasn't just a dream?"

"You tell me," he said, his voice intense.

She took a deep breath. "I'm not sure where to start."

"Maybe at the beginning."

Wouldn't that be nice? "Well, that was sometime before I met you. How long before, I'm not quite sure."

"That's a little confusing," he said.

She sat up in bed and pushed a hand through her tangled hair. "I'm in trouble. I don't know why but I am. The problem is, I don't think I can get myself out of it."

"Because?"

"Because I don't know what went wrong. I don't know who else is involved. I don't know how big this is but something tells me it's big. Really big. And that terrifies me. I don't know who the bad guys are. I don't know what they want." She took a breath.

"Okay. Anything else you don't know?"

She nodded. This was the hardest part. "When I looked in the mirror yesterday, I didn't recognize myself. Not because my hair was different or anything dumb like that. I didn't know who the woman in the mirror was." She swallowed hard. "I don't even know who I am."

Chapter Five

"I knew Mary Smith was bogus," he said.

Her dark eyes got big. "That's it? That's it?" she repeated, her voice rising. "I tell you that I don't know who I am and all you can say is 'I knew Mary Smith was bogus.' Of course it was bogus. I. Don't. Know. My. Name."

"And you're pretty freaked out about it," he said.

Now she gave him a look that would have made most people run for the door. It made him want to smile but he resisted. If he didn't watch out, she'd land another punch.

"A little," she said sarcastically.

"I get that," he said. "But I don't think it's helpful for both of us to be freaked out. And I've been around a few people who have had short-term memory loss. It comes back."

She didn't say anything for a long minute. "But what if it doesn't?"

And that simple question, asked in a small voice, pulled at his gut more than any full-blown tantrum could.

"You can't worry about that. Right now, you need to focus on staying safe." He meant that. While he was trying really hard to be calm, listening to her talk about some ghost that scared her and tied her to a bed had made him sick.

"You woke up asking the day of the week. Saturday seemed important. Why?"

"I don't know," she said, frustration in her tone. "In my dream, I knew that something very bad was going to happen on Saturday. That I had to stop it."

"Something bad to you?"

"I don't know." She shook her head. "This is going to sound crazy but even now that I'm awake, just saying the word *Saturday* makes my heart rate kick up in my chest."

"Okay. It's just Wednesday. If something bad is going to happen on Saturday, we've got a couple days. I think our best bet now is to get the hell out of Dodge," he said.

"We? Our?" she repeated. "This isn't your problem."

No, it wasn't. But he'd made his decision on that the minute he'd circled back to warn her about the Mercedes Men. "I'm between jobs right now so I've got some time on my hands."

She stared at him. He could read the questions in her eyes. She wanted to trust him but with no memory to guide her, she probably felt that any value judgment she might make was suspect. "What was your job?" she said finally.

"Navy SEAL for eight years. Got my discharge papers six months ago."

"So you haven't worked since then?"

He shook his head. "Nope. I signed on for more of the same with a private contractor. The money was really good but—" he paused "—I'm just ready for something else." There was no need to tell her that he'd come home to have a conversation with his brother, a conversation that was probably going to be difficult for both of them.

"What brought you to Missouri?" she asked.

"Family. I was raised about a hundred miles from here in a small town. Ravesville. Ever heard of it?"

"No." Her cheeks got pink. "At least I don't think I have."

He shrugged. "No worries. Don't try to force it."

She shook her head. "There are men looking for me. And I don't have any idea why. That's pretty frightening."

"I can keep you safe," he said confidently. "Now let's roll. There's a piece of apple pie in my car that we can split for breakfast."

She reached out and touched his arm. Her hand was warm and soft. "Thank you," she said softly.

She was lovely. But he couldn't forget the wedding dress that she'd wadded up in the corner wastebasket. She was someone's fiancée for sure. Maybe someone's wife. "You can have the bathroom first," he said. He had a call to make.

She got out of bed, looking like a waif in his T-shirt and sweatpants. They needed to get her some clothes, some boots. When the bathroom door closed, separating them, he reached for his phone.

Chase answered on the second ring. "Hello," he said, his tone almost a whisper.

"It's me. Cal."

There was a pause. "Are you okay?"

"Good. I'm good. You?"

"Fine." Chase took a breath. "Where the hell are you?"

"In Missouri," Cal said. "I could be at the house for dinner."

"That…that would be nice. But I'm in St. Louis. With Raney."

"Who's Raney?"

Chase laughed softly. "Don't worry. You'll get to know her. I'm going to marry her."

Cal felt a rush of emotions. He swallowed hard and managed to say in a fairly normal tone, "It's a good thing my heart is strong. Congratulations," he added.

"Thanks," Chase said. "It's a long story but Raney is testifying this week and maybe next. That's why I'm whispering. I'm at the courthouse for an early morning meeting with attorneys before testimony begins later today."

The pieces were clicking together. Raney was the witness that his brother had been protecting.

"Just as soon as she finishes, we'll be back at the house. In the meantime, you're welcome to stay. There's an extra key in the garage, in a coffee can under some nails and screws, on a shelf on the rear wall."

He laughed. "Old habits," he said. As kids, there had always been an extra key to the house somewhere in the garage. It was comforting to know that some things never changed. He thought about telling his brother about Stormy. Knew it wouldn't change Chase's mind about offering up a place to stay. But it might divert his attention from where it needed to be—on the woman who'd evidently turned the confirmed bachelor around. "I'll take you up on the offer and I'll have the coffee on when you and Raney get back."

"You do that," Chase said. He cleared his throat. "I'm really glad you're home, Cal. I'm really glad you called."

THE APPLE PIE was really good. And she enjoyed the bag of chips that came afterward. "Breakfast of champions," she said. They were in his SUV. He'd brushed the snow off and scraped the ice away and was now sitting next to her. The vehicle was warming up nicely.

The only activity at the hotel since they'd left their room was the arrival of a pickup truck that had a plow attached to the front end. The driver was clearing the parking lot again, working around the cars as best he could. He had waved as he'd taken his first pass by them but otherwise ignored them.

Cal had watched him closely for several minutes and evidently decided he wasn't any threat because he'd started in on his own breakfast. "Yep, beats an MRE any day," he said, biting into his half of the pie. "And a restaurant is out of the question right now. I don't want to take a chance on the wrong people seeing you."

The wrong people. Who the hell were they? Would she suddenly recognize them if she saw them? Maybe that would work. Maybe she should chase after the Mercedes Men and force a confrontation. It dawned on her that maybe that was exactly what Cal had planned. "Where are we going?" she asked.

"To Ravesville," he said.

"Where you grew up?" she said, remembering their earlier conversation.

"Yes. Just talked to my brother." He turned to her. "Who's engaged. Unbelievable."

She laughed. "Is he twelve?"

He frowned. "Of course not."

"Then why is it so unbelievable? People get engaged and married all the time."

He looked over his shoulder at the wedding dress

he'd retrieved from the trash can and once again thrown into the backseat. "Obviously."

Now it was her turn to stammer. "I mean…people do…but even so…I don't think I did."

He stared at her, his gaze piercing. "Why is that?" he asked finally.

"I think I would know. I think I wouldn't forget something like that."

"At the risk of stating the obvious, you don't even remember your name."

He hadn't said it unkindly. Just matter-of-fact. She totally understood his skepticism. But married? She would not have forgotten that. But it was a waste of time to dwell on it when her mind was blank. "So we're going to your family's home?"

"Yes. My brother's been living there, getting the house ready to sell. He's away right now but we can use the house."

She would be alone with this man in a strange place. She could feel her skin warm suddenly and she felt ill, as if the pie might make a return appearance. What the hell was her body trying to tell her?

Was she making a mistake? Was this the wrong thing to do?

"You look a little green," he said.

Probably because her body was trying to tell her no and her brain, which knew she had no other option, was saying *full steam ahead*.

"I'm fine," she said, dismissing his concern.

He didn't look convinced. "I imagine you'd feel better in clothes that fit. Once we get to Ravesville and you're settled at the house, I can take care of that."

The idea of him buying her clothes made her heat up

again. That was an intimate thing for a man to do for a woman. She didn't know what to say.

He didn't seem to expect an answer. Maybe he bought clothes for women all the time.

She didn't think so. He'd been a SEAL. Not a lot of department stores where they worked.

Would he ask her about sizes or simply do a visual inspection? Oh boy. She was edging toward hot.

"It normally wouldn't be that far in good weather," he said, oblivious to her temperature-control troubles. "It will take us longer today. But first there's something we need to do."

"What's that?"

"Remember last night I told you that I thought the Mercedes Men were going to come back. We need to see if I was right."

That was a bucket of ice water. "How do you propose we do that?"

"We need to get somewhere where we can see them and they can't see us."

She looked around. The palette was white with a little gray from the bare trees. But then she saw what might be a possibility. The hotel was on a service road, off the Interstate. It went for about a half mile before it reconnected with the highway.

Down the service road, about halfway to the Interstate, were two other buildings. She hadn't noticed them the previous night. Of course, it had been dark when they'd arrived. It wasn't another hotel. No, these were one-story cement structures, each with three big garage doors. The building closest to them had a partial second story made of wood, painted white, as if it had been added at some time.

From that vantage they would certainly have a good view of the hotel parking lot but would need binoculars if they wanted to see anything in detail. She realized she was tracking when he reached into the backseat, unzipped his bag and pulled out a pair. She looked at them closer. Military issue. Very nice.

"We still need to get into the building," she said.

He put the binoculars to his eyes and took a long look. When he pulled them away, he said, "There are only two cars in the parking lot for two big buildings. Both are snow-covered. I suspect the cars were there all night. Now, it's possible that somebody spent the night at work. More likely, I'd think, that the drivers were too nervous to drive their own vehicles and got a ride with a coworker."

"What if you're wrong? What if there are people inside."

He shrugged. "Hopefully, we can avoid any interaction."

"Hopefully," she said drily. "But there may be more people coming. It's a workday."

"In Missouri, two inches of snow can bring the economy to a standstill. Eight to ten inches like this is a hundred-pound gorilla. People won't be able to get out of their driveways. Anyone who can won't want to travel any farther than the local store to get bread and milk. I'm going with the relatively safe assumption that anybody who works there has the day off."

"There's still the issue of the building being locked."

He smiled. "Locked doors aren't generally too much of a problem for me. Alarm systems, now, they can be a bit trickier. Let's just hope there isn't one."

"So we're just going to drive down there, park and hope for the best?"

"Something like that," he said.

She had to admire his confidence that bordered on cockiness. And it certainly felt good to be doing something versus hiding out in a hotel room. She glanced at the road again. "A plow must have come through sometime during the night."

"At 4:18 this morning," he said, proving that she really had slept like a log once she'd finally relaxed. "The road is drifting shut again but we'll be able to get through."

It appeared the plow had done two swipes on the service road, one in and one out. It would have been a stretch to say they'd cleared both lanes. On each side of the road, snow was piled up high, probably four or five feet, making it look as if the road was a tunnel.

He was probably right. Most drivers would decide to stay home today.

She watched the plow driver finish clearing the hotel lot. "But their parking lot hasn't been plowed. We'll get stuck for sure if we try to pull in."

"I know. That's where I'm hoping we get a little luck."

"In the form of…?" She let her voice trail off.

"In the form of this guy," he said, indicating the man driving the plow. "I'm hoping that he's a smart entrepreneur and has a contract to plow out all the businesses along this service road."

That would make sense. It would make his drive to this area worthwhile. On a day like this, to a person who did that kind of work, time was money.

It took the plow driver another ten minutes to finish

the hotel lot. She realized she was holding her breath as she watched him drive to the exit of the hotel. When he turned right, she let out a breath. Two minutes later, when he made another right into the other parking lot, she smiled. "Today's our lucky day," she said.

"That would be nice," Cal said. He turned off the engine. "We're going to be here a little while," he explained. "I don't want to raise suspicion if somebody looks out of their hotel room and sees us idling here for a long period."

It made sense but without heat pouring through the vents, the SUV quickly chilled and she was grateful for Cal's warm coat. Even though she'd protested, Cal had given it to her before they'd left the hotel. "No way to avoid your feet getting wet," he'd said. "I'd carry you but somebody might see it and think it looked odd. We don't want to draw any unnecessary attention."

Her feet had gotten wet on the way to the car and now they were cold. But she didn't complain.

It took another fifteen minutes before they saw the plow driver exit the parking lot, turn right and head away from them. They waited until they saw his truck merge back onto the Interstate. Then Cal started the SUV again. He put the vehicle in Drive and took off.

When they got close, she could see that the plow driver had done a pretty good job pushing the snow to the sides, although the people who owned the cars weren't going to be happy. He hadn't been as careful to go around the cars as he'd been in the hotel lot. Instead, there were big piles behind each car, effectively pinning them in.

Close-up, she realized that the two buildings were attached, similarly to how some houses were connected to garages. There was a small wooden breezeway between the two cement buildings. "That looks new," she said.

"Probably has more to do with summer than winter. Missouri gets hot and the people who work here probably want to be able to move from building to building without ever having to go outside when it's ninety-five degrees."

Just that quick, she could see herself in a sleeveless linen dress, briefcase strap over one shoulder, walking down stone steps, relishing the hot, humid air. *Don't get me wrong,* she was saying. *I'm grateful for the air-conditioning but do they have to keep it at sixty?*

Who was she talking to? Where was she?

"Stormy?" Cal asked.

She shook her head. "It's nothing," she said. She wasn't really lying. It was worth nothing.

Cal shrugged and pulled close to the building that had the second story. In addition to the three big garage doors, there was a regular door at the end closest to them. "That's our best bet," he said. "Wait here while I check it."

He got out of the SUV, moving fast. He tried the door but it didn't open. He reached into his pocket, pulled something out and went to work on the lock. Within seconds he had the door open. She was impressed. She'd jimmied open a few locked doors in her time but not that quickly.

She put her hand to her mouth. How did she know that?

The knowledge had literally just popped into her head when she'd seen the door swing open. She wanted to launch herself out of the vehicle and tell Cal that she'd remembered something that might be important.

At least it seemed more important than some vague recollection of walking down steps, conversing about the weather. However, she immediately dismissed the idea. She wouldn't offer up the information until she knew for sure what it meant.

Maybe she was a thief?

The idea sat heavy on her heart. She didn't want to wake up from this nightmare and find out that she was a bad person.

Cal stuck his head inside the building. In just seconds, he pulled back, turned, locked eyes with her and motioned for her to wait. Then he went inside, closing the door behind him.

It dawned on her that this was her chance. The keys were in the ignition, the SUV was running.

It would be easy to be on the road before he knew what was happening.

She put her hand on her door. Opened it. Drew in a breath. A mad dash around the rear of the vehicle would do it. She could slip into his seat, put the car in Drive and be on her way.

She pushed the door open enough to get one foot out. His socks were dull against the much whiter snow.

Mother Nature. Purity. In the rawest sense.

Yet it would have killed her.

If this man had not saved her.

Not once but probably twice when he'd come back to the hotel to warn her.

But if she didn't go now, it might be too late.

Chapter Six

She pulled her foot back in, closed her door and let out the breath she'd been holding. She wasn't going to steal his vehicle and leave him stranded. He didn't even have his coat.

A bad person would do that. And if she'd been bad in the past, she was turning over a new leaf, beginning immediately.

She waited another five minutes before she saw anything. Then all three of the three big garage doors that lined the front of the first building started to open. Her heart beat fast in her chest and didn't slow down until she saw Cal poke his head out of the closest opening.

He walked back to the SUV and swung into the seat. "Place is clear. I'm going to pull my SUV inside. The Mercedes Men are likely to see this building as well and may want to come take a look. I don't want to make it easy for them by leaving my vehicle in the parking lot. They've already seen it once. Unless they're really a bunch of goons, somebody is going to remember that."

He put the SUV in Reverse, not Drive. It took her just a minute to realize that he planned to back into the empty space. That was smart. Easier to get away quickly if all one had to do was pull out.

She could see that there was enough room for his SUV but that was about it. There were similar empty spaces in front of the other two garage doors. Once they got the vehicle inside and she stepped out of it, she saw that the rest of the building, which was probably the size of a football field, was filled with big boxes. "What's in all these?"

"High-end sleds. Wood toboggans. They produce in the other building and warehouse in this space. I opened one of the boxes. Quality stuff."

She started to laugh. Couldn't help it.

"What's so funny?" He pushed a button on the wall and all three garage doors closed. The space was suddenly darker, colder.

"It's like we found the Missouri branch of Santa's workshop. I'm waiting for the elves to jump out, to tell us to skedaddle, that time is a wasting and the big guy in the red suit can be a real taskmaster."

"Abominable Snowman? Elves? Santa? I'm seeing a theme here."

She nodded. Would she have her memory back by Christmas? Would she be alive at Christmas? If the Mercedes Men meant to do her harm, could she evade them for that length of time?

"Are you still going to be in Missouri at Christmas?" she asked.

"I have no idea," he said. "I'm not thinking that far out."

That was undoubtedly a good approach. She would try not to worry about anything beyond her immediate control. "What's upstairs?" she asked.

"Offices."

"Is there a good view of the hotel parking lot?"

"Yes. We won't miss them."

The stairs to the second floor were at the far right side of the building. When they got there, she realized he was right. Even without the binoculars, they could probably see what was going on. With the binoculars, they could pick out fine detail.

Good. She wanted a close-up look at the men. If life was fair, she'd have an epiphany of sorts and know exactly who she was. A couple things had already popped into her head. Perhaps…she looked around…perhaps a visual would be the push that got the sled going down the hill at warp speed.

"Don't touch anything," he said. "We don't want to leave any fingerprints behind, just in case."

She sat in one of the chairs, with her hands folded together, resting on her lap. The office was warm and soon she was nodding off. She got up, took off Cal's big coat and started walking around the room to stay awake. "I need something to do. I'm going crazy."

He was slouched in the chair, arms behind his head, feet crossed at the ankles. "How about sports trivia? What year did Tiger Woods begin golfing professionally?"

"That's easy—1996."

"Your turn," he said.

She studied him. "The first World Cup was held in what country in 1930?"

"Uruguay," he said. "How many wins did Muhammad Ali have?"

"Fifty-six wins. Five defeats," she added.

"There's no extra credit," he teased. "Who did Wayne Gretzky play for in the 1980s?"

"Edmonton Oilers. Who is the only pitcher to lead

both the National and the American League in shut-outs, in the same season?"

He scratched his chin. "CC Sabathia. Played for the Indians, then the Brewers." He smiled at her.

"You're really good," she said.

"You're not so bad yourself," he said. He was quiet for a few minutes. "There are a lot of women broadcasting professional sports these days. Do you think that might be your job? Or maybe you're a sportswriter."

"Just the idea of standing up in front of a camera and talking to thousands of people makes my knees shake. I don't think that's my job. I suppose I could be a writer. I feel like that's more realistic but it still doesn't seem right."

"Okay. Maybe you're just a sports geek. We're trying to make lemonade out of grapefruit."

She sat back down. "We could have slept longer," she said.

"Yep. But I didn't like the idea of being surprised by your cousins."

"I don't think we're family."

"I hope not," he said. "It's going to be a real buzz killer if you see them and the first thought that comes to your head is what you're supposed to bring to Thanksgiving dinner."

She stared out the window. "Thanksgiving. Is that why you're headed home?"

"Yep. A few months ago, I decided that this was going to be the year…the year I joined my brothers for Thanksgiving dinner."

"You told me about your brother Chase. How many others?"

"Just one. Brayden. Everybody calls him Bray. He's

four years older than Chase, seven years older than me. He left for the marines when I was in middle school. Now he's a DEA agent and lives in New York." He was silent for a minute. "It will be good to see them," he added.

It wasn't all that unusual for family to get together on holidays but the way he said it, she had the distinct feeling that there was more to the story. She wanted to ask but decided not to. She settled for something less personal. "Do you cook?"

"Uh, no. Not really. You?"

She tried to remember if she liked to cook. Had no idea. "I will definitely be out of your hair by Thanksgiving," she said instead.

He shrugged. "Thanks for not driving off earlier."

She stared at him. "You left the keys on purpose. It was a test, wasn't it?" she challenged.

"I figured it was better for both of us if we knew the answer to the question early on."

"The question being, will she run if she gets the chance?"

"Exactly. At least here, I had access to heat and there's more snacks in the vending machines. There are lots worse places to be stranded."

She wanted to be angry, to be outraged that he'd baited her. But something told her that she would have done the very same thing. She stood silently, watching out the window. Finally, she turned to him. "Where exactly were those vending machines?"

He laughed but quickly silenced it when they saw two Mercedes sedans drive into the hotel parking lot. He put the binoculars up to his eyes.

With her naked eye, she could see that no one got

out of the one car. They parked in the back row, facing out, so that they had a good view of the office. Two men got out of the other car that had taken a front-row parking space.

"Do you think the clerk is in danger?" she whispered, before realizing how foolish that was. The men couldn't hear them. Now that it was happening, now that the men were actually back, it made her chest feel tight. What the hell did they want with her? If they had bad intent, was it possible that innocent bystanders would be caught in the fray? That was unacceptable.

"I thought of that," he said. "I don't think so. A dead hotel desk clerk in the middle of Missouri will get some attention. Every hotel in the state will be on hyperalert. It would seriously hamper their abilities to inquire about you at other places. I think they'll use other means of persuasion to get his attention."

"A new cell phone?" she asked drily. "Unlimited downloads?"

He smiled and handed her the binoculars. "My guess is old-fashioned cash. Take a good look at the two men when they come out of the office."

"You're awfully confident that the clerk will show them the rooms?"

"He's barely voting age and certainly no match for these guys. He'll take the cash and when they tell him to keep his mouth shut about it, he probably will because not only would he lose his job, he'll have to worry about these guys finding him and that their weapon of choice will no longer be Ben Franklins."

"Is that what you'd do?" she asked.

He shook his head. "Hell, no. I'd lead them both into an empty room and take them out. Then I'd wait for the two goons in the car to get impatient and come check on why their friends are no longer visible. Then I'd take those two down."

If another man had made that boast, she'd consider it false bravado. But Cal said it factually, without emotion, as if it was all in a day's work.

Navy SEALs were well trained. That was a given. And, she suspected, very confident of their abilities. Otherwise, they wouldn't have the guts to do what routinely needed to be done.

The door of the hotel office opened. She stared through the binoculars. The Mercedes Men walked on each side of the front desk clerk, who hadn't even thought to put on a coat. He would be freezing by the time they looked at every room.

Cold but hopefully alive. She stared at the faces of the men, waiting for some memory to return. But there was nothing. She could see the scar that Cal had described. It was very noticeable and seemed familiar. Why, however, was beyond her grasp. She studied the shorter man. The way he walked, how he swung his leg from the hip, was eerily familiar.

"Know them?" Cal asked.

"Both the scar and the way the other one is walking seem familiar. But I'm wondering if it's because you mentioned both things last night when you described them. Maybe I pictured that and now I think I've seen it before." She looked at him. "I think I've lost my confidence to sort out what is real and what isn't."

"Okay," he said.

"You say it like it's no big deal," she said, angry at herself. "I don't know any more than I knew ten minutes ago. We wasted all this time."

"It was a long shot," he said, "that simply seeing them would jump-start your memory. One we probably needed to take but not the basket to put all our eggs into. I got what I needed."

"And what was that?"

"I wanted to verify that the two cars were still traveling together and that they hadn't split up. I think we can assume that this is going to be their pattern. One car and two men are always backup. I also wanted to see how long it took them to come back. It was about six o'clock when they were here last night. It's almost noon. That's eighteen hours. I think we have to assume that they probably took turns sleeping so that they didn't lose any time looking. It gives me a feel for how they've identified their search area."

"They're looking for a needle in a haystack. Even if I had been out there somewhere, in the dark, in the snow, it would have been virtually impossible to find me."

"I know. But they kept looking. That gives me some idea of how determined they are."

"This is absolutely crazy," she said, watching the desk clerk knock on doors. If no one came to the door, the clerk would unlock the door, the men would step inside, only to reemerge a minute later. Some of the rooms were occupied. When the knock was answered, there was a brief conversation before the two men stepped inside, out of view. Like before, in less than a minute, they'd be back. "What do you think they're saying to the guests?"

"I suspect it's some line about the men being inspectors of some sort and they have to make a quick visual inspection of the room. The guests are probably irritated but as long as the men get in and out quickly, will probably not make too big a fuss."

"Good. If they do, this could turn ugly." And that would be on her conscience forever.

The men looked at all eight rooms on the first floor and started upstairs. "Are we going to stay until they finish?" she asked.

"We have to. We can't risk the men in the second car seeing us leave."

But that would make them sitting ducks if the men decided to search the warehouse next.

She watched as the trio made progress. The hotel clerk had his arms wrapped around himself and he looked miserably cold. The other two men, in their big black coats and dark pants, simply looked miserable. They both had square faces and flat noses.

"Do you think they might be brothers?" she asked, handing him back the binoculars.

He watched for a few minutes. "I think you're probably right," he said. "I didn't see that right away because I was focused on the one guy's stride."

They watched in silence for a few minutes. The trio got to the door of the room where she and Cal had spent the night. They knocked. Waited. Opened the door.

If Cal had not come back to warn her, she might still be in the room, oblivious to the fact that danger was on her heels. "Thank you," she said. "I probably can't say it enough."

"You'd have done the same for me," he said.

She liked to think so. The men came out. Checked the final two rooms. Their mouths were set and their posture tense. The trio walked back toward the office.

Please, just go, she thought. She did not want the young hotel clerk harmed.

She let out her breath when the men returned to their car and the young man went back inside the office. They were leaving. She was grateful.

Until she realized that the Mercedes Men were headed toward the warehouse. She and Cal had nowhere to go.

Chapter Seven

Cal moved quickly. "I'm going downstairs. Stay up here. No matter what, stay up here."

"What are you going to do?"

"Whatever it takes," he said. He grabbed the coat that Stormy had shed and tossed it at her. "Lock this door behind me. Hide in that closet," he said, pointing across the room.

"Shouldn't we call 911?"

"Won't do us any good. By the time they get here, it's going to be over, one way or the other." He could tell she didn't like the sound of that.

"But—"

"No time," he said. The Mercedes Men were half-way down the road. He pulled up his pant leg, reached inside his cowboy boot and came out with the knife that he kept strapped to his ankle. He pressed a button on the handle and the blade extended. He handed it to her.

She didn't recoil or throw up her hands. She took it, tested the weight in the palm of her hand, then gripped the handle.

"Do you think you could stab someone?" he asked.

"I'll do what I have to do."

"Good. If anybody besides me opens that closet door,

let them get close and then go for center body mass. Don't hesitate. You'll only get one chance."

He took two steps toward the door.

"Cal," she said.

He turned and she was close. Close enough to reach her arms up, pull his face toward her and kiss him hard. It was unexpected and explosively hot. He opened his mouth and their tongues battled.

When she pulled back, he felt as if he'd been hit by an incoming missile. Dazed.

"Be careful," she said.

He was generally never careful but almost always successful. "I'll do my best," he managed.

He ran lightly down the stairs. If the Mercedes Men followed their pattern, two would enter. He would have the advantage of surprise. It would be enough unless one of them got off a lucky shot. The trick was letting them get far enough inside that the other men waiting in the car didn't realize that their buddies were under attack and come running. That would change the odds.

He absolutely could not let any of them get upstairs. While the knife gave Stormy a bit of protection, it was an inefficient weapon against a gun.

He stood flat against the wall, near the door that they would either pick the lock or simply knock down. He listened hard. Could hear the first set of tires. The car engine. Second set of tires. That engine. Then nothing for a minute.

Car door slam. Second car door slam.

He breathed normally, in and out, in and out. He needed to get steady fast. Needed to get that kiss out of his head.

His buddies would be laughing their tails off knowing that his knees were practically knocking together. Not because of the Mercedes Men. Them he could handle.

The doorknob jiggled. It had been an easy door to unlock. If they had any skill at it, it shouldn't take them long.

He listened for the lock to tumble.

What he heard was a muffled cry, the voice deep. Then fast conversation at the door in a language that he didn't know. Then the sound of running feet. Two car doors. Engines changing gears.

The cars were both leaving.

What the hell?

Then it made sense. He heard the sound of another approaching vehicle, coming from the direction of the hotel. Big rumbling engine.

The engines from the two cars were fading. They'd turned right out of the parking lot, headed back toward the Interstate.

He needed to see. He ran back upstairs to the windows.

It was a big delivery truck. The sign on the side said Wardman Toboggan Company.

It was a "good news, bad news" kind of moment.

Good news in that the Mercedes Men had decided a confrontation wasn't in their best interests. Bad news in that the likelihood that the truck would pull into the garage and see their rental car was pretty high.

He'd had no compunction about taking out the Mercedes Men but didn't want to have that same fight with an unsuspecting employee.

"Change of plans," he said, turning. Then smiled when Stormy didn't immediately open the closet door. Good girl. "Just me," he said. "Mercedes Men backed off when a company truck started down the road. Let's roll. We need to be in our vehicle and ready to go if those garage doors open."

She opened the closet door and tried to hand him back the knife. "You keep it," he said.

She shrugged, retracted the blade and put it into the pocket of his coat that she'd once again put on. She didn't ask any additional questions, just followed him down the stairs and got inside the SUV. He could hear the engine of the truck. It needed a tune-up.

He started the SUV. Counted to five. The garage doors started rising. All three of them. He saw the nose of the big truck in front of the third door. Waited until the door in front of the SUV was open far enough that they could squeeze under.

Gunned it. And they were out of the building and sliding around the edge of the big warehouse, likely before the man in the truck had any idea what had happened.

He went the opposite direction of the Mercedes Men, heading back toward the hotel. But he didn't stop there. Just kept going until he was also back on the Interstate.

She didn't say a word until they were safely back on the road with nobody following them. "That was fun," she said.

He turned, trying to figure out if she was being sarcastic. He didn't think so.

It was oddly endearing and very attractive. "Ready for the drive?" he asked.

"Sure. But what about the people at Wardman's?"

"Well, I suspect it'll go sort of like this. When they first saw my SUV pulling out, they probably would have tried to figure out if there was a legitimate reason for me to be inside. For example, did the SUV belong to someone who works there? When they came up empty on that, they might have tried to get a plate number. But they wouldn't have. We got out of there pretty fast and this morning before we started, I made sure there was a nice mud and snow mix on the plates, obscuring the information."

"They'll call the police?" she said, more fact than question.

"I imagine so. First, they'll call the boss. He or she will tell them to call the police. Then there will a quick look around to see if anything is missing or disturbed. When everything looks okay, they'll probably calm down, and quite frankly, the cops won't put any time into it."

"Cameras?" she asked.

"Didn't see any. Those are getting more sophisticated by the minute, however, so it's possible. Nervous about seeing your photo splashed across the internet or the local news station?"

"Nervous?" She put her hands on the borrowed sweatpants. "Why, do these make me look fat?"

He laughed so hard that he almost couldn't drive. He might not know her name but he was slowly fitting together the pieces of Stormy. And liking the image he was creating.

Which was a problem considering she was somebody else's woman.

He turned on the radio. "I'm going to try to catch some road reports," he said.

SHE WATCHED THE miles roll by. They'd left the Interstate behind and turned off onto a two-lane highway.

In most places, it was plowed wide enough to cause no worry for cars going opposite directions. There were places where it had blown badly and had they met a car in exactly those spots, it might have been an interesting game of chicken.

That didn't happen. In fact, they met very few cars. Fewer than ten so far and none of them had been a black Mercedes.

The lack of activity gave her plenty of time for reflection. Perhaps too much.

She'd kissed him. Couldn't put it out of her mind.

She'd grabbed his face, pulled him close and laid one on him. What the heck did that tell her about the kind of person she was?

She was a kisser? A wanton kisser? A nondiscriminating kisser, looking for any pair of available lips?

Or was it possible that she was very discriminating and had simply found something unique and interesting and worth her time? That was certainly something to chew on.

She fought the urge to ask Cal how he felt about it. That would have been such a female thing to do—to want to talk it to death. He hadn't resisted. Had participated quite nicely, in fact.

But hadn't mentioned it and apparently wasn't inclined to want to talk about it or anything else. He'd fiddled with the radio for a few minutes and settled on a talk radio station that was debating the use of drone technology in the public sector.

She could tell the roads were still slick although no new snow was falling. Once the plows and the salt trucks were out and about, it would be fine to travel. There would be nothing to slow down the Mercedes Men.

But how would they be able to trace her to Ravesville? Maybe once she got to Cal's family home, she'd truly be safe. Her mind would heal.

She'd had the two flashes of memory. They seemed incongruent. Her in a pretty dress with a briefcase and the ability to pick a lock. Figuring out how these seemingly disjointed memories went together was difficult.

Equally challenging was sorting through the new information that she was learning. Just this morning, she'd discovered two rather interesting facts. One, when Cal had handed her the knife and told her not to hesitate, she'd known that she would do what she had to do to protect herself. She would fight. And the second thing that had become abundantly clear when she'd been hiding in the closest, sweltering in Cal's big coat, was that she didn't like being left behind. When Cal had ordered her to hide, her first impulse had been to tell him to think again. But she'd decided to go along.

While she'd been waiting, her heart had been beating hard. At first, she'd thought it was in fear. Then she'd realized that it was in anticipation.

Of what, she wasn't sure. But she wasn't scared of it.

She wasn't scared now. She closed her eyes, comfortable in the warm SUV, confident that Cal could handle the roads just fine.

She woke up when she felt a gentle tap on her shoulder. She opened her eyes.

"We're getting close," he said. "Thought you might want to get a glimpse of the town. We have to go through it to get to the house."

"Will anyone recognize you?"

"I wouldn't think so. I haven't been home since my mom died eight years ago."

"Did you…did you see her before she passed?"

"I did. We had a couple days together. She was in and out because of the meds they had given her but it was still good." He was silent for a few more minutes. "Where do your parents live?" he asked.

"Fort Collins, Colorado," she said. Then turned to him. "How the heck do I know that?" she asked, hysteria hovering at the edge of her very slim grasp on sanity. She closed her eyes. Then after a long, frustrating moment opened them again. "This is crazy. I can't picture them and I don't know their names but I'm confident that it's Fort Collins. How can this be?"

He shrugged. "I'm not a physician but I've seen this before. When you try to force it, it won't come. But random things will be there. It should make you feel good, that it's not all gone."

She rubbed her forehead. "It's like my brain is a crossword puzzle and the edges have been rubbed off the pieces so I can't see how everything fits together."

"It'll come," he said. He slowed the vehicle down. "Well, this is it. Don't blink or you'll miss it."

She smiled. It was sort of charming. A big main street, a couple blocks long, with four-way stop signs at the end of every block. Lots of red brick. Diagonal parking. There were a few cars in front of the Wright Here, Wright Now Café. She looked in the windows as they passed. "Cute little place," she said.

"Uh-huh."

"You lived here your whole life?"

"Yep."

"Your mom and dad must have liked the community."

He didn't answer right away. Two stop signs later, he said, "My dad died when I was eleven."

"I'm sorry," she said.

"My mom remarried a couple years later. Brick Doogan. He wasn't a nice guy. He's been living in the house since Mom died. He was in a fatal car accident very recently."

"Which is why your brother is fixing up the house to sell."

"So you were listening?" he teased. "I'm not sure what the house will look like. I got the impression from Chase when we first spoke about it that it was worse than he expected."

"It's got to be better than a snowdrift," she said.

He nodded. "A woman with low expectations. My kind of girl."

She felt her stomach tighten. His kind of girl. Was she?

As nice as that might be, there was a reason she could not be involved with Cal. Felt it. Sadly enough, knew it had something to do with the wedding dress in the backseat.

Chapter Eight

As they passed the Fitzler house, he pointed it out. "Gordy Fitzler and his wife have lived there forever. They had two daughters. They were older than me but that didn't stop me from teasing them mercilessly on the school bus. Gordy owned a roofing company and Chase worked for him for several years."

"Is that a for-sale sign?" she asked.

Cal squinted. The sign was in the front yard and the snow was high enough to almost obscure it. But Stormy was right. The Fitzlers were selling. "I wonder if that will hurt our chances of making a sale, to have two houses on the same road up for sale at the same time."

"Or maybe help it. Someone will come out to see this house and it won't be quite right and then they'll realize your house is for sale, too."

"Maybe. Fitzler has a nice outbuilding that he used for his business. That may make his a more attractive property."

He drove another five hundred yards. "That's ours."

"It's big," she said.

"Big enough," he said. There'd been times in the past years when his whole living space wasn't as big as one of the rooms in this rambling white farmhouse.

The driveway to the house was drifted badly and even with his big SUV and a running start, Cal thought there was a possibility that they might get stuck. But he wasn't inclined to leave his vehicle on the road and walk the rest of the way.

So he accelerated, made the turn and tried to plow through it. The back end slid and the tires grabbed. He didn't let up on the gas and managed to get close to the house before the vehicle stopped forward progress.

He looked at Stormy and at her feet in his white athletic socks. "I'll carry you," he said. "Let me get the key out of the garage first."

He pushed open his own door, stomped through the snow and then used his hands and feet to move snow away from the side door of the garage. When he could get it open, he slipped inside. Flipped the light on and from there, it was easy to find the key. Just where Chase had said it would be.

He grabbed a shovel on his way out and noted with relief that there was a snowblower. That was new. When he and his brothers had lived here, they'd shoveled. Missouri rarely got snow like this so it hadn't been all that difficult.

Today, he sincerely hoped the sucker worked.

He waded back to the car, got Stormy's door open, and gathered her up in his arms. His coat came almost to her knees and he knew it had never smelled better, some combination of hotel lotion and Stormy.

There was a moment of excitement when he got to the steps and his foot sunk deeper than expected. He pitched forward. "Whoa?" he said.

She squealed. It was delicate and feminine and it made him laugh.

"Sorry about that," he said. He yanked his foot free and managed to get up onto the porch, where the snow was significantly less.

"Put me down so you can unlock the door," she said.

He ignored her. Instead he shifted her so that one hand was free. Unlocked the door and pushed it open with his foot. Stepped inside the dark cold house, still holding her.

She stretched out a leg and used her toes to flip up the light switch.

When light flooded the entryway, he grinned at her. "We're a good team," he said. Then he carefully set her down.

The house was much the same yet felt very different than the last time he'd been there, when it had been filled with death. It smelled different. The light seemed different.

Chase had been busy. The living room and dining room both had fresh paint. The carpet in the dining room had been ripped up, exposing a real nice wood floor that he hadn't realized was there. There was a neat pile of wood flooring in the corner of the living room, a good match to the dining room, just waiting to be laid down.

He walked toward the kitchen with Stormy following. He remembered the appliances. White, sturdy, and more than thirty years old, they'd been a part of Hollister dinners since before he was born. The table was the same, too. But the kitchen felt warmer, more welcoming than he remembered it feeling eight years ago. Maybe it was the paint? It was different. Maybe it was because it was sparkling clean?

Maybe it was because Stormy was beside him?

He shook his head to clear it. He might have carried her over the threshold but she was somebody else's bride.

"Great house," she said. "I love the big windows."

"The one in the front room was replaced about seventeen years ago. After my stepfather put my hand through it. My punishment."

He heard her gasp and immediately regretted his frankness. It was unexpected, really. He was generally much more careful about sharing anything personal. But somehow his usual defenses were on the fritz when it came to Stormy.

"What did you do?"

"Didn't get the dirty clothes off my bedroom floor quite fast enough."

She was silent for a few minutes. "How old were you?" she asked.

"Fourteen."

Another bout of silence. "I'm sorry that happened to you," she said finally.

He appreciated that she didn't seem inclined to want more information. Such as how did that make him feel about his stepfather? His mother? What was it like after that? Those were complex questions with even more complex answers.

"So that makes you thirty-one," she said. "I wondered. You must have gone to college before you enlisted?"

"Chase and I moved to St. Louis the day I turned eighteen. He got a job with the St. Louis Police Department. Busted his ass so that I could go to school and get an engineering degree."

"And then you decided to enlist? After all that? And become a SEAL?"

"Seemed like the thing to do." He wasn't going to tell her about the conversation that he'd had with Brick Doogan, about how the man had tossed his world upside down in a matter of minutes.

He hadn't had the guts to confront Chase with the truth at the time. Had simply left home and proved time and time again that he was tough enough to take anything that got thrown at him. Proved that nothing scared him.

"Now what?" she asked.

"I'm going to go see if the snowblower works. The car needs to be dug out." He thought that they were safe in Ravesville but he wasn't taking any chances on getting caught unawares with no means of escape.

"What should I do?" she asked.

"Whatever you want," he said, smiling. "You're a guest."

AN UNINVITED GUEST. For sure.

He had to be regretting that he'd ever pulled her out of the snowdrift. Yet he was being really great about it. Acting as if it was no big deal that he was suddenly saddled with a woman who didn't even know her own name but apparently had done something to give four guys a reason to chase her around the Missouri countryside.

She was going to remember everything and get the heck out of his hair. She was.

She had to.

The alternative was too awful to contemplate.

But in the meantime, she could earn her keep. She was hungry. He had to be more so. So far, she'd seen him consume a good amount of licorice, chips, candy bars and apple pie.

She suspected that wasn't all he normally ate. He was incredibly buff. He'd picked her up and *carried* her several times, as if she weighed twenty pounds rather than a hundred and twenty pounds.

At thirty-one, he was young to have lost both of his parents. And his stepfather, too, although the man certainly didn't sound like a prize. What kind of person shoved a fourteen-year-old's hand through a window?

Her stomach grumbled, reminding her that it was time to eat. She walked over to the cupboards and started opening them. There was a good supply of the staples: flour, sugar, salt, dried pasta and cereal. She opened the refrigerator. It was practically bare. No eggs, no milk, none of the things that would allow her to cook much of anything.

She heard the roar of the snowblower and knew that Cal would be occupied for a little while. There was a lot of snow. She looked again at the cupboards. She was going to have to figure out how to deliver on her end, as well.

Ten minutes later, she was waiting for water to boil. Something about standing at the stove felt familiar. Was she a cook? Did she spend time in the kitchen? She closed her eyes, willing her mind to find something that would tell her just one small thing about her past.

But it was as if she'd been born yesterday, in the middle of a snowstorm, wearing a wedding dress. But she hadn't been. She had parents. And she'd remembered that they lived in Fort Collins, Colorado. If she got really desperate, maybe she could put a picture of herself in the paper with the hopes that they'd see it. Sort of like a lost-cat advertisement.

She shook her head. She was really starting to feel sorry for herself, wasn't she? Enough of that. It was going to get her nowhere.

She opened two cans of tomato sauce. She added a liberal amount of dried basil, oregano and garlic. She found a jar of mushrooms and threw those in, as well.

Then she opened the freezer, saw the frozen rolls and grabbed them. By the time Cal came back inside, she'd set the table and there was a steaming bowl of spaghetti and warm bread from the oven. She'd poured them both water to drink.

He was snow-covered and his jeans were wet. He sniffed the air. "Smells great," he said.

It felt good to do something for him, even if it was as simple as throw a quick meal together. "So the snow-blower worked?"

"After a little gentle coaxing," he said, shedding his coat.

"You must be the handy type," she said.

"My background is mechanical engineering. I'm a total geek."

"You don't look like a geek," she said, immediately wishing she'd kept her thoughts to herself.

"Oh yeah?" He lifted his chin.

In his faded blue jeans that he wore low on his hips and his flannel shirt, he looked sexy and just a little dangerous. The cold air hung around him and his cheeks and nose were red from the wind.

"I always loved figuring out how things worked. Mechanical engineering was an easy choice. After I enlisted, I realized that I had something I could offer to the rest of the guys on the team. As long as I had some string, duct tape and a sharp knife, I could get most anything running again."

"Good skill," she said.

He sniffed the air again. "Looks as if you've got your own skills."

"It's just a little something," she said. "But it's ready if you are."

He followed her into the kitchen, washed his hands and sat down at the table. He looked up at her. "This is amazing," he said, as if she'd done something special. She felt warm.

"Thanks," she said. "We're going to need to get some milk, eggs and fresh produce at some point."

"No problem," he said, taking a big serving of the spaghetti. "I'll go to town tomorrow," he said. "Just make me a list."

He said it as if he expected her to stay. "I might remember everything by tomorrow," she said.

He nodded. "I hope you do."

"I'll be out of your hair just as soon as I do," she said. "Okay."

"And if...if it doesn't come back," she added, realizing that she needed to vocalize her greatest fear, "I'll still move on. I know this is just a temporary stop," she said, assuring him that she wasn't going to overextend her welcome.

"Great," he said.

She laid down her fork. "I know I'm putting you at risk by being here."

He sighed. "Do I look concerned about that?"

She shook her head. "Maybe you should be," she said. "Maybe you should just tell me to get the hell out."

He looked at his half-eaten lunch. "When you can cook like this? You think I'm crazy?"

Maybe. He was inviting trouble into his life. "I just want to be clear on my intentions," she said stiffly.

"Crystal clear," he said. He pointed at the bread basket. "Can you pass the rolls?"

AFTER LUNCH, THEY cleared the table. He washed and she dried the dishes. "Let's take a look at the rest of the house," he said.

There was a master bedroom off to the side of the kitchen. It had also been freshly painted but there wasn't a stick of furniture in it. The attached bath had been cleaned and emptied of all signs of Brick.

He wondered if that had been the first thing that Chase had done. It wasn't as if Chase didn't have a reason to hate Brick Doogan, to want to exorcize his spirit from the premises. He'd taken the brunt of Brick's hateful nature, protecting everyone else in the house.

Cal had let him. And that knowledge still rubbed him raw with guilt.

When he and Stormy went upstairs, it was easy to see that Chase had plans for the second story but had not yet had time to implement them. Bray's room was empty save a gallon of new paint in an unopened can. He opened Bray's closet. It was filled with old winter coats. He recognized them as coats his mother had worn over a period of many years. She'd been dead for over eight years and Brick still hadn't done anything with them.

Maybe he'd been sentimental. Maybe he'd simply been lazy. It didn't matter but perhaps one of them would fit Stormy.

Chase's room was also empty and his closet was bare. There was a gallon of paint there, as well.

He was starting to get the pattern. He wasn't surprised when he opened the door to his old room and saw the gallon of paint. The bed in the middle of the room did give him pause. There was no frame. The mattress and box springs sat on the floor. Sheets and a blanket, looking freshly washed, were folded and sitting at the end of the bare mattress. He opened the closet door. Women's clothes and men's clothes.

Not his mother's or Brick's. These belonged to Chase and Raney. He turned to Stormy. "Will any of these fit?"

She glanced at several of the items, looking at the size tags. "Well enough," she said. "But I hate to use someone's things without their permission."

He shook his head. "Chase won't care and while I don't know Raney, if my brother loves her, then she's the type who won't care, as well."

She nodded. "I suppose you would like your sweatpants back," she said.

His sweatpants and T-shirt had never looked or smelled better. "I'm glad they served a purpose," he said. "I'll let you have some privacy to pick something out." See, he could be a gentleman. Even when his libido was spiking at the mere thought of her getting naked to change clothes.

When she nodded, he walked out of the bedroom and went downstairs. The fifth stair squeaked, the way it always had. It brought back a sudden rush of memories. Being fourteen or fifteen, waiting for his brother to come home. Hoping that Chase would get inside without Brick hearing that he was late or realizing that he'd been drinking. And he'd cringe when he heard the step squeak, wishing that Chase had been more careful, wishing that Brick slept more soundly.

And then digging deeper under the covers when Chase and Brick would go at it. There'd be yelling and then worse when Brick stopped talking and got his point across with his hands.

He'd just lain there. Afraid.

And later, when he got Chase alone and begged him to be more careful, his brother had just smiled.

He'd been such a dumb ass that he'd never even questioned why Brick went after Chase with a vengeance and left him alone. Until Brick had told him why.

That was the day everything changed.

But that was more than eight years ago and he needed to forget it. If not forget it, then at least get past it. That was why he had come home for Thanksgiving.

He sat down on the couch in the living room and watched the road. There was generally little traffic on the rural road and none today. The sun was shining and made the living room, with its big windows, feel warmer than the rest of the house.

He closed his eyes and let himself relax. He was home. For better or worse. Back in Ravesville.

Five minutes later, he heard the upstairs bedroom door open and close. Then light steps on the stairs. He smiled when Stormy came into view.

She'd put on a blue jean skirt, a black sweater and black knee-high boots. She had some kind of black nylons or tights on, too. She looked fabulous. Sexy.

Maybe she should have stayed in his T-shirt and sweatpants. *Married*, he reminded himself. Or close to it.

"Looks as if the clothes fit pretty well," he said.

"They're wonderful. I had underestimated the psychological boost of having clothes on that actually fit."

Psychological boost for her maybe. Psychological torture for him. "What do you want to do with your bridal gown?" he asked, needing to quickly get his head back in the game.

She looked startled. "I...I don't know."

"I don't think we should leave it in the SUV. If we need to abandon that vehicle quickly, I don't want to have to deal with it."

She nodded. "Of course. I guess we should bring it inside." She paused. "I don't want it," she added. She pointed at the brick fireplace on the far side of the room. "I suspect it would burn pretty well."

He stared at her. "How can you be so sure that the dress isn't important to you, that it isn't a good thing?"

She shrugged. "I don't know how to explain it. All I can say is that I think I would know if I was recently married. I would feel it."

Not the best logic he'd ever heard.

"I'm not wearing a ring," she said.

He knew that. He'd checked, of course. "You don't have any rings on. Maybe you're the type that doesn't like jewelry."

She studied her hands. She'd clipped her nails very short to repair the damage. Still, her hands were very feminine, with long, graceful fingers. When she looked up, he could see the frustration in her eyes.

"There's something not right about that," she said.

"About what?"

"I have a ring. A favorite ring. Silver. Wide band. Heavy. I can see it. But I don't have any idea how I got it or where it is now." She sighed. "I swear, I want to just claw my brain apart."

He laughed. "Well, it's a good thing, then, that you can't get to it. Don't push it. It's something that you can remember the ring. The rest will come." He stood up. "I'll get your wedding dress. I don't think we should burn it. There may be evidence on it that shouldn't be destroyed."

"I guess I could hang it in the closet upstairs."

He shrugged. "Maybe we shouldn't be so quick to push it aside."

"I'm not sure I'm following."

"Do you know if it was a new dress or do you think it had been borrowed from someone?"

He could tell the question surprised her. She closed her eyes. "It was hanging on a white padded hanger, the kind you might find in a wedding dress store. There are straps inside some dresses… I don't know what they're called, but you use them if you're hanging up a dress that has a wide neckline and won't fit on a hanger very well. Somebody had hung the dress on the hanger using those straps. They were perfectly wrapped. I never saw a tag but I think it's very possible that it was new." She opened her eyes. "Where are you going with this?"

"Stores sell certain brands of clothing. Even wedding dress stores, right? By looking at the brand, do you think it's possible that we might identify the store that it came from?"

"Maybe. But I'm pretty sure that I didn't go there and pick it out. They aren't going to be able to tell me anything about me."

"But one of the Mercedes Men must have picked it

up. They would have paid for it, maybe with a credit card. Maybe we can find out something about them."

"We don't have much else to go on," she admitted. "But where would we start?"

"We know where you ended up. We have to work off the assumption that they didn't get you into a wedding dress and put you on a plane. We can use my phone to search for all the bridal stores in Missouri. Then we call them to see if they carry this particular brand."

"That could work," she said. "But there could be several. It's a big state, maybe a popular brand."

"We'll start with those that are closest to us. Ready to try?"

She nodded. "If I thought standing on my head in the corner would help, I'd try that."

Chapter Nine

According to the pink tag sewn into the back of the dress, it was a Jenna McCoy. That meant nothing to her.

But when they searched the brand, they realized that it was carried by seventeen bridal stores in the state of Missouri. And upon further investigation, they realized that there were more bridal stores in the state that didn't list their labels.

It was daunting to say the least. "Seventeen that we know about," she said.

"Eight if we consider the major markets of Kansas City, Colombia and St. Louis. Those are the closest geographically to where you were found."

"Eight," she repeated. "Do we call them and describe the dress? See if they've recently sold one?"

"That might work. Maybe we could get a contact name and email address and send them a photo?"

"I think they're going to think we're nuts. I can just hear them now. *Hey, lady, you got the dress. Why the heck don't you know where you bought it?*"

"I never said it was a perfect plan."

She couldn't help it. She laughed. He was going for innocent and it was a look that he simply couldn't pull off. "Let me think about this," she said. "In the meantime, I'm going to make dessert."

"A real dessert?"

He might not be able to do innocent but he could do hopeful really well.

"You'll see," she said and left him alone in the living room.

In the kitchen, she found a can of cherry pie filling and a can of crushed pineapple. She opened them, mixed them together in a 9x13 pan and spread a box of cake mix on top. She dotted it with butter she found in the refrigerator. She was just opening the oven when Cal called out, "How's it going in there?"

"Good. Forty-five minutes," she said.

"It's been about five years since I've had homemade dessert. I guess I can wait a little longer."

He said it lightheartedly but it reminded her of the tremendous sacrifice that soldiers made. She wiped her hands on a towel and walked back into the living room. He was sitting on the couch, looking at his cell phone.

"Thank you for your service," she said, her tone serious. "I imagine it was difficult at times."

He nodded. "Sure. Difficult. Wonderful. Frustrating. Exhilarating. Any given day it was different. Sometimes any given hour. Got to see a fair amount of the world."

She laughed. "I'll just bet you did."

"It wasn't as hard on me as it was on the guys who had a wife and kids at home. I don't know how they did it."

She shouldn't pry. Really, she shouldn't. "You didn't leave anybody behind?" she asked, losing the internal battle quickly.

"Nobody special," he said.

She should let it go. "What's that they say about sailors? A girl in every port?"

"Maybe not *every* port," he said, laughing. "I was a lot of places."

She bet he'd broken his share of hearts.

"You look tired," he said gently. "Why don't you go take a nap?"

"I need to watch this," she said, waving a hand in the direction of the kitchen.

"I got this," he said. "I'll pull it out in exactly forty-five minutes. I promise, I won't forget."

He was right about her being tired. While she'd gotten some sleep the night before, her body felt fatigued, as if she'd been running on empty for a long time.

"Thank you," she said.

"No problem. If you're real lucky, there will be some left when you get up."

She hoped so. Her appetite seemed to be coming back. She no longer felt ill, which was a huge relief.

She walked upstairs, kicked her boots off and lay down. She should sleep when she could. She could see herself, hands on her hips, smiling at someone. *First rule, sleep when you can.*

That had her practically jackknifing in the bed. First rule of what? And who the hell was she talking to?

She took a deep breath, then another. Think, she told herself. Reason it out. What had she been wearing? Blue pants. A lighter blue button-down shirt, tucked in. Tennis shoes.

She stared at her bare feet. She didn't wear tennis shoes. She was sure of that. And the blue pants and shirt had been plain, almost ugly. She liked herself in the pretty linen dress better.

She'd been giving advice. Lightheartedly. But still, she was in a position to offer advice.

She tried to envision the room that she'd been in. Gold wall behind her. Some kind of wallpaper. That was all she could visualize.

She lay back on the bed, all thoughts of a nap gone. Things were coming back. They were. She just hoped it was in time. She hadn't said anything more to Cal but every time she thought of Saturday, she started to feel ill.

She pretended to sleep for an hour before she got up and walked downstairs. She saw a ladder at the bottom of the steps. That was new.

She found Cal in the kitchen. He had indeed pulled the cobbler out. It was nicely browned and there was a large square missing.

"Hi," he said. "Did you sleep?"

"Some," she lied. "What's the ladder for?"

"If the opportunity presents itself, I may tackle the painting while we're here. The ceilings are pretty high upstairs. I'll need a ladder for sure."

"That will be a nice surprise for your brother."

"Trust me on this," he said, "it's the least I can do."

She heard something in his tone, something that didn't quite match the carefree phrase. It was the same thing she heard every time he talked about his brother. Anger. Maybe. Hurt. Possibly. Sorrow. Certainly sounded like it. A myriad of emotions. But whatever it was, he was still lucky.

What she would have given to have her sister back.

Her knees buckled and Cal caught her before she hit the floor. "What the hell?" he said.

She ran a shaky hand through her hair. "I had a sister.

She died when I was seven. She was five years older. I can see her."

He led her from the kitchen to the living room and sat her down on the couch. He crowded in next to her. Then he rubbed her back. Gently. "What's her name?" he asked.

"Mia. I called her My Mia. She was my everything." She could feel hot tears run down her face.

He gathered her into his arms. "What's Mia's last name?" he asked, his lips close to her ear.

"Mia…." She closed her eyes. Damn. Why wouldn't it come? "I don't know," she said.

"It's okay," he said. "How did she die?"

"I can see her. She's running down the stairs, her backpack hanging off one shoulder. She's late."

"For?"

"I don't know."

"Maybe a car accident?"

She shook her head. "She was only five years older. If I was seven, then she was twelve. Too young to drive."

"Someone else could have been driving. One of your parents."

How horrible that would be. But that didn't seem right. "I can remember my parents coming home, walking in the door together and telling me that Mia was dead. My grandmother was there and she was crying."

"Did your grandmother live with you?"

"I don't know."

"What was her name?"

She stared at her hands. She could see herself as a seven year old. Sitting at a table while her grand-

mother stood at the counter, making bread. "Nana."
She looked up.

He was looking at her with such gentle concern that
the dam, the fragile dam that she'd constructed to hold
back her tears, her emotions, her ice-cold fear, dissolved
and she sobbed.

She sobbed for the sister she could not remember.
She sobbed for all the other things that were out of her
reach. She sobbed for the woman who had been wearing a wedding dress and nothing else in the middle of
a snowstorm. She sobbed because she didn't know if it
was ever going to be better.

He pulled her into his chest. Stroked her hair. Rocked
her. Absorbed her grief. Gave her his strength in return.

And when she couldn't cry any more, she stopped.
She felt absolutely empty.

She pulled back and he let her go. She sank back
against the couch cushions. "I'm sorry," she said.

"Don't be," he said. "You've probably been saving
that up for a while."

"I hope the bank is empty," she said, hiccuping once.

He smiled. "Can I get you anything? Water? Coffee?"

"Maybe some water," she said.

He got up and she took advantage of the moment to
pull herself together. He certainly hadn't signed up to
have a hysterical woman on his hands.

When he came back with a glass, her hands were
almost steady. "I'll be fine," she said, assuring both
of them.

He nodded, looking thoughtful. After a minute he
asked, "Want some cobbler?"

She laughed. "Maybe later." She licked her lips. "It's

hard," she admitted. "To just wait. Not knowing if it's ever really going to happen."

"It's only been a little more than a day," he reminded her.

"It seems much longer," she said. "I guess it's like watching water, waiting for it to boil." She looked around the room. "You know what would be helpful right now?"

"Name it," he said.

"A paintbrush?"

"Huh?"

"Can I help you paint? I need something to do. I am going to go crazy just sitting around waiting for my memory to suddenly return."

"You should probably be resting. Letting your mind totally shut down."

"I can't sleep," she said. "Please."

He studied her. "I don't like to trim. How do you feel about that?"

"I'm taking the 'glass is half-full' route. I'll just tell myself that I love it. How will I know the difference?"

"There is that."

HE DECIDED TO start painting in Bray's room. He didn't bother with drop cloths. The carpet was old and would no doubt need to be replaced before they put it on the market.

He had found a stir stick, a paint tray and several brushes in the bathroom attached to Brick's bedroom. He picked up the can of paint and looked at the color.

"Summer Burst," he said. "What kind of color is that?"

"It sounds lovely," Stormy said.

He pried the lid up, gave the paint a stir and said, "Green."

She peered over his shoulder. "It's not green. Green is in-your-face, like it or not. This is lovely. It's soft sage with a hint of violet-blue undertones."

"That's what I said. Green. What's wrong with good old-fashioned white?"

She rolled her eyes and picked up a roll of masking tape. "White? I guess they didn't have HGTV where you were."

He feigned shock. "I know desert chic. Khaki and sand are the new neutrals."

"And Kevlar is all the rage," she added. "Don't be gauche and leave home without it."

"A gentleman is never gauche," he said. He picked up a roller. She was being a good sport but it pained him to see the traces of tears on her cheeks. She'd lost her sister. *My Mia.* That sort of told the whole story.

While it was a tragedy, it was also their first solid clue as to her identity and that was important. Especially when instinct was telling him that she was still in danger. The Mercedes Men had come back to the hotel and had been persistent enough to attempt to look in the warehouse. Cal regretted that the company truck had come along. He wanted to force the altercation with the Mercedes Men, to once and for all figure out why they were in hot pursuit of Stormy. But he certainly hadn't been willing to do that when there was a great likelihood that innocent bystanders would get hurt.

Over the next several hours, they worked in companionable silence. She slipped out of the room several times after hastily explaining that she was working up an appetite and she probably should throw something together for a late dinner.

"Something" ended up being medium-rare roast beef with potatoes and carrots. It was delicious. When he carried his plate over to the sink after dinner, he was amused to see the careful list she was keeping of all the food that she'd removed from the cupboards, the refrigerator and the freezer. One roast, 3.5 pounds. Four potatoes. The list went on.

He walked into the living room and stood at the window. He'd been right about the roads. A plow had come through around eight, which meant that the primary roads were clear or close to it, otherwise the secondary roads would not have received any attention.

The Mercedes Men would make better time now. Would they have thought to take down license plates at the hotels? He thought so. It was basic and what else were the guys in the second car doing while Dumb and Dumber were asking the questions.

Unfortunately, because he'd been out of the country for the better part of the past eight years, he'd never taken the time to establish a residence or update his driver's license. So, when the rental company had asked to see his license and then asked if the address in Ravesville was his current address, he'd taken the easy way out and said yes.

That might come to bite him in the ass but it couldn't be helped now.

If he and Stormy were lucky, there'd be other names that would get checked first.

His cell phone buzzed and he pulled it out of his pocket. "Hi Chase," he said.

"I just wanted to make sure that you'd gotten inside and that everything was okay," Chase said.

"Everything's good," Cal said. "I had a couple free hours so I started painting in Bray's room. I figured that might help get the house ready to sell faster."

"Was that the Summer Burst? How's that look?"

Cal started to say that it was a lovely soft sage with a hint of violet-blue undertones but stopped. His brother would call 911, thinking the paint fumes had gotten to him. "It's good."

"About the house," Chase said, his tone hesitant.

"Yeah?"

"I want it. I want to buy out yours and Bray's shares. I want it for Raney and me."

Cal didn't think there was much in the world that could surprise him but this had. "Of course," he said. "I never figured you'd want it." He laughed. "I'll paint more carefully, make sure I don't get any on the wood-work."

"You do that. Thanks, Cal."

After Chase hung up, Cal continued to stand at the window. Chase was coming back to stay. Wow.

The fifth stair squeaked when Stormy hit it. "Did I hear you on the telephone?"

"Yeah. Talking to Chase. He wants to buy Bray and me out. He wants the house."

"How do you feel about that?"

"I think it's great. He sounds happy. Settled."

"That would be a nice feeling," she said. She didn't sound as if she was whining, just stating a fact. "I'm tired," she said. "I think it's an early bedtime for me."

"Good night," he said. "Thanks again for dinner. It was great."

She smiled and went back upstairs. He sat down on the couch, reached for the book that was in his duffel bag and read for an hour before finally admitting that the book, a biography of Teddy Roosevelt, wasn't holding his attention. He put it down, stretched out, which meant that his feet were hanging off the couch, and closed his eyes.

He didn't wake up until he heard the squeak of the fifth step. Immediately on full alert, he sorted through the possibilities, assessing the danger. His body told him that he'd been asleep for roughly four hours. He breathed in the air. No temperature change to indicate that a door or window had been breached. There'd been no other unexpected noises.

It had to be Stormy. Was she trying to sneak out?

He rolled over, blinked several times to let his eyes adjust to the dark and slowly sat up.

She was poised on the stairs. Enough moonlight shone through the big living room windows that he could see that her long dark hair was wild around her face, making her look both very vulnerable and very alluring. She was once again wearing his sweatpants and T-shirt.

"It's a little early for breakfast," he said.

"I have to tell you something. And it couldn't wait until morning."

Chapter Ten

His heart was beating fast. He knew it wasn't from getting awakened from a sound sleep. No, it was Stormy, in his house, becoming a bigger and bigger part of his life, that was making it speed up.

He stood up. "Have a seat."

"I remembered how I got into the snowdrift."

He wasn't sure he wanted to know. But still, he motioned again for her to sit on the couch. She looked too frail, like a good breeze might blow her down the rest of the stairs.

She sat, with her back against the pillow he'd been using and her legs bent at the knees. He tossed her his blanket.

"Let's share," she said, holding out a portion. "It's chilly."

He sat back down, a full foot away from her toes. He let the blanket fall across his lap. "I'm listening."

"I was in the trunk of a car," she said, her voice emotionless. "I must have been sleeping or knocked out or something because I woke up, feeling sick to my stomach. The car was stopped and I could hear some noise around me but not voices. I knew I had to get out. My hands were tied but I...I'm pretty flexible and was able to turn my body enough and get my arms in a position where I could reach the emergency trunk release. They should have disabled it," she added, shaking her head.

He felt a hot burn in his stomach. She'd been bound and stuffed into the trunk of a car. She could have easily died. They'd probably drugged her, which was why she woke up feeling sick. It was her lucky day that the Mercedes Men had underestimated how long she'd be passed out or that she'd be able to engage the release with her hands tied.

"I got out of the trunk. I was wearing the wedding dress." She said it as if it still surprised her.

"Where were you?"

"A parking lot. Some cars. Lots of semis. It took me a minute to realize it was a truck stop. There was a gas station and a little diner."

"Dawson's Diner, I suspect. You remember the apple pie you had for breakfast yesterday? I got it at that same diner."

She let out a sigh. "I wish I'd known that you were inside. It would have made things so much easier."

"I think we might have just missed each other. The waitress who served me mentioned that right before I'd arrived, there'd been some commotion in the parking lot. It had quieted down fast when two state troopers happened by for afternoon pie."

She thought about that. "They probably did go a little crazy when they came back outside and I was gone. I wasn't there to see it."

"Where exactly did you go?" He held up a finger. "Wait. First tell me if the car you climbed out of was a black Mercedes."

"It was."

He'd assumed so but he'd been trained to not make assumptions. "Okay. Now tell me how you managed to disappear."

"As I said, I was feeling really sick and it was hard to think. But I knew that I needed to get away. I assumed the people who had put me in the trunk were inside the diner. I wasn't going there. I saw a semi that was open in the back and I was going to climb inside. But then I couldn't do it. I couldn't willingly put myself inside another dark space."

He nodded. He understood.

"Then I saw the second truck. It was a big horse trailer, probably one that could carry fifteen or twenty horses. It had horizontal slats. I knew if I could get up onto the side and get my hands and feet into the slats, that I'd have a chance to hang on."

It was a crazy idea but he liked it. And based on the little he knew about Stormy, it seemed to fit her character. And the lack of interest in another dark space was totally understandable. He'd been pinned in a cave for three days once by enemy fire and it had taken him a while before he could even tolerate a dark room.

"I kicked off my shoes. I had these little heels on and I knew that I would be able to grip better with my bare feet."

"It was cold."

"I know. But I figured that was the least of my problems. I wasn't going to die of the cold, at least not for a while. I wanted away from that parking lot, from that horrible trunk. I got lucky. I wasn't hanging on to the outside of it for more than five minutes before the driver came out. I couldn't see his face because he was all bundled up in a hat with earmuffs and a big coat.

He started the vehicle and when I could feel it vibrating under me, I suddenly realized how precarious my situation was. But before I could come up with an alternate plan, he was pulling out of the lot."

"It's amazing that you were able to do this without anybody seeing you."

"The car I'd been in was parked toward the back of the lot. So was the horse trailer. If somebody had been watching, they'd have probably seen me but it was snowing heavily and the wind was blowing. I guess it was lucky that I had on that awful dress. I blended in."

Awful dress. The irony was not lost on him. They both hated that dress. He understood his reasons just fine. And this glimpse of a memory helped him better understand her reaction. She'd been locked in a trunk. That was certainly not the way the happy bride got to the church.

Or back from the church. That was certainly a possible reality. "Do you remember anything from before you were put in the trunk of the car?"

She shook her head. "No."

"Okay. What happened after the truck driver started his rig?"

"I remember being so frightened that he was going to see me clinging to the side of his truck and stop the vehicle. But he either wasn't a very careful driver or his mirrors weren't adjusted at the right angle to see the back of his truck. For whatever reason, he didn't stop and I simply hung on. I was doing pretty well even though it was much colder when we were moving. We took the exit off the highway and went around the corner. The back end of the truck slipped on the slick road. I should have been expecting it but I wasn't prepared. I remembered losing my grip and flying...flying through the air."

She took a deep breath and let it out slowly. "I must have screamed. At least in my dream, I was screaming. That's when I woke up."

He considered the explanation. The room was very quiet. The only sound he could hear was the wind blowing and a stray branch from the tree scratching the back side of the house. "Is it possible that any of it was just a dream, that it didn't really happen?"

She shook her head. "I don't think so. I was dreaming, yes. But my mind was reliving what had occurred. I know it."

"Then I think we need to go back to the truck stop, back to where it started."

Now her breath was coming fast. "I want to do that. I do."

"It might be a dead end," he warned her, his tone serious.

"It might be the answer to everything," she countered. She wanted him to understand that she could handle either outcome, that she wasn't going to fall apart regardless. "At the very least, we can score some truly excellent apple pie."

"Well, I was happy enough with that until I tasted your cobbler."

She blushed. He was glad that he'd been able to tease her. He didn't ever want to see her cry again. "We'll go as soon as we both get up." He stood. He didn't want her to leave. Knew that she should. "You should probably get back to bed."

She hesitated and he almost offered to share the couch.

Then she slowly moved. "It seems as if in bed is the only time my mind is relaxed enough to remember anything."

It wouldn't be right of him to try to convince her to let him hold her through the night. "Your memory is coming," he said. "Be ready," he added.

"Is that some form of *be careful what you wish for*?"

He knew what he was wishing for. And now that he knew that even if she was married, it had been under duress, that should have cleared the path. But she was still bewildered, definitely off her game. He needed to keep himself in check and not add to the stresses in her life.

"Something like that," he said. "Good night, Stormy."

He watched her walk up the stairs. Then he held the portion of the quilt that had covered her close to his face, breathing deep. He didn't close his own eyes again for a very long time.

SHE WAS AWAKE well before dawn but she stayed in bed. It was warm and she wasn't quite ready to face Cal yet. Something had happened between the two of them as they'd huddled in the darkness, sharing the quilt.

He hadn't touched her and unlike at the toboggan factory, she'd managed to keep her fingers and her lips to herself. But still, there had been a connection. It had comforted, warmed, while at the same time, it had brought her to the edge of her control.

That was why she'd gone quietly upstairs when he'd suggested it. Because she'd known that he was trying to do the right thing, trying to keep things from getting more complicated.

She was a guest in his home. He deserved that she'd at least try to leave it *and him* unscathed.

Perhaps if the memory of waking up in the trunk of the car had come to her in the daytime, it might have been different. Maybe she'd have been able to process it alone. But in the middle of the night, she'd needed someone else. On her way down the stairs, she'd deliberately stepped on the fifth step, knowing that it would loudly creak. It was her way of announcing that she was coming.

Her way of giving him the opportunity to decide how he wanted to play it. If he continued to lie on the couch, pretending to still be asleep, she would have gotten a glass of water from the kitchen and returned upstairs, as if that had been her whole mission.

But he'd rolled over, invited her to share his couch and listened. And she'd been very grateful. She'd needed to talk about what she'd remembered. When she'd told him about being locked in the trunk, she could feel his anger. He'd seemed almost amused by the fact that she'd chosen to hang on to the side of a truck in the middle of a blizzard. Even now, she thought she'd likely done the right thing. It had gotten her away from the men, even if getting tossed from the truck and hitting her head had caused a whole lot of other problems.

Between what she remembered about the ghost and the wedding dress and now this, knowing that she'd been locked in the truck of a car, was proof positive that she hadn't been the happy bride-to-be. She knew that Cal had been bothered by the wedding dress and what it meant. It hadn't been the same for her. She'd *known* that it was nothing. Still, it had been a bit hard to ignore.

Yesterday, when she'd remembered her silver ring,

it had given her a reason to pause. Something told her that silver ring was very important to her. Was it a wedding ring? An engagement ring? She could see it clearly and it didn't look like that but maybe the giver had been unconventional. It looked old. Maybe it was a family heirloom?

When she thought about her ring, her body seemed to have a reaction. She felt hot and slightly nauseous and very angry. It was just crazy.

Cal had said, *Your memory is coming. Be ready.* Was she? Or had something so horrible happened that she was blocking it out. Maybe it had nothing to do with the bump on her head? Maybe it was simply her way of coping.

She needed to get over it.

They would go to the truck stop today. She would stand in the parking lot, breathe in the cold air and will her memory to return. She swung her legs over the side of the bed.

Once she finished a quick shower and dried her hair, she dug into the closet for some additional clothes. She found a pair of black leggings and a long red sweater. She pulled on the black boots that were a little big but a huge step up from going barefoot. She looked at the knife that Cal had given her the day before. She slipped it into the pocket of the red sweater.

When she walked downstairs, Cal was standing in the kitchen, his rear end resting against the counter, drinking a cup of coffee. He looked fresh and capable and once again, she thanked her good luck that he'd been the one who'd found her in the snowdrift. "Good morning," she said.

"I'd make you some toast with your coffee but there's no bread."

"Maybe we can actually get breakfast at the diner," she said.

"The cook, or I should say chef, is a good one. We go for information, maybe get an omelet as the icing on the cake."

She shook her head. "Based on the apple pie, I'd rather have the cake."

He drained his coffee. "Let's go." He picked up his coat and under it was another black wool jacket. "I got this out of the closet upstairs. It belonged to my mom. Will it work?"

"Perfect," she said.

The road in front of the house was still snow-covered but once they got back to the highway, it was much better. They drove through Ravesville, dutifully obeying all the four-way stops. Cal accelerated as they left town. It was definitely better driving. Easier for them and easier for the men chasing her.

Almost as if he'd read her mind, Cal turned to look at her. "Nervous?"

She shook her head. "Anxious. Hopeful." She turned to stare out the window. Out of the corner of her eye, she saw him turn on the car radio.

She didn't want to listen to talk radio. She wanted to know more about Cal. "Will you stay in Missouri?" she asked. "After your visit with your brothers?"

"I don't know. I haven't thought much about it."

"You don't have a job to go back to?"

"Nope. Gave them my notice. I've been thinking about starting up a small engineering company, taking on projects that really interest me. Maybe contract with the government on building ships and submarines. Every time I was on one, I'd find all kinds of things that could have been designed better, more efficiently, so that it would work better. I think I'd find that worthwhile, making sure the next generation of sailors has it better."

"That sounds very cool," she said. "You could probably do that work from anywhere."

He shrugged. "Maybe I should buy the Fitzler property, live just down the road from my old house."

He was joking. But the idea didn't seem all that crazy to her. "It has that big outbuilding," she said. "Certainly big enough for creating prototypes or whatever it is you engineering types like to make."

He scratched his head. "You know what they say, you can never go back home again. Somebody very wise probably learned that the hard way."

"That's just something that parents try to tell their kids when they're graduating from college. Come on. It would be cool. You'd be in one house and Chase in the other. It would be as if you owned the road. Like the road might really be called Route 6 but everyone in the community would refer to as Hollister Road."

"Now you're getting crazy," he said good-naturedly.

She let it go. It was his decision. She would be long gone. With that unsettling thought heavy on her heart, she reached for the radio knob and started looking for something to listen to.

They didn't talk again until Cal said, "Five minutes out."

She rubbed her hands together in anticipation.

"It's possible that the Mercedes Men may have the location staked out," he said.

She'd thought of that. The risk was worth it. For some reason, the Mercedes Men had stopped at Dawson's Diner. She didn't think it was as simple as they suddenly had a hankering for a ham sandwich. "I'll get down on the floor. You check out the parking lot. If we see their cars, we leave."

"That should work."

She unbuckled her seat belt and got on the floor. "I hope they're there," she said.

He chuckled. "Ready to bust somebody's chops?"

"Maybe."

"Even if the lot is clear, I should probably go in first, just to make sure that they haven't gotten smart and changed vehicles. Give me a three-minute head start."

She could tell when they turned into the lot. It was rougher and Cal slowed way down. The SUV made a big circle. He was going around the building. "Anything?" she asked.

"Nope. I'm going to park. Three minutes," he reminded her.

"Got it," she said.

He parked, shut off the vehicle and got out without another word. She looked at her watch.

The first minute went fast. The next sixty seconds dragged on. She held her breath for the third minute. Then she straightened up, opened her door and calmly walked into the diner.

Cal was sitting in a booth and smiled at her. She sat down.

He pushed a menu in her direction. "See anybody interesting?" he asked, his voice low.

She shook her head. As she'd walked in, she'd looked at everybody. There hadn't been a flicker of recognition in her blank slate of a mind and nothing alarming on anyone else's faces.

"The same waitress is working today. Her name is Lena. Maybe she'll be helpful. I left a really good tip."

Despite her anxiety, she smiled. When the waitress came up, she was wearing a bright fuchsia smock and white pants and her hair was pulled up into a lopsided bun. She was probably midforties.

"Hey," Lena said, looking at Cal. "I remember you."

A woman would have to be dead not to remember Cal Hollister. Big tip or not.

He smiled up at her. "The apple pie was so good I had to come back."

"Glad the storm didn't get you," Lena said. She turned toward Stormy. "Can I get you some…" Her voice trailed off. "Coffee?" Lena finished stronger.

She had to take the chance. "Have we met?" she asked. "You look so familiar." She did her best *I'm sweet and harmless* imitation.

"I…uh…" Lena stammered and looked at Cal. He had a relaxed look on his face and was looking at the menu as if his greatest ambition in life was to discover the morning breakfast special.

"I don't think we've met," Lena said. "But I saw a picture of you. Just the other day."

"Oh really, which one was that?"

"You were sitting at a bar. Wearing a royal blue dress that crossed in the front."

She could see the dress. Could see herself at the bar. She'd been nursing a glass of white wine. Waiting.

Damn it. Who was she waiting for?

Who the hell had taken a picture of her there?

And how in the world had this woman seen it? "Love that dress," she said.

"Your fiancé was flashing it around when he came in to talk to Pietro about the food for your wedding reception. He's pretty proud of you."

She was glad no one had yet poured her coffee. She would have surely choked on it. She couldn't very well ask her fiancé's name or for a description. She put a finger up to her lips and tapped thoughtfully. "I'm trying to remember how he knew Pietro," she said.

"He told me that the two of them had worked together at Moldaire College. I got the impression that they hadn't seen each other for a while." Lena lowered her voice. "I know Pietro and his wife moved here about four years ago. Unfortunately for him, she and their son left about a year ago, moved back to Kansas City. He stayed, though, said he liked the area."

"That all rings a bell," she said. "You know, I'd love to say hello to Pietro. Is he working today?"

"Nope. It's his day off."

"Shoot." She waved her hand in Cal's direction. "My stepbrother helped me pay for the wedding. We'd both appreciate having the opportunity to thank Pietro personally for making it such a special day. Does he live nearby?"

"A couple miles down on Summerfield Road," Lena said. "Big yellow house on the hill."

Cal gave an almost imperceptible nod.

"Great," she said.

Lena smiled. "He's a nice guy but his ego does need to be stroked. He'll enjoy hearing how the food was at the reception."

Her tongue felt too big for her mouth. Just because

he'd fixed food for the wedding reception didn't neces-sarily mean there'd been a wedding. "Delicious," she said. "It was delicious."

"You two going to have breakfast?" Lena asked.

She could hardly wait to follow up on the two leads. Pietro and Moldaire College. But it would look odd if they didn't eat. "Absolutely. I'll take a short stack of pancakes and a big cup of coffee."

Cal ordered eggs, bacon and hash browns along with coffee. He waited to speak until Lena was at the other end of the restaurant.

"Nicely done," he said.

"Thank you. We probably better leave her another big tip."

Chapter Eleven

Stormy ate half her pancakes before pushing her plate aside. He figured that was as good as he could have hoped for.

He hadn't been exaggerating when he'd told her that she'd done a nice job. She'd struck just the right chord with Lena and the two of them had been chatting like old friends.

Lena came by, dropped off the check and cleared their plates. He took one last swig of coffee. "Ready?"

Stormy nodded.

He saw her glance at the check amount and knew that she was likely going to add it to her list of expenses to reimburse, somewhere between basil and flour.

He left Lena a tip in line with what he'd left the first time. Her information had been golden but there was no sense letting on that they were too grateful.

He led the way out of the diner and, after opening the door, stood in the entrance and scanned the exterior. Nothing too different than when they'd come in. Different vehicles getting gas, of course, but none of them was a black Mercedes. Of course, it was possible that they were being observed from a distance. He and Stormy had done just that at the toboggan factory. He glanced off into the distance. There wasn't anything close enough to warrant concern. He stepped away from the doorstep and started walking. He shortened his stride so that Stormy could easily keep up.

"Pietro or Moldaire College?" he asked.

She opened her door and slid in. He walked around the SUV.

"Pietro," she said, buckling her seat belt. "Even if Moldaire is a small college, it will still be like looking for a needle in a haystack because I won't know where to start."

"The first time I met Lena, she told me that Pietro was a chef at a restaurant in the student union at the college. Catered all the significant events."

"That helps," she said. "Still, let's see if we can find him. Maybe he can start to fill in the missing pieces."

"He might be in on it. Maybe one of the Mercedes Men is his best friend. His brother."

She sat back in her seat, evidently considering his comment. He appreciated that in her excitement at having a lead, she didn't immediately dismiss his concerns. She was a thinker.

"Lena said they worked together at the college. She didn't say they were old friends or any kind of relative."

"Maybe she doesn't know the extent of their relationship," he countered.

"Maybe. I need to take the chance. But you're right. There is a risk. I'm going alone."

"Like hell you are," he said.

"It only makes sense," she argued. "If he's in on it, then we don't want him to know anything about you. If that happens, your home will be compromised."

"What if he tries to detain you until his friends come

back?" He didn't know why he was bothering to even discuss it. It wasn't going to happen.

"Let me see your gun," she said.

That surprised him. "Why?"

"I want to see if it feels familiar."

He didn't care if she'd given shooting instruction to the military. "Do you know how to shoot a gun?"

She shrugged. "I think so."

"The fact that you *think* you know how to shoot a gun is not terribly comforting."

She waved a hand. "I promise I won't shoot myself or him, unnecessarily," she added.

He could feel his breakfast rumble in his stomach. He, who never got nervous about anything. "I'm not giving you my gun." He started the car. Pulled out of the lot.

"I assume you know where Summerfield Road is?"

"Sort of. I think it's only a few miles from where I found you. There won't be that many houses. We should be able to find the yellow one on the hill."

"Okay. Get me close and then I'll let you out. Once I talk to him, I'll be back to get you."

"No. You let me out, give me ten minutes to get into position and then drive up to the house."

She didn't say anything. Then finally she sighed. Loudly. "Fine. Let's just do this."

He took the same exit off the Interstate that he'd taken just two days ago. When he made the sweeping turn, he couldn't help but look at the place where he'd found Stormy. The wind had whipped the snow around and there was no sign that he or anyone else had tromped through the ditch.

"Was that the place?" she asked, her voice soft.

He slowed down. "Yeah. Want to have a closer look?"

She shook her head. "I am amazed that you saw me from the road. I…could have easily frozen to death."

She could have. That thought made his knees feel as if they were made of jelly. But she didn't need to be dwelling on the what-ifs. "I think you were probably knocked out when you hit your head on the fence post. You were just regaining consciousness when I arrived. I suspect you'd have gotten up and thumbed a ride from the next car."

"I'm not sure," she admitted.

She was quiet for another two miles before she turned in her seat. "I'm glad it was you," she said. "I'm glad and very, very grateful it was you."

His throat felt tight. He was falling for Stormy. He didn't know her real name or her real story but none of that mattered.

"Did you recall that picture that Lena was describing, the one where you were wearing the blue dress?"

"Oddly enough, I did. I can't remember my own name but I could see myself in the blue dress, sitting at the bar."

"What bar?" he asked casually.

"The Blue Mango." She turned to him wide-eyed.

"Who were you with?" he followed up quickly.

SHE TRIED TO visualize it. But it made her feel sick. She shook her head. "It appears my subconscious is onto your tricks."

"At least we got The Blue Mango," he said. "That first night, in the hotel, you smelled like mangoes."

She felt warm. "It was the hotel lotion."

"I'm fond of mangoes," he said.

She wasn't sure what to say to that. "Have you ever heard of this place?"

"Nope." He pulled his cell phone from his shirt pocket and tossed it into her lap. "See if you can find it."

His browser was fast and it took less than a minute. "There are three Blue Mangoes. One in Connecticut, one in Los Angeles and one in Kansas City."

"Focus on the Kansas City one," he said. "Proximity should never be ignored."

"It's on Lager Avenue. They have their menu posted. It's a restaurant, too, not just a bar. Looks good," she added, rather stupidly, she thought. His remembering how she'd smelled that first night had shaken her.

He slowed down to take the turn off onto Summerfield Road. It was a roughly paved road with large potholes at the edges.

Heck, maybe she'd only remembered The Blue Mango because she'd used mango lotion post injury. She certainly couldn't explain why some things were there and most things were not.

But maybe they wouldn't need The Blue Mango after all. Maybe everything would fall into place after their visit with the chef.

She knew that Cal was worried but she intended to be very careful. The knowledge that she'd been tied and drugged just days ago was still very fresh in her mind. But she'd push the man for answers if she had to. Time was ticking away. It was already Thursday.

Two miles down the road, she saw a yellow house on the hill. "Think that's it?"

"I'm sure it is. I'll do a pass-by first," Cal said.

"Good idea," she said. Cal didn't speed up or slow down as he drove by the two-story farmhouse. There were no cars in the driveway. That didn't mean much. There was a separate two-car garage. Pietro could be parked there. Visitors, too, she supposed.

What was clear was that there had been some activity at the house recently. The driveway was partially cleared of snow, the work of a shovel probably, versus a snowblower. Someone had made a path wide enough for one car that led up to the garage.

She couldn't tell if there were footsteps in the snow leading from the garage to the house but she assumed so. When she got close, she'd be able to tell if it was one set or multiple.

Once they crested the hill and were out of sight of the house, Cal slowed down quickly and stopped the vehicle. "I'll walk from here, through that field, and circle around behind the house. Ten minutes should be plenty."

He was going to be walking in knee-high snow, with waist-high drifts in places. He was going to get soaked. "Are you sure you want to do this?"

"Absolutely." He pulled on his gloves. "If something goes wrong," he said, "your job is to get the hell out of here. Don't worry about me."

"Nothing is going to go wrong."

He turned toward her and before she realized his intent, he'd pulled her toward him. He kissed her hard. It was fast, intense and made her want more. "You got that right," he said and opened his door.

If she'd thought it was difficult to wait three minutes before going into the diner, ten minutes was an eternity. In the entire time, no cars came from either direction. That was good in that there was no one to see Cal sprinting across the field.

She couldn't believe the man was running through

the snow. He was clearly in amazing shape. It would have been quicksand to her but he was acting like it was warm surf.

At seven minutes he was too far away to distinguish from the trees that ran the perimeter of Pietro's property. At exactly ten minutes, she put the car into Drive and took off.

The driveway leading up to the house worried her and something told her that she didn't drive in snow very often. As she made the turn, the back tires lost traction and the rear end swerved. She got the vehicle under control, stayed in the path and drove up to the house.

She did not see Cal but she knew he was there.

She got out, listening carefully. She didn't hear anything unusual. She studied the footprints in the snow. It was hard to tell whether it had been one person making multiple trips between the house and garage or multiple people making one trip. She stepped up onto the porch, looked for a doorbell, didn't see one and started knocking.

About a minute later, the inside door opened. A middle-aged man with dark hair cut short and heavy, black-framed glasses stood beyond the screen door. He was wearing gray sweats and a white T-shirt. That almost made her smile because that was what she'd been wearing when she'd borrowed Cal's clothes. If she hadn't changed, they'd have been twins.

The man was holding a yellow pepper in his hand. That boosted her courage. Men with yellow peppers were harmless. This had to be Pietro, the chef.

He looked around her, as if he was trying to figure out how she'd ended up on his porch. He didn't show any signs of recognizing her but if the Mercedes Men had showed Lena her picture, it was a good hunch that they'd also shown the chef.

"Can I help you?" he asked.

She smiled. "I'm sorry to bother you but you recently catered my wedding and I just wanted to tell you what a wonderful job you did."

There was no change of expression. She started to get very nervous.

"I…uh…got your name from Lena at the diner," she added.

"How was the pork?" he asked.

"Delicious," she said.

"The rosemary potatoes?"

Uh. "Fragrant. Wonderful."

"Good." His tone was flat.

She remembered that Lena had said that he needed his ego stroked. Maybe *delicious* and *wonderful* weren't enough. *Fragrant* probably didn't even count. She should have gone for something more. *Awesome. Best ever. Cooking-show worthy.* "I was wondering if you had a card or something that I could give to my girlfriends. A couple of them are getting married soon."

He scratched his head. "No. Listen, I don't mean to be rude but I'm in the middle of something."

She understood why he'd become a chef and stayed in the kitchen. He didn't have the personality to interact with customers. "But—"

He slammed the door in her face.

She wanted to kick it open and demand more information. But that didn't necessarily seem like the thing to do.

She walked to the SUV and got in. He hadn't cleared

enough of the driveway to pull around, so she had to back down the lane. It allowed her to keep an eye on the house. She still did not see Cal.

She turned, drove over the hill, slowed and stopped. It was almost twelve minutes before she saw Cal coming across the field. Once he got close, she got out of the driver's seat and into the passenger seat. He entered the vehicle in a burst of cold air and pure male.

"Did you hear?" she asked.

"Every word," he said.

"Where the heck were you?" she asked.

"Behind the garbage cans next to the garage. I wanted to see what vehicle was in the garage and then I wanted a position where I had a clear shot at the front door."

He said it without emotion and she knew that had Pietro presented any danger to her, Cal would have stepped in quickly and taken care of things.

"I didn't get anything," she said. "I'm sorry."

"You got something. I don't think Pietro and your groom—"

"He's not *my* groom," she interrupted.

He smiled. "Okay. How about we just call him G for short. I don't think Pietro and G were friends. He pretended not to recognize you but when you mentioned the food, you didn't surprise him. That was plain. And it was smart to try to reel him in with the mention of friends who might need catering. But he was so clearly done with you. That has to mean something. And I think it speaks to his relationship with…ah, you know who."

It struck her that he was being deliberately a little provocative and silly to make her feel better. He had realized that she'd be bitterly disappointed and had wanted to head that off at the pass.

Cal Hollister was a very nice guy.

"Maybe G and his friends have given up looking for me," she said.

"Maybe," he said. They reached the highway. Cal made the required stop. "I stuck around for a few minutes to see if he was going to make any phone calls. He didn't. Just picked up a big knife and attacked the pepper with a vengeance. You coming to his house bothered him. I don't know why. But I think it might be important."

"Should we go back? Should we get the truth out of him?"

"Are you willing to hurt him to do that?"

"I… No. No, I'm not."

"Then I don't think so. It would take some persuasion. Our best bet is to go to Moldaire College. It's just a little east of Kansas City. That's a ninety-minute drive from here. We could check it out. There are also four bridal stores in the area."

"Let's go," she said.

They got back on the Interstate and it was smooth sailing. They didn't talk. Yet the silence was comfortable. She closed her eyes. The next thing she knew he was gently shaking her shoulder. The vehicle was stopped.

"We're here."

She blinked. "I don't know why I can't stay awake."

"Well, there's probably a good reason. Earlier you said that you woke up in the trunk feeling sick. You do realize that you were probably drugged. That takes a toll on the body if it happened repeatedly."

She swallowed hard. "I thought of that," she said.

"That first night in the hotel, in the shower, I... I looked for...signs to see if I'd been raped."

The car started to roll and he slammed his foot on the brake and shoved it into Park. "I should have taken you to the damn hospital," he said, clearly angry with himself.

She reached out and touched his arm. "I wasn't. I know I can't be sure but I really don't think anything like that happened."

"I want to kill them all for making you even have any doubt."

If she hadn't already started to love Cal Hollister, that would have been the push that sent her tumbling down the slide. "Thank you," she said.

He still looked so troubled. "Where to now?" she asked, hoping to get him refocused.

He looked around. They were in a parking lot, surrounded by stone buildings of varying heights but none over four stories. The buildings were solid structures with heavy, arched windows and big doorways. These were buildings that had been here for a long time, probably a hundred years.

"I don't know much about Moldaire," he said. "It's private and very expensive. It was way out of my price range when I was looking at colleges. It's not Ivy League but probably somewhere in the second tier of that group."

"How big?"

"Maybe six to eight thousand students. Liberal arts focus if I remember correctly."

She looked around. There were huge trees, bare of leaves, beautiful with fresh snow clinging to their branches. There were heavily bundled-up students walking fast, their heads down to avoid the cold.

"See anything that rings a bell?" he asked.

There was something but she couldn't put her finger on it. "You said that Pietro was a chef here at the student union. Let's go have lunch there."

"You didn't answer me when I asked if anything rang a bell. Talk to me."

"I have been here before," she said slowly. "I'm not sure when or why but this place is familiar to me. And I think I was here recently."

"Okay. That's exactly why we're not going to the student union. Too big, too many potential casualties if something goes wrong."

"But—"

He shook his head. "We'll drive around the campus. Give you a couple more vantage points. That's the best I'm willing to do today. Maybe this will be enough to trip that little wire in your brain and everything will be clear as mud tomorrow."

"I hope so," she said.

He stopped at four more places around the picturesque campus. Once near the dorms, once by the science building, once down the street from the administration building and once near the student union, which was one of the larger buildings. There was a sign advertising the restaurant inside and a telephone number to contact if someone was interested in renting a room in the Union Hotel, which by the looks of the building were probably the upper floors. Nothing felt more or less familiar. "I'm sorry," she said.

"No problem."

He didn't even sound disappointed and she wanted

to cry. After the encounter with Pietro, she'd had her hopes pinned on this. "We're running out of clues."

"That's the glass half-empty. You might say we're narrowing the possibilities. Half-full."

"Does my glass have alcohol in it?"

"A truly excellent scotch."

She wrinkled her nose. "I don't think I drink scotch."

"Ah, but I do." He picked up his cell phone. Pushed a few buttons. "Let's go dress shopping."

"Four words I never expected to hear Cal Hollister say," she muttered. "Maybe you've already been drinking."

He smiled. "Maybe I love shopping."

"And maybe I love cleaning fish." She paused for effect. "I think we're both lying."

It was a crazy little conversation to be having on a cold day in the middle of the nowhere but it had accomplished exactly what she suspected Cal had intended. There was no time for a pity party. She needed to keep moving forward. The answers were somewhere. She just needed to turn over the right rock.

Chapter Twelve

Jo-Jo's Bridal Boutique was in a strip mall, in between a dry cleaner's and a nail salon. They parked in front and watched for a few minutes. Two women, probably a daughter with her mother, came out of the shop carrying a garment bag. No one went in.

"We should be prepared for the possibility that your picture was flashed around here. If G showed your picture to Lena and Pietro, there's a possibility of that. Sort of a *see my beautiful bride, now give me the perfect dress for her* kind of moment."

"How do we play this?"

"As close to the truth as possible. Our goal is to get information on G and the rest of the Mercedes Men. How about we tell them that you recently got married after your fiancé surprised you with a wedding dress but now you're attempting to resell the dress and you have a buyer who won't pay the price you're asking unless she sees an original invoice?"

"They might not be inclined to want to be helpful. After all, every resold dress is one less new dress they might sell."

"You'll pull it off," he said confidently. He opened his door. "Let's do this."

The store was small and stuffed with mostly white and ivory bridal gowns. On the far wall was an assortment of colored dresses suitable for bridesmaids.

There was one store clerk, a middle-aged woman with her glasses on the far end of her nose. When she greeted them, she looked over the top of her glasses. "Good afternoon. My name is Ann. What can I help you with?"

"Hi. My name is Mary and this is my stepbrother, Tom. I recently got married. My fiancé surprised me with this gorgeous dress." She held out Cal's phone so that the woman could see the picture of the dress and the close-up of the label. "I think he bought it here. It was so sweet. And now I feel terrible but I don't want him to know about some of my credit card bills. I need to get them paid off before the next statement comes. I'm hoping to resell my dress and I've got a buyer but she won't pay the price I'm asking unless she sees the original receipt. I can't ask my husband," she finished.

Ann pushed her glasses up and took another long look at the picture. Then she walked over to one of the racks and flipped through the long dresses. Finally, she turned. "I wish I could help. We sell that designer but not that particular dress. I don't think he bought it here."

She bit back her disappointment. "Oh, I'm so sorry to have bothered you, then. You don't happen to have any idea where he might have gotten it?"

"You might try the Dream a Little Dream on Cleveland Avenue. They're our biggest competitor."

She recognized the store name from the list she and Cal had created. "Thank you so much," she said.

She and Cal walked back to the SUV. He started the

car and pulled out of the parking lot. "Nicely done. You took my story and made it better."

It had been effortless and it made her think that she was accustomed to doing things like this. "I think I must be an accountant. Lying doesn't seem to bother me."

He laughed. "Figures lie and liars figure."

She looked at his phone. "How far away is Cleveland Avenue?"

"We'll be there in fifteen minutes."

They had to wait for a train so it took them seventeen minutes. The two-story store was on the corner of a busy intersection. The area was more commercial and more upscale. There was an art studio next door and a big bank across the street.

They parked and went inside. There were several salesclerks, all helping customers. She and Cal pretended to look around until another salesclerk walked out of the back room.

"Can I help you?" the girl asked. She was young, maybe not even twenty, and she wore a very short skirt.

"I'm Mary and this is my stepbrother, Tom," she said, launching into her story. When she got to the part about the credit card debt, the salesclerk nodded, as if she understood that particular predicament.

"I was here that day," the salesclerk said. "I wasn't waiting on your fiancé but I did see your picture. He was showing it to everyone."

Just like Cal had thought. "It's embarrassing," she said, rolling her eyes.

The girl laughed. "We all thought it was cute but we weren't sure when he said he was going to surprise you with the dress. Most of our brides like to pick out their own dresses. I know I'd want to."

"It was a lovely gown." She gritted her teeth.

"One of my favorites. And that's saying something since we have over 200 different styles. You must have had a real spur-of-the-moment wedding."

"Because...." She let her voice trail off.

"Because hardly anyone wants to buy a gown right off the floor," the salesclerk said. "They want to order a new gown, one that hasn't been tried on by other customers. But when we told your fiancé that was how it generally worked, he said that he had to have the one off the rack."

"It was really sweet of him to take care of it. That's why I feel awful now. But do you think you'd have the original invoice? Maybe if I could just take a quick cell phone picture of it so that I could send it to the buyer."

The girl scratched her head. "We might have it back in the office." She glanced around the store. "I guess everyone else has been waited on."

"I know that I'm taking you off the sales floor and you probably work on commission. I'll make it worth your while." It was just one more thing to add to the list of items that she needed to repay.

"I appreciate that," said the salesclerk. "I'll just be a few minutes."

Without having to ask him, Cal stuffed a fifty-dollar bill into her hand before moving toward the front of the store and taking a spot near the cash register, where he could keep watch on both the store and the parking lot.

She wandered around the store, casually looking at the various dresses. She was on her second cursory lap when she saw a dress that made her stop. It was ivory. A smooth satin. Off the shoulders and fitted through the hips, it gently flared at the knees with a swirl of the skirt. Stunning. There was no other word.

She couldn't help herself. She lifted the hanger off the rack, walked over to the mirror and held the dress up to her body.

An older woman, knitting while she waited, looked up. "That's lovely dear. My granddaughter should look at that one."

She smiled and took another quick glance in the mirror. Out of the corner of her eye, she saw that Cal was watching her. Embarrassed, she hurriedly stuffed the dress back onto the crowded rack.

It took the salesclerk another five minutes. Finally she came out of the back room holding an invoice. "Found it," she said. The girl held out a yellow five-by-eight receipt, the kind that gets torn off a book of receipts.

She reached for it and willed her hands not to shake. She realized that Cal had very quickly and quietly come to stand next to her.

Next to customer name, some earnest salesclerk had written Golya Paladis. Next to address was written Moldaire College. The dress had cost fourteen hundred dollars.

"That's odd," said the salesclerk.

"What?" she asked. Her head was whirling. *Golya Paladis*. Did the name mean anything to her?

"We're supposed to get an address and a contact number," the girl said. "But maybe because we weren't ordering the dress that wasn't necessary."

She pointed to a small circle with an X inside. "What does this mean?"

The salesclerk smiled. "That he paid cash. The very best kind of sale."

She pulled out Cal's cell phone. "May I?" she said at the same time she discreetly pushed the fifty-dollar bill in the salesclerk's direction.

"I don't see why not. It's your dress," the girl said.

She took the picture, thanked the girl again, and she and Cal left the store. Back in the SUV, neither of them said anything for a minute.

"Golya Paladis," Cal said. "When we called him G, we were right all along."

She rolled her eyes.

"Mean anything to you?" Cal asked.

"Not at the moment," she said. "Maybe you could kick me in the head, knock everything loose and that would all change."

"That'll be our backup plan. Let's see if we can find out a little more about him." He started punching info into his smartphone. After a few minutes, he frowned and shook his head. "I don't like this."

"Now what?" she asked.

"There's nothing. And I have access to some sites that not everyone would have because of my work as an independent contractor and even those are coming up empty."

"It's an alias."

"Probably. But Golya—"

"Let's just keep calling him G. I don't really want to think of him as a real person. He's shallow, worthy of only an initial."

"Okay. G bought the dress on Sunday. Two days before the wedding. That was the same day that Lena at the diner said that he contacted Pietro. Remember that she said Pietro was upset and she assumed it was because he had very little notice to get food ready for the reception."

"So I somehow fell into his hands before that."

"Yes. And I don't think too far in advance of that. He seemed to be moving fairly quickly, like his plan was coming together very fast. I think it's possible that you fell into his hands, that perhaps marrying you was an impulse that wasn't well thought out. Like you said earlier, what would have made him think that he could keep you once you were no longer drugged?"

"Maybe he'd been stalking me. He had a picture of me. I remember the picture. I remember sitting at the bar at The Blue Mango. I was having fun. It had to be before G. But maybe he was there. Watching."

She couldn't control the involuntary shudder.

"Doesn't matter how he got it. It's helped us. People remember you and they trust our story," he added with his usual optimism.

"Half-full?" she said.

"Always." He pulled out of the lot. "What do you want to do? We could go home or we could try The Blue Mango. Your decision."

She was exhausted. As Cal had suggested, she suspected that she was still feeling the effects of the drugs in her system. Plus it had already been a day of ups and downs, starting with the visit to Pietro's, the trip to Moldaire that had left her unsettled but no wiser and now this, a success to find out the full name of one of the Mercedes Men, only to discover that he didn't really exist.

She had to keep going. "The Blue Mango."

It took them forty minutes to find the place. It was

in a section of Kansas City that had become gentrified within the past twenty years and cute little businesses were springing up in the hundred-year-old shopping district. The Blue Mango was on the corner, a two-story brick building that appeared to be an apartment on top, restaurant/bar on the bottom.

There were no lights on in the building and many empty parking places nearby.

She looked at her watch. It was just before four. "It says on the website that they're open for lunch and dinner. It doesn't say anything about them closing in between."

"There's a note on the front door," Cal said. "Wait here while I go read it."

He was back in the SUV in less than a minute. "It's handwritten, apologizing for being unexpectedly closed today. They will reopen tomorrow at normal time."

She rubbed her head. "Do you think that their being closed has anything to do with me?"

"I don't know. It's a nice place. Doesn't look like the type that posts a handwritten note on the door."

"I'm going to call them," she said. "It doesn't look like anyone is inside but maybe the number is to someone's cell phone. Maybe we can get some information." She needed to keep pushing. She felt it.

He handed her his phone. She found the website and dialed the number. It rang and rang. Finally, she hung up.

"Now what?" she asked.

"Let's go home," he said. They were sixty miles down the road when he turned to her. "I'm going to get gas. I think you better get out of view. There's no telling how many resources they have and how many places they're watching. Once I fill the tank, I'll go into the grocery mart inside. I can probably get milk, bread and eggs. The basics."

She understood what he wasn't saying. There were probably a number of grocery stores in the small towns surrounding the Interstate but he wasn't taking a chance that the Mercedes Men hadn't effectively spread the word in the small communities to look for someone like her. "I should cut my hair. Dye it blond."

He shook his head. "Not yet," he said, his eyes amused. "I like your hair. It feels like silk."

That was nice. A little flustered, she hurried to unbuckle her seat belt and get on the floor so that her head would not show above the windows.

She felt him slow, then turn, then slow some more. She sensed that he was probably driving around the gas station before pulling into one of the bays. "How's it look?" she said.

"Nothing unusual," he said. He stopped the car, got out, and soon she could hear the sounds of fuel pouring into the vehicle. She would need to add gas to the list of items to reimburse him for.

The mileage reimbursement rate was 57.5 cents a mile.

She jerked up, almost forgetting that she was supposed to hide. She could remember having a conversation about the mileage rate recently. She'd been laughing. She could see herself. Sitting in a chair, in front of a plain table, a laptop computer in front of her. She was pointing at a screen. "Just use the form," she said. "It's online."

She'd been talking to someone. With someone. Who?

She heard the door open and barely stifled her squeak. Cal swung into the seat. He put the sack of groceries he was carrying on the floor of the backseat. "Everything okay?" he asked, already pulling away.

She waited until he told her she could safely get up before telling him everything. When she finished, she added, "I was kidding before but maybe I really am an accountant."

"You'll be handy to have around at tax time," he said easily. "Tell me about the chair."

The chair. He wanted to hear about the chair. But she realized that he was asking about exactly what she'd been trying to work through in her head—the details.

"Blond wood. With arms. Padded seat. Some kind of mauve print."

"Hotel issue?" he asked.

She nodded. "Maybe."

"What were you wearing?"

The very same thing that she'd been wearing in the one other brief vision that she'd had. But she'd never mentioned that one to him and didn't think it was prudent to do so now. She didn't want him to think she was hiding things. "Blue button-down shirt. Tucked in. Blue pants. Not blue jeans. Maybe khaki." She hadn't been able to see her shoes. But the other time, she'd distinctly seen that she was wearing tennis shoes. "White tennis shoes. I had my hair in a ponytail. That seems weird. I feel like it was unusual for me to have my hair like that."

"Anything else about your appearance?"

"No. But there was something next to the laptop. A blue lanyard, attached to a plastic badge. You know the kind. You would use it to clock in or open a door."

"Yours?"

She shook her head. "I don't know. It was turned over. Maybe the person's I'm talking to."

"Maybe. Any idea who that might be? Man or woman, even?"

She shook her head. "This is going to sound weird but it makes me sad to think of that person. I don't even know who it is. How can I be sad?"

"You know the person. You just can't remember him or her right now. But there's emotion connected to that knowing. Are you sure it's sadness? Could you be mad? Disappointed?"

"Sad. And maybe angry. Those don't seem to go together."

"Tell me about the laptop?"

She closed her eyes. "A big one. Maybe a seventeen-inch screen."

"What was on the screen?"

"I don't know. Information. I don't know what. I was pointing at something. Telling somebody to go online for the mileage form."

They were both quiet for several more miles. She turned to him. "What do you think it means?"

"It means that things are coming back. It's only a matter of time."

"It's hard to be patient when I feel so anxious. When I feel that I'm fighting time."

STORMY WAS PROBABLY right to feel as if she was fighting time. With every hour that went by, the Mercedes Men had more of an opportunity to track him to Ravesville. He wondered if he should move Stormy now. Take her a couple thousand miles away, where he didn't have to worry about pulling into a damn gas station and the potential of somebody seeing her.

The idea was certainly attractive. But he suspected maybe counterproductive. Her memory was coming back. And it was impossible to know what sight or sound might break the logjam in her head. But he was fairly confident that the stimuli weren't a thousand miles away.

What he was more confident of was her reaction if he mentioned getting away from it all. She'd refuse. She dealt with things head-on. From that first night in the hotel, when she'd casually walked past him with shampoo in her hands, ready to disable him the first chance she got, she'd shown her considerable backbone.

She'd hung on to the side of a damn truck, in the middle of the snowstorm, no coat, no shoes, probably still partially drugged up. She was a fighter.

And he'd yet to hear her whine or complain about *why me?* Sure, she'd expressed frustration over her inability to remember but there'd been no prolonged pity parties. She was handling this about as well as anybody might hope.

By the time he pulled into his driveway, the sun had set. Still, with a full moon, it was a light night. Everything looked the same. No fresh tracks in the snow from someone else approaching the house. He backed into the garage and they got out. Just to be sure, he carried the groceries in one hand and his gun in the other.

They were shutting the front door behind them when he heard the sound of an approaching vehicle.

Chapter Thirteen

"Go," he told her. "Upstairs. Not your room. Use the first bedroom. It has a deeper closet. Get all the way in the back. Don't come out, no matter what you hear."

There was no time to argue. The engine was closer. The vehicle was turning into the driveway.

She was halfway up the stairs before she made the decision that she wasn't going to let him fight the battle alone. He was in danger because of her. She glanced over her shoulder and he was watching her, making sure she got to safety before he opened the door.

She wasn't going to screw with his concentration but she also wasn't going to hide like some scared third grader. She opened the first door. It smelled of fresh paint. She closed it behind her just as she heard a car door slam.

She glanced at the windows across the room. They did her no good. They faced the backyard, giving her no view of the driveway and who might have come to the house.

She waited for a second slam, thinking that was the pattern of the Mercedes Men. Two approached. Two waited behind in backup. But there was only one car door.

She heard a knock at the front door, then the quiet rustle of Cal moving toward it. Just as he opened the front door, she quietly opened the bedroom door and slipped down the hall.

Hidden crouched behind the half wall, she now could hear everything that was being said. Of course, if they came up the stairs, she was a sitting duck. There was no place to run.

"Hi," she heard a feminine voice say. "I...uh...was looking for Chase."

"He's not here," Cal said. His voice was polite, but not friendly.

"Where is he?" she asked. Her tone had a little more edge.

There was a pause. "Who wants to know?" Cal asked.

She risked a look around the edge of the wall. From her angle, she could see the woman who still stood in the doorway. She was beautiful. Tall. Slender. And she had the most amazing red hair. It flowed to her waist. She was staring intently at Cal.

"Oh my gosh," the woman said. "You're Calvin, aren't you? I haven't seen you for almost ten years."

"Trish?" he said, his voice warmer. "Trish Wright?"

"Wright-Roper," she said. "What are you doing here?"

Cal stepped back, enough that Trish could step into the house and close the door behind her. The flow of cold air that had been making its way up the stairs was cut off.

She had no idea who Trish Wright-Roper was but clearly, Cal didn't think this woman was a threat. She started to breathe a little easier.

"Just got out of the navy," he said. "Came home for Thanksgiving. How's your sister?" he asked.

"Summer is good. Divorced recently. But she's got two great kids that I spoil rotten."

"And you're married?" he said.

"Widowed," she replied softly. "Listen, I don't want you to think I'm crazy since we're just reconnecting after a really long time but Summer and I own the Wright Here, Wright Now Café in Ravesville. Just a little while ago, some men came in, asking for directions to the Hollister house."

That wasn't good.

"There was something about them. Summer and I both had the same feel. They said they were looking for their cousin and asked if we'd seen a dark-haired woman. Now, that certainly didn't sound like Raney but still, it was an odd exchange. We've gotten to know Raney and wouldn't want anything to happen to her. So when I gave them the directions, I gave them good ones, but the long way around. The minute they left, I tried the house phone but there was no answer. I realized I didn't know Chase's cell phone. I jumped in the car and came here to warn him. You've probably only got about fifteen minutes before they show up."

"How many men?" Cal asked, his voice even.

"Two. I saw two."

"Okay," Cal said. "Thank you. This is very helpful. But you need to get out of here."

"Do you want me to go to the police? Of course, my ex-brother-in-law is probably on duty and he's not likely to be helpful."

"Nope. I've got this," Cal said. "But you're right. These men aren't friends of the Hollister family. But you and Summer need to be careful around them. Don't give them any reason to believe that you'd side with us."

She heard the door open, felt the cold air whoosh in.

"Be careful, Cal. Men like you, men like my Rafe, you think you can handle anything but sometimes it's just too much." Her voice was full of emotion.

"Don't worry," Cal assured her. "I got this covered. I'll be in for breakfast soon. Be careful driving in the dark."

"Good to see you again, Cal," the woman said, her voice fading away.

"You, too, Trish. And thanks again." Cal shut the door.

She was debating how best to get back to the closet when she heard Cal's boot on the first step.

"You can come out from behind the wall now," he said.

She stood up. He didn't look mad, more resigned.

"How did you know I was there?"

"Really excellent hearing," he said. "I heard the click of the door, saw just a shadow of movement as I was opening the front door and realized what you were doing. I had some level of confidence that you'd figure out a way to stay hidden," he added.

"I did," she said somewhat unnecessarily.

He nodded. "So you heard everything?"

"Yes. Who is she?"

"Trish Wright. I guess, Wright-Roper now. My brother Bray dated her sister Summer for years. We all thought they'd end up married but it didn't happen that way. Bray went away to the marines and Summer married somebody else. I appreciate the fact that they've still got kind feelings toward the Hollister family." Cal looked at his watch. "We've got less than ten minutes. This time, I really do need you to hide. Will you do that? Please?"

"Tell me your plan first," she said, not answering his question.

"I don't have one," he said. "Other than to get more information out of them than they get from me and to keep you safe. Everything besides that is fluid."

She let out a loud breath.

"I can't focus on them if in the back of my mind I'm wondering what you're doing," he said.

"Fine," she said. "I'll be in the back of the closet, hidden behind the clothes." She started to walk toward the bedroom.

"Stormy," he said.

She stopped. "Yes."

He put his hand on her shoulder, turned her and kissed her. All the emotion of the moment was packed into ten seconds of scorching pleasure.

Then he stepped back. "We're not finished," he said.

CAL WAS ON the porch, swinging in the old hammock, whittling on a stick when the Mercedes Men drove into the yard. He turned the outside porch light on, making it easy for them to see him. He wore an old military jacket that he'd gotten soon after he'd enlisted. After Stormy had gone upstairs, he'd quickly pulled it from his duffel bag. It had seen better days but he'd always been reluctant to part with it.

One car drove in. Two men inside. He figured the second car was probably just over the hill.

Both men opened their car doors. They appeared to be unarmed but Cal figured they had plenty of fire-power on them and in the car.

"Hello," the driver said. He was the man who had done the talking in the hotel. Cal was confident that this was G. On the passenger side was the guy who walked funny, the one he'd coined Bad Knee.

"Hello," Cal said easily. He kept whittling. Small pieces of wood littered the snow-covered porch.

"Kind of cold to be outside," G said.

"I'm watching for 'em," Cal said.

The two men looked at each other. "For who?" Bad Knee asked.

Cal looked up, his eyes darting fast. "The jerks in the woods. I'll blow this place up before I'll let them take it." He held up his knife. "I'm ready."

"You were in the military," G said, focusing on his jacket.

Cal nodded. "Just got home. Had to drive through a storm to get here. I told everybody I saw along the way that they were coming."

The two men exchanged another glance. He wasn't sure if they remembered him from seeing him by the vending machines. They had barely given him a glance that night. But now, Cal was pretty confident that they thought he was relatively harmless. "Our car is having trouble," G explained. "We barely got it here. May we use your phone to call for help?"

"I guess," Cal said, getting up. "You two from around here?"

"Nope. Just passing through," said Bad Knee.

Cal showed them the phone in the kitchen. As they walked through the house, they looked in every room. Bad Knee was eyeing the upstairs.

"Big house for a single guy," Bad Knee said.

"My brother lives here, too," Cal said. "Cried like a little girl about the snowstorm. We had to stop driving and spent the night at a hotel." He was pretty confident the hotel clerk might have told these two about the man and his brother who had stayed in room 14. "He went to get beer."

"I see," said Bad Knee. "We're in the area looking for our cousin. She ran away from home."

"I did that once," Cal said, grinning big.

"It's not a good thing," G said. "She's young. Foolish. Has dark hair. She's very beautiful," he added somewhat bitterly.

"She better be careful. They can see in the dark. Like a damn cat," he said. He took his knife and drew a line down the dark woodwork, marring it. "Ticktock, goes the clock." He tapped his knife against the woodwork.

The two men walked toward the door.

"You can stay here and wait for a ride if you want," Cal said.

"No. That's okay. We'll be going," G said.

"You got any matches?" Cal asked.

The driver frowned. "Matches? Why?"

"I got to start a fire. They don't like fire."

G chuckled. "Sure. I got some matches." He pulled a half-used matchbook from his pocket. "Make it a good one," he added, flipping it toward Cal.

The men walked back to their car, got in and drove off. Cal sat back down on the hammock and continued his whittling. He didn't move for three minutes. When he was sure the cars had moved on, he got up, walked inside and locked the door behind him. He took off his coat and tossed it on the couch in the living room.

Unfinished business. That was what he had with Stormy.

Halfway up the stairs, he called out her name. "Stormy."

She didn't answer. He walked into the room, strode over to the closet and ripped the clothes out of the way. Held out a hand and hauled her out of the small space. Once she was out, in one smooth movement, she wrapped her arms around his neck, her legs around his waist, and kissed him for all he was worth.

He could have kissed her all day. But all too soon, she unwrapped her legs and slid down his body. He was painfully aroused and he doubted that she wasn't fully aware of the fact.

"I was scared," she admitted, her hand resting on his chest. "I thought you might kill them."

"I would have," he said, "if it had been necessary. But the other two would have come looking for them eventually and then I'd have had to kill them, too. Even though I really wanted to beat the crap out of them for what they did to you, it just didn't seem like the most prudent action to take right now. They're a clue to your identity. The more we ultimately learn about them, perhaps the more we learn about you."

"I appreciate your restraint," she said, sounding half serious, half amused.

Restraint was not ripping her clothes off and taking her with her back against the wall. He shrugged. "Maybe they'll give up."

She shook her head. "You don't really think that, do you?"

"No. I bought us a little space. They'll be back or we'll run into them somewhere along the way."

"But they won't be back right away." Her tone was suggestive and he could feel hope rise in his chest. But this was too important to have any potential misread of the situation.

"I want to make sure I'm clear here," he said, his damn voice cracking. "I want to take you to bed, Stormy. And if you don't want that, we need to stop. Now."

She moved the hand that had rested on his chest to the back of his neck. She pulled his head down, met him halfway, her lips still wet from the earlier kisses. When she stuck her tongue into his mouth, he felt the answering surge in his body. When the kiss ended, she pulled back just a little. "Don't stop. Please don't stop."

"Just so you know, we're about one minute shy of doing this on the floor versus on a soft mattress."

She threw her head back and laughed. Then she jumped and wrapped her legs around his waist one more time.

HE CARRIED HER into his old room, gently dumped her down onto the mattress and fell in beside her. And it took almost no time for them to be naked. And for him to be inside her.

It was…amazing. He had his hands under her rear and his strokes were long and purposeful and she was just this close to—

She came explosively, her internal muscles clamping down.

"That's my girl," he murmured in her ear.

And when she was finally spent, he spread her even wider and went deeper. Minutes later, he tightened, groaned and emptied into her.

Or rather the condom. He had had the good sense to have one in his pocket.

"That's my boy," she said, slightly modifying his comment. She patted his back, which was damp with sweat.

He smiled against her shoulder. He was careful to keep his weight off her. After a minute, he said, "That was pretty fast. You okay?"

"Wonderful. Thanks…uh…for having protection."

He shifted, withdrew and rolled to his side. He pulled on her hip, turning her, so that they were facing. "I need you to understand something," he said. "I'm a young, single guy. So I keep some condoms in my bag. But I need you to know, I don't…" He stopped and shook his head. "I don't go through that many," he finished.

She wanted to laugh but he was so serious. "I get that, Cal. You're not promiscuous. I…I don't think I am, either."

In fact, it felt as if she'd used some muscles that didn't get used all that much. But it had been worth it. And while it had been fast, it hadn't been too fast.

Truth be told, she'd have let him take her on the floor.

Now she couldn't wait to share with him what had happened while she was in the closet. "I remembered something," she said.

HIS HEAD SNAPPED UP.

"It was hearing the voices. The one who said that it was a big house for one person."

"That's the guy with the bad knee."

"Yeah. That makes sense. Remember that I told you about the ghost. And that I was afraid of him. It was him. He's the ghost."

Cal propped himself up on one elbow. "How do you know?"

"He's the one who drugged me. Shots in the arm. After I saw the wedding dress in the corner of the room, he gave me a shot. When I woke up, I was wearing the dress and my head hurt. I didn't realize it was a veil until they let me up. I tried to pull it off and he slapped me."

"I should have killed him," Cal said.

She patted his arm. "That's my boy," she said, repeating what she'd said earlier.

He managed a grudging smile.

"Anyway, then he dragged me down some hallway. I tried to resist but they'd put these stupid shoes on me and I couldn't get any traction. But I saw the way he walked. The way he swung his leg from the hip. I think…" She stopped, closing her eyes. "I thought he was a ghost but he was just a stupid man wearing a sheet that he'd cut eye and mouth holes into. He never wanted me to see his face."

There was only one reason for that. They hadn't intended to kill her. Drug her, yes. Keep her captive, sure. But they weren't going to kill her because one of them intended to marry her.

It was a crazy plan. And didn't seem well thought out. What did they think she was going to do once they got complacent and stopped drugging her? Be happy that she'd been forced into a marriage?

No. That wouldn't happen. They would know that she would run the first opportunity she got.

Unless there was no place to run.

Where had they intended to take her? Why?

There were so many questions. But it was good to finally have some solid proof that there hadn't been any plan to kill her. Maybe that would work in her favor if they found her.

Not that he intended to let that happen.

But bullets killed and something could happen to him. "Listen," he said, "I'm going to get you my brothers' phone numbers. You need to memorize them. If something happens to me, go to them. Brayden Hollister. Like I said before, he's DEA and one tough son of a gun. He's in New York. And Chase Hollister. Detective with the St. Louis Police Department."

She put her hand on his arm. "Don't worry," she said. "We're both going to be okay."

She's very beautiful. That was what G had said. It was the same thing he'd said to the hotel clerk. In his gut, Cal knew that this was the man who had not only purchased the wedding dress but had also been the one who intended to marry Stormy. When he'd described Stormy, there had been deep emotion. Not love. Obsession, perhaps. Tinged now with a heavy dose of anger.

A dangerous combination.

"Maybe it's time to go to the police," he said. "Your memory is coming back. You've got enough to tell them."

She shook her head. "I can't trust the police."

"Why?"

"I don't know. But in my heart, I know that to be true."

He could call Chase. Maybe Chase could put some feelers out, see if there was any information within the law enforcement world circulating about Stormy.

But Chase had his hands full. Someone he loved was testifying at a murder trial. Cal wasn't going to ask him to put his own interests second again in favor of Cal's interest. He just wouldn't.

The Mercedes Men surely wouldn't be back for at least another couple days. He'd give Stormy another forty-eight hours and then they had to do something.

"I should get up," she said. "It's close to eight. You've got to be hungry."

"You bet," he said, leaning down and nuzzling her pretty breast.

Chapter Fourteen

Cal was very talented with his mouth. No debating that, she thought, as she cracked eggs in a bowl. She was making French toast for a very late dinner.

It had been an amazing day. It seemed only fitting that the day had culminated with several hours in Cal's bed.

She was slightly sore and deliciously satisfied. It was a nice combination.

"Hey," he said, coming up behind her. He was freshly showered and he smelled of soap and mint from the toothpaste he'd used. He wrapped an arm around her waist and turned her to face him. Then he kissed her.

"Your French toast will burn," she said, pulling back.

"I don't care," he said.

She gave him a gentle push. "I think we need to go back and see Pietro. He wasn't happy that I knocked on his door. That must mean something."

"It's probably worth a try."

She flipped three pieces of French toast onto a plate. She handed it to him.

"Thank you," he said. He waited until she'd gotten her own serving and sat down at the table before he cut into his food. "Good," he said between bites.

She could probably feed him dog food and he'd be appreciative. She took a bite and chewed slowly.

"I need to ask you something," she said.

"Okay."

"Don't ask me to hide in the closet again," she said. "I don't think I can do it. I need to be able to help."

He looked her in the eye. "I understand. I do. But I'm not going to let you get hurt. I can't."

"I feel the same toward you," she said.

He seemed to consider that. Something changed in his eyes. She saw a bleak look of what might have been disgust.

"I'm sorry," he said. "I made a mistake."

She'd wanted him to understand, not to be defeated. "I understand, I do. It's just—"

"I need to tell you something."

Something in the tone of his voice told her that this was her opportunity to be strong for him. "I'm listening," she said.

"I told you that my stepfather wasn't a nice guy. That was an understatement. He was a mean bastard."

She kept her mouth shut. She'd sort of figured that.

"I haven't always looked like this," he said.

That made her smile. "You weren't born 6'2" and 200 pounds?"

He shook his head. But he seemed to have relaxed just a little. "I didn't hit my growth spurt until college. I was thin as a rail in middle school and high school."

She wasn't sure where this was going.

"Chase was three years older and a foot taller and seventy pounds heavier. But he was still no match for Brick."

Things were becoming clearer.

"Brick used to beat him," Cal said. "Sometimes badly."

Her heart broke for the young boy he'd been. He'd had to have seen that. Probably had to worry that he was next.

"He didn't hit me."

"That was good. Right?" she asked.

"You know why? You want to know why?" his voice rose.

She wasn't sure she did but she figured he was going to tell her. "Why?" she asked softly.

"Because Chase made a bargain with him. Brick could beat on him all he wanted. Chase wouldn't fight back and he wouldn't turn him in. In exchange, Brick was to keep his hands off me."

Oh my. "I think your brother must have loved you very much," she said finally.

He ignored the comment. "You know how I found out? Brick told me. He and my mother came to my college graduation. The college that Chase had paid for, sometimes working three jobs at a time. And that was my present from Brick Doogan. He told me the truth."

"Why?"

"Because I think he knew that it would tear Chase and me apart. And that made him happy."

"Did it? Tear you apart?"

"I was so angry with Chase. So angry with myself that I hadn't been smarter, that I hadn't seen what was happening. That I'd ignored the clues that I'd seen. Because I was afraid."

"You were a child."

Cal didn't say anything for a long minute. "When I

asked you to hide in the closet, I was doing the same thing that Chase had done for me. Protecting. For good reason, perhaps. But it was the wrong thing to do."

"I'm not angry," she said.

"I was. After Brick told me, I couldn't keep my head on straight. The underlying message was clear. *You can't protect yourself so I'll do it for you. No matter what the cost to me.*" How the hell was something like that supposed to make a guy feel?

Emasculated. Impotent. "What did you say to Chase?"

"Nothing. I couldn't. As fast as I could, I enlisted in the navy and left home. Chase was shocked, to say the least. I'd just graduated with a mechanical engineering degree. I'd never talked about enlisting. And suddenly, I was in and on my way to basic training."

"Why did you do it?"

"I had to. I had something to prove. That I didn't need anybody fighting my battles. I was determined to be the best, the toughest. Nobody would ever have to take care of me again. When an opportunity came up to become a SEAL, I didn't hesitate."

She sat quietly, processing everything that he'd said. "And you and Chase have never talked about this."

"Nope. I sort of stopped talking to him at all. Look, I'm not proud of that but I was twenty-two and very angry with him. Yet, I loved him and knew that I owed him a great deal. With those conflicting emotions, I felt it was better to just be away. Chase and I have communicated over the years but we've never really talked. That's why I was coming home this Thanksgiving. It's time. Past time."

She understood much better that myriad of emotions she heard in his voice whenever he talked about his brother. "I'm betting that's going to be a really good conversation," she said. "You'll handle it beautifully."

He shrugged. "We'll see. He needs to understand that I'm not angry any longer. I get why he did what he did." He looked her in the eye. "And I will try very hard to never ask you to hide in another closet."

"Thank you," she said softly. "And thank you for telling me about Brick and about Chase. You know, you've got your head on pretty straight."

He shrugged. "I thought you should know, especially since we…"

"We did it," she teased, wanting desperately to lighten the mood.

"Yeah. Since we did it." He stood up and stretched, yawning widely. "I'm still real happy about that, you know."

She felt warm. "I'm probably going to turn in shortly," she said. "I'm hoping that you're not planning on sleeping downstairs." She wanted him in her bed. She wanted his heat, his strength, his incredible maleness to surround her. To insulate her from the rest of the world.

She wanted him inside her again.

She held out her hand. "Come with me."

WHEN SHE WOKE UP the next morning, Cal was already awake. He was watching her. "Hi," she said, a little self-conscious. "What are you looking at?"

He smiled. "Dessert."

She raised an eyebrow. "As I recall, you had a couple *helpings* last night."

"There are certain times when it's just damn foolish to count calories."

She'd been counting orgasms. Four.

"Remember anything else while you were sleeping?" he asked, his tone gentle.

She shook her head. "Today will be the day. I just know it."

"I know you have your hopes pinned on what we might get from Pietro but I don't want you to be disappointed."

She sat up in bed. When the sheet dropped to her waist, she pulled it up fast but not before Cal gave her a look of pure male appreciation. "Of course I'll be disappointed. But not devastated. There's a difference." She smoothed down the sheet, running the palm of her hand over it several times. "It's Friday. I think I'm running out of time."

He nodded. "So we should get up and get going."

She would much rather stay in bed and play. "Yes," she said, already swinging her legs over the side.

They ate a quick breakfast of cereal and toast. When they walked outside, she could tell the weather had warmed up considerably, probably to the midforties. That, combined with the sunny day, was making the remaining snow and ice melt quickly.

When they passed Fitzler's, she didn't tease him any more about buying the property. But she saw him take a long look, as if he might be sizing the place up.

When they got to the spot where Cal had found her, there were spots in the vast expanse of land where the ground, an ugly green-brown, showed through. It looked so different than it had just forty-eight hours before.

But then again, she was very different, too.

A woman couldn't leave Cal Hollister's bed unchanged.

Cal had touched her heart, too. Of course she was different. When he'd listened and really *heard* her request to not be shuffled to the back of the closet, she'd known that something powerful had happened. It had been a connection that she still wasn't sure she understood but it had told her everything she needed to know about Cal Hollister and the kind of man he was.

They pulled into the diner parking lot and went through the same routine as before. She got out of sight, Cal checked the parking lot, then entered the diner alone. At three minutes, she followed.

Unfortunately, Lena wasn't working. It was a younger waitress who was hurrying back and forth with coffee and heaping plates of food.

She slid into the booth, anxious to see if there was any sign of recognition. It was impossible to know how many people G had shown her picture to. "Coffee?" the waitress asked, barely giving them a glance. Her name tag said Laura.

They both nodded and Laura hurried away, presumably to get them cups. Cal got up from the booth and snagged a newspaper off the stack that was haphazardly lying at the end of the counter. He sat back down and started quickly scanning the contents, flipping through the pages.

"Looking for something in particular?" she asked.

"Nope. Just looking," he said.

She didn't believe that. Cal probably never did anything without intention.

He pushed the newspaper in her direction. "Why don't you take a look?"

She shrugged. "Can't hurt," she said. The front page

was primarily devoted to national news and then it turned more local on the inside pages. She scanned the obituaries and passed up the food ads. The second section of the paper was Sports.

And the hair on the back of her neck stood up. Her hand hovered over the page, anxious to flip, not able to complete the action.

"What?" Cal asked immediately.

Laura chose that moment to return to the table, two coffee cups in one hand, setting them down with a thud.

She watched as Laura took a pen out of her pocket. At least somebody was acting in a normal, expected manner. Not like her, who practically had a panic attack over a newspaper. What the hell was wrong with her?

"What can I get you this morning?" Laura asked.

Instead of ordering, Cal looked toward the kitchen. "We were hoping to catch up with Pietro while we were here," he said.

"Good luck," Laura said. "He didn't show this morning."

Her hand started to shake. She put down her coffee cup before the liquid sloshed over the rim. "Is he sick?"

Laura shrugged and looked toward the door as a table of four came in. "Not sure. But he hasn't called in and the owner is really pissed. He's acting like Pietro does this all the time. I've worked here for over a year and have never seen it before. The guy is a jerk."

"Pietro?" Cal attempted to clarify.

"No. The owner." She tapped her pen on the order pad. "What would you like?"

Cal pushed the menus to the edge of the table. "We'll take four of your cinnamon rolls to go and if you could put these coffees in some paper cups, that would be great." He pulled a twenty out of his shirt pocket. "You can keep the change."

Laura scooped up the money and their coffee cups. "I'll be right back."

"What do you think?" she asked once the woman was out of hearing range.

"It's odd," Cal admitted. "And when odd things happen, we should pay attention. But first, tell me about the newspaper."

"There's something here," she said, her voice soft. "I can feel it."

"Which article?"

She looked at the Sports section again. There was a big article about the St. Louis Blues hockey team, a smaller article about coaching changes in the National Baseball League and several blurbs about local sporting events coming up on the weekend.

"None of them," she admitted. "It's just an overall sense of unease."

"You have a lot of sports knowledge," he said. "For a girl," he added, his tone teasing.

As always, Cal had the most amazing way of adding just a little humor right when it was desperately needed. "We need to find Pietro."

"Agreed. That's why we're taking our stuff to go."

In less than three minutes, they were in the car. Once they got out of the parking lot and back onto the highway, Cal drove with one hand and held a cinnamon roll in the other. She felt too nervous to eat but she sipped her coffee.

"How do we play this?" she asked as they got closer.

"I've been thinking about that." He took a big drink of coffee. "I think we need to be prepared for the possibility that something happened to him. After all, to unexpectedly not show for work and not call…"

Her coffee started to roll in her stomach. "You think something happened to him because he talked to me?"

"I don't know. But it does seem odd that your conversation was yesterday and today, this."

"I'm like the damn plague," she said, so irritated with the whole situation that she could barely stand it. She wanted to thump her head against the window, to shake loose the memories that refused to come back.

"You might be the catalyst but you're not the person responsible for anything that's happening," he said. "And I could be way off. I said we simply needed to be prepared."

He wasn't wrong. Something had happened to Pietro and it likely had something to do with her and the Mercedes Men.

When they got close to Pietro's house, Cal did a pass-by, the same as the day before. Nothing appeared different. The snow had melted enough that the car tracks from the day before were no longer visible. Now there were simply patches of snow, split by long strips of gravel.

She expected Cal to stop like before, so that he could get out and she could drive. Instead, he did a U-turn and headed back toward Pietro's. "We're going in together?" she said.

"Yeah. I would prefer to leave you alongside the road while I go check but I figured you wouldn't be too happy about that."

He had remembered that she'd asked him not to leave her out, to include her in her own defense.

"Thank you," she said.

"Don't thank me yet," he said, his tone disgusted. "This could be the stupidest thing I've ever done. We need to be prepared for the possibility that the Mercedes Men found out about your visit and that they are betting that you'll come back. They may be waiting for us."

"Then we deal with them," she said. "We need to stop this before more people get involved."

He didn't respond. When he made the turn into Pietro's driveway, he glanced at her. "Be ready," he said.

"I am." She sincerely hoped that they did not find Pietro dead in his house. She wasn't sure how she felt about a potential confrontation with the Mercedes Men. She'd been truthful when she'd said she wanted this over with. But she certainly didn't want to put Cal in danger.

"I go first," he said. "Stay behind me."

"Okay. What if he's inside, on the couch, with the flu? What are we going to tell him?"

"We'll have to think of something."

Nobody shot at them as they walked from the SUV to the front door. Cal knocked sharply. She listened carefully for any telltale noise from inside and knew Cal was doing the same.

But they heard nothing.

Cal tried the door. It was locked.

He hesitated for just seconds before removing the tool from his pocket and picking the lock. Then he wrapped his hand in his shirttail before turning the knob.

The interior was dark. Quiet. They went into the kitchen, which looked out into the backyard, similar to the Hollister house. But the similarities ended there. While the Hollister appliances were thirty years old, these were brand-new stainless steel. There was a six-burner stove with double ovens. Big pans with copper bottoms hung from hooks in the ceiling.

All of that was interesting but not as interesting as the plate on the counter. It was a sandwich, with four or five bites out of it. There was a half a slice of fresh pineapple.

It appeared that Pietro's lunch had been interrupted.

"I'm going to look in the bedrooms," Cal whispered.

She nodded. The kitchen smelled like…cinnamon. Yes, that was it. She opened the oven. Inside was the remains of some kind of crumble. It looked half-baked.

Pietro had had the presence of mind to shut off his oven but he hadn't wanted to waste any time waiting for the dessert to finish cooking.

Cal came back into the kitchen. "The house is empty. No signs of struggle. I'm going to check the garage."

His car wasn't going to be there. She was confident of that. When Cal came back in just a minute, he shook his head. "He's gone," he said.

"He was in a hurry."

"Looks like it," Cal agreed. "There's no way of knowing what he took for clothes or where he might be headed. Let's get out of here."

"Wait," she said. She walked over to the desk in the corner of the kitchen. She used a pen to pick through the mail, flipping envelopes over.

"What are you looking for?" he asked.

"Two things. His last name. There's an electric bill here for Pietro Moroque. And—" she stopped and smiled at him "—this." She pointed to a bright orange envelope. Like Cal had with the door, she used her shirt-tail to pull out the card from inside. It was a Hallow-een card. A child had scribbled his name inside. It was hard to read but she thought it said Jacob. She didn't care about that. She looked at the envelope. The return address in the corner was a preprinted address sticker. *Tika Moroque. 519 Feather Ave., Kansas City, MO 64110.*

"This has got to be his wife and child," she said. "If he's running, will he go there first to say goodbye?"

"Or to make sure they're safe?" Cal said.

With her shirt, she carefully wiped off the pen that she'd touched. She tossed it back onto the desk. "Let's go."

Chapter Fifteen

It took a couple hours to reach Kansas City but they had no trouble finding Tika Moroque's house. Their GPS led them right to it. It was a modest ranch on a quiet street. There was a swing set in the backyard with a big slide.

They made a pass-by in both directions before parking on the street, across from the house. They got out, crossed the street, walked up the short sidewalk and rang the bell.

It was almost noon on a Friday and there was no reason to believe that anyone would be home. Still, they waited. And rang the doorbell a second time.

Just as they were about to return to the car, the front door swung open. A woman, dark short hair, maybe midthirties, wearing a gray business suit, answered the door.

Before Cal or she could speak, the woman held up her index finger and pointed at them. "You need to get the hell away from my house."

"We just want a minute of your time, ma'am," Cal said.

"No, you don't," she said. "You want to screw up my life. And the life I've built for my son. But I'm not going to let you. Get off my porch." She tried to close the door but Cal was faster.

He stuck his foot in the door and pushed forward. In just seconds, they were inside the small house.

The woman had her back against the wall with her hand up to her mouth. She looked scared to death.

Now it was Cal's turn to hold up a finger. "We are not going to hurt you. Or your son. Let me be clear about that. But I didn't want to have this conversation on the street."

"I have nothing to say to you," she said.

"Well, we have something to tell you." Cal motioned to the small living room at his right. "Perhaps we could sit?"

Tika finally nodded. She took small sideways steps, never taking her eyes off them. When they sat on the couch, she lowered herself into the chair opposite of them.

"My name is Cal Hollister. This is Stormy. I call her Stormy because I found her three days ago, injured and alone, in the middle of a snowstorm."

They had the woman's attention. Her eyes were big.

"Unfortunately," Cal continued, "Stormy doesn't remember her real name or how she ended up in the snowstorm. She had a head injury."

Tika didn't say anything but her face looked less frightened.

"We went to see your ex-husband yesterday. We had reason to believe that he might be able to help us. But he wasn't helpful. And today, when we tried to talk to him again, he's suddenly gone from his house and missing from work."

Tika showed no reaction to the news. They weren't surprising her.

"We need your help. That's all we want." Cal sat back on the couch.

She felt like squirming under Tika's stare. But she sat still, with her hands calmly folded in her lap.

"You really can't remember who you are?" Tika finally asked.

She shook her head. "I'm hoping you can help me with that."

"I have no idea," Tika said.

She tried not to let the disappointment swamp her. She needed to think. "But our visit here didn't surprise you," she said.

Tika shook her head. "My ex-husband was waiting for me as I left the day care this morning after dropping off my son. I was on my way to work but after we talked, I decided to come home. I wasn't up to facing the office. He told me about your visit to his house yesterday."

"What did he tell you?"

Tika hesitated. Then she shrugged. "He said that he'd catered a wedding reception for an old acquaintance from Moldaire College. That he hadn't wanted to but he owed the man and this would pay the debt."

"Owed?" Cal asked.

Tika shook her head. "I don't know the details. I don't want to know. There were things about my ex-husband that I discovered after we were married that didn't make me happy. That's one of the reasons we're no longer married."

"He said the man had showed him a picture of his fiancée and when you came to his door, he knew that you were the same woman. He also knew that something had gone wrong. The man had come with some friends to pick up the food. They made one trip out to their car but there was more stuff. He was waiting for them to come back for the second load. They didn't. Finally, he went outside to see what was going on. They were very agitated. They didn't realize that Pietro speaks Russian. They were talking about how the woman had disappeared. About that time a couple cops drove in and the men got the hell out of there, without ever getting the rest of the food."

"Pietro asked me about the roast pork and rosemary potatoes."

"Yeah," Tika said. "That's what they left behind. When you said it was good, he knew you were lying."

"Can you tell me the names of the men?" Cal asked.

She shook her head. "I don't know their names. I don't want to know their names. He referred to the man who had contacted him as Golya. I don't know if that's a first or last name."

Cal showed no reaction to the name. She understood. There was no reason for Tika to know that it meant something to them. "Did he contact Golya and tell him that we'd been at his house?" she asked.

Tika shook her head. "No. That's why he decided he needed to disappear for a few days. He said that if Golya found out that the missing woman had been at his house and that he'd simply let her go, he would be very angry. Maybe angry enough to kill him."

"Why did he let me go?"

"I got the impression that he thinks Golya is crazy. Like really crazy as in mentally ill. He did say the man is a mean son of a bitch and he didn't want any part of sending you back to him. I really do think my ex is trying to be a better person."

"How would Golya have found out Stormy was there?" Cal asked.

Tika pointed her finger in their general direction. "Even without his help, Pietro was confident Golya would find her. And then he assumed that she would probably tell Golya about the visit, not realizing the jeopardy it would put Pietro in. Unfortunately, he didn't think about this until he'd let her drive away."

"So he was simply going to hide forever?" Cal asked, shaking his head.

"Not forever. He seemed to think that Golya was headed back to Russia very soon, maybe within days."

"Why did he think that?" she asked.

"Something Golya said about his bride learning to love Russia when it was her new home."

She looked at Cal. If she hadn't managed to get away, would they have somehow managed to get her out of the United States and into Russia?

"We really need to know more about Golya," Cal said. "Surely you can contact your ex-husband. He would have given you some way to do that in the event something happened to your son."

Tika shook her head. "There was no need. I have sole custody of my son. I am his mother. Pietro is not his father. Another reason why our marriage didn't work. My son does not understand the particulars yet. He is too small. The truth is known by just a few people. But if something happens to my son, I would call his real father, not Pietro."

"Given that, it seems odd to me that he came here this morning," she said. "Why tell you all this?"

Tika shrugged. "I don't think he has anybody else. And to tell you the truth, I think he just wanted somebody to know in case he did suddenly turn up dead. I wish he wouldn't have. I'd rather not know." Tika stood up and looked at her watch. "When I saw the two of you on the porch, I wasn't going to answer the door. I don't want any of this ugliness touching me. But then I figured that you'd probably just come back and Jacob might be here then."

Tika walked over and opened the front door. "I've told you everything I know. Now I'm asking you nicely. Please just leave my house and forget that we ever had this conversation because that's what I'm going to do."

She stood up. "I know you said that you couldn't get a message to Pietro. But if you could," she added, "you can assure him that I won't say anything about seeing him to the men who hired him to do the catering. It's not my intent to put anyone else in danger."

Tika shrugged. "I got the impression from Pietro that these are not nice people. You should probably be worried about yourself."

SHE AND CAL were back in the car before Cal spoke again. "It's starting to make some sense," he said.

"How's that?" she asked, shaking her head.

"Most of the time, kidnappers never intend to return the victim. They keep the person until they are no longer valuable to them and then dispose of them. For that reason, they rarely care if their victim can describe them. But in your case, it was different. The person who interacted with you, the Ghost, was careful that you couldn't identify him."

"He never hurt me. Just kept me drugged up and then

got me dressed in that awful wedding dress. I don't understand why G would think that I would be any happier being his bride in Russia than in the United States."

"Tika said that Pietro thought he was mentally ill. Maybe he was confident that he could win you over. Maybe he thought you'd fall in love with Russia. Maybe he was going to keep putting pills in your coffee so that you were a little doped up for the next twenty years."

"But why?"

"That's easy," Cal said. "You're very beautiful. To a man like him, having you as his wife would be a great accomplishment."

She looked at her still-bruised wrists. "He would have had to tie me to the bed for the next twenty years."

"There are other forms of coercion that make a person stay in a bad marriage," he said, his tone gentle.

She didn't need him to spell it out. What would have happened if she'd gotten pregnant? Even if she despised the father, she would never have left her child behind.

"We need to go to Moldaire. I know it's dangerous but time is running out."

"If indeed there is something significant about Saturday," he countered.

"There is," she said. "I know it."

He put the car in gear. "We can be there in forty-five minutes. We may want to make a stop on the way."

"Where?"

"When G and Bad Knee were at the house, I could smell cigar smoke on them. I asked if they had any matches. They tossed me a half-used book. It was from someplace called Raftors. I did a quick search this morning. It's a lingerie shop."

"Lingerie? Is that code for something?"

He shook his head. "Appears legit. At least the front of the house. Not sure what goes on in the back rooms."

"Why didn't you say anything before this?" she asked.

"I thought you might get a little freaked out thinking about G buying lingerie."

"It makes me sick," she admitted. "Because it was probably going to be presented to me on my wedding night. But it's a clue. I'm glad you told me."

"I'm not sure there's much to be gained by going there."

"Maybe not, but it's on our way. We shouldn't ignore it."

"Okay," he said and started driving.

They were fifteen minutes from the college and passing a small private airstrip when a memory so strong, so poignant, had her clenching her stomach.

"What's wrong?" Cal asked immediately.

"Mia. Mia died in a plane crash."

"Okay." His voice was steady, which was good because she felt about ready to spiral right out of her body.

"Tell me about it," he said. He kept driving but she could tell that he reduced his speed, as if he was getting ready to pull over or stop suddenly if necessary.

"Her best friend's dad was a pilot. She frequently flew with them. They were going to their cabin at the lake one summer evening when their plane crashed. Mia, her best friend, both the parents. Everyone died upon impact."

He was silent for a few minutes.

She could feel herself get more in control.

"What was her friend's name?" he asked.

"Misty. It was always Misty and Mia. M&M, like the candy."

"What was Misty's last name?"

"Wagner. Misty Wagner." She shook her head. "How can I remember her best friend's name and I can't remember Mia's?"

He shrugged. "Easy. You probably heard your parents say a hundred times things like *make sure it's okay with the Wagners* or *the Wagners will drop Mia off later*. They probably never referred to Mia by her last name."

It made sense. Suddenly something else was making a lot of sense. "It was a plane crash. Four people died. It had to have made the papers. There has to be some record. If I can find that, I can find Mia's last name. I can find myself."

He nodded. "It's a possibility."

She hadn't surprised him and she realized that he'd been going down that path from the minute she'd said that her sister had died in a plane crash.

"Where did the crash occur?" he asked.

She thought. "I don't know. I'm not sure it's something that I've forgotten. It's possible that I never knew. At seven, it probably didn't matter to me. And my parents never talked about it."

"Where was the lake house?"

She shook her head. "On a lake?" she said, throwing both hands up in the air. It was so frustrating.

He smiled. "We can find it." He held out his phone.

"I hope so. I know the month and year of the crash and I'm pretty sure that Mr. Wagner was a big shot in business. He ran some company."

"What was his first name?"

"Steve. I think. Look, I know it's not much but I

think the crash got lots of press. I can remember my mother, years later, talking about what vultures some reporters could be. I guess a few camped out in our front yard, wanting a quote."

She opened the browser on the phone and searched. Nothing. Damn it. She'd been so sure.

After ten minutes, he said, "If it happened twenty-five years ago, then perhaps the news coverage was never in digital form. We may need to dig deeper, to actually look for a hard copy of an article. We should probably try the library in Kansas City."

She nodded. "It's worth a try. But not the public library. Let's go to the library at Moldaire College. The college is at the center of all of this. I know it. It's time to figure this out."

But before they got to the campus, Cal followed the directions on his GPS to Raftors. The lingerie shop was in a strip mall, on the very edge of the Moldaire campus. There were fast-food restaurants on both sides, with a vacuum cleaner repair store at one end and a cash store at the other end of the retail cluster.

There were thirteen cars in the parking lot. Once Cal shut off the car, she sat very quietly in her seat.

Cal stared at her, concern on his handsome face. "Maybe we should just forget this. You just had that memory of Mia and you're probably still a little shook. We're probably not going to get anything here anyway," Cal said.

"I've been here before."

"Really?" he said. "Just when I thought you couldn't surprise me anymore," he said.

"I have been in this parking lot. Sitting. Waiting."

"For who?"

She closed her eyes. "I don't know." She put her hand on the door. "Now I'm really glad we came. Maybe G got those matches from me."

"I guess that's a possibility. Do you think you might have come here with him?"

She shook her head. "I came here with someone. We were eating chicken fingers in the car." She turned to him. "Chicken fingers. How is it that I can remember something like that and I don't know who I was with?"

"I have no idea. Ready to go inside?"

She opened her car door in response. When she got close, she could see that Raftors was a small store, probably not bigger than twenty feet wide by thirty feet deep. When they opened the door, a bell tinkled. There was a woman behind the counter who looked up.

Even though it was spelled differently, Raftors might have gotten its name from the fact that there was merchandise all the way up to the rafters. Bras, bustiers, corsets and panties. Every color. Many materials. Even fur.

When they got to the counter, she saw that there was a glass bowl of matchbooks. She glanced at Cal. He shrugged.

The woman behind the counter was frowning at her. "I told you I'd call if Jessica came back into work. She hasn't. That's why I didn't call," the woman finished, her tone acidic.

She was so surprised that she was literally speechless. But that was okay because the woman wasn't done.

"I run a legitimate business here. And whatever Jessica has done, she did it on her own time. Not through me and not through this store."

She decided it was one of those times to go for broke.

She looked at the woman's name tag. "Marcy, I'm sorry to bother you. I was in an accident a few days ago. So, you have me at a slight disadvantage. You remember me but I don't remember you. I don't remember ever being in this store."

Marcy rested her crossed arms on her ample stomach. "So you've got…brain damage?"

She hoped not. "Temporary amnesia," she said. "Can you tell me who Jessica is?"

Marcy looked at Cal. "Who is he?"

"A friend who helped me after the accident. Jessica?"

"Jessica worked here, up until about two weeks ago. You came in here about a week ago asking for her. I told you the truth. She quit without notice and I didn't expect to see her. She never even came in to pick up her last check. You asked me if I would call you if she came back in. I said I would."

"Why did I want to talk to Jessica?"

The woman shook her head. "I ain't never had a conversation like this before. You said she was your sister and that you hadn't seen her for some time."

"Thank you. Ah…one last question, I promise. Did I tell you my name?"

"Yeah. You said it was Jean."

She looked at Cal to see if he had any other questions. He shook his head. She smiled at the woman. "Again, thank you. You've been very helpful."

They were three feet from the door when Marcy called out, "I hope you get your memory back. That has to be really weird."

"Really weird," she repeated when they were back in the car. "I'll tell you what's really weird. I don't have a sister named Jessica. I know that. Mia was my sister. My only sister. Yet, for some reason, I'm trying to find some woman, claiming that she's my sister." She slammed her hand against the dash. "I told that woman my name was Jean. My name isn't Jean. That's another lie. I know it."

"I don't know what I expected," Cal said, "but it wasn't that. I think you did the right thing by telling her the truth. Otherwise, you wouldn't have gotten anything out of her."

"I got something but it doesn't make any sense."

"It will," he said. "Let's go to Moldaire."

Chapter Sixteen

The college library was one of the formidable stone buildings on the square. Now the open green space in front of it was no longer snow-covered but rather snow-spotted. In many places, patches of grass were visible. It was almost forty-five degrees outside and the remaining snow was melting fast.

There were many more students walking around with lots of the female students wearing colorful rain boots so that they could stomp through the slush.

Her tennis shoes had gotten really wet walking across campus.

"I…"

"What?" Cal asked.

She had started to tell him about the tennis shoes, about having one more memory. But he was already skittish about them being on campus. She didn't want to give him a reason to demand that they get the heck out of there.

But this was Cal. She trusted him.

"Stormy?" he prodded.

"I…I just know we're going to find something," she said. She'd already told him that Moldaire felt familiar. She didn't need to tell him about walking across the campus in tennis shoes.

He studied her. But then he focused on parking the SUV.

They walked into the library. There were two people behind the circulation desk who didn't even look up as they passed. There was a big sign with arrows that directed library patrons to various sections.

To the right of the big sign was a bank of computers. "Let's try the computer first, just in case," he said.

He sat down at one, followed the directions to log in as a library guest and typed in *Steve Wagner plane crash*. Nothing came up. He typed in *Misty Wagner*. Nothing. She started to look around for someone to ask for assistance. Cal kept typing, trying search terms. Finally, he got it with *Stephen Wagoner*.

She had been mostly right, even though the name was just a little different. Stephen Wagoner had been a big enough deal that the *Wall Street Journal* had covered the story. They followed the link and started reading the three-paragraph story.

When Cal finished, he looked at her. She was rereading the portion about the others who'd died in the crash. Mia Akina.

"That's her," she said.

Cal put his hands on the keyboard. "Ready?" he whispered.

She nodded.

He typed *Mia Akina obituary* into the search field.

In three more clicks, she was transported back twenty-five years and learning that Mia was dead. The pain ripped through her and she must have made some sound because Cal's arm went around her back.

"Steady," he said, his mouth close to her ear.

She drew in a deep breath. At almost the very end of the relatively short obituary was the information she'd been searching for. *Mia Akina is survived by her parents, Rafal and Jacinta Akina, and her seven-year-old sister, Nalana Akina.*

"Nalana," he said.

If she had been expecting an epiphany of sorts upon learning her name, she would have been bitterly disappointed. She felt no different.

"I guess," she said. Although when Cal had pronounced it with the accent on the second syllable and a soft *a*, it had seemed right. "I knew it wasn't Jean."

She read the remaining paragraph. *Rafal and Jacinta Akina, both sports journalists residing in Los Angeles, were in New York covering the US Open at the time of the plane crash.*

"Sports journalists. That explains a lot," Cal said.

"I'm not sure it matters," she said, unable to keep the disappointment out of her voice.

"Of course it matters," he said. "Every piece of information is a piece of you. It leads us to something else. Now we can easily find out where you live and where you work, Stormy. I mean, Nalana."

"For right now, let's just stick to Stormy. I'm getting used to it." She looked at her watch. "In less than twelve hours, it's going to be Saturday. We need to figure out why that's important."

"We—"

A blaring alarm drowned out anything else he might have said. Library users pushed back chairs, gathered books and started toward the entrance. "Fire," she said.

"Let's get out of here," Cal said. He did a couple

fast clicks to clear the browser history and then he shut down the computer. Then it was a fast but casual walk out the front entrance. People were milling outside the building, as if they anticipated it was simply an irritating drill rather than a full-blown emergency.

She didn't smell any smoke or see any fire so she assumed they might be right. Two campus police cars pulled up, sirens adding to the noise level. Two officers got out of each, two women, two men. As one of the men brushed past her, he gave her a look and might have stumbled just a little but then he kept on walking.

She and Cal got into their SUV. "Did you see that?" she asked. The brief interaction with the campus police officer had shaken her more than she'd expected.

"Uh-huh," Cal said. "I'm trying to decide if it was just a double take to look at a pretty woman or if it meant something. Is it possible that your concern about the police is because of some interaction with the campus police?"

"It's possible," she agreed. "What do you think we should do?"

"Maybe he recognized you because he's seen you around campus. No big deal. But if he recognized you because of some association with the Mercedes Men, then it's going to be relatively easy for them to look at the security camera tapes and realize that the two of us are together. That means G will no longer buy the story that I'm a crazy veteran chasing bad guys in the woods. The house won't be safe."

"I don't want to go back," she said. "I don't want anything bad to happen in that house. It's going to be Chase's home. Nobody needs those kinds of memories.

Plus, we need to be here. I can feel it. Something is going to happen. We need to be close to try to stop it."

"Let's get the hell out of here, at least," he said. "No sense making it easy for them. Where to?"

"We need to go back to The Blue Mango."

"Call them first. See if they are open." He tossed her his phone. He pulled out of the parking space and started driving.

She dialed. When the phone was answered on the second ring, she almost dropped it. "I was just calling to see if you were open," she said.

"Yes. Until ten tonight."

"Thank you," she said and ended the call. She turned to Cal. "Let's go."

IT WAS SIGNIFICANTLY more difficult to find a parking spot than it had been the day before. The Blue Mango was evidently a popular restaurant.

Cal finally found a spot a block away and they walked. He walked nearest to the street, keeping Stormy closer to the buildings. That provided some protection, although there could always be someone lurking in a doorway, ready to attack.

Danger could come from anywhere and for some reason, perhaps it was Stormy's certainty that something bad was going to happen on Saturday, he was running at full alert. The idea of something harming Stormy was eating at him, making his normal confidence feel shallow and cracked at the edges. He was this close to ignoring her insistence that the police couldn't be trusted. He wanted her protected.

He'd been trained by the best of Uncle Sam's navy to always consider all the possibilities. That meant that he couldn't ignore the possibility that Stormy was afraid of the police because she'd done something bad. Maybe at this very moment the police were hunting her. Was that why the campus cop had done a double take? Was her picture circulating because she was wanted?

What the hell would he do?

He knew the answer to that one.

Whatever it took to keep her safe. He had money saved. He could afford to hire a good attorney.

For now, he'd honor her wishes to stay away from the police. He could not take the risk that she'd be taken into custody and never forgive him for the betrayal.

When they got close, he motioned to Stormy to let him enter first. It wasn't gentlemanly but it was prudent.

The interior of The Blue Mango was filled with dark wood, black-and-white tiles and soft lighting. There were big plants in the entryway and a young man stood beside a high table that had two stacks of large, leather-bound menus.

Cal took a quick inventory. Bar off to his right. Oval. Stools on three sides. Sixteen seats. Two lone males, drinking beer. Male bartender. Four other patrons, split into two tables of two. Three empty tables.

Restaurant to his right, booths alongside the far wall, tables in the center, waitstaff station along the back wall. There was a family of four at one of the tables, and he could see the tops of heads in two booths. None of them had the jet-black hair that Golya sported.

"Two for dinner?" the young man asked. He had given Stormy a quick glance, the kind of look a guy gives an attractive woman, but Cal didn't see any flicker of recognition in his eyes.

Stormy stepped forward. "Yes. Could we have a table in the bar?"

"Of course," the young man said, reaching for two menus. He led them to one of the open tables.

When he left, Cal leaned forward. "Anything?" he asked.

Stormy nodded. "Maybe. It seemed very familiar when we walked in." She opened her menu. "Let's order," she said. "Maybe it will come to me."

Cal got a steak, Stormy got the salmon in a lemon butter sauce with capers. Both got baked potatoes and clam chowder to start. Neither one of them ordered a drink, choosing to stick with water instead.

They were halfway through their food when the bartender, on his way back to the bar with a tray of clean glasses, passed by their table.

"Hey, how's it going?" he said, looking at Stormy. "Nice to see you again."

Stormy smiled and the bartender kept walking. When he was behind the bar, Stormy leaned forward.

"He knows me."

Her voice was filled with hope and Cal was reminded of how frustrated she must be to be living in a void, not having the comfort of a past, an identity.

"Seems so," he said, cutting a piece of his steak with perhaps a little more force than necessary. The bartender was probably midtwenties and a good-looking guy. The idea that Stormy may have sat at the bar and flirted with him was not a happy thought.

"I think we're going to have an after-dinner drink at the bar," she said.

For the next five minutes, she pushed her salmon around on her plate. When the waiter came by, she gratefully gave it up. He offered dessert and they declined. Cal asked for the check and paid in cash once the waiter brought it.

"I think I should go to the bar alone," she said.

Like hell. "Why?" he asked.

She rolled her eyes. "You're...imposing. And I don't think that's going to encourage him to talk to me."

Tough. "What happened to the stepbrother story? That's what you told everybody else."

She shook her head.

He didn't like it. Not one bit. But she was probably right. She might be more successful in getting information if he wasn't there. He remembered his promise to never ask her to hide in the closet again. Damn.

He studied the windows, the angles. He pulled a twenty out of his pocket and slid it across the table. "Sit at the end stool. Order a drink. Keep it on your left side, far enough that I can see it from behind you. If at any time things start to go south, move it to your right side. I'll be there in thirty seconds."

She picked up the money. "Got it," she said. She stood up. He thought she was going to walk away without another word. Instead, she leaned forward and brushed a kiss across his cheek.

It might have been a familial good-night kiss that a woman reserved for a favorite stepbrother. But her lips were warm, her breath sweet and lemony, and she lingered just a moment too long. It was a kiss of reassurance, a kiss of promises. "Thank you," she whispered.

Cal walked out of the restaurant thinking that Stormy could probably ask him to stand naked in the middle of the street and flag down buses and he'd do it. He crossed the street and stood under the awning of a dry-cleaning store that was closed. Through the far window, he could see into the bar. Could see the back of Stormy as she sat on the last stool.

Could see the bartender approach and smile.

He congratulated himself on not reaching for his gun.

SHE SLID ONTO the stool. She picked up the bar menu, flipped to the Cordials and Liquors tab and scanned the possibilities. None of them looked particularly appealing.

The bartender was busy filling an order for one of the servers. She left with a tray of wineglasses and two margaritas. "Thanks, Joe," she said.

The bartender gave one of the men at the bar another beer. Then he headed toward her, a smile on his face.

She had to take the chance. "How's it going, Joe?"

"Good," he said. "I thought maybe your consulting assignment had ended," he said, "when I didn't see you and Tim here on Monday night. I know how he loves the oysters."

Who the heck was Tim? "We got busy," she said. "Just couldn't fit it in."

"That's good. Megan," he said, tossing his head in the direction of the server who was taking drinks in the bar area, "thought that you might have thrown us aside in favor of Strawbridge Bay. She'd heard Tim talking about the food there."

"We like it here better," she said.

"Well, you were probably wise not to come in. It was crazy here. We had all our frozen drinks at half price. I blew up two blenders." He put a napkin in front of her. "Want your usual, Jean?"

Jean. Again, the mysterious Jean. Sure, she'd take

Jean's usual. She was going to have to start writing down her names to keep track of all of them. "Absolutely," she said, smiling. She pushed the twenty in his direction.

He took it and came back with a Bailey's on the rocks and nine dollars of change. He set the glass in front of her and she casually moved it to the left, beyond her body. Then she picked up the five, leaving the four ones on the counter. "Tim and I are working different hours right now and haven't seen much of each other. He hasn't been in?"

Joe shook his head. He picked up a knife and began slicing limes into wedges. "No, but there were some people in on…let me think, was it Wednesday? Yes, definitely Wednesday night because we were closed unexpectedly yesterday due to a little water problem. Anyway, they were asking about the both of you. Said they worked with you at Moldaire College. I guess I didn't realize that's where you and Tim were working. You know, I graduated from there."

"I guess we must not have mentioned it." People looking for her. It had to be the Mercedes Men. "Was it two men, both with dark hair?"

He shook his head. "No. Man and a woman. He had light brown hair and she was a blonde. Heavy on the makeup." He paused for effect. "I like the natural look myself," he said, his tone suggestive. "You do it well."

She smiled, really grateful that Cal wasn't here. He'd commandeer the knife and Joe would be missing a finger. "Hmm," she said, her mind whirling. Man and a woman. Coworkers. "You didn't happen to catch their names, did you?"

Joe stopped slicing. "I didn't. I think they left a card,

though. Asked me to give it to you if you came in." He put down his knife. "I'm sure I threw it in the cash register."

She could feel her heart start to beat fast in her chest. This was it. The break that she'd been waiting for.

He opened the cash register and picked up the drawer in the front, where they stuffed the larger bills. "It was right here," he said. He kept looking.

Finally, he turned. "Sorry, Jean. Somebody else must have thrown it away."

She tried to not let the disappoint swamp her. "Well, if there are other consultants in town, I'd really like to look them up. They didn't happen to mention anything else, did they? Like maybe where they were staying?"

"No. But maybe I could take your number and if they come back, give you a call."

"That would be great." She held out her hand and he pulled a pen from behind his ear. She wrote Cal's cell phone number on one of the bar napkins. He picked it up and put it in his shirt pocket.

"I'm off next weekend," he said.

"Give me a call," she said. She felt bad leading him on but she needed his help if the man and woman came back to the bar looking for her.

"I thought maybe you were with that guy you were having dinner with," Joe said.

"My stepbrother," she said. She'd have crossed her fingers if she was the superstitious type. "He's just visiting."

WHEN SHE CROSSED the street, Cal discreetly motioned for her to keep walking and he fell into step next to her. "Well?" he said.

She told him about Jean and Tim and the strangers who were asking about them. He listened carefully. When they got to the car, he opened her door. Once he'd slid behind the wheel and pulled out, he said, "I saw him hand you a pen."

"I gave him your number," she said.

"My number?" he asked, turning his head.

"Well, he thinks it's mine," she said.

There was a pause. "Well, good. He's not my type."

She punched his arm. "Right now, I just want him thinking that he's Jean's type."

"So you and Tim have been frequenting this bar. And you've been going by the name of Jean. And you were coworkers."

"Yes. He referred to our consulting assignment. But why would I be using a false name for a consulting assignment? Why wouldn't Joe have known me as Nalana Akina. That's my name. We know that for a fact."

"Because maybe it's not your run-of-the-mill consulting assignment. It's something else. You're in this area for some other reason."

"But at the center of everything is Moldaire College. Joe said that he was surprised that Tim and I never mentioned that we were working at Moldaire. But the brown-haired man and blonde woman said we were coworkers at Moldaire." She shook her head. "This is impossible. How can I figure out my past when I'm lying to everyone?"

"I don't know. But your disappearance, and Tim's disappearance, have caused other people to start looking for you, to start asking questions. To be bold enough to leave a card. That's good."

"Maybe. I have two different groups of people looking for me. And I don't know why. And it's seven o'clock on a Friday night and I think something bad is supposed to happen on Saturday. *Good* isn't the adjective I would choose."

"It's a challenge," Cal conceded.

"We have to go to the Strawbridge Bay. Joe the bartender said that Tim told one of the servers that he liked their food. Maybe Jean and Tim went there together. Maybe the man and woman that are looking for Jean and Tim will know to check there, too."

Cal tossed her his phone. "I hope it's close."

It was six miles away. The traffic was heavy and it took twenty minutes to get there and another ten to find a parking spot. They squeezed into one, between a BMW and a Lexus. They watched the door for a few minutes. "I think we're underdressed," she said.

"But our money is good," Cal countered. "I think that's what they care about." He opened the car door for her. "Are we eating again?" he asked as they walked down the sidewalk.

"How about dessert and coffee?" she whispered.

It was smaller than The Blue Mango. Just one dining room with a service bar at the rear of the restaurant. That was discouraging. There would be no talkative bartender here.

"Table for two?" the young hostess asked. She could not have been much more than sixteen.

"Yes." She looked directly at the girl and smiled. The girl smiled back but showed no sign of recognition. "We're just interested in your dessert menu."

"That's fine," the girl said.

She led them to a table in the middle of the restaurant. Cal sat so that he could see the door.

She looked around. No Mercedes Men. No brown-haired man or made-up blonde. Their server was a young black man who took their order for cheesecake and coffee politely but with no personal exchange.

"I have the craziest urge to stand up on the table and yell, does anybody here know me?"

"It's a bust," Cal said. "We had to try." He took a bite of his cheesecake. "And they have really excellent desserts."

"Thanks for trying to make me feel better," she said.

Cal finished his coffee. "We should get going. We have a long drive ahead of us."

"No. I don't want to go back to Ravesville. Let's go to Moldaire College instead. We can get a room in the student union."

"Did you forget that I wasn't even willing to have lunch there two days ago?"

"Nope. But it's different now. We have to stay close, where we can respond quickly. We aren't going to let G sneak up on us. And maybe they're not even here any longer. He's leaving the country. Maybe he's going to be long gone before whatever bad thing that's supposed to happen on Saturday actually occurs."

"The student union is a huge building. Difficult to secure even a small space. An attack could come from multiple directions," he said, still not convinced.

"There's no place better to stay. It's like hiding in plain sight." She was not going to back down.

He seemed to sense that. "Oh, what the hell," he said.

It took them forty minutes to drive back to the campus. It was now close to nine o'clock. They parked and walked into the pretty stone building. There was an imposing foyer with marble walls and intricately tiled flooring. Up four steps, to the left, there was a large restaurant that was open but didn't look busy, probably because it was past the dinner hour. In the middle was open space for students and visitors to gather. Lots of small groupings of chairs. The colors were soft in blues and violets, the lighting was good, and the overall effect was warm and comforting. There was a gas fireplace that was lit.

To the right was a big oak registration desk. They headed that direction and waited while the young man behind the desk finished his conversation. His name tag said Devon.

"We'd like a room," Cal told him once he'd hung up.

Devon started laughing. "You guys should buy some lottery tickets."

Huh?

Devon held up a hand. "Sorry. It's just that we've been sold out of rooms for a month. I've personally turned away at least thirty people today. But that call was to cancel a room. So I guess you guys can have it. I just need a name and a credit card."

"Mary Smith," she said. "And we'd like to pay with cash."

Devon nodded. "I guess that's okay. Hardly anyone does that anymore."

It took him another couple minutes of clicking computer keys before he picked up a plastic key card, ran it through a machine to activate it and handed it to them.

"Why is the student union so busy?" Cal asked.

"The game." The young man looked at them as if they were stupid.

"What game?"

Devon reached out an arm and pulled a newspaper off the stack at the end of the counter. It was the college newspaper. The headline read Secretary of State to Attend End of Season Game.

Her pulse started to race and she felt very warm.

She scanned the article quickly. Secretary of State Dane Morgan, who was an alumnus of Moldaire College and a fraternity brother to President LaTrope, would be the honored guest at Saturday's end-of-season game between Moldaire and rival Rollston College of Omaha, Nebraska. Following the game was a $200-a-plate, invitation-only dinner, emceed by Morgan to raise money for the college. LaTrope had promised that the dollars would go toward long-overdue repairs needed on the school's infrastructure.

"Cal," she said, her voice sounding strange to her own ears.

He leaned over her shoulder so that he could see what she was looking at. "Sounds like fun," he said nonchalantly. "Thanks," he said to Devon. Then he put his hand on her elbow and propelled her toward the elevator.

"Breathe," he whispered.

She wished it was that easy. She was dizzy and nauseous and her head felt as if it was going to split open. Her heart was pounding in her chest. She was going to pass out.

When the elevator door closed, she sagged against the wall.

"Hey," Cal said, putting his arm around her to support her. "What's going on?"

She gulped for air but it wasn't enough. Gulped again.

"Honey, you're hyperventilating," he said. With one arm around her, he cupped his other hand around her mouth. "Slow down."

"This is it," she managed. "Something bad…going to happen…secretary of state…at game."

The elevator dinged, indicating they'd reached the fourth floor. The door opened.

And in walked the Mercedes Men.

Chapter Seventeen

Cal did his best. But he'd lost a valuable second because his arms had been full of Stormy. But still he managed to take out two of them with quick sharp blows and he was going after the third one, Bad Knee, when the odds shifted quickly. He saw that G had Stormy's arms wrenched behind her back with the barrel of his gun resting against her neck.

"Don't hurt her," he said, putting his own hands in the air.

G said something in another language to the two men on the floor and they managed to get themselves up. Then, with one on each side of him, holding him tight, Bad Knee punched Cal in the face. It was a good swing.

As his head whipped back, he heard Stormy's cry. G barked out another order and they were moving fast down the hallway. Cal saw that one of the men had picked up the key card. He used it to unlock the room that had been assigned to Cal and Stormy.

He was pushed up against the wall and roughly searched. They tossed his phone to the floor and stepped on it, destroying it. Then they found his gun and they tossed it across the room before he took a hard hit to the right kidney. They flipped him back around and

Bad Knee got two more punches in, one to the face and one to the gut.

Then one of them, who was pretty good with a rope, yanked his arms back and tied his wrists together. Once he was tied, they shoved his head back, cracking it against the wall.

His two attackers took their positions, one on each side. They were being smart. Not taking it for granted that he'd be out of commission with his arms tied behind his back.

G still had his gun up against Stormy's neck. She looked frightened but he was grateful to see that she wasn't hysterical. She had pulled it together.

G leaned his face close to Stormy's. "You have caused me a great deal of trouble," he said. "I am not happy. And in my country, when a husband is not happy with his wife, he disciplines her." He motioned Bad Knee to approach. "Not her face," G said.

Bad Knee hit Stormy in the stomach, hard enough that he could have broken some ribs. Stormy's knees gave out but G held her up, until she managed to catch her breath.

Then G nodded and Bad Knee hit her again.

"That was for embarrassing me in front of my friends," G said. "They were expecting a wedding."

Fury, blind naked fury, swept through Cal. He was going to kill them all. Rip them apart with his bare hands.

Stay alive. Just stay alive until I can get us out of this. He willed the thought to her as finally Bad Knee stepped out of the way and he could make eye contact with her.

She gave him a weak smile then turned to G. "You're not my husband."

He pushed the barrel of the gun harder into her delicate neck. Using his free hand, he pulled at a chain around his neck. There was a silver ring with a wide band hanging on the chain. "I already wear your ring, my sweet. And soon you will wear mine."

Cal saw Stormy flinch and it was as if she could not take her eyes off the ring that G wore around his neck. She looked across the room to Cal. "That was Mia's. My grandmother gave it to her before she died. I got it when Mia died."

"Silence," G ordered. "You need to learn, even if it's the hard way, that I'm nobody's fool. Your partner already learned that lesson."

At first, Cal thought G was talking about him. But then he saw something cross Stormy's face and realized that he was wrong. G was talking about someone else. Stormy's partner.

It had to be the person that Stormy had said she couldn't remember but the emotion connected to the person made her sad. He could tell that Stormy was remembering exactly what had happened and it was something horrible.

G either wasn't as perceptive or he didn't care. He yanked on Stormy's arm and dragged her to the bed in the middle of the room. Then shoved her hard so that she fell upon the mattress.

She quickly scooted up, so that she was sitting with her back against the headboard.

Cal could tell the movement hurt her newly injured ribs. They would pay for that. Slowly.

There were tears in her eyes but he didn't think it

was because of her injuries. She was remembering and it was painful.

"Your plan is full of holes," she said.

G laughed. "I don't think so. Our bomb is already in place. The timer is ticking. What's the line?" he paused for effect. "That's right. Bombs bursting in air. Right about the time they're singing your disgusting national anthem, they'll get to experience the real thing."

The men in the room giggled as if they were thirteen-year-old girls.

Cal was confident that Stormy hadn't remembered or hadn't ever known about the bomb. Her comment about the plan had been a trick to get G to reveal more. She was brilliant.

"I will admit that you and your partner were an unexpected complication. Bad timing," he said, "on your part."

"Very," she said. "But we were able to get word to others. They know."

"Oh, I don't think so, my dear. As I expected, your people came nosing around, with some crazy story that that were trying to find you because an elderly relative had died. It was obvious that they were looking because you and your partner hadn't checked in as expected. I had to play the role of the trusted yet perplexed supervisor who didn't have a clue why you hadn't shown up for your job on the office cleaning crew. While all the time, I wanted to strangle every single person who asked a question about you and say, I want her just as badly as you do."

With his gun still pointed at Stormy, he motioned toward the remaining rope that was on the floor. Bad Knee picked it up, then roughly jerked first one arm, then the other, tying them to the headboard corner posts. Then he yanked on her legs, pulling her onto her back. He frowned at the boots she wore. He unzipped them and tossed them both aside. Then he tied each ankle to a footboard post.

She was spread-eagle on the bed. Fully clothed still but in the most vulnerable position a woman could be in. They wanted to humiliate her.

But damn her, she kept her chin in the air. *Take your best shot.* That was what her attitude said.

He'd never loved her more.

"I'll admit," G said, "you were more difficult to find than I expected. A woman in a wedding dress is easy to remember but no one seemed to know." He turned to Cal. "You were quite convincing, Mr. Hollister. You might have had a future in the movies that you Americans love so much."

Cal was rapidly clicking through the information that G was spewing out. *Your people came nosing around.* He'd been right. Stormy was in some kind of law enforcement, probably working undercover. *I had to play the role of the trusted yet perplexed supervisor who didn't have a clue why you hadn't shown up for your job on the office cleaning crew.* Stormy's disjointed memories made perfect sense. She'd been dressed in blue pants and a blue polo shirt. That was likely the uniform that the cleaning crew wore. But she'd remembered working on the computer for hours every night. She'd probably been documenting a case file or reporting information back to a superior.

But why had she been on the Moldaire College campus? Who had she been investigating? And how did that person figure into all of this?

Was it G that she'd been investigating? Somehow, Cal didn't think so. G had said something earlier that it had been bad timing on her part. Had she stumbled into something and before she could report it up the food chain, she and her partner had been captured?

He needed G to keep talking so that he could piece it together but G was evidently done with that. He motioned at Cal's two guards and suddenly they were pulling him toward the small bathroom. The student union had been built many years before and while the bathrooms might have been remodeled, some of its original *charm*, in the form of old fixtures, still existed. They pushed him onto the floor, tied his ankles together and then tied him to the thick steel leg of the pedestal sink.

He was sure they intended to kill him before it was all over. But for whatever reason, they were waiting. He suspected that G was still hoping for some cooperation from Stormy and if he killed Cal now, that wasn't likely to happen.

He was surprised they hadn't gagged him.

But then he understood why when Bad Knee came up behind him and he felt the sharp prick of a needle in his arm. "I gave him enough to knock a horse out," Bad Knee said to someone.

He heard G laughing.

Damn was his last thought.

SHE WOKE UP feeling sick, just like before, and the memory of what had happened swamped her. She hurt and it was difficult to take a deep breath. The room was dark and she wondered if it was nighttime but then realized that the shades had been pulled down and the curtains closed tight.

"Cal," she called out. Her voice was weak, barely a whisper. She swallowed hard. "Cal," she said louder.

Had they killed him? The thought paralyzed her. She loved him. It was like losing Mia all over again but this time with the knowledge that it was her fault. She'd dragged Cal into this mess.

She was going to make G and his friends pay.

For Cal. For Bolton, the best partner she'd ever had.

"Help," she yelled. "Help." Over and over again, until her voice was hoarse. But no one came. She cursed the century-old plaster walls and thick wood door that kept sound in.

She had to get free. And keep the secretary of state from getting blown up along with twenty-five thousand other football fans.

She pressed her rear into the mattress. There it was. In her pocket. The knife that Cal had given her.

They'd searched Cal but hadn't thought to search her. Now she needed to figure out how to get it out of her pocket and use it to free herself.

She pushed her rear against the mattress, trying to push the knife up. Again and again. It was painstakingly slow progress and she was sweating with the effort by the time the knife was finally free.

Now came the hard part. If she could get the knife up to one of her hands, she had a chance of gripping it in her fingers and sawing through the rope.

But how the hell was she going to get the knife anywhere near her fingers? And then she thought of Cal. She could not let him have died in vain.

She pulled again at all of her ropes. She twisted her wrists and her ankles, testing to see if there was any give. Nothing with her wrists. But maybe, the right ankle. She had good flexibility and strength in her ankles and feet. She needed to use that to her advantage.

She twisted her foot, back and forth, desperately trying to stretch the rope around her ankle. The braiding dug into her skin, cutting into her. It hurt but she kept going. It was her only chance.

It seemed to take forever but finally, the rope seemed loose enough. She flexed her foot downward, pushing it to an angle that it wasn't ever meant to go. But when she smoothly pulled her knee up, her foot slipped through the rope.

One leg was free. She lifted her head off the pillow. The skin around her ankle was bloody and raw but none of that mattered. With the use of a leg, she could do a lot.

"Cal," she said again, her poor voice spent. There was no answer, not even a rustle from the bathroom.

She had never felt so alone. It was even worse than the first time the Mercedes Men had taken her.

But Cal would not expect her to give up. He'd expect her to keep going. To be optimistic. "Half-full," she whispered. "My damn glass is half-full," she said.

She used her rear to push the knife down, toward the foot of the bed. When she got it as far as it would go, she bent her knee, bringing her foot as close to her rear as possible, and picked up the knife with her toes.

The sweet rush of success fueled her. She had a ways to go but she'd come further than the Mercedes Men could have ever contemplated.

Now came the tough part. She raised her leg, the knife clenched between her toes. She was going to have to toss it across her body and have it land close enough that her fingers could grab it.

It was going to have to be a perfect throw.

If she overshot, the knife would be on the floor. Might as well be on the moon. If she undershot, it would be just as frustrating. She'd be able to see it but it would be in a spot that she wouldn't be able to reach, even with one free leg. There was a limit to the amount of flexibility she had.

She judged the angle, the distance, took a deep breath and tossed it. It bounced off her hand and would have clattered to the floor if she hadn't been able to snag it at the last second. She turned it in order to get to the button. She pushed it and the blade extended.

She bent her hand at more than a ninety-degree angle at the wrist and set about the business of sawing through one of the ropes. It was tedious and her fingers cramped but she hung on to the knife and kept going.

And finally, one wrist was free. She pulled it down, wincing at the pain in her shoulder from having her hands pinned above her head for hours.

How many hours she had no idea. She didn't have a watch and there was no clock in the room, not even an alarm clock on the bedside table.

She needed to untie her other wrist. This was easier and in just minutes both wrists were free. Then she cut the final rope on her left foot. She was groggy, sick to her stomach, bleeding, and felt as if she'd been run over by a truck.

But there was no time to waste.

She stumbled her way into the bathroom. Cal was on the floor. Tied.

She knelt down. Felt for a pulse. It was there. Slow but steady. He was alive. Her heart soared with the knowledge.

The two of them needed to get out of there before the Mercedes Men came back.

She shook him. Hard. No response.

"Cal," she pleaded. "You have to help me."

Wildly, she looked around the bathroom. The bathtub was an old one, with claw feet and a shower curtain that wrapped all the way around it. She pulled it back. Saw the pipe for the shower and the showerhead on the hose.

She grabbed it, turned the cold water on full blast and aimed it at Cal's face.

Chapter Eighteen

Cal sputtered and spit. He was being water-boarded.

He must have been captured. They could try but they weren't going to get anything from him.

It took him a full minute before he realized that he was lying on the bathroom floor of the student union and Stormy was next to him, tears running down her face.

She was also trying to drown him.

"Wake up, damn you," she said. "Wake up."

"It would be helpful, darling, if you'd get that hose out of my face."

She dropped it and the clang seemed to echo through the small room. She fell on him. Hugging. Crying.

"It's okay," he said. "Now get this rope off me."

She efficiently sawed through the rope and the minute it was loose, he pulled his arms free. Even with the cold shower, he felt fuzzy and light-headed, as if he'd gone days without sleeping.

He looked at his watch. Hell. It was more as if he'd been sleeping for days. It was just after eleven. He'd been asleep for almost twelve hours. G and his merry men had shot him up with a massive cocktail.

He sat up. Reached out and gently touched her ribs. "Are you okay?"

She nodded.

Then he saw her bloody ankle and heel. "What the hell happened?" he asked.

"It's nothing. We have to get out of here before they come back." She started to cut through the ropes on his ankles. "Listen, Cal, I don't have time to explain but I'm an FBI agent."

"Figured something like that. What were you doing here at the college?"

"A clerk in the college accounting department had discovered that something looked odd with the financials. There was over two million dollars missing. She followed the trail as far as she could and she was confident that it was someone of substantial authority because money had been transferred from account to account and not everyone could do that. She went to her supervisor, who contacted the FBI. Bolton and I were sent undercover. Because we didn't know whom we could trust at the college, we told no one. We applied for jobs and the only open positions at the time were on the cleaning crew. That was perfect in that it gave us access to every executive's office at the college."

She made a final swipe with the knife and his ankles were free. He stood up and gripped the edge of the sink for support.

"I was Jean and Bolton was Tim. Even when we went to dinner on our off time, we stayed in those personas. We drove into Kansas City, thinking the distance between there and Moldaire reduced the likelihood that anybody would recognize us. He took that picture of me at The Blue Mango. It was on my cell phone. G must have gotten it off of it when he took it from me after Bolton and I were captured."

"What's missing money have to do with a bomb in the stadium?"

She put her arm around him, as if she was afraid that he was going to fall down. He didn't shake it off because it felt good to touch her.

"We didn't know anything about a bomb." She shook her head. "Trust me on this, I'm not the agent they would have sent. As it turns out, I'm not an accountant but close. My specialty is white-collar crime, specifically embezzlement. It took weeks but my partner and I were able to access most of the information we needed. Some if it was hard copy. That was easy. People who have locked offices rarely lock up information in their offices. The computer records that we needed were harder to get but not too hard." She looked up at him. "You'd be amazed at how many executives write their passwords on a scrap of paper and stick it under their keyboards. While we were supposed to be cleaning their offices, we would access the computer, copy off all activity on a thumb drive and analyze it back at our hotel."

Cal walked out of the bathroom and over to the window. He moved the shade and curtain just a fraction of an inch and looked outside. The room was still whirling but it was slowing down. "People are heading to the stadium. We have to get out of here, get to the police. Where do they fit in this?"

"I think the real police are fine. It was the campus police that my subconscious knew we couldn't trust. My partner and I had decided that we needed to get into the president's office. We had eliminated most everyone else as suspects and there was a paper trail that was leading to the president's office. He's married but had a young girlfriend."

"Let me guess. Jessica from the lingerie store." He did a couple deep knee bends to get the circulation moving in his legs.

"Yeah. Several hundred thousand dollars had been transferred into her account. And suddenly she was missing. There was no evidence that she was harmed. I think she basically got what she wanted from the guy and booked it out of here."

"What did you find in the president's office?"

"More than we should have. We were inside when we heard someone outside. We hid in the closet." She gave him a quick smile. "I know. A closet. Anyway, people came in. I recognized the one voice. It was G, who was the supervisor of the cleaning crew. From day one he'd made my skin crawl, always looking at me, brushing up against me. We didn't recognize the other voice but soon it was clear that it was the president. G was blackmailing him. Giving him money so that he could pay back what he'd stolen from the college. In exchange, the president had invited his friend and former fraternity brother, the secretary of state, back for the end-of-the-season football game. I remember being really angry that they were going to use a sporting event as the venue."

"G is a terrorist. So is the president of the college."

"Yes. They never talked about a bomb. We assumed that they were going to shoot the secretary. Anyway, after they left, my partner and I got the hell out of there. But what we didn't realize was that the office was being watched by a campus police officer on G's payroll. We left, he followed and tried to apprehend us. He killed

Bolton. I'm not sure he meant to or if his gun went off accidentally. Anyway, he took me hostage. They retrieved the computer from Bolton's hotel room. Our transmissions were always secure but they evidently got enough to realize that we were federal agents. I think that might have been when the plan to go back to Russia got hastily thrown together. I have no idea why a real wedding was necessary."

Cal was looking for his gun that they'd tossed aside. He looked up. "Pride, Stormy. To a man like G, pride is important. He wanted his friends to believe that he was marrying a very beautiful woman." His gun was gone. He'd expected as much.

He grabbed her boots and tossed them to her. "Stormy, you need to contact your people so that they can get the local police involved. They're going to have to mobilize very quickly to make sure the secretary of state is in a safe spot and get everyone away from the stadium."

"What are you going to do?"

He cracked open the door of the room and looked down the hallway. It was empty. He looked back over his shoulder and smiled at her. "I'm going to see if I can figure out how to shut down that bomb."

THEY TOOK THE elevator down to the registration desk. After doing a quick check to make sure they didn't recognize anybody in the lobby, they approached the desk.

"We have an emergency," she said to the clerk, this time a young woman. "I'm an FBI officer and I need to use your phone."

The woman didn't even ask to see any identification.

Just got off the stool she'd been sitting on and stepped away from the desk. There was a second empty stool and draped over it was a black jacket. There was a college ID badge pinned to the pocket.

"Whose jacket is that?" Cal asked.

"My supervisor's. He stepped away for just a minute."

Cal picked it up and put it on. It was a little small and the picture didn't look anything like him. She looked closer at the badge. Geoff Larkin, Manager.

"You can't take that," the clerk said.

"She will explain," Cal said, his voice polite.

She felt his hand on her shoulder. Cal leaned in and gave her a hard kiss. "No heroics," he said. "Promise me."

"You're the one going off to disarm a bomb," she said.

"I have to," he said simply. "I love you, Stormy," he added, already moving. "And I'm going to marry you and you're gonna wear that pretty ivory dress you saw in the wedding dress shop."

Then he was out the door.

The desk clerk was staring at her, her mouth open. "Wow," the woman said.

Wow, indeed.

She pressed her hand over her mouth. She wanted to call him back, to make him promise to stay by her side. But Cal Hollister had been a soldier, one of the best of the best. He could not sit back and wait while a terrorist killed innocent bystanders. She could not ask him to do that.

She needed to do her part. She went behind the counter, picked up the phone and started dialing.

CAL HAD SEEN his share of bombs over the years and had a pretty good idea of how he'd engineer a large explosion in a football stadium. Explosives would have to be planted at multiple locations and tripped simultaneously by an electric charge. He needed to find the source of that charge. It was possible that there could be multiple sources but that heightened the possibility of discovery. He was betting on one.

And he was betting that it was in an area that most people never saw. An area that was off-limits to most people but not to the maintenance personnel. The area under the stadium.

When he got to the stadium, he didn't hesitate. He walked to the front of the line, vaulted over the turnstile and flashed his badge with his thumb partially over the picture in the direction of the kid taking tickets.

"Manager Geoff Larkin. We've got a water problem," he said and kept walking. In the distance, he heard the sounds of approaching sirens. Lots of them.

Good. Stormy had made her call.

And there was no doubt a bomb squad in Kansas City. But it would take them a little bit to mobilize. They'd want to look at blueprints. They'd need to debate the options. The preferred method was never to have an actual person defuse the bomb. They'd want to send a robot in to remove the bomb and transfer it to a safe location to deal with it there. Dealing with it could take the form of a robot defusing it, letting it detonate in a controlled environment or even taking their own bomb to blast this one to hell.

They'd act according to protocol and that was all well and good in certain circumstances but protocol took time, and that was one thing he was confident they didn't have.

He found the freight elevators and got in. There were two lower levels, B1 and B2. Damn it. Two levels meant it would take twice as much time to search.

He stabbed B1 and prayed that he was right.

He would have felt much better with his gun. All he had was the knife that he'd given to Stormy. The knife had already come in very handy earlier today. It would have to be enough.

The door opened and he stayed inside the elevator. Edged his head out. He didn't want to meet up with any of the Mercedes Men if he didn't have to. They would slow him down.

The floor and walls were cement, the ceiling was a mass of white PVC pipes and encased electrical wiring. There were wire-fronted storage units, probably ten feet wide, against one wall. Some were filled with cardboard boxes, one had stacks of yellow cones and a pile of orange flags, one had what appeared to be brand-new toilets. On the other side of the room were two big rooms. Meeting spaces.

He closed his eyes. Breathed deep.

Then he stepped back into the elevator. He was going lower.

The B2 level looked a little like the floor above it in that it was all gray cement. But in the middle of the large space was a fully enclosed structure.

The power plant.

He could hear the hiss and crack of big boilers that were heating water that would ultimately supply heat and more to the upper levels. He tried to open the door. It was locked.

Damn it.

Then he saw the badge reader next to the door. His only hope was that the security processes at Moldaire weren't overly sophisticated and that all management personnel had access to all areas of the campus. He ripped Geoff Larkin's badge off his coat and slid it through the narrow channel.

He heard the click, grabbed the door and was inside.

It was a sea of commercial boilers, huge generators and chillers. He glanced at his watch. Time was running out. He had to find the power source and find it fast.

On his second loop around the room, he saw it. A small box, taped to the underside of one of the boilers, with a wire leading up to the ceiling and then beyond. He squatted down and used the edge of his knife to flip open the metal box.

He examined the three wires, all the same color. Why was it in the movies they always made it look easy by having a red, white and a green wire. And the guy always had somebody on the phone, walking him through the process. *Now cut the red one.*

He had nobody. And no way of knowing how much time he had left. In the movies, there was always a ticking clock. Not one here. All he knew was that the national anthem was sung at the very beginning of the game. Which had to be just about now.

He pulled all three wires at the same time.

Chapter Nineteen

After she had contacted her supervisor, things had moved quickly. The man had quickly called in both local and state police departments. He'd also reached out to one of the agents who'd been dispensed to Moldaire earlier in the week, looking for Nalana and Bolton. Within minutes, that male agent had arrived, moved her to the manager's office that was behind the registration desk and stood guard at the door.

She'd begged to go to the stadium but her supervisor had expressly forbidden it. Nalana was to stay put until the terrorists could be apprehended. She'd hated that she knew he was right. She wanted to be with Cal but she could not take the chance that the Mercedes Men would somehow intercept her and she'd be in a position of being a bargaining chip that might allow the terrorists to escape.

And Cal had said no heroics. She owed it to him to be careful, to be here when he came back.

She had just started to dial the phone to express her condolences to Bolton's family when she heard the explosion. She sank down in the chair and dropped the receiver. It hit the desk with a thud.

The bomb had gone off. It was unthinkable.

She'd been so confident that Cal would be able to do it, that he would come back to her in one piece, with his slightly cocky attitude and his killer grin. She hadn't allowed herself to contemplate any other option.

But the explosion had to mean that he had not been successful. And she quite frankly had no idea how she would bear it.

She put her face in her hands. Her head, her heart, her whole body felt heavy, as if she would never again have the strength to lift it. *Oh, Cal. I did so love you.*

She would have to call his brothers and tell them that Cal had died a hero, trying to save innocent people. She remembered the day that he'd been insistent that she memorize their numbers. He'd done it to ensure that she wouldn't be left defenseless or without resources. She would tell Chase how much Cal had loved him, how he had known the sacrifices that Chase had made for him and how he'd come to terms with that knowledge over the years, and how he'd challenged himself to be the kind of person who could act in the same selfless manner.

She could stay to help them with the funeral. And the people would come and point to her and wonder whether she was somebody important in Cal Hollister's life.

And she would try to find some comfort in knowing that while their time together had been short, they had connected in a way that most people never had the joy of experiencing. It had been brief but it had been love.

And she would wrap that around her for the cold days that were sure to come. It would take time but in his memory, she would make sure her glass was half-full again. "I will," she whispered.

"Will what?"

Her head whipped up. Cal. Sweet, sweet Cal. She leaped up from behind the desk and ran to him. He held out his arms, she jumped and wrapped her legs around him. She gripped his face in her hands. "I thought you were dead," she said. "I heard the explosion."

"I'm harder to kill than that." He held her tight. "They had a second, much smaller bomb, in the president's office. It's trashed but nobody was in the building. No casualties there. No explosion or casualties at the stadium. The secretary of state is in his car, on the way back to the airport."

He said it as if it was no big thing. All in a day's work. He was amazing. "What about G and the others?"

The agent who'd been at the door was smiling. "I don't want to intrude but I just heard. Golya Paladis and his comrades have been apprehended on their way to a small airport outside of Kansas City."

Cal held up a finger. "Golya is wearing a silver ring on a chain around his neck. We want it back."

"I'll see to it," the agent said. "We also have word that a campus police officer has just surrendered outside of the stadium. The president of the college was picked up at his house."

It was over. She leaned her forehead against Cal's lips. "Now what?"

"Now we go shopping. Let's get that wedding dress on order or whatever crazy thing we need to do to ensure that it's here and ready for you within a couple weeks. That's all the longer I'm waiting."

"If it's not here on time, I'll wear your T-shirt and sweatpants."

He smiled. "Okay by me. They're easy to get off."

* * * * *

"I'm going to get to my truck and take the gun out of the back. Do you want to wait inside it?"

She flashed him a wry smile. "What do you think?"

"I think you want to come with me, but I also think you'd better consider what's good for Charlie. He needs his mom."

"Point taken," she conceded. They ran to the truck, and Lily slid inside while Chance took his revolver out of the locked case and handed her the keys. "If anything goes wrong, get yourself out of here, okay, Lily?"

"Chance, I—"

"Not now, sweetheart," he said. "I'm in a hurry. Lock the doors. I'll be back." He leaned inside and kissed her. Her lips were cool and wet and perfectly delicious. He tore himself away and ran toward the back of the church.

COWBOY
UNDERCOVER

BY
ALICE SHARPE

This book is sold subject to the condition that it shall not, by way of trade or otherwise, be lent, resold, hired out or otherwise circulated without the prior consent of the publisher in any form of binding or cover other than that in which it is published and without a similar condition including this condition being imposed on the subsequent purchaser.

® and ™ are trademarks owned and used by the trademark owner and/or its licensee. Trademarks marked with ® are registered with the United Kingdom Patent Office and/or the Office for Harmonisation in the Internal Market and in other countries.

Published in Great Britain 2013
by Mills & Boon, an imprint of Harlequin (UK) Limited,
Eton House, 18-24 Paradise Road, Richmond, Surrey, TW9 1SR

© 2012 Alice Sharpe

Published in Great Britain 2015
by Mills & Boon, an imprint of Harlequin (UK) Limited,
Eton House, 18-24 Paradise Road, Richmond, Surrey, TW9 1SR

© 2015 Alice Sharpe

ISBN: 978-0-263-25327-6

46-1215

Harlequin (UK) Limited's policy is to use papers that are natural, renewable and recyclable products and made from wood grown in sustainable forests. The logging and manufacturing processes conform to the legal environmental regulations of the country of origin.

Printed and bound in Spain
by CPI, Barcelona

Alice Sharpe met her husband-to-be on a cold, foggy beach in Northern California. Their union has survived the rearing of two children, a handful of earthquakes, numerous cats and a few special dogs, the latest of which is a yellow Lab named Annie Rose. Alice and her husband now live in a small rural town in Oregon, where she devotes the majority of her time to pursuing her second love, writing. You can write to her c/o Harlequin Books, 233 Broadway, Suite 1001, New York, NY 10279, USA. An SASE for reply is appreciated.

I'd like to dedicate this book to all readers who, just like me, love a good story.

Chapter One

Chance Hastings couldn't sleep. This in itself wasn't unusual, not lately anyway. Between the extra ranch work
an early fall demanded, his brother Frankie's antics and
his own personal chaos, his mind was just wound up too
tight. What was unusual was that instead of being in his
own cabin two miles over the ridge, he'd elected to spend
the night at the main ranch house in the home in which
he'd been raised. His father and his new stepmother,
Grace, had taken a short trip to Oregon and Chance had
volunteered to watch over the house as Frankie was rarely
around anymore.

Finally admitting there was no point lying in bed
with his eyes wide open, he got up and dressed by the
light of the full harvest moon shining through the generous window. He'd always loved autumn in Idaho, especially around the ranching community of Falls Bluff.
The golden fields rising to the mountains and the decid-
uous trees bleeding yellow, orange and red into the high
evergreen forest engaged him at every turn.

His plan for the coming day included traveling out toward the mountains with his brothers Pike and Gerard to
round up the heifers they wanted to move closer to the
ranch for the coming winter. He might as well get a head

start on things by saddling up three horses and loading them into the trailer. He paused in the kitchen to start a pot of coffee and leave his brothers a note about meeting him in the barn. He pinned the note to the corkboard by the door.

The perking coffee created a warm ambience in the kitchen that he rarely experienced anymore. Lily, who had shown up under mysterious circumstances nine months earlier and left after a sudden fright six months after that, still dominated the room, at least for him. He could almost picture her at the stove, an enigma of a woman who had wormed her way under his skin. He waited for the coffee to perk, but the more aromatic it became the less he wanted it. Instead, he headed for the mudroom where he retrieved his Stetson from the shelf on which he'd stashed it hours before, grabbed his coat and snagged his truck keys from the hook. As he clasped the doorknob and twisted, the phone back in the kitchen rang. His first instinct was to ignore it. He didn't really live here. However, calls in the middle of the night always telegraphed urgency.

"Hello?" he said as he grabbed the receiver.

He heard breathing but nothing else.

"Hello?" he repeated.

A child's voice said tentatively, "Is Mommy there?"

Was this someone's idea of a joke? "Who is this?" he demanded.

"Charlie."

Lily's five-year-old boy? At three thirty in the morning? "Charlie, this is Chance Hastings. Where are you? Where's your mom?"

"I don't know," the child wailed.

"Calm down, big guy. Are you lost?"

"I want Mommy."

Chance's brow furled as his imagination suggested all sorts of reasons for the child to have lost track of his mother. None of them were good. "Charlie? Your mom and you don't live here anymore, remember? You guys left. Do you know where you went?"

Soft sobs filled Chance's ear. "That's okay," he crooned. He could picture the boy's blond hair and blue eyes, freckles scattered over tearstained cheeks. "I'm trying to help you. When did you see Mommy last?"

"Yesterday," Charlie managed to choke out.

"Then what happened?"

"I went to school on the big bus."

"That's great. What's the name of your school?"

"Miss Potter's kindergarten."

Chance doubted that was the actual name of a school. "Do you know where it is?"

"On the little hill."

"Do you remember the name of the hill?"

"No."

"Do you remember the name of the town you and your mom live in or maybe which state it is?"

"I forget. I want my mommy."

"Okay, we're working on it. What happened at school yesterday?"

"I made a picture."

This was like pulling teeth. "Charlie, who are you with now?"

"Daddy."

The phone in the kitchen was the old-fashioned rotary type. Chance's grip on the receiver tightened. He didn't know much about Charlie's father, Jeremy Block, except that he'd done something severe enough in Lily's eyes that she'd run from him with their child in tow and hid out here until Block sent someone to abduct and kill her a few months before so he could reclaim his son. The man had been adamant he was working for Jeremy Block.

The night that went down, Lily left Hastings Ridge Ranch, Charlie in tow. Chance didn't know where Block lived and he didn't know what had happened in the weeks following Lily's departure.

He hadn't wanted to know. He'd avoided the topic like the plague. "Where is your dad right now?"

"Asleep."

"Has he hurt you?"

"No."

"Okay, that's good. Can you tell me anything about where he lives?"

"In a house."

"What city?"

"Bossy."

"Could it be Boise?"

"I guess."

Another thought jumped to the foreground of Chance's mind. Lily would never willingly let her son go unless she had no choice and that meant almost anything from abduction to murder.

"When did you go with your dad, Charlie?"

"Mommy wasn't at the bus stop," Charlie said, talking fast now, his voice wavering as he apparently turned his head and compromised the signal on a cell phone. "A man said he knew where she was. He drove the wrong way and I was scared. I told him to stop but he frowned at me. I fell asleep and it got dark and then we were at Daddy's house but I want Mommy and he says I can't see her and—"

"Charlie!" A masculine voice boomed from Charlie's end of the line. "What are you doing, boy? Is that my phone? Who did you call?"

"I want Mommy," Charlie squeaked.

The man spoke into the phone. "Lily? Do you really think you're ever going to see him again?"

"This isn't Lily," Chance said.

"Then who—"

"I'm a friend of Charlie's. Are you Jeremy Block?"

"What's it to you?"

"The boy sounds upset. What's going on?"

"Nothing that concerns you," Block said, and severed the connection.

The ranch phone didn't have a caller identification screen so Chance dialed the code to find out the number of the last call, jotted it down and dialed it. The call was answered by Block's terse message to leave a number but now Chance knew that Charlie was in Boise or a nearby community with the same area code.

Chance called a Hastings family friend on the police force next, Detective Robert Hendricks, who had a knack for sounding alert and on the job no matter when you yanked him from slumber. Chance told him about the call. "Give me the number," Hendricks said.

"You've got to rescue the boy," Chance said.

Hendricks was quiet for a beat or two. "Gerard told me you didn't want to know anything about Lily Kirk after she left the ranch. Was your brother mistaken?"

"No. I didn't want to know anything. I still don't. But it's different now that Charlie is in jeopardy."

"Charlie isn't in jeopardy," Hendricks said slowly.

Chance straightened his shoulders. "What? How can

you say that? Are you forgetting Jodie Brown and what he did to Kinsey thinking she was Lily?"

"Stop for a minute, Chance. Jeremy Block is a respected district attorney in Ada County down in Boise. Lily ran out on him and took their child with her. She has a documented history of being unstable. He filed for and won temporary custody in her absence. It sounds as if he finally got his kid back. As a father, I can understand how good that must feel. The fact is Lily is the loose cannon, not him."

"But Jodie—"

"Jodie Brown was a career criminal with a record as long as your arm. Block sent him to prison for drug trafficking twelve years ago. He says that's the last time he saw him. He figures Jodie was out to take revenge on him by abducting his wife and demanding a ransom. Block denies having anything to do with Jodie since years before when he won the conviction. There is no indication he isn't telling the truth."

"What does Jodie Brown say about this?"

"He's dead. His truck ran into a tree a couple of days after he left your ranch. His blood alcohol was .20. Case closed. Except that there's a warrant out on Lily but I understand she's disappeared."

"If Jeremy Block knew where to find his son, he knows where to find his ex-wife," Chance said, and despite Hendricks's insistence that Jeremy Block was Man of the Year material, felt a chill.

"Not ex," Hendricks said. "There's been no divorce."

Chance blinked away that momentary shock. "Charlie said a man took him from the bus stop and drove him to his father's house. Doesn't that remind you of what Jodie

Brown tried to do? Do you really believe Jeremy Block is telling the truth?"

"I really do," Hendricks cautioned. "But more importantly, it's all happening two hundred miles from here. The police in Boise are satisfied with his story so that's the end of it although I will contact them about the child's call so they can look into it."

Chance slammed down the receiver. His father had taken Lily in nine months earlier and not said a word to anyone about her past but there was a good chance he knew something that might help. Chance had to know she was safe and not fighting for her life somewhere. He dialed his father's cell and when no one answered, his stepmother's. Both phones went straight to voice mail and he left the same message, an insistent request they call home as soon as possible.

Now what? Where was Lily? How did he find her?

He heard a vehicle outside. Undoubtedly Gerard or Pike had arrived early to help get ready for the Bywater trip. He dashed into the mudroom, glad for the company. He was betting Gerard knew all about Lily's past from Hendricks. He switched on the floodlights before opening the door and exited the house as a woman stepped out of a red coupe.

The car looked familiar but the small woman standing in the glaring light did not. The three resident dogs had roused themselves from their beds in the horse barn to welcome the newcomer who didn't seem alarmed by the excited attention of the two shepherds and the part-Labrador retriever milling around her legs. She wore her light brown hair parted in the middle and pulled back. Heavy black glasses dominated a pale face while a long shapeless gray cardigan dominated an equally drab dress that fell all the way to the top of brown cowboy boots.

"Chance?" the woman cried, taking a halting step forward and then stopping.

Chance's mouth almost dropped open as he recognized Lily's voice. For the tick of a heartbeat he tried to reconcile the woman before him with the sassy, blonde firecracker who had left here months before, and then he came out of his stupor and stepped toward her. "I just had a call from Charlie," he said.

"You heard from my baby? When?" Her hands flew up to cover her face and her knees buckled. He reached her before she hit the ground. The dogs yipped with uncertainty.

"I'm okay," she insisted. "Where is Charlie? Who has him?"

"His father," Chance said.

"I thought so. Damn."

He still couldn't believe she was here and right on the heels of the past thirty minutes of revelations. He was touching her, almost holding her. He'd only done that once before and at that time, he hadn't known she was still married. And at that time, at least at first, she'd melted into him...

"Come inside," he said. "I just made coffee."

"I need to talk to your father."

"Come inside," he repeated. "You're trembling."

"How did Charlie sound?" she asked as she allowed him to guide her up the stairs.

"Not bad," Chance said because he couldn't bear to tell her how frightened the boy had seemed. "I don't know why he called here looking for you."

"It's my fault. I drilled this number into his head last summer when my cell phone died."

The dogs hung back at the door. Chance led Lily to a stool and she sank down with a shuddering sigh. He found mugs and poured coffee. "I contacted the local police and asked a detective friend for help."

"The police?" She took off the thick glasses and closed her eyes, squeezing the bridge of her nose with thumb and forefinger. "I wish you hadn't done that," she said, looking back at him. Without the glasses, her rich brown eyes came into focus and she looked more the way he remembered her.

"Yeah, I can understand why you'd rather not have to discuss your husband with the cops," he said. "Did you know there's a warrant for your arrest?"

"It doesn't surprise me. It's probably the first thing Jeremy did when he realized I wasn't coming back."

"What's it for?"

"I'd lay my money on kidnapping my own child."

"Because of your troubled past?"

She narrowed her eyes and he saw a flash of the old Lily. "I don't have a troubled past. That's Jeremy's story, not mine. Where's your dad?"

"He's gone. He won't be back for a few days. Tell me why you stole off into the night with Charlie. Not the time you did it three months ago when you left here. Before that, when you left Jeremy."

She shook her head as she undoubtedly picked up the anger his words hadn't been too successful at disguising. "You don't need to know."

"Listen, Lily. Jerk me around all you want but in the end, who else is going to help you? Dad is off in Oregon. There's a good chance he's out of signal range. Unless you have legions of friends I don't know about, maybe we should just level with each other."

"Don't start this, Chance. You and I can't agree on anything. There's no point in involving you—"

"Involving me?" he snapped. "You come here in the middle of the night dressed like you're auditioning for the role of the prim librarian in *It's a Wonderful Life*. Your son, the best thing you've ever done as far as I can see, has been taken by his psycho father and you're so frightened your eyes are spinning. Trust me, I'm involved."

"I don't want you—"

"I know. You made that real clear last summer. I'm not asking you to sleep with me, I'm asking you to let me help Charlie. Now, what do you say?"

She rubbed her forehead and he wondered how long she'd been driving. Where had she gone after she left the ranch? He waited for her to make up her mind, and when it seemed they would sit there in silence forever, he decided to wade in. "Block told the police Jodie Brown was acting on his own to take revenge on him for convicting him twelve years ago. By the way, Jodie died in a traffic accident before the police could question him. The case is closed as far as they're concerned.

"Furthermore, Block is claiming you had a history of being unstable and that you took your son without giving him a chance to work something out with you."

"He didn't want a chance to work things out," she said. "You don't understand—"

"Of course I don't," Chance said. "You haven't given me the opportunity to understand because you haven't said anything. Start with something easy. How was Charlie snatched?"

Her fingers tightened on her mug as she leaned forward. "I had a flat tire yesterday so I was running late to meet him at the bus stop. Everything just seemed to go wrong and it got later and later. I called the school but the bus had already left so I called one of the other mothers and she said she would pick him up when she got her own child. I went to her house but Charlie wasn't there. She said she'd arrived a minute late and seen him getting into a car with a man but he was smiling so she figured I sent another friend. She described him. It sounded enough like Jeremy—I could guess what was happening."

"But it wasn't Jeremy. Charlie told me a man he didn't know told him he'd take him to see you but he drove to Boise instead."

"Poor Charlie," she cried. "He must have been frantic. Why didn't I have a better plan for days like that one? Why did I live so far away from his school that he had to ride a bus? He hates buses. I should have found a different job closer to his school—"

"Calm down," Chance said, patting her hand. "Is he in any danger from his father?"

She stared at him for a second. The look in her eyes twisted his heart but he ignored it. Then she finally shook her head. "Not immediate danger, no. Jeremy is in love with the idea of having a son, making a legacy, although the reality of it bores him. He can be violent, but mainly toward me. Near the end the violence was trickling down to Charlie. He's not suitable to raise a child."

"I guess that's what he says about you, too," Chance observed.

"I know. He's twenty years older than I am. When you're adrift and all of nineteen, that kind of attention from a man like him is pretty exciting. He could do anything, or so I thought. He raced cars, he rode horses, he flew a plane—anything. Long story short, I wound up pregnant. He insisted we get married and I thought I'd hit the jackpot. At first I barely noticed the way he didn't want me associating with my friends or holding down a job. I just thought he wanted to take care of me. My father was an alcoholic. It was…nice…to have a man take charge for a change."

"But eventually?"

"After Charlie was born, Jeremy started taking on high-profile cases to make a name for himself. It wasn't enough to just be a prosecutor anymore. He wanted me as arm candy at parties to impress the 'right' people. I hated those parties and he knew it. In fact, I suspect he knew my heart wasn't in our marriage anymore. At some of those parties, I felt so light-headed and disconnected I was afraid I was going to pass out. People looked at me funny and made comments I wasn't supposed to hear about how I was a drunk like my father. The thing was, I didn't drink anything but seltzer. Jeremy told me it was my nerves and for a while I kind of believed that. I was so blasted stupid I made things easy for him.

"Then one day I found a bottle of barbiturates in Jeremy's desk drawer and I knew in a flash that he'd been drugging me so I'd appear intoxicated in front of other people. I worked up the courage to ask for a divorce. He said I was welcome to leave as long as I left alone. I protested, of course. I planned to take Charlie, but Jeremy promised that would never happen. He said everyone knew how paranoid I'd become, and that I drank. He said I'd trapped him by getting pregnant and everyone knew that, too, and felt bad for him. He said it would be better all the way around if I just died. That way he would get total control of Charlie and be a sympathetic widower to boot. He laughed when he said it, but you have to know Jeremy. His laugh has nothing to do with humor."

"So you bolted," Chance said. With her now austere hair and colorless clothes, she actually looked like the kind of person life beat into submission. He suddenly missed her bleached hair and dangling earrings and then it occurred to him that perhaps that persona had been as much a facade as this one.

"More or less," she said. "I started gathering every scrap of paper I could find, every receipt, anything that looked potentially valuable. I found a few photographs, made copies of records… Anyway, they're all in a safety-deposit box in Boise. I've never tried to make sense of them, there was never time. I just knew I needed something on him if I was ever going to win custody of Charlie. I was hoping I'd find evidence of collusion or something. But then he came home one night and he had had a horrible day. He'd been riding high after winning a conviction against a child murderer and his name was being discussed in political circles. But then a kid hanged himself in his cell and the prosecutor's office came under investigation. Jeremy was livid.

"Anyway, I didn't say the right thing or look the right way, who knows? Jeremy hit me so hard I blacked out and when I came to, Charlie was sitting beside me, crying. I'll never forget the look on his face. A week later, I'd made my plans and Charlie and I left. The mother of an old school friend took me in for a day or two and then she called your father and he offered me a job and refuge so that's how I ended up here."

"You never called the police?"

"No. I'd tried that before and wound up looking like a nutcase trying to ruin my husband's reputation. It wouldn't have done any good. Jeremy was respected, and feared, by so many people and I was a nobody."

They both startled and got to their feet as engine noise came from the yard.

"I hope that's not the police," Lily said. By now they were at the back door and could see through the small window.

"It's Gerard's truck," Chance said. "We're going up to get the heifers today." He opened the door and watched his brother approach. Gerard had had a couple of rough years, starting with the tragic accident that had taken the lives of his wife and daughter, followed by a spell of amnesia. But he'd come out on top when he fell in love with Kinsey Frost, the woman who helped him find himself in both a literal and figurative way.

Gerard stopped walking as Lily stepped out onto the porch beside Chance. He tipped his hat and said hello the way a cowboy does to a female stranger.

"It's me," Lily said, moving down the steps to intercept him.

He still looked confused.

"Lily," she added, coming to a stop in front of him. Gerard looked from her to Chance. Chance knew that his older brother and Kinsey were probably the only two people in the world who understood what it had meant to him when Lily left and he crossed mental fingers now that Gerard wouldn't spill it. He should have known he wouldn't. Gerard gave her a hug and then looked around. "Is Charlie asleep in your car?"

"He's not with me," Lily said.

"Come inside," Chance added. Lily turned to come back up the steps. In a moment of clarity, he saw the terror lurking in back of her eyes.

"Kinsey is going to be so sorry she missed seeing you," Gerard added as they once again closed the doors on the three dogs. "She flew back to New Orleans to help her grandmother for a couple of days. How long are you going to be here?"

"I'm leaving in a few minutes," Lily said. "I wanted to ask your father for advice. I thought maybe… Oh, I shouldn't have come."

"We can give advice, too," Gerard said as they entered the house.

"A lot is going on," she said, picking up the glasses she'd taken off when she first arrived. She folded them into a pocket and added, "Chance can fill you in after I've left."

"No, Chance can't," Chance said but he suspected Gerard didn't need too much filling in.

"Why?" Lily demanded.

"Because I'm coming with you."

"You don't even know where I'm going," she protested.

"You're going to Boise. You're going to see Jeremy Block. You'll need someone to bail you out of jail."

A defiant expression crept onto her face. "You don't have to do that," she said, thrusting her chin high in the way the Lily he'd known before used to. That woman he had chided and baited and given a rough time and she had returned it all with a spirit that intrigued him to this day. "I don't need someone to take care of me," she added.

"Yeah, right. Anyway, we'll stop at my place so I can throw some clothes into a duffel, tuck a big fat gun under the front seat and then we're off."

"What is it about men?" she asked no one in particular. "You all think you can rescue the damsel in distress."

"Well, when the damsel shows up so early in the morning, what are we supposed to do?"

"Listen when she says no thanks."

Silence ensued until Gerard cleared his throat. "May I say something?"

"Sure," Lily said.

"Just take him along for the ride, will you please? He's impossible when he gets like this and he might actually come in handy."

She looked at Chance, who silently returned her scrutiny. She was beautiful under all that drabness, delicate and feminine as long as she didn't start arguing. But he couldn't wrap his head around the thought of her leaving on this mission all by herself. If she refused to let him come with her, he'd follow on her tail.

"Oh, all right," she said.

"Unless Frankie shows up, you and Pike will have to get the heifers on your own," Chance told his brother.

"We'll manage," Gerard said as he poured himself a cup of coffee and added with a wink, "You two kids be careful."

Chapter Two

"Explain one thing to me," Chance said.

Lily had been staring out the dark passenger window, her eyes gritty from fatigue. She'd asked Chance to take the wheel because she'd been driving for hours and knew her judgment was impaired. She turned her attention to Chance whose strong profile was undeniably spectacular, a fact she found irritating. She didn't want to like him or need him or want him around and the fact that she felt all those things to some degree just plain irked her. "What do you want to know?"

"Last summer when Block sent Jodie Brown to take you, he had murder on his mind. If he had a warrant and had established custody of Charlie, why didn't he just turn you in? Why all the drama and hysterics? Why take such a risk?"

She shrugged. "How am I supposed to know that? All I can figure is that he doesn't want to share custody with me. Maybe Jeremy has the police in his pocket but if we end up in court, twelve ordinary people will get to hear my side of things. That might bring out distasteful facts about his true character. Plus, he's no doubt looking ahead to his future campaign for governor. That's his goal, you know. I could pose a liability to him."

For a second she heard her father's voice in her head. In a moment of sporadic sobriety he'd warned her not to look back, to keep focused on the future. *You can't change the past*, he'd said, and he was right.

But you couldn't run from it either and that's exactly what she'd done.

"Does Block know about those papers you gathered?"

"Probably. I raided his file drawer that last day. Maybe he's afraid I have something on him. Wouldn't it be wonderful if I actually did? I need to get them out of my safe-deposit box and take a look."

"Before you see Block?"

"I have to have some kind of ammunition."

Lily closed her eyes, hoping to find a few minutes' respite, but Chance had other ideas. "If he had murder on his mind before, why did he take Charlie this time and leave you free to continue causing trouble?"

Weariness had long ago seeped into every cell of her body. Talking was a struggle. She cradled her forehead with her hand. "I don't think that was his plan," she said. "Remember I told you about all the mishaps that made me late? I think he was not only making sure he could nab Charlie but that I would arrive home alone. But I didn't go home. I called a neighbor who promised to call immediately if Charlie showed up. For hours I just drove around and then I thought of your father."

"One more question," Chance said.

"Please, I'm exhausted."

"I know you are, Lily." He put his hand on her arm and even through the sweater, his touch made a warm spot that spread toward her shoulder.

"One more," she agreed.

"Where did you go when you left the ranch?"

"Reno. I figured hiding on a remote ranch hadn't worked, so I decided to try a bigger city. I drove to Reno because I had a friend there who said she was leaving town for a few weeks to visit her boyfriend in Florida. She said I could use her apartment and sub at her old job as a waitress at one of the casinos outside of town. Now I'm wondering if my friend ran low on funds and told Jeremy where I was to collect a little quick cash."

"She's like that?"

"She could be. For all I know Jeremy set the whole thing up with her just to nail down my location. I don't know. I try not to be paranoid."

"With a warrant out for your arrest, you probably shouldn't have taken Charlie over a state line."

"I didn't know about the warrant," she said. "You just told me about it. It wouldn't have made any difference though." She turned in the seat. "I think that's how Jeremy found me this summer. He must have accessed Idaho school records. My decision to send Charlie to summer school could have gotten me killed."

They fell silent. She leaned to the side until her forehead rested against the passenger window and closed her eyes. For a few moments she waited for Chance to think of something else he wanted explained, and then she stopped worrying about it. The next thing she knew, Chance was shaking her shoulder.

"We're here," he said as she rubbed the sleep from her eyes. "What now?"

They were in Boise, downtown somewhere. She'd been gone for almost a year but she'd lived here most of her life. She finally recognized the café on the corner and placed their exact location. "My credit union is a few blocks that way," she said, pointing north. "I want to get that stuff out of my safe-deposit box."

Chance glanced at the clock on the dashboard. "It won't be open yet. Let's grab something to eat."

"Not in this district," she said. "Jeremy's office is pretty close to here."

"Just give me directions."

Despite commuter traffic, they were soon approaching the suburbs and a plethora of fast-food establishments. Settling on one, Chance ordered himself a full breakfast but she stuck to coffee, knowing her nervous stomach wouldn't take kindly to food.

What was Charlie doing right that moment? Had Jeremy employed someone to help him take care of him? Was Charlie afraid he'd never see his mom again? The poor little kid had a fragile spirit that she'd no doubt fostered by putting up with Jeremy's abuse for so long. She wanted him to be braver about life than she'd been.

Chance plowed his way through half the menu, proving what Lily knew from months of cooking on the ranch: Cowboys could eat. As he was wadding up wrappers and tossing them into the bag, he met her gaze. "You should have something besides coffee," he said.

"Maybe later. Is it still too early for the credit union to be open?"

He turned the keys and the clock flashed on. "Yeah. Let's stay right here in the back of this dark little parking lot until it's time."

"I guess," she said. What else were they going to do?

"Great." He smothered a yawn with his fist as he pushed the lever to half recline the seat. "I'm going to catch forty winks. You okay?"

Did he mean beyond the gnawing nerves and the constant worry? "I'm fine," she said.

With a little smile, he tipped his dark brown Stetson down over his face, crossed his arms over his chest and seemed to go to sleep in about thirty seconds flat.

For a while, she stared at the comings and goings in the parking lot. Who knew so many people bought their breakfast at a drive-through? That made her think of Charlie who loved fast food and her eyes burned. She wanted to be on the move, not stuck here waiting.

She looked over at Chance when he made a soft little sound as his hand slipped from his chest. She caught it before it landed on the gearshift, carefully returning it to rest beside his other hand.

In a way she wanted to remove his hat and gaze at his sleeping face. Without the cynical glint in his dark eyes that often caused her to look away, would she glimpse the man she'd felt pull at her heartstrings so many months before?

She allowed herself to remember the night last April when they'd been walking alongside the river. Wildflowers had perfumed the air and the still-cold water gurgling against the rocks sounded like music. They'd stopped beside a tree and she'd leaned against it and before she knew it, he had cupped her face with both of his hands and told her she looked beautiful in the moonlight. His gentle voice and soothing caresses had been a balm to her broken spirit so that when he finally kissed her, she was flooded with feelings she'd given up hope of ever experiencing.

Eventually, he'd unbuttoned her blouse and lowered his head to kiss her throat, his lips warm against her cool skin. She'd wanted him with every fiber in her body, yearning for the moment when he stripped her bare. That moment never came because she'd been yanked back to reality when the plaintive call of a coyote rose from the ridge. The terrible decisions she'd made concerning men and desire all seemed to storm through her head as the lonely cry echoed over the valley. She'd withdrawn emotionally and he hadn't been so far gone that it escaped him. With a sigh, he'd raised his head and looked down into her eyes and she'd bolted, running back to the ranch house like a scared rabbit.

Their budding romance had died that night and eventually turned into an acerbic interchange of half-veiled insults and sarcasm.

Yet here they were.

"Knock it off," she scolded herself. "Think of something pleasant."

"LILY? LILY, WAKE UP," Chance said for the second time that day, he shook Lily's shoulder.

She was slow to respond at first and then she sat bolt upright. "Oh, God, I fell asleep. What time is it?"

"Almost one. We slept for hours."

She rubbed her forehead. "Well, at least the credit union will be open. Let's go."

Once inside the building, Chance looked askance at all the security cameras and wondered if anyone there knew about the warrant out for Lily. Thanks to the black glasses and baggy clothes, she looked more like a refugee from a homeless camp than a patron of a downtown banking establishment, but would someone call the cops as soon as she announced her identity? He decided to keep his fears to himself and just stay alert for any sign of trouble.

She went through the security measures to access her

box and disappeared with the attendant. A few minutes later, she returned, a couple of fat manila envelopes peeking from the top of her oversize handbag. He took her arm and they left together. The whole thing had taken less than fifteen minutes.

"We need to find someplace private to go through and sort all this," she said as she hugged her purse as if it was a precious baby. "I'd forgotten how much stuff I collected."

"Let's get a room somewhere," Chance said.

"Good idea."

They found a room and paid using Chance's credit card and name. Once inside, Lily removed the thick glasses before upending both envelopes onto the small round table. The contents came spilling out.

"Yikes," Chance said. The thought of trying to make sense of all that paper was mind-boggling. Maybe he should have stayed at Hastings Ridge and rounded up heifers, which was a lot more fun than pushing papers around. Of course he didn't say any of this to Lily who would just remind him he was here because he'd wanted to be.

She flashed him an understanding smile and sat down. "I think we should get the clippings into one pile, receipts into another, memos into a third and miscellaneous off over there."

For more than an hour they sorted and organized in near silence. Chance was anxious to do something about Charlie and he knew Lily was, too. It made sense to try to find something she could use against Block in some way, but it seemed unlikely they had sufficient time to make such a discovery.

"Let's go to your husband's house," Chance finally said. One more useless receipt and he was going to scream.

"No. He doesn't get home from work until six thirty or so."

"So we'll get there before he's home."

"Not a good idea. I want to catch him unaware."

"You said earlier that he knew you'd come after Charlie."

"I know, but he doesn't know when or how. Be patient."

"We're not going to be able to wade through all of this in one afternoon," Chance said, gesturing at all the bits and scraps of papers before them.

"You're probably right. I'm going to go take a shower and change clothes. I hope the clothes in my emergency escape suitcase still fit."

Chance walked over to the window. He stood looking out into the parking lot for a few minutes. Was she getting gussied up for Jeremy Block? That was a disquieting thought.

With a sigh, he returned to the papers. Thirty minutes later, his heartbeat quickened as he detected the first clear pattern he'd come across in the form of several orders from a florist shop in Boise. He stacked them apart in order of ascending dates. The deliveries were spaced at intervals of seven days and all went to the same address. Without knowing his way around this city, he had no idea if they went to an individual or a business. For all he knew, they could be flowers Block purchased for his office or his secretary's desk or even for the house he'd shared with Lily.

For a second he rubbed his eyes. The long nap in the car had taken the edge off fatigue, but he was still tired. Sleep had been so elusive lately. He felt if he laid his head down he'd fall into slumber for a hundred years and wake up ready to punch Block in the nose, reunite Charlie with his mother and take them both back to the ranch and…

Wait a second. Was this about Lily and the fantasy he entertained on long nights that someday he and she…

Oh, please, don't go that route, he cautioned himself. *Don't pretend because she needs your help she actually wants you.*

He looked up when a noise at the bathroom door caught his attention. Lily emerged with her soft brown hair waving around her heart-shaped face. Gone were the baggy dress and long, limp sweater, and in their place, tight black jeans, a black form-fitting top and a brown leather belt that matched her boots. She'd gone from plain Jane to a country-Western knockout and he swallowed a jolt of desire that shot through his body like a lightning bolt.

"Feel better?" he managed to say in a voice that sounded remarkably steady.

"A lot better," she murmured. Her gaze dropped to the stack in front of him. "Did you find anything?"

He tore his mind from the lovely curves and dips of her body around which the top had molded itself. "I don't know. Where is Vance Street?"

"Vance. I'm not sure."

He punched the address into his phone and showed her the resulting map. "That's over in the Tower District," she said. "Mostly condos."

"But you and Jeremy didn't live there?"

"No. His family had money of its own. When his father died, he left Jeremy a house and a little land right outside the city. Jeremy pictures himself lord of the manor."

"He sent flowers to this address once a week for several months near the end of the period when you lived together."

"Flowers? Really?" she said as her huge brown eyes came alive. "Jeremy hates cut flowers. I don't think he ever bought me a single rose. There must be a special reason why he did that."

"It could be nothing," Chance cautioned.

"Or it could be he was seeing someone else," Lily said. "Oh, my gosh, I bet he was having an affair. This is great!" She started pacing the room again, gesturing, suddenly animated. "If he's involved with someone else, maybe I can use that as leverage." She grabbed her handbag off the back of a chair and the baggy gray sweater from the bed. "Let's go check out that address."

He took the keys from his pocket, ready for action of any kind.

1801 VANCE STREET turned out to be located within a small villa of condos arranged around a central courtyard, all encased within the confines of an ornate iron fence. At this time of year, the pool had been drained and covered in preparation for cold weather. The trees were a riot of color, leaves drifting to the ground as the wind teased them loose.

They found a row of brass mailboxes built into a small arch near the street. The name on 1801 was V. Richards.

"Vicky, Valerie, Vivian?" Lily mused.

"Or Vincent, Victor, Val," Chance said.

"How do we find out?"

"We ask."

She looked around at the complete absence of other people and raised her eyebrows.

"Look, at the risk of making you mad, how about you let me knock on the door and see what I can find out."

"Why you?" she said. "I'll do it."

"What if this person is actually home and what if you know them or they recognize your face? You aren't disguised, remember?"

"I know. But so what?"

"So they call Block, Block calls the cops, Charlie spends the next twelve years living with daddy dearest."

"Oh."

"Just go sit in the car, okay?" he coaxed.

"Okay, but don't mess this up."

"Your faith in me is truly heartwarming," he said. "Here, take my hat with you so I don't stand out so much." He waited until she got back in the car, then he walked down the narrow path to 1801. He wasn't surprised when no one responded to the doorbell as it was a late weekday afternoon. He imagined the tenant of the condo was still on his or her commute. He walked around the grounds looking for someone, anyone, and finally spied a middle-aged guy raking leaves out by the pool/patio area.

"Excuse me," he called. "I have a delivery out in the truck for 1801, V. Richards. They're not home. Is there a manager here or anything?"

"I'm the manager," the man said, leaning on his rake. He gave Chance a once-over, probably deciding he didn't look much like a delivery man but glad for anything that interrupted the raking, especially as the fading light must make the job a tough one. "What can I do for you?"

"Is it safe to leave a package outside the door? It's pretty heavy. I wouldn't want it to be a problem for the recipient to get it inside by themselves."

"Yeah, it's safe enough. That door doesn't face the

street. If Valentine needs help, all she has to do is ask for it. She's a nice enough kid."

"Kid?"

He laughed. "Everyone under thirty is a kid to me and she's way under. Probably nineteen or so."

"Does she live alone?" Chance asked and immediately wished he hadn't. But the manager didn't seem to find the question intrusive.

"Oh, you mean how does a gal her age afford this place? Easy. She's a student. Her parents pay the bills and they wanted her someplace safe."

"So she lives off her folks and goes to college," Chance said, hoping he sounded like a jealous guy who had had to support himself his whole life and begrudged Valentine her address on easy street.

"Yeah, tough, right? She's been here for two years now. Well, kids these days, you know." His gaze suddenly focused over Chance's shoulder and he straightened up. "Hey there, Mr. Hasbro."

Chance turned to see a grumpy-looking man in his late sixties. "The circuit breaker blew again. You need to fix it pronto."

"Sure thing, Mr. Hasbro. As soon as I finish raking…"

"No, now. Betty is in the middle of making my dinner."

"I'll be right up, sir. Just have to get my tools."

"Don't dawdle," the older man said and stalked off.

"His breaker wouldn't blow if his wife didn't overload it," the manager confided to Chance. "Just leave the package," he added as he set aside the rake and hurried off.

"Well?" Lily asked as he slid into the passenger seat.

"You were right, it's a woman, but I don't know. The manager said she is a nineteen-year-old student."

"She sounds perfect," Lily said. "Jeremy likes his women young and innocent."

"Her name is Valentine Richards," Chance added. "The manager seems to think she's a nice kid."

"That's all he said?"

"Pretty much."

"It's going to have to be enough," Lily said.

"Enough for what?"

"Leverage. You don't send a woman flowers for weeks on end without there being a motive."

"Maybe, but Lily, even if he was having an affair, you left him. Unless this woman is a convicted criminal, he's just an abandoned husband with a girlfriend."

"But it appears he was seeing her while we were married."

He shrugged. "Today's morality doesn't necessarily blink at infidelity."

"It's all I've got," she added. "Are you coming with me or not?"

"Let's get it over with," he said as he felt around under the seat with his right hand, reassured when his fingers brushed the smooth leather of the holster into which he'd slid his .38 over twelve hours earlier when they'd stopped at his cabin.

SHE KNEW HER way around the city, taking backstreets, avoiding long-winded lights, anxious now to get this over with.

"You can't just walk into his house and have a simple conversation with him, you know," Chance said.

She flashed him a quick look. He'd all but disappeared in his dark clothes in the dark car. Just the glint of the whites of his eyes and the occasional street lamp illuminating his face. "That's exactly what I'm going to do," she said. "I'm going to tell him I know about his affair with Valentine. That's my leverage."

"He'll chew you up and spit you at the police department."

"Doesn't matter. It's a chance I have to take. Maybe he'll listen to reason."

"Maybe he'll listen to Smith and Wesson," Chance said, and took the gun from under the seat. The thought of the two of them eye-to-eye with a gun in the middle made her anxiety level shoot through the roof.

She pulled the car over to the side of the road, parking between street lamps where darkness prevailed.

"We're here?" Chance said, looking around.

"No. The house is a block over. I didn't want anyone to recognize my car. Come on."

They walked quickly. She knew a shortcut that consisted of a nature trail owned by the home owners' association and took him that way. They erupted onto the street she'd called home for five years. The thought of stepping foot on Jeremy's property made her physically ill. The only worse scenario was losing Charlie. She would not leave here until she'd at least seen him. "I'm going to try reason," she muttered to herself as they drew closer.

Chance sighed. "Nothing you've said about this guy screams reason, Lily. Listen, let me go in first," he added. He shoved the gun into the back of his jeans. "I'll be reasonable. He won't know who I am so he won't be expecting anything. I can at least make sure Charlie is in the house and—"

"No," she said softly but with fire in her tone, pulling on his arm to stop him from proceeding. "The house is right up there. Someone could be guarding the gate. You stay back here so he doesn't see you."

"Have you forgotten what your husband did to you, Lily? Are you crazy?"

"He's not going to risk killing me in his own home."

"You are crazy. You've told me what he did to you in his own home."

"I was a lot more timid back then. And I didn't have Valentine Richards to use as ammunition. Please, Chance, just wait for me. Like you said on the ranch, I might need someone to bail me out of jail."

With that, she continued walking, relieved beyond belief when Chance didn't follow. She didn't look back until she reached the gate. There was no sign of Chance.

"Evening," a man said.

She turned to face the gate. She'd never seen the man standing there.

"May I help you?" he asked.

"Who are you?"

"Name's McCord," he said. "Who are you?"

"I'm Jeremy's Block's estranged wife. I need to talk to him."

McCord's face registered surprise as thick eyebrows wrinkled his brow. He was a stocky, fifty-year-old guy with an ex-boxer's nose and a smoker's gravelly voice. "I reckon he'll be surprised to see you." He rolled open the gate for her and she followed him up the walkway to the big black door.

"Mr. Block is probably in the study," McCord said as he gestured for her to enter the house. Stepping inside felt like entering a time warp.

"Is anyone else in the house?"

"Besides me? Just the gal Mr. Block hired to watch the kid."

"Then Charlie is here," she said, her gaze flying up the stairs. She veered that direction but McCord stepped in front of her.

"He's here. But you came to see his father, right?"

"After I say good-night to my boy," she said.

"No can do," McCord said and started to reach for her arm to prevent her from climbing the stairs. She dodged his grasp, walked to the study and yanked open the door.

Jeremy glanced up from his seat behind his desk. He was on the phone.

"Wait outside," he barked, his gaze traveling from Lily to McCord. "I'm in the middle of something important." He turned in his swivel chair so that his back was toward them. McCord grabbed Lily's arm and pulled her out of the room. He closed the door and pointed at a chair set against the wall.

Could she get past him and run up the stairs? Charlie was up there, so close now she could almost feel him in her arms.

"Don't try it," McCord said, accurately reading her body language."

"Please, Mr. McCord. Charlie is my child."

"I don't want to hurt you," McCord said and firmly pushed her down onto a chair. He planted himself square in front of her. "But that doesn't mean I won't."

Chapter Three

For twenty-one minutes, according to the clock in the foyer, Jeremy kept them waiting. Lily had no choice but to accept the fact she wasn't getting past McCord, but that didn't keep her gaze from repeatedly traveling to the second floor and the open balcony railing that surrounded it. She was so nervous and stressed her hands trembled in her lap and she had to clench them together to keep herself from exploding. More than once, she caught Mc-Cord casting her a distasteful glance.

What exactly had he been told about her?

At last Jeremy's voice told them to come into his study.

"You can leave," he told McCord as they entered. Mc-Cord turned and left, closing the door behind him.

Looking straight at Lily, Jeremy trotted out what she called his campaign smile. "Well, look who came home," he said. He did not get to his feet. His sandy-colored hair showed a few gray streaks, his eyes were so blue she knew he wore contact lenses to boost the color. He was dressed for the office in a custom-made gray suit. It was one of the more expensive worsted wools, which probably meant he had been in court that day.

Was he handsome? Not in the way Chance was, not with classic features, broad shoulders and a devilish smile that ignited the color of his eyes. But he was command-ing. His cold eyes could look warm when he put in the effort and he knew how to twist words more adroitly than a clown manipulating balloons into giraffes.

She stepped to the far side of his desk. "First of all, this is not my home. Secondly, of course I came. You stole my son."

"The law sees it the other way around." He nodded at his phone. "I should warn you. The police will come as soon as I ask them to. They have a warrant—"

"I know about that." She'd had twenty-one minutes to cool her heels and face reality and what she'd decided was that she was going to have to do the whole thing the legal way and that meant going through the system. "Listen, Jeremy," she pleaded. "Just let me see Charlie. I have to know he's okay."

Jeremy chuckled. "How very melodramatic. Of course he's okay. He's back where he belongs and no longer at the mercy of his unpredictable mother."

Lily's chin tilted. "You might be able to fool other people, Jeremy, but you can't fool me. I'm the one who lived here. I'm the one you set up to look like a lush. I'm the one you knocked unconscious. And then there's that minion you sent to kill me, Jodie Brown."

"You're delusional," he said. "I think you always have been. Well, you know what they say drugs and alcohol will do to a person."

"I found the barbiturates in your desk."

"So what? The prescription is in your name, pre-scribed by your physician to relieve anxiety. I was very troubled when I discovered you were mixing them with booze. I even talked to him about it. He was going to hos-pitalize you for observation, but you disappeared about then. I swear, getting custody of Charlie was a walk in the park."

"If it was such a walk in the park then why did you employ Jodie?"

"I knew nothing about what he did," Jeremy insisted.

"Did you kill him when he failed?"

"I believe he died in a drunk driving accident. Surely you're not blaming me for that, too?"

"You think you've covered all the bases, don't you? Let's try this one. I know about your affair with Valentine Richards."

He leaned back in his chair, a man in his domain, a confident man who could lie without effort. "I suppose you found out about her when you snooped through my files."

"It doesn't matter how I know about her. You were cheating on me. I wonder what your precious community would think of you if they knew that."

"As usual, you have it wrong. Valentine was an intern in my office. Sweet girl. Lost her grandmother while she worked here. I wanted to cheer her up so I sent her flowers."

"You hate flowers."

"But she loved them."

"I love them, too. That never made a difference to you."

"Are you jealous?"

"Oh, please. I just find it interesting that you've finally met someone who makes you think beyond yourself. Maybe you're ready to give me a divorce now."

"No," he said.

"Why?"

He smiled. "Because you want it so badly."

"I don't need your permission," she said.

"If you're hiding from me, it's going to be tricky to show up in court. And oh, then there's that nasty warrant."

Bantering with Jeremy was wasting time. Maybe that was the point. Maybe the police were about to arrive. If that was the case, then she was going to at least see Charlie before it was too late. She walked across the room, grabbed the doorknob and advanced on the staircase.

Jeremy caught her arm and pulled her around. She stumbled on the stair and fell against him. A visceral wave of distaste filled her body as she struggled to stand on her own. He slapped her face so hard her neck snapped to the side. She put a hand up to her stinging cheek and stared into his flat eyes. "Get away from me."

He lowered his head until his mouth was close to her ear. "I could kill you tonight and explain it away however I want. No one on earth would give a damn, not even Charlie, not after a while."

"You never give up, do you, Jeremy. Stop trying to bait me. It doesn't work anymore."

Pounding footsteps from the top of the stairs broke a stalemate. They looked up to see a young woman rushing across the open mezzanine. She stopped short at the head of the stairs and looked down at them.

"What's going on?" Jeremy said.

"It's the boy," the woman responded.

Lily tore herself from Jeremy's gasp and ran up the stairs. Jeremy was right behind her. "What about Charlie?" Lily demanded as she reached the quivering woman who glanced at Jeremy, then back at Lily.

"I've looked everywhere," she said. "He's not in his bed. I don't know… I don't know where he is."

Lily tore down the hall. She entered Charlie's room. It was filled with toys, many of them still in their boxes. The bed was empty. The other two appeared in the doorway as Lily stared at the rumpled sheets. She set her palm against the pillow. It was cool to the touch.

"Is he hiding somewhere? Did he run away?" Jeremy asked.

"I don't know," the woman responded. Lily walked to the window and examined the sill. Then she looked at the wooden window casing. Scratch marks clearly revealed the window had been pried open from the outside. She looked out the open window and saw nothing but the blackness of night. The light that should have illuminated this side of the yard wasn't burning and the moon hadn't yet risen high enough to help.

Her baby had been taken from this room. Had Chance done it? It was possible and if so, at least Charlie was safe. She'd been inside the house for more than thirty minutes, so he could have had time to do this. Her heart slammed against her ribs. Was Chance that rash and impulsive? Yes, at times. But he was smarter than that, she was sure of it. The thought of him trying to help her and actually jeopardizing his freedom—for surely if he had done this and was caught he would wind up in jail—well, it made her sick inside.

"Damn that spoiled brat," Jeremy said under his breath. "If he ran away—"

Lily whirled around, ready to slap him as hard as she could. "How dare you call Charlie—"

"How dare you?" He caught her raised hand and twisted it down to her side but didn't release it. For the first time he seemed to be interested in what she'd been staring at. He pulled her out of his way and turned to examine the window in silence. She knew the gouges on the wood were unmistakable. At last, through clenched teeth, he addressed the other woman. "I employ you to watch my son. You're his damn nanny. Where the hell were you while this was going on?"

"In the other room," she admitted. "I know you said to sit here with him, but my eyes kept drifting closed. I don't know why I'm so blasted sleepy. I knew I had to do something so I went to my room to find a book. I guess I sat down on the bed. The next thing I knew I was yawning myself awake. I wasn't out that long, I swear I wasn't."

"You were gone long enough for this to happen, you nitwit."

"Yes, sir," she said, looking down at the floor. She bent and picked up a piece of paper. "I didn't see this before," she said. "Maybe it fell when I threw back the blankets. Oh, my gosh! It says: *A son for a son. White—*"

Jeremy snatched the paper from the nanny's hand before she read another word. "Give that to me," he said as he released Lily's wrist.

"What does it mean?" Lily demanded. She couldn't believe Chance would leave a message as inflammatory as that. In fact, she knew he wouldn't. That meant someone else had taken Charlie. But who? "Who is White?" she asked.

Jeremy met her gaze but didn't respond, at least not to her. Instead he turned to the nanny. "Get downstairs and tell McCord to search the grounds. I want to know exactly how my son was taken from this room."

She nodded nervously and began to turn. Jeremy cleared his throat. "And Janet? Don't say a word about this to anyone else, do you understand? Not even the police. It's your fault the child is missing. Don't make it worse for yourself by blabbing to anyone but McCord."

"Yes, Mr. Block," she said as she scurried away.

Lily planted her fists on her hips. "What does that note mean, Jeremy? Who is White?"

He looked at the paper again, then folded it in half. "Don't you have enough problems of your own?"

Had he always been this much of a nutcase? Did he really think anything that happened to her mattered in the face of what was happening to their son? "Why aren't you calling the police? And you shouldn't be touching that paper. There may be fingerprints—"

"I will handle this my own way," he interrupted.

"You know something, don't you?" she said in a burst of understanding. "You know who took him and why. Someone named White. Tell me."

The hateful look in his eyes as he raked her over went straight to her gut. He tore the note into pieces and opened his hand to let them flutter to the carpet. She wanted to catch them and paste them back together. She couldn't understand how he could destroy the only link they had to Charlie's abductors.

"It's some enemy of yours, isn't it?" she implored. "Oh, my poor Charlie. How can you stand there and let this happen? Don't you care anything about him? Please—"

He grabbed her shoulders and shook her. "God, you're annoying. I'll get Charlie back safe and sound but I'll do it my own way in my own time. No police. Not unless you want Charlie dead."

Lily swallowed a lump of air. She wasn't sure what to do except get out of that house.

"Now I have to figure out what to do about you," he added.

"No, you don't. I'm leaving."

He stepped in front of her. "I don't trust you. You aren't going anywhere."

"Move out of my way."

"So you can run to the police and in some misdirected gesture of sacrifice, tell them everything you've seen and heard? I'll have to waste time quieting them down and by then it will be too late for Charlie. If you want him to live, you'll stay out of this and you won't involve the police. For now, I have things to do and you're in the way."

His fist connected with her cheekbone and she stumbled backward. Grabbing her arm, he pulled her from the room and all but ran her down the stairs, his fingers digging into her arm. He propelled her into his office, opened the closet, tore her purse from her shoulder and pushed her inside. The door slammed in her face, encasing her in blackness. The click of the lock echoed in her ears.

And then it was silent.

CHANCE WAITED UNTIL he heard the front door close behind Lily and the man she'd called McCord, then jumped over the gate. He dashed to the cover of the trees and hunkered down for a minute as his eyes adjusted to the dark. It seemed odd to him that the outside was so poorly lit but at least he didn't think he had to worry about cameras picking up his every move.

The gun constituted a last-resort measure not to be taken lightly. Bravado aside, he had no intention of shooting anyone if there was any other choice.

Eventually, he knew his sight was as good as it was going to get and he made his way across the manicured lawns to the house where he carefully peered in through a low window. It turned out to be the kitchen—empty. The next window opened onto a dining room that was dominated by a black lacquer table and the most pretentious-looking candelabra he'd ever seen. For a second he stared inside, wondering what bothered him so much, and then he had it. There were two chairs at the table, one at either end, like on a movie set when they wanted you to understand that the people who dined there didn't have much to say to one another.

Had Lily endured dinners in this setting? Chance, who had grown up with four other men and a rotating roster of stepmothers, couldn't imagine the numbing silence and the thought that Charlie might soon eat a peanut-butter-and-jelly sandwich in this mausoleum was just flat-out depressing.

Farther along, he found a living area that looked as though it had never been lived in, and then popped his head up to find himself peering into a smaller room that seemed to be a den or a home office. It, too, appeared empty and he was about to turn away when the chair in the corner suddenly spun around and a man appeared.

Chance immediately ducked out of sight, but the impression of the man stayed vivid behind his eyes: late forties, stern, arrogant. Blue eyes like Charlie's. He held a cell phone in one hand and avidly tapped a pencil against the wooden arm of the chair with another. The window was slightly open, but try as he might, Chance couldn't make out what was being said. He scampered away, careful to keep his head down.

That had to be Lily's husband. But where was Lily? And where was McCord? He decided to skirt the entire perimeter of the house. The harvest moon that had seemed to illuminate the world on his ranch in the mid-

dle of the night was subdued here by the massive size of
the house and the shadows it cast. Maybe in a couple of
hours it would rise high enough to overcome this obsta-
cle, but Chance fervently hoped he and Lily were back
in the motel room by then.

And maybe Charlie, too. Maybe Jeremy Block would
come to his senses and be reasonable.

Sure. And pigs could fly.

Careful to avoid the patches of light that shone through
the windows, he almost tripped when he turned the corner and came across something in the grass. He knelt
down to investigate. Someone had left a metal ladder
lying on the grass. By the feel and heft of it, a long one.

Why would anyone leave a ladder lying on the grass?
He looked up at the bank of windows overhead and saw
two lights placed far enough away from each other to suggest two different rooms. Probably upstairs bedrooms;
one of those might be Charlie's. He played around with
the possibility of raising the ladder and checking it out
but decided against it.

Besides, maybe someone had been washing second-
story windows today and got lazy or put the ladder down
flat so a small boy wouldn't be tempted to climb it and
fall. Who knew?

Like a moth drawn to a flame, he retraced his steps to
the office window and chanced another peek. This time
the door was opening. He shrank back against the rock
siding, then slowly inched his face close enough to see
inside. Lily stood in front of the desk, her body so taut
she almost vibrated. Block stayed seated and managed
to look bored as she spoke.

Did he dare nudge the window open farther? No, he
decided, too risky. Besides, he could pretty much guess

what they were saying. One thing was clear: there was no love lost between them.

After several minutes, Lily turned on her heels and rushed to the door. She ripped it open and slammed it behind her. That was his girl, temper, temper. But Block was out of his chair in a flash, hurrying after her and the look on his face chilled Chance's blood. The door swung closed behind them so whatever happened next occurred without Chance witnessing it. And in his gut he knew nothing good was going on inside that house.

Self-preservation kicked in and he began to wonder where McCord was. If the older man did carry out a cursory patrol of the yard every once in a while, shouldn't he be showing up soon? And exactly how was he going to get out of this yard when the time came to escape? He found the answer to that when he literally ran into a tree growing close to the tall fence. He could shimmy up the trunk and jump down on the other side.

Desperate to know what was going on, Chance crept around to the garage side of the house and smelled smoke. The lights were still off, but he stopped short when he saw the glow of a cigarette as someone sucked on it. Squinting, he could just make out the figure of a man leaning against a white car, an acrid pale cloud hanging in the air around him.

A door opened from the house into a nearby carport. A woman stood framed in the light. "Mr. McCord?" she called with an edge of panic in her voice. She flipped on a weak outside light and McCord pushed himself away from the car and swore.

"Turn the damn light off," he said.

"The little boy is missing! There's a note and everything. Mr. Block said you should find out how the child was taken or if he's still on the grounds. And we're to tell no one about this."

"Have you called the cops?" McCord asked as he emerged into the light. He was a stocky man with an almost bald head.

"Mr. Block insisted no police. He's furious with me."

"What about the kid's mother?"

"Is that who she is? He's furious with her, too. I think he hit her. I better get back inside. Hurry, check the grounds."

She ran back inside the house. Chance expected McCord to turn on the outside floodlights if they had them and sure enough, within seconds the yard jumped from black to living color. He moved at once into one of the few remaining shadows but he had the feeling McCord had witnessed the movement. The older man would come looking and chances were he packed a firearm.

Even more to the point, Lily was apparently trapped inside the house. The maid said Jeremy had hit her. His fists clenched. How badly was she hurt? How could he get her out of there?

Slinking behind a grape arbor still thankfully covered with drooping yellow leaves he could hide behind, he pulled his gun, but paused to try to think.

Who in the world had taken Charlie?

LILY GRASPED OVERHEAD for a light cord to pull. She couldn't find one and there was nothing on the wall. Then she remembered the switch outside the door. The shelves behind her felt like they were covered with office supplies. What could she do when Jeremy returned? Give him a bad paper cut?

She kicked at the door until her foot hurt. She pounded her fists against the heavy wood panel to no avail. She yelled and shouted and had the horrible feeling no one could hear her or that if they did, they would simply ignore her.

Who had taken Charlie and what did they want with him? Her stomach clenched into a knot as she pictured his eyes filled with fear. How could Jeremy be so cavalier about his child's safety? If Jeremy wasn't blowing smoke, then going to the police might prove deadly for Charlie... How did she chance that her lying, cheating husband might actually be telling the truth for once?

She swore under her breath.

A sound on the other side of the door froze her solid for a second and then she frantically started patting the shelves again, feeling for something, anything she could use as a weapon. Her fingers brushed the cool metal of an aerosol can. She grabbed it and another one next to it. She depressed the nozzle sprays and was rewarded with nothing but puffs of air. That's what they were: compressed gas meant to blow the dust from a computer keyboard. Their contents were useless, but they were heavy enough to buy her a moment or two if she used them as projectiles.

The lock clicked and she jumped. This was it. Raising the cans to face height, she squinted against the sudden infusion of light and threw the cans as hard as she could. She opened her eyes in time to see one strike a dark head while a tanned hand caught the other.

"Damn!" Chance said. "Ouch."

"Chance! I'm sorry, I thought you were Jeremy!" She threw herself against him and he caught her, hugging her close for a second, then he raised a hand and gently touched the uninjured part of her cheek. "When I get my hands on that man—"

"Not now," she said. "How did you get in here?"

He gestured at the window. The yard beyond was brilliantly illuminated. "But I don't know how we're going to escape," he said. They heard a yell from outside. "I bet they found the ladder over on the far side of the house. Is that how they took Charlie? Through the window?"

"Yes." She wasn't sure how he knew Charlie was missing but now wasn't the time for conversation.

"We'll have to make a dash for that tree over by the fence. Are you up to it?"

His gaze studied her face and she could imagine what he saw. She knew one eye was swollen because she could feel it with her fingers and she suspected the warm sticky substance on her cheek was blood from Jeremy's last punch. "Don't worry about me," she said. "But Chance, if I'm stopped and you're not, promise me you'll find Charlie."

"Lily…"

"Promise me."

"I promise. Come on."

He stuck his head out the window, then turned to look back at her. "The tree is about twenty feet to your right. Can you climb trees?"

"If I have to."

"Then go. I'll be behind you. I have something to do here."

"What?"

"Lily. Go." He picked her up, and swung her outside.

"See if you can find my purse," she whispered. "It has the car keys."

"Will do." He released her. She dropped to her feet and took off at a dead run. She found the fence and kept going until she got to the tree. Chance showed up earlier than she'd anticipated and hoisted her onto a limb over her head. She scrambled along until she got close to the top of the iron fence and threw herself to the ground on the other side, landing facedown, all but knocking the wind out of her lungs. Chance landed a few seconds after her, but he came down on his feet and absorbed the shock in his legs. He immediately stood and pulled her upright. She saw with relief that he held her purse in one hand.

They ran across the street, thankful to be out of the light.

"I don't know how we avoided being seen," Chance said as Lily led them to the nature trail.

"I don't, either. What did you do in Jeremy's office besides find my purse?"

He pressed her bag into her hands. "Wiped my prints away and kicked in the closet door from the inside. I didn't want your husband knowing you had outside help. You didn't tell him I was with you, did you?"

"No," she said as she extracted the car keys. Would Jeremy believe she was capable of kicking open a door? Maybe, maybe not, but at least he'd wonder.

Lily took the passenger seat. A few seconds later, Chance directed the car onto the quiet road. "Where's the nearest police station?" he asked. The moon illuminated the pavement and they drove without lights for several seconds before they'd turned away from Jeremy's neighborhood and traffic began to appear. The headlights went on and they sped up.

"We're not going to the police," she said.

"But the man hit you, Lily. He locked you in a closet..."

"I'm not important. It's Charlie we have to worry about. Jeremy says if the police get involved, the kidnappers will kill Charlie."

"And you believe him?"

"I don't know what to believe," she said. "But for now, no police. I have to find out who took Charlie. It's someone named White, I think."

"We'll find him," Chance said.

Too caught up in her thoughts, she didn't respond. *A son for a son...* That implied revenge. It had to be tied to Jeremy.

Chapter Four

"Jeremy knows who took Charlie," she said. "And for some reason, he's keeping it to himself, which to me implies he has something to hide." They were digging through the papers Lily had gathered before leaving her husband. The former neat stacks were now in a state of disarray as she grabbed one reprinted article after another. "Look for the death of a man," she coaxed.

Her voice was too highly pitched and the papers seemed to slip through her fingers. Chance wanted to tell her to calm down but he knew better than to even suggest such a thing.

"There was no demand for ransom, right?" Chance asked.

"No."

"Is it possible Jeremy staged the kidnapping to throw you off?"

"Why bother? I'm just a pesky gnat to him."

"Don't underestimate yourself," Chance said. "You can be a hell of a lot more than pesky when you put your mind to it."

"Thanks," she said with a sudden smile.

"What's to keep us from calling the cops?"

"Jeremy said—"

"The man lies as easily as a duck quacks."

"But this time he may be telling the truth. I can't risk it until I know more."

Chance stopped arguing. All it took was one glance at her bruised and bloodied face to make the veins pop in his forehead. No one knew better than he how focused and relentless she could be, but the fact that Jeremy felt he had the right to strike her made his blood boil.

Boiling blood aside, the bigger issue was Charlie. Little Charlie, stolen from his bed, held…well, why? As a hostage? As retribution? What did a five-year-old kid have to make retribution for? Who in the world would take out their hatred for a man on his very young child?

No one sane. Ergo, a lunatic had Charlie. And a lunatic might harm the boy if threatened.

"Here's something," she said, holding up a piece of newspaper. "A man Jeremy prosecuted died of cancer while serving a life sentence. It says, 'Levi Bolt, 68, expired Wednesday—'"

Chance cut her off. "*His* parents would have to be in their eighties. Keep looking."

They fell silent as they searched. "Look at this," she said a few minutes later. He glanced at her face to find that the blood had congealed and her eye had swollen almost closed. He stood up.

"Lily, let me help you clean those wounds."

"Not yet," she said. "Read this to me. It's not long."

He took the paper from her hand and read the article aloud.

"'Police today reported an inmate apparently committed suicide early Saturday morning by hanging himself in his cell. Darke Fallon, estimated age eighteen, was found at 3:25 a.m., January 14. He was being held pending proceedings that were to have started on Monday to determine competency. Prison medical staff attempted life-saving measures before transporting him to Charity Hill Medical Center where he was pronounced dead. Results of toxicology tests were unavailable for review.

"Fallon is accused of the January 10 murder of Mr. Wallace Connor, 21, of Greenville, Idaho, who was found knifed to death in a Boise motel where he had reportedly traveled for a job interview. Twenty-four hours later, police spotted Connor's truck. The driver, Darke Fallon, confessed to the murder but shortly after arrest, ceased cooperating with police. He claimed Connor picked him up while Fallon was hitchhiking from his home in Bend, Oregon, but that could not be confirmed. State appointed attorneys swore to fight demands for hypnosis to establish identity. It is unknown if Mr. Fallon leaves any survivors. The prosecutor's office, headed by Jeremy Block, refused comment.'"

"How could the police not find a trace of him?" Chance mused aloud. "Apparently no fingerprints, no family stepping forward, no Social Security number, no one has ever seen or heard about him before? That seems so unlikely in this day and age."

"I know, I know," Lily said, "But *his* parents would be young enough to steal Charlie."

"If he had any. Did Jeremy talk about this suicide to you?"

"I'm not sure. What's the date again?"

"January 15."

"That's right around the time Jeremy finally knocked me out and I decided to leave. I told you there'd been a suicide at the jail in a cell before he came unglued. This must have been the one."

"Was there a follow-up investigation after his death?"

"Probably."

"There must have been fallout over the suicide," Chance said. "Did you ever hear why the kid killed himself before his trial?"

"No."

Chance skirted through other clippings. "There's nothing else here."

"I'll search the internet," she said, and picking up her phone, went to work. After a half hour they knew a little more but not much.

"Wallace Connor came from Greenville, right? That's pretty close to an area called White Cliff," she finally said. She sat for a moment, then looked up at him. "*White.* Maybe the word *white* in the note wasn't a name of a person but a place." She scanned the screen. "White Cliff appears to be a survivalist community." She groaned and closed her eyes. "Talking kind of hurts," she admitted. "I must have bitten down on the inside of my mouth when Jeremy hit me."

"Wait here," Chance said, and taking the ice bucket, walked to the machine near the outside stairs. Back in the room he gave her a cube to suck on and made a compress by wrapping the rest in a hand towel she held against her face. "I'll take over the search," he added.

"There's a lot in here about that survivalist community you mentioned," he said after he'd continued reading. "One reporter tried to find out if Fallon had ever lived in White Cliff but got nowhere. Apparently the police had the same lack of success."

"How about Wallace Connor?" Lily garbled around the ice cube.

"They say he left behind his parents and a younger

sister. Robbery was the supposed reason for the murder because his wallet was empty and a lapis lazuli ring the desk clerk noticed when he checked in was missing from his hand. The police caught Fallon the next day. He was driving Connor's truck. He told the cops his name, admitted he killed Connor and then shut his mouth and never said another word to anyone about anything. His lawyers were court-appointed. His competency hearing was scheduled for the Monday after he died. His suicide seems to have been the end of it."

"It's a dead end," Lily said bitterly.

He set aside the phone. "No, not a dead end, just a twisty road. We'll figure something out. Come on, let me wash your face and get some antiseptic and a bandage on that open cut. No, don't argue with me." He pulled her up by clasping her arm, grabbed his toiletries kit from his duffel and gently pushed her ahead of him into the bathroom.

She sat on the edge of the tub as he bathed her face in warm water, dabbed on the ointment and covered the open wound with a bandage. The occasional whimpers that escaped her lips made him furious. How dare that jerk touch her.

"Am I pretty again?" she asked as she stood, a little playfulness creeping back into her voice.

He put his hands on her shoulders and studied her face. "Not yet, but you will be."

"Hold me," she said softly.

He drew her closer and put his arms around her. She fit perfectly, as he knew from experience, and though he swore to himself he would not react to her closeness or the way she clung to him, he could feel his body stirring.

"I'm so scared," she whispered against his neck.

He drew back to look at her face, but his gaze landed on her mouth, and mindful of her injuries, he leaned forward and gently touched her lips with his.

They'd kissed a few times several months earlier. To him, her lips had been everything delicious and tasty in the world. Honey and scotch, summer nights, a good dinner. He'd wanted to bed her with a vengeance and had worked on seducing her for weeks, but one torrid fifteen minutes had led to her bolting away from him for good.

So what? There were more women in the world than men and he'd known his share. Frankly, he seemed to have a knack for finding women who wanted what he wanted—a satisfying romp in the hay, no heartstrings engaged. His father had been married seven times. Seven times! Women came and went, the trick was not to block the door.

And then came Lily.

Tricky, complicated, troubled, on the run, dangerous.

She pulled away from him and studied his face. "Thank you for rescuing me from the closet."

"You're welcome." He touched her good cheek. Her skin was so soft.

She nodded briskly and disengaged herself from his embrace. He longed to keep his fingers linked behind her back, longed to hold her in his arms all night. He knew she was distracted and sick with worry and so was he… *Oh, give it up*, his brain scolded, and he withdrew his hands.

"We need to talk to those survivalists ourselves," he said as they returned to the room. He looked away from the bed, which suddenly seemed to take up almost all the floor space. She sat down in the chair in front of the table and shook her head. "I know. It's wild land up there, people are scattered and many are suspicious of outsiders. I guess we start by finding White Cliff."

"Yeah," he said. His voice sounded too loud.

"I'm going to go back over everything in the files. We must have missed something," she said.

"Now?"

"Right now."

He shook his head. "It's late, Lily. You need sleep. There's always tomorrow…"

"You go ahead," she said, her attention on the papers she held in her hands. "I'm not sleepy yet."

Maybe she didn't want to crawl into bed with him. Maybe that was too risky for her. He stripped off his clothes and got under the covers, noting as he did all this that she didn't look at him once. Man, as soon as Charlie was safe, he had to somehow get to her.

He knew he couldn't sleep even though she'd switched off most of the lamps. A few minutes later when he glanced at her, he found her sitting in the sole pool of light, head bent over the table, a solitary figure obsessed and afraid. He sat up and reached out to touch her shoulder and she pulled away. He laid his head back on the pillow to consider what his next move should be. Against all odds, he fell asleep instead.

THE WORDS BEGAN to blur in Lily's eyes. There was just so much unrelated stuff. Copies of papers detailing Jeremy's courtroom victories, memos to office staff including several to Valentine Richards, who apparently worked for Jeremy just as he claimed, which didn't preclude a personal relationship. Still, maybe lightning struck twice tonight. Maybe he'd told the truth about Valentine and the danger of police involvement, too.

And so what if they'd had an affair? She should have known it wouldn't matter. Going to his house thinking the knowledge of his infidelity would give her leverage seemed terribly naive in retrospect. And Chance had warned her but she hadn't had any other options so she'd refused to listen.

Where was her boy? How did she keep breathing not knowing if he was in danger? *Keep focused…* She found receipts from the dry cleaner's and the bakery and the shoe store. There were photographs as well: a large boat, the day's catch from some fishing trip, buildings she didn't recognize, women wearing suggestive clothing…

Oh, what was the point of all of this?

She got up and paced. Chance's breathing was steady and deep—he was down for the count. The thought of sitting here for seven more hours while Charlie was in trouble made her shiver inside.

And then she knew that she couldn't wait, not another minute. Working quickly but quietly, she gathered all of the papers and stuffed them back in their envelope. She sat down to write Chance a note explaining why she had to leave and why it was better if she went alone.

It wasn't fair to keep dragging him into the minefield her life had become. She knew what he wanted from her—a quick, easy fling that would be over for him the moment it became real for her.

But it was more than that. She was asking him to climb out on a limb with her because she had no intention of returning Charlie to Jeremy. She would be on the run forever and Chance was a guy with roots so deep they touched the center of the earth which was, for him, his three brothers, his father and a ranch that had been in the family's hands for over a hundred years.

Now that she'd made up her mind to go off on her own, it was clear she should never have allowed him to accompany her even this far. She reread her note. It all sounded like a lot of half-baked excuses.

She looked back into the room before closing the door, half hoping Chance would stir, that he'd sit up, that he'd see her, but his breathing remained steady, his body still. She whispered goodbye under her breath and closed the door behind her. She drove away without looking back, certain she was doing the logical, reasonable, all-around best thing for everyone. It had to be right because it felt so terrible…

CHANCE WOKE UP, yawned, then sat up abruptly.

There was no sign of Lily.

"Damn," he swore under his breath. Why in the world had he chosen now to turn into Rip Van Winkle?

He got out of bed and dressed in a hurry, looking around as he pulled on his boots. Not only was Lily not in the room, there was no sign she ever had been. She'd taken everything with her.

"Damn," he said again. He tucked his gun out of sight under his shirt and opened the outside door. Morning light seemed to shine straight down on the empty spot where he'd parked her car the night before.

For a second he tried to tell himself she'd gone out to bring back breakfast, but he knew it wasn't true. There was a total feeling of abandonment. She was gone.

Back inside, he searched every horizontal surface for a note that might explain why she'd run out on him…again. He finally spied a wadded-up piece of paper in the garbage can and sat down as he smoothed open the paper.

After reading the first sentence, he swore under his

breath and stood. A minute after that, he picked up his duffel bag and locked the room behind him.

It took him six hours to hitchhike the two hundred miles home and that was because he was eventually lucky enough to catch a ride with a guy who lived in Falls Bluff. Once in town, he walked to the feed store where he knew Patty Reed, the pigtailed girl who worked behind the counter, would lend him her truck so he could drive himself home.

However, she did more than that. She actually insisted on getting someone to cover for her and driving him herself. Chance knew this had little to do with his own charisma; Patty was hot for Chance's younger brother, Pike. However, a ride was a ride.

They arrived at the ranch house to find his father and his new stepmother, Grace, still off in Oregon. Gerard and Pike were unloading bales of hay into the feed barn using a combination of brute strength and a forklift to get the job done. Kinsey had not yet returned from New Orleans, though Gerard had pinned many of her rough sketches to the walls in the barn because he liked looking at them. Horses peered over a fence; a looming tree sat alone on a hilltop. A herd of deer grazed in a field at twilight. There was even one of the ghost town that existed on ranch property, and though it had been the site of tragedy for Gerard, it was situated front and center. Maybe it was his way of domesticating the pain, of reclaiming good memories as well as bad.

Gerard told Chance that Kinsey had made this switch from portraiture to scenery and still life because she'd finally found a real family to belong to: theirs, and a real home in which to plant roots. Seeing as she and

Gerard were going to be married next summer, it made perfect sense.

Gerard, busy driving the forklift, looked up as Chance walked into the barn followed by Patty who immediately veered over toward Pike and leaned fetchingly nearby. Chance supposed his scholarly-looking brother made an attractive picture to a kid barely out of high school. Lots of girls thought glasses made a guy look smart. It didn't hurt that in Pike's case, he could back up the advertising with an agile brain.

"You leave with one girl and come back with another," Gerard said as he turned off the noisy machine.

"I just caught a ride with Patty. She's here to ogle Pike."

They both looked over at the truck. Pike seemed to be ignoring the girl.

"He's preoccupied right now," Gerard said. "His mom in LA called this morning. There's some issue with his stepsister."

"You know," Chance said, "every once in a while, I kind of wish we all had the same mother instead of different ones, but then I think she might have been like Pike's and I'm okay with things the way they are."

"No kidding," Gerard said. "Where's Lily? What happened? She's not really in jail, is she?"

"Not yet," Chance said and gave Gerard an abbreviated explanation of the past twenty-four hours.

"Charlie is missing? Again? Lily must be worried sick. Even that louse of a husband has to be concerned."

"I don't know. He seems to know more than he's telling. Lily said he acted as though he knew exactly who had the boy. The word *white* was mentioned in the note. We thought it was a name at first but it's also a survivalist camp or something up in the panhandle. It might be that someone from there took Charlie or it could be a complete red herring."

"You let her go off alone to a survivalist's enclave?"

"Enclave?"

"Yeah. White Cliff isn't just a camp, it's an unincorporated community. There are lots of places like it across the country. This one is dominated by a guy named Robert Brighton. He and the others call themselves true patriots, devoted to knowing how to defend and take care of themselves in the event of a military or natural catastrophe."

"I'd never heard of it before yesterday. How do you know so much?"

Gerard shrugged. "Remember Gary Stills from high school?"

"Sure."

"He got disgusted with rising taxes and government involvement in their ranch a few years back and took his wife and kid and moved up that way. I heard from him a year or so ago. He ranted on about getting ready for Armageddon so I read up on it."

"Hell, it's hard to imagine Lily in that kind of situation," Chance said, wondering how in the world she expected to uncover anything on her own. "And it's hard to believe those people would kidnap a little boy and subject themselves to police involvement. They don't sound like the type."

"As long as you don't cross them. Anyway, you said Lily's husband refuses to involve the police so they have little to worry about."

"Yeah, and how exactly did they know he'd react that way? It seems totally out of character for him. If all he's interested in is free press and sympathetic votes, why doesn't he jump on this chance to get his son's plight on every news channel in the country?"

"All good questions," Gerard said. "When are you joining Lily?"

Chance took off his hat and pulled it on again. "I'm not."

Gerard stared at him, his brilliant blue eyes thoughtful.

"Don't look at me like that," Chance protested. "She left me high and dry. I don't even know for sure she went to White Cliff. She might have found another lead after I went to bed."

"Why did she go alone?"

"She said something about not wanting to involve me. If that's the way she wants it, then fine."

"I guess it's out of your hands," Gerard said. "It's her son, right? Well," he added as he turned the forklift back on, "I'd better get back to work. Pike is waiting on me."

Chance took a deep breath. "I'll go help him. After a day with Lily, picking up bales of hay will be child's play."

By nightfall, he'd worked until his muscles ached. Unfortunately, they weren't the only parts of him that hurt. He went outside the main ranch house where he'd decided to spend the night. If that was the phone number Charlie knew, then it was best there be somebody here to answer it. He sat on the bench, breathing in the cold autumn air. Forty-eight hours before, Lily had driven back into his life.

A vehicle pulled into the parking area and he stood abruptly. Had she had second thoughts? Seconds later, the headlights dimmed, the door opened. And then he recognized Pike's lean frame walk toward him as the interior light peeking through the open door sparkled against his glasses. As usual, the dogs provided an escort.

Swallowing disappointment, he sat back down on the bench. "How's it going?" Pike asked as he leaned against the railing.

"Okay. Gerard said you heard from Mona. She all right?"

"My mother is never all right, you know that," Pike said. "The woman isn't alive unless she's neck deep in drama. Her boyfriend seems to have cheated on her."

"Gerard also mentioned Tess."

"Yeah. Apparently when she heard about what her father had done, she stormed off. She's only eighteen, you know, and LA can be a rough place when you're alone."

"I met her the summer before last when you flew her here for a visit. She's a smart kid."

"I guess," Pike said.

"Yeah. Well, I know you're worried about her,". Even in the half-light, he could see the strain on Pike's face.

"Yeah." He took off his glasses and pinched the bridge of his nose. "But you know how I feel. Maybe you're inexperienced when it comes to worrying about a little sister, but you're positively preoccupied with Lily."

"No, I'm not," Chance said.

Pike's eyebrows inched up his forehead.

"No, really," Chance insisted. "She's made it clear she thinks I'm a bumbling oaf. I could save that woman's life once a day from now until hell froze over, and she'd still second-guess everything I did or said."

"That doesn't sound like you," Pike said.

"What do you mean?"

"Since when do you let anyone scare you away?"

"You know Lily. She's a lot easier to look at than to deal with."

"Maybe. I just keep thinking about Charlie."

As if on cue, the phone rang. Chance hurried inside and picked up on the second ring. "Yes," he said, tense with anticipation.

But the call was from one of his father's friends. Chance disconnected and went back outside where the sound of the nearby river rushing over rocks mimicked his hammering heart. Why was he so disappointed that the call hadn't been from someone in trouble? Was he a ghoul?

No, he decided. But sitting here on the ranch waiting to hear if Charlie was okay, not knowing what was going on…it was eating him up inside.

"I'm going to bed," he announced.

"Sounds like a good idea," Pike said, and getting to his feet, ambled back to the truck. Chance locked the door and climbed the stairs.

After four hours of lying on his back and staring at the moonlit ceiling, he swore under his breath. He sat up and walked downstairs, stared at the silent phone, then grabbed his tablet computer and went back on the internet where he eventually found a reference to White Cliff that called the proposed community a fortress. Sounded formidable. It couldn't be that hard to find, could it?

Well, it was wild country and a lot bigger than it appeared on a map. You could drive down endless unpaved forest roads if you didn't know which to take…

There was only one person Chance could think of who might be able to help. But why would Jeremy Block offer any information? He wouldn't. Chance needed a bargaining tool. Did they have anything in common? No, nothing, except maybe Lily.

Lily. It always came back to her.

He put down the tablet and walked outside. For a minute, he let his mind wander the ranch. The fields, the big old hanging tree, the ghost town, the generations of people who had lived and worked, ranched and mined, fished the rivers and hunted for food, built homes, given birth and gasped their last breath right on this land. Sounds of the river filled the night. A horse whinnied nearby. The ponderous full moon stared down at him. Wind rustled the boughs overhead. The ranch was peaceful on this autumn night, demanding nothing. Come first light, another busy day of ranching would commence. The list of things to do stretched on for eternity. This was his life, his home.

"Damn her," he muttered yet again.

It was too early to make any phone calls, but it wasn't too early to go home and pack a bag. He left a note on the board for his brothers and took off for his own cabin. A half hour after that, dressed in the clothes he'd worked in all day, he tucked the handgun and a rifle into a locked case behind the seat of the oldest vehicle on the ranch, a thirty-year-old Ford pickup. He wanted to look inconspicuous. He wanted to be able to change his story whenever he needed to, be invisible or all over the map.

The cattle guard rumbled a goodbye as he drove off Hastings land and headed south. It was time to be someone else for a while, time to go undercover.

Chapter Five

Chance had debated how to present himself. Unkempt, drunk, angry? Somehow he doubted any one of those alone would work on Block. But crafty and sneaky wouldn't work, either. He decided on a mix of characteristics and knew he would depend mostly on luck.

He parked the truck on the other end of the path he and Lily had used to escape and locked his wallet in the box with the guns. He wasn't sure what he would find at the Block house and he didn't want any ties to the Hastings name. What he knew was that going off to northern Idaho without knowing what Jeremy Block had already set in motion was too dangerous. Chance didn't want to get blindsided but even more than that, he didn't want Charlie caught in the middle of a situation where everyone around was armed to the teeth.

Maybe Block wouldn't be home. Maybe he'd gone after his kid. That would be good to know, as well, because if Lily got in Block's way, she was toast.

McCord didn't show up at the gate so Chance marched up to the front door, punched the doorbell three times fast in a row with his knuckle and banged his fist against the dark wood. No prints in knuckles and fists. This guy was a DA with law enforcement ties and Chance did not want to leave any tangible proof of his identity behind.

The door was opened by the woman Chance had seen come to the kitchen door to tell McCord that Charlie had disappeared.

He took a deep breath. Showtime.

Before she could utter a word, he pushed the door open with his shoulder and barged past her. "Where is she?" he demanded. He strode to the stairs and started to climb them, hollering, "Lily?" at the top of his lungs. Hopefully Jeremy Block was somewhere in the house and would hear him.

A door behind him opened and Chance turned to see the man he'd glimpsed through the window "What in the hell is going on?" he demanded.

"Where is she?" Chance said, coming back down the stairs. "I know she's here."

"Where is who?"

"Lily Kirk. She talked about you sometimes. Is she here?"

Block cut him off with a barking laugh. "That woman is poison."

"Amen."

"And I should know, I'm married to her."

Chance allowed his expression to register surprise. He made a big deal of looking around the opulent surroundings and whistling low in his throat. "I knew she'd lived with you and all but she never said a word about being married. Brother, I can't believe she ran out on all this. I didn't know she was that stupid."

Block seemed to suddenly notice that the woman who had opened the door was still standing nearby. "For heaven's sake, Janet, close the door and get lost," he commanded. She did as he asked and hurried up the stairs, giving Chance a wide berth.

"Just tell me. Is the bitch here or not?" Chance demanded.

"Come into my office," Block said. "Let's have a civilized drink and discuss this." Chance preceded him into the den. He paused to stare at the closet door he'd splintered two nights before. "What happened?"

"Nothing important," Block said but his teeth stretched tight over his teeth as though tasting something bitter. "What's your name?"

"Pete Reed," Chance said, digging up the moniker of an old school pal. "At least that's the name I'm using right now. My real name is none of your business."

"Why are you so angry with Lily?"

"She stole two thousand three hundred bucks from me, money I had to get from a guy who is twice as mean as anybody I ever served with in the army. The dude almost killed me but I got what he owed me, I always do. And then that bitch stole it."

"You're really mad," Block said.

"Hell, yes, I'm mad."

Block narrowed his eyes as though assessing what he was seeing. "How mad?"

"Mad enough to make her wish she'd never met me."

"She has that effect on men," Block said. "Have you ever done any time?"

"Twice. Trumped-up assault charges. I was a little out of sorts after my discharge from the army. I've got a temper, I admit it."

"Where do you work now?"

Chance emphasized an impatient sigh. "I was a bouncer at a strip club until I blew town to find Lily.

How is this getting me any closer to that goal and why the third degree?"

"You a good shot?"

"Give me a gun and a knothole a hundred yards away and I'll show you."

Block poured two small glasses of amber liquor out of a crystal decanter he kept on the desk and handed one to Chance. "Cheers," he said, hoisting his glass to his lips. Chance did the same and downed it in one gulp, trying to get a handle on where Block was coming from. He sure didn't act like a guy whose kid had been taken.

Block sat behind his desk and motioned for Chance to take a seat opposite him. "If I know Lily, and I do, she's trying to get our son back."

"Charlie?"

"You know the boy?"

"Sure, I saw him around now and again. Lily didn't encourage us to be friendly if you know what I mean." He grinned and added, "Maybe she thought I'd be a bad influence. Who is she trying to get him back from? You?"

"No. I had him for a day or two but then someone stole him away in the night."

"So that's why she left Reno? Because someone took Charlie from her?"

"Yes. Me."

Chance looked around again. "The kid will be better off here than in that dump in Reno."

"Of course he will. But a third party decided they wanted to hurt me so they took Charlie."

Chance shook his head. "I don't get it. Why isn't this place swarming with cops? What kind of ransom do they want?"

"No ransom demand has been made and I didn't call

the police. I don't want them involved. Too dangerous. What I want to do is steal him back."

"Then go do it. If he were my kid I wouldn't be sitting here yapping about it."

Block's lip curled in anger but he quickly covered it with a self-deprecating smile. "I can't. If I show up, who knows what they'll do to the boy. I need someone else to take care of it. Maybe someone like you."

"Me?" Chance scoffed. "Ha." He paused as though thinking and added. "If they don't want money for the kid, then why did they take him?"

"I have no idea," Block said. *Like hell you don't,* Chance thought. "The only thing I have to go on is a note they left. That's why I'm pretty sure where he is."

"And where's the note?"

"Lily took it with her when she left," he said. No trace of the lie he'd just told surfaced in his eyes. "But like I said, she'll charge in and mess up everything."

"A specialty of hers," Chance said. "But I still don't see how any of this gets me closer to my money."

"I'm going to be honest with you," Block said. "I need help. I need someone I can trust—"

Chance shot to his feet and laughed. "Trust? Hell, you don't even know me."

"Sit down, Pete, please. I'm an excellent judge of character."

Chance grabbed his glass and gestured at the decanter. The glass he could break before he left, but he didn't want his prints on the liquor bottle. Block took the hint and poured him a shot that Chance knocked back as he reclaimed the chair. "You want me to go get him, is that it?"

"Yes."

Chance stared at Block, who didn't flinch. After a long

pause, he shook his head again. "Excuse me, but looking around it's hard not to notice you must be loaded. Hell, hire yourself a private detective."

"Listen to me, Pete, it isn't that simple. These aren't ordinary people. It's going to take someone with finesse and cunning and you strike me as a man with both those qualities."

"Flattery won't get you anywhere," Chance said. "Use one of your own people."

"I had to fire the only man I would trust with a job like this."

"Why'd you fire him?"

"He failed to protect my son and I do not tolerate failure. Listen, just come up with a convincing story, fit in for a few days and then when the time is right, do what needs to be done and extract my kid without getting him hurt."

"Lily will know I'm ready to do whatever I have to in order to get my money back. If she's there, she'll turn me in as a liar the moment she sets eyes on me."

"Not if you take care of her first thing," Block said softly.

Chance had come here hoping to get a lead on finding Charlie and by default, Lily. But he wasn't prepared for what he thought he'd just heard. "Are you talking about killing her?" he said.

Block shrugged. "I have a bottle of her barbiturates. Assuming she's there, all you have to do is get the pills down her throat. It will appear she committed suicide. But if something goes wrong and she does finger you, off you go, no harm, no foul." He cleared his throat. "I don't expect you to risk yourself for nothing. I'll give you what she stole from you and a bonus, too. If she still has your cash on her it might be best to leave it with her so no one gets suspicious. When you bring Charlie back to me, I'll add another twenty grand."

Chance whistled. "Murder, though. I haven't killed anyone since the army."

"And you did it then because you were fighting a war. This is war, too. The victory is freeing a child. Do you have a gun?"

"Not on me, but I can get one. Where do I find Lily and all the rest of these people?"

"An area called White Cliff."

Bingo, Chance thought. Confirmation. Lily was right. Hell, she often was which was just another irritating thing about her. "Where's that?"

"Up in Idaho's panhandle, almost to the border. It's one of those commune things. The leader is a guy named Roberts. He's a fast talker and a hard hitter but I heard he's not around the place as much as he used to be. There's a woman up there who runs a small store located outside the walls of the community. She calls herself Maria Eastern. If Charlie is living there, she'll know about it. You can't ask her straight out, though, and you can't mention my name or she'll put a bullet through your brain."

"The price just went up ten thousand," Chance said. Block opened his mouth to speak but closed it without saying anything. "And I'm going to need more cash up front," Chance added. "I have to buy the gun I told you about and my truck needs a tire. I don't plan on spending my own money."

"I'll add another thousand," Block said.

"Two thousand," Chance countered.

Block gritted his teeth. "Be warned that these people are heavily armed and know how to handle themselves."

"Sure."

"Wait for me in the entry."

Chance had already folded the tiny shot glass in his fist and took it with him when he left the office. Block soon appeared and handed over an open envelope stuffed with cash Chance assumed he'd retrieved from a hidden safe inside the office. There was also a slip of paper with a crude map naming roads and estimated distances. In the end he was supposed to look for a red no-trespassing sign.

"There are going to be a million of those," Chance said without touching the note.

"Look at the spelling."

Trespassing had been spelled *tresspassing*. "That's intentional," Block added. "That's the sign that points out the right road or so I'm told."

"Is this place some kind of secret?"

"Not at all. It's located close to a town called Greenville but the less you show your face or ask directions, the better for you if things go wrong."

Chance stuffed the envelope of money in his pocket. "You must really love that kid," he said.

"He is my son. Once I have him back, I won't lose him again even if I have to send him out of the country to school."

"Then nobody better get caught," Chance said, implying, he hoped, that this meant him, too.

"You'd be smart to keep something in mind," Block said. "I'm an important man in this state. If it comes to whose word will be believed, it will be mine, not yours. If you double-cross me, I'll find you."

So much for all that baloney about trust. On the other hand, Chance didn't have to pretend to feel the chill in Block's icy gaze. His fear did not originate from concerns for himself. It was Lily and Charlie he worried about. The fact the tough older guy wasn't at the house was troublesome, too, as was the quick way Block had bought and enhanced Chance's original scheme, almost as though he'd read the script beforehand.

Was it possible he knew who Chance really was? Could this be a trap? Was he being played by the guy he was playing?

And where was McCord?

Block opened the front door. At the last second, he caught Chance's arm and Chance turned. "Don't forget this," he said, pressing a prescription bottle into Chance's hand. "And be sure to give Lily my best."

Chance took the crystal shot glass out of his pocket where he'd wiped it clean on a bandana. "Thanks for the drinks," he said and walked away.

THE DRIVE WAS long and lonely and it was dark by the time Chance finally found the misspelled sign along with an arrow pointing down a dark tunnel of unpaved road and huge trees. After a mile or two, he came across a small community of very old houses where only a few looked inhabited. The rest were falling apart with sunken porch roofs and moss-covered fences. There was a small store on the other side of the road that looked downright festive in comparison, seeing as it had a neon soda sign in the window and a big old ice machine out front. It appeared to still be open.

Chance itched to stop there, for perhaps that was Maria Eastern's store. But first he wanted a glimpse of White Cliff. All the internet had had to offer were artists' drawings of walls and buildings. He had no idea how much if anything actually existed. If it was in the same state of disrepair as this little settlement, then everyone was barking up the wrong tree.

A half mile farther along the road, he came upon a wide spot backed by a nine-foot-high rock wall. He got out of the truck but left the headlights burning. That old moon he was so fond of shone enough that he could tell a huge area of land had been cleared beyond the wall. Other than that, all he could see was fence. There was no sign announcing that this was White Cliff but what else could it be? Well, the gate in the wall was firmly closed so there was no use standing there staring at it. Tomorrow he'd have to find a way inside.

Back in the truck, he retraced his route to the store, this time noticing another sign pointing out a place called Freedom Lake. The road was an offshoot of the one he was on, consisting of heavily rutted dirt and ghostly looking trees.

The parking lot at the store was empty but an open sign hung in the door so he went inside. A gangly young man with dark hair cut very short stood behind the counter, flipping through the pages of a catalog. He wore a camouflage long-sleeved shirt.

"Howdy," Chance said.

The kid nodded once and went back to his catalog. Chance grabbed a can of juice from the refrigerator section and a package of chips off a rack. When he got to the counter, the kid registered his purchases with a disinterested flicker of his eyes, punched in some numbers and gave Chance a total.

"It's pretty country up here," Chance said as he counted out the money. "Real peaceful." He glanced at the catalog, which was open to a page dedicated to shotguns. "I bet you do a lot of hunting up this way."

"Yeah," the kid said. He didn't look much over seventeen, maybe not even that old.

Chance gestured at the catalog. "When I was about your age, my dad got me a BB gun."

"That's for little kids," the boy scoffed.

"I guess. I had fun with it though. Until I killed my first songbird. Didn't feel too macho over that."

"Killing animals for sport is wrong," the boy said. He picked up the catalog and turned to an earmarked page. "This is my next gun. I've almost saved enough to buy it." The item he pointed to was an assault rifle.

"That's not really a hunting gun," Chance murmured.

"No siree, but if you have trouble with people, this is the weapon you want."

"And your parents will let you buy it?"

"It's just Mom, my brother and me. And sure, she doesn't care. I've been proficient with automatic rifles since I was twelve. In fact, I can shoot a human-size target nine out of ten shots."

"I'm impressed," Chance said.

The kid smiled. "It's no big deal. Everyone in White Cliff over the age of thirteen has to be able to do that. And you have to qualify with a handgun, too. You know, in case."

Chance opened the bag of chips and offered them to the boy who took a couple with a shy grin and a hasty thanks. "Mom won't let me eat the junk food we sell in here. If we can't kill it ourselves or grow it, we barter for it."

"Sometimes there's nothing like a bag of salty goodness," Chance said.

"Yeah. My favorite are pretzels. My aunt bakes them herself, but they're not the same. My cousin used to have a thing for sunflower seeds. His mom planted whole rows of plants in the garden, but sometimes, I'd smuggle him a bag or two from the store."

Chance laughed and offered more chips. "Do you have a large family?"

"Not that big. Now it's just my mom and brother and a bunch of step-cousins and an aunt and a uncle, you know."

"Sure. You said you needed to be proficient with a weapon just in case. In case of what?"

The boy swallowed his chips and took a few more. "Well, let's say terrorists knock out our country's power grid," he said. "Everything crashes. Everything. Your money in the bank is gone in the blink of an eye. Pretty soon you run out of food and gasoline and everything else. You got no electricity to keep your freezer running. You can't trust your city's water. But us here at White Cliff won't be affected because we're preppers."

"Preppers?" Chance said.

"Yeah. That's just a name for people who prepare for the inevitable trouble ahead. You know, we stockpile food and ammo. We take care of ourselves. Anyway, so all those panicked people start trying to take what we have and they're so scared, they're dangerous. We need to be able to protect ourselves."

"That sounds reasonable," Chance said but he had to suppress a shiver. The thought of children shooting other children to protect their food was nauseating.

"Or say the government decides to impose undemocratic laws and come after us for no reason? I mean, it could happen. Heck, we just got a new teacher at the school whose uncle was gunned down in Texas a few years back by a government agency."

"How many people live up there?

"A couple hundred. Maybe more like three now but someday it will have thousands. We have our own stores and schools and just about everything a person needs."

"Do you know a family by the name of Fallon?"

The boy ate the last chip and brushed the salt off his hands. Chance offered him the unopened juice and he took it with a nod of appreciation. "You're talking about that guy who murdered a Greenville man down in Boise."

"You know about that?"

"Sure. Police came and asked questions. Everyone knows about him up here but nobody had ever seen him and there's no trace of him having a family here or in Greenville, either." He opened the juice and took a long swallow.

A noise at the door made the kid look up and Chance turn round. A woman wearing a long black coat entered. The boy slammed the can down on the counter and whipped the empty bag off to the side. The woman watched him do both, a suspicious frown twisting her lips for a second. "Dennis? What are you doing?"

"Nothing, Mom," he said.

The woman was tall and stern-looking with very straight graying black hair that fell almost to her waist, dark eyes and an old scar on her forehead.

"Best you go on home now, I'll close up the store," she said, sparing Chance a lingering perusal as she strode around the counter. The kid grabbed his jacket from the back of a chair, stuffed the rolled-up catalog into a pocket and hurried out of the store without looking at Chance again.

Chance offered the woman his hand. "Pete Reed," he said. "You have a nice boy."

"Maria Eastern," she replied. "I know he's nice. Too nice, sometimes. He needs to know when to keep his mouth closed. People take advantage of innocence." She took off her coat and hung it on a hook. She was almost as tall as his six feet one inch. "What are you, one of those reporters come sniffing around for a story?"

"No," Chance said. "Do you get a lot of reporters up here?"

"Some. Mostly they treat White Cliff as a novelty."

"I did drive up to the end of the road when I first got here," he said. "I wanted to look around but the gate appeared to be locked."

"It's late," she said. "We tend to rise and set with the sun in these parts and we don't like strangers driving by our homes after dark."

Or any other time, he bargained. "I used to know some people who moved up this way. Their last name is Fallon. Do you know them?"

"Are you sure you're not a reporter?" she asked, her hooded eyes veiled.

"I'm sure."

"There is no one named Fallon here and never has been."

He needed to up the ante and give himself a reason to hang around. "It was just a thought. Listen, ma'am, I'm sure you don't want to hear my story, but I was living on land my grandfather homesteaded and when my daddy died the government took so many taxes we had to sell off half the land just to stay out of the slammer. I told them those were the last taxes they were taking from me and now they've taken everything except the cash in the ground. My woman used to talk about relocating to

White Cliff, but I always had my family's land to consider. Now that's gone and so is she. I've got nothing."

"And what do you want from us?"

"A fresh start. I just want to look around. I dug up the last of the money Grandpa buried under a rock and it's just enough to buy a place up here. Maybe if Dorrie hears I've turned myself around she'll come back to me."

Maria stared hard at him with those dark, dark eyes. Her vision seemed to snake through his skin, along his arteries, straight to his lying heart. "I'll think about what you've said," she finally muttered. "We take turns at White Cliff dealing with interested parties who show up on our doorstep. This week it's my turn. Come back here about one o'clock tomorrow. But I should tell you that I can often see through lies and self-delusion. I've had a lot of practice. So, I suggest you spend your night being honest with yourself and tomorrow being honest with me."

Her comment surprised him. "I'll do that," he said. What would happen if he was honest with her right now? If he asked if Lily had shown up, if he asked about Charlie being here, if he admitted he was scamming Jeremy Block?

And risk a bullet to the brain?

He needed to think about this. He left the store without saying another word and drove slowly back to the last town he'd driven through to find a motel.

Something told him he was in for another sleepless night.

Chapter Six

Okay, she'd done it. She'd found White Cliff, she'd come up with a convincing story to elicit enough sympathy to buy her a few days' hospitality and even managed to ingratiate herself into the community by volunteering to take over a fifth-grade class for an ailing teacher. All this in a little over thirty hours. Not bad.

She looked around the small room of ten-year-olds. One student stood in front of her desk reading aloud from a history book. This particular volume had been published sixty years earlier and there was the taint of revisionist history in the curriculum, but the kids sat calmly at their desks and appeared to listen.

A beautiful new school was under construction next door and the sound of hammers and saws made their way through the windows. Most importantly, Lily had learned that a kindergarten class was held in the adjacent building. Her plan was to dash down there and check it out as soon as her class went to what the school called recess but which she'd learned consisted of laps around the track.

She had one goal: find Charlie. If he was here, it figured he'd be in that kindergarten class, sitting right out in the wide-open. She was hoping the fortress nature of this place might breed complacency. When you are surrounded by like-minded people who all know and support you, to say nothing of two walls between you and the rest of the world, it might be easy to assume you were safe.

She could see why someone would exact revenge against Jeremy—boy, could she. She could even see why they might go so far as to kidnap his son if they felt he'd "kidnapped" theirs by facilitating his death. What fueled the anxiety eating at her gut was that revenge would go too far and Charlie would become part of some insane sacrifice.

Her subtle attempt to find out if someone had recently "acquired" a five-year-old boy had been thoroughly ignored. She was afraid to mention Darke Fallon or Wallace Connor, afraid to push too hard. It was all so frustrating. She had to struggle every minute not to begin pounding on doors or give in to the longing to call the FBI and beg them to find her son.

What would Chance do? For a second she remembered him as she'd last seen him, asleep and peaceful. In another life, if they'd met first, maybe they could have found a way to build a future. Even if she'd managed to leave Jeremy in such a way that he hadn't decided killing her was preferable to divorcing her, she might still have found Chance and then she and Charlie could live with him and play with him and work with him…and love him.

She finally realized the whole classroom had fallen silent, including the child who had apparently finished reading. With horror, she felt a tear sting the gash on her cheek as it rolled down her face.

"Sorry about that, kids," she said. "I was thinking about our country's…great history. I guess I got emotional. Emma, you read the chapter very well. It's almost time to go run around the field a couple of times. Be back in twenty minutes."

The kids got up eagerly and filed out of the classroom. Lily made herself sit there for a moment in case one of them came back for something, and then she got to her feet and walked briskly down the hall toward the door. She crossed a small courtyard and opened another door directly into the kindergarten room. Her hope she could spy on the class without being seen evaporated as more than a dozen kids and two adults turned to face her.

Her gaze swept the children as her heart almost beat out of her chest. Several were blond—none were Charlie.

"May we help you?" one of the women asked. Lily had been told all the teachers were parents who took turns teaching the kids who attended this organized school but many parents chose to homeschool their kids themselves in their own homes. She told herself that Charlie might be with such a family; his not being here didn't absolutely mean he wasn't at White Cliff.

"Sorry to barge in," she said. "I'm new and I was just looking around. I thought this doorway led to the restrooms."

The other woman spoke up. "They're in the main building."

"Thanks," Lily called and left the classroom. She returned to her own class to finish the teaching day but she did so with a heavy heart. Where was Charlie and what did she do now?

MARIA TOLD CHANCE she'd decided to give him a personal tour and he could leave his truck parked outside the wall. He wasn't flattered by her attention—he figured it had more to do with keeping an eye on him than because she liked his company. She drove him around the perimeter first and he was duly impressed by the organization set out in front of him.

As she drove, she delivered a well-rehearsed spiel about the community being the vision of a solitary man. Since his death, his son, Robert Brighton, had assumed leadership. Chance saw signs of building going on everywhere.

Eventually, they ended up walking onto a broad expanse of grass, pausing by a large central water fountain. "Where's the gunfire coming from?" Chance asked as the sound of bullets flying competed with the splattering of water.

"There's a target range to the east of us," Maria said. "When the clouds are low like they are today, the noise seems louder than usual, but you get used to it. It's the sound of freedom, after all."

"That's a good way to put it," he said. He gestured at a series of grassy mounds and then a row of what appeared to be bunkers against a hill, five of them in all. "What's all of that?"

"The mounds are a memorial for fallen patriots. The bunkers are used for storage now. Food, ammo, weapons, water, things like that. Originally they were intended as living quarters for new settlers. It was a time of high tension with Russia and they were intended to substitute as bomb shelters should the need arise. The big white house across the way there belongs to Richard Brighton. He lives with my sister and their—his—kids. My boys and I live in an extension near the back. It's a beautiful place." She checked her watch and added, "We better keep moving. My boys are out of school by now." As she led the way back to her car, she posed a question.

"What are your plans? Are you thinking of starting a small a business, for example? We could use a good mechanic."

"Not me," Chance said with a laugh. "I'm not the business type."

"Okay, well, then, for example, would you prefer a quiet neighborhood filled with children or a bigger parcel of land on which to raise crops or animals?"

"Children," he said quickly, determined to walk through any door she opened no matter how hard he had to squeeze through.

"Do you have any?" she asked.

"Not yet, but a man can dream. All I need to do is find my Dorrie."

"Then I'll drive you through one of the neighborhoods first."

"How many are there in all?"

"Three. They're all very pleasant."

It crossed his mind that he should ask a financial question or two. "How does the money part work?"

She smiled. "That's a discussion to be had with Mr. Brighton. Perhaps we can arrange a meeting for tomorrow.

"Mind if I ask why your store is outside the walls?"

"Not at all. It's a temporary location while I construct a new store one street over. See, my sister moved here years ago when she met and got involved with Robert Brighton. I used to visit her. I liked how uncomplicated things seemed. When my husband died a few years ago, I was left with two boys to raise. I thought what better place to do it than White Cliff." She drove under a small arch and added, "This is the first neighborhood."

The houses all looked relatively modest to Chance

while the land around them was utilized to the last degree. Dried cornstalks and pumpkins were about all that were left of the seasonal harvest, though some trees still held scattered apples and pears. Cords of firewood had been stacked against most of the fences. There were several windmills in evidence, used no doubt for power, and almost everyone had solar panels on their rooftops and propane tanks in their yards.

Several adults working outdoors and kids playing on the street added a comfortable ambience to the environment, but Chance's heart almost stopped beating when he spied a small blond boy sitting on a curb by himself. A second glance revealed it wasn't Charlie. He'd only just begun to recover from that disappointment when he glanced up to see a woman walking on the sidewalk in front of them. By the way she moved her head, it was obvious she was searching for someone or something.

"Stop!" Chance yelled and Maria instinctively applied the brakes. "It's a miracle," he said as he opened the door and ran after the woman. He hadn't seen her face but that shapeless gray sweater and the way she moved made it clear to him that he'd found Lily. His pounding footsteps must have alarmed her because when she turned, her eyes were huge.

"Chance! What are you doing—"

She didn't get a chance to finish because Chance grabbed her around the waist and hoisted her off the ground. He twirled her around, put her back down and bent his head to kiss her. It had been intended as a show of his enthusiasm to assure Maria he was an up-and-up guy, but the instant his lips touched Lily's, all bets were off. All the anxiety, anger, worry and pure raw emotion he'd been trying to tame for days raged inside his body as he claimed her.

She resisted for a half a heartbeat and then surrendered. She hadn't kissed him like this since the night out by the river. All the stories he'd told himself that one woman's kiss was much like another shot up in flames as he lost himself in the soft, moist oasis of her mouth. He blocked out everything but the sensation of having her to himself for what couldn't have been more than a couple of seconds but seemed to last forever.

But just as before, she broke the connection abruptly, breathlessly, though this time she didn't run away. Instead she looked up at him and slowly raised her hand to gently touch his cheek with her cold fingers. He felt the unexpected tender caress shoot through his body. "What are you doing here?" she whispered.

"What do you think I'm doing here?" He wrapped his hand around hers, trying to warm her. He finally remembered Maria and looked up as she pulled her car forward.

"Quick," he added. "There's not much time. You're my wife, my name is Pete Reed and you're Dorrie."

Maria exited her car and approached with a stately walk and a disapproving glance at Chance. "Lily, you know this man?"

"Yes," she said. "Pete is my husband."

"Lily? Is that what you're calling yourself?" Chance asked, staring into Lily's eyes, one of them still black and blue. He could almost see the imprint of Block's knuckles. "That was your mother's name," he added.

Lily touched Maria's arm. "I kind of thought Pete might show up. It's fine that he's here."

"You said *your husband* hit you," Maria said, her gaze

searching Lily's battered face before glancing again at Chance. "I don't like to pry, but she was in bad shape when she got here and we offered a temporary sanctuary."

"Now wait a second," he said, putting up his hands and backing away a step. "Dorrie knows I never hit her."

Lily smiled at him and then looked at Maria. "He didn't hit me," she mumbled.

"But you said your husband—"

"I said it wrong. What I meant was that after I left Pete, I went to my ex-husband's house to ask for money. He did this to me, not Pete."

Maria didn't look convinced. She'd been haughty the night before, friendly that day and now she looked suspicious. "Is there actually a warrant out for your arrest?"

"Yes. I didn't lie about that or Uncle Hank, either. I'm not ashamed of those things. May Pete stay in the apartment with me?"

"If that's your choice." Maria seemed to think for a second before speaking again. "The teacher you're subbing for needs help until the end of the week. That's three days. When she's ready to return, it would be best if you and Pete leave. If you've decided our community and way of life appeals to you, then submit an application. Mr. Brighton will review it and respond within ninety days. That's how it's done." She turned to Chance and added, "You can bring your truck inside the wall. Do you two want a ride back to Lily's, I mean Dorrie's apartment?"

"No, we'll walk," Lily said.

"Thanks for everything, Maria," Chance added.

"I better get back to work," was all she said.

They watched her drive away. A few children had gathered round them and Lily made it clear there could be no frank discussions in front of them. "Let's walk to the gate and get your truck," she said.

So holding hands like a reunited couple might, they walked the mile back to the gate so Chance could get his things out of the truck. Eventually, the kids petered out and they were alone. "Finally, we can talk," Lily said.

He put his arm around her shoulder to make sure they were close enough to speak in whispers as there were other people coming and going, most on foot as they were. "What were you doing walking around that neighborhood?" he asked. "And what did Maria mean when she said the teacher you're subbing for? And who's Uncle Hank?"

"I was searching the neighborhood for Charlie. As far as the teaching thing goes, I lucked into that. My class is full of ten-year-olds, but I managed to sneak down to the kindergarten room this morning. Charlie wasn't there. I don't even know if he's here."

"He's here," Chance said.

She turned her head and looked up at him. "He is? How do you know that for sure?"

"Because your husband sent me to get him back."

Her expression turned horrified. "You went to see Jeremy?"

"Yeah. Not right away. I had to get over being mad at you first."

She bit her lip. It was on the tip of his tongue to chastise her, but he held off.

"Jeremy actually said Charlie was here?"

"He seemed pretty damn sure. He told me Maria Eastern would know but warned me not to ask her outright."

"Maria? Well, she does seem enmeshed in things."

"She said today that she's here in White Cliff because her sister has a relationship with Robert Brighton."

"Really? What have you learned about Charlie from her?"

"Nothing. I wanted to ask her outright. I figured when she found out I wasn't working for Block she'd be open, but I didn't know what you had set up so I decided to wait to talk to you first."

"Maybe we should just go talk to her."

"I don't know," he said. "If she's responsible for taking Charlie then she's involved in kidnapping. If she knows who did take him, then she's an accessory after the fact. Either one of those charges are very serious. It seems unlikely she'd be chatty about it if she knows you're Charlie's mother and might bring charges."

"You know what's been bothering me? How did they even know Charlie was at Jeremy's house? He and I had been gone almost nine months."

"Maybe there's a neighbor someone paid off to report when and if Charlie returned."

"Or maybe Jeremy set this whole thing up to get rid of me forever," she said.

He squeezed her shoulder. "Okay, you'd better tell me what you told the people here so we don't trip each other up."

"I remembered a friend of my father's from a long time ago. He joined a cult down in Texas. There were rumors children were being abused. When the cult refused to submit to a government investigation and took up arms, there was a big invasion of sorts. My dad's friend was shot along with two kids and a policeman. In the way that can happen with these things, Dad's friend became a sort of legend. When I got here, I told them Hank Miller was my uncle. It was obvious his name was familiar to them. I said my husband had beat me up and I'd been on the run for a while. I asked for help."

Two men walking toward them scanned them uneasily. One was carrying an AK-47 slung over his back. Lily and Chance both smiled. They got zero response from the men who passed them by without saying a word. Chance hugged Lily closer to be able to whisper to her. "That must be why Block warned that police involvement with Charlie's kidnappers could be dangerous. He's afraid if law enforcement shows up, these people might defend their home turf and create a situation like the one down in Texas."

"But law enforcement showed up after Wallace Connor's death and asked about Fallon. Nothing terrible happened."

"They asked about someone who apparently doesn't exist. Coming to look for a kidnapped child is a whole different ball game."

"The key to this has to be Maria," Lily said. "We have to find out more about her. But who do we ask? I haven't spoken to a single person here but Maria, a couple of the teachers and a few kids. Everyone else just looks at me funny."

"Well, if we can't ask anyone in White Cliff, we'll have to ask elsewhere."

LILY SLID INTO the old red truck. She'd never seen it before, but having spent six months serving as a cook and housekeeper for the Hastings men, she knew there were barns and sheds aplenty with years of accumulated equipment tucked away here and there and everywhere. She doubted they even knew exactly how much stuff they had.

Instead of starting the truck, Chance sat with both hands on the steering wheel and stared through the windshield as if he was in a daze. She loved his strong profile and admired it for a bit, remembering the kiss of a few minutes before with a rush of pleasure. She could only imagine what it would be like to sleep with him, to have all his heat and power focused on her to the exclusion of anyone else. It was a very provocative concept.

He turned to face her and for a moment she wondered if her thoughts had somehow entered his consciousness.

"What are you thinking?" Lily asked.

"Neither Maria or her son, Dennis, knew anyone named Darke Fallon. They've all heard of him because the police came calling after the Connor shooting. Have you met Maria's other son?"

"No. I haven't even met Dennis. But Maria said her sons were less than a year apart in age."

"What I'm thinking is this. We've been concentrating on Fallon because he killed himself under your husband's watch, so to say. But the guy Fallon killed in that motel, he must have been someone's kid, too. If I'm remembering correctly, he was in his early twenties. I also remember he lived in Greenville and left a couple of family members behind. Greenville is roundabout six miles from here. I stayed there last night."

Lily had already started a search on her cell phone. "No one named Wallace Connor is listed but there is an O. Connor and there's also a place called Connor's Greenville Bakery, both in Greenville."

He glanced at his watch. "What time do they close the gate here?"

"Nine o'clock," Lily responded. "Are you suggesting we drive to Greenville?"

"Sure. We have plenty of time and we need to rule the Connor family out when it comes to taking Charlie."

"I know…but—"

"But what?"

She shook her head. "It feels wrong to leave here and drive into Greenville on a wild-goose chase. Charlie has to be behind one of these closed doors…"

"There are dozens and dozens of closed doors in White Cliff, Lily. Very few of them will actually open up to let you in."

"But there are more neighborhoods to search. I've only walked through two of them."

"Listen to yourself. You're looking for Charlie out in the open while all the houses sit up away from the road. He could be behind any one of the hundreds of windows and how would you know? This isn't the regular world where you can pretend to go door to door with a survey and look for him. These people are wary of strangers—"

"You think I don't know all of this?" she interrupted, her voice rising.

He took a deep breath. "Okay, I'll come with you and look through the other neighborhoods. There will still be time to hit Greenville when we finish with—"

"No, Chance, no. Two unknown adults walking side by side are intimidating to people. Remember the looks those men gave us? A lone woman just kind of disappears."

"Then I'll wait—"

"No, that's okay."

"But we should stay together."

She curled her fingernails against her palms. "This is the very reason I came alone," she said.

"Why?"

"I knew you'd try to micromanage me."

He took a deep breath before speaking carefully and she could hear the effort he put into holding his temper. "You're right. Charlie is your son and you didn't ask for me to come find you, in fact you went out of your way to make sure I didn't. But I'm here now, and I think we should take advantage of that. Since we can't walk the neighborhoods together, let's split up and cover twice the ground."

"I guess so," she said, getting out of the truck. "The next neighborhood isn't far, I'll walk." She shut the door louder than she had to.

She heard him start the engine as she walked stiffly toward the gate and then she stopped and turned. He hadn't moved the truck an inch. A debate raged inside her head. Some of what he said made sense. Instinct and love weren't always enough. Giving in to fear wasn't going to help. And what else had Jeremy told Chance that he hadn't yet shared that might help her figure this out?

She walked back to the truck, opened the passenger door and got inside. "I've decided we should drive into town," she said.

He didn't utter a word, just backed up the truck and headed out on the gravel road. Lily closed her eyes for a moment. Days of worry were taking their toll. She finally took a deep breath. "Chance? Are we going to talk?"

"About what?" he shot back as they finally hit pavement and turned toward Greenville. He didn't even glance at her as he asked.

"Listen, I'm sorry I seem ungrateful that you've come to help."

He spared her a quick glance. "I'm not here to undermine you, Lily. I'm only here because two heads are better than one. Charlie needs as many people on his side as he can get. And I knew that if I wasn't here helping I'd never know how this ended."

"What do you mean? I would have called you when this it's resolved."

"Really? Because with your track record, I was pretty sure I'd never hear from you again."

"My track record?"

"You're a quitter, Lily. You run away when things get scary."

She opened her mouth to refute his comment, but he interrupted her.

"You ran when I kissed you that first time. You ran when Jodie Brown came to the ranch. You ran when you decided I would be too much trouble to bring with you to White Cliff. And you want to run now."

"I didn't ask you to follow me here," she said.

"No, you didn't. You seldom ask anyone for much of anything. Is there a person in this world you trust?"

"Your father," she responded immediately.

"And yet even with him you didn't come clean and admit how serious your problems were with your husband. It's like you're afraid to give up any control at all."

She turned her head and stared out the passenger window. He thought he knew all about her! He thought he had her figured out. Couldn't he see it had taken her six years of a bloody, soul-draining marriage to finally grasp the raw edges of self-destiny? And now she was supposed to share it, to give it away?

"Maybe I do run when I feel threatened, but don't you think you do the same thing?" she said.

He looked perplexed. "What do you mean?"

"You're almost thirty-five years old. You've never had

a serious relationship. As soon as a woman starts to feel the slightest bit comfortable, poof, you're gone."

"That's not true," he said, but the shifting in his eyes revealed he wasn't so sure about it.

"Maybe we're more alike than you want to admit," she said.

He stared at her for a long moment before speaking again. "I never thought of myself as a quitter," he said. Was that pain in his eyes? Was it possible he'd actually considered what she said? He took a deep breath and added, "I guess when it comes to you I should have minded my own business right from the start. I don't know why I keep bugging you. But now it's about more than you and me, it's about Charlie. I like that kid. I want him to be safe, with you. Don't ask me to turn away from doing anything I can to make that happen." He cast her another wary glance. "Truce?"

"Truce."

Chapter Seven

"The bakery is straight down Main Street, left on Franklin," Lily said. She put the phone in her purse and added, "The residence is two blocks over on Lincoln."

"Let's start with the business," Chance said.

The bakery was in the middle of a block that looked as though nearby strip malls had exacted their toll on commerce. Parallel parking existed on either side of the two-way street that had been planted with numerous sugar maples. Their colorful leaves seemed to wage war against the increasingly gray skies, though defeat was inevitable.

There was a chill to the air that promised winter was soon to become a force to be reckoned with, and Chance saw Lily pull her sweater closer around her body and shiver.

The bakery itself was awash with pink. Pink walls, pink counter, pink trim. Most likely, he thought, the glass-fronted display cases would be filled with a decent variety of goodies in the morning. But this late in the afternoon, there were only a few loaves of bread and some tired-looking pastries to be had.

A girl who didn't look a day over sixteen stood behind the counter. Unsurprisingly, she wore a pink apron over her T-shirt and jeans. "Betsy" was embroidered in white over the pocket. Her face was round and lightly freckled, her eyes a pale blue. "Can I help you?" she asked, pausing in her chore of wiping fingerprints off a case door. There was a guarded look in her eyes.

"How about a loaf of bread?" Chance said.

"Wheat or whole grain. That's all we have left."

Chance looked at Lily who supplied the answer. "Whole grain. Boy, those pastries look good."

"They are," the girl said.

"Let's get the last three," Chance said. "Did you bake them?"

The girl shook her head causing the straight reddish-blond locks to slide across her shoulders. "No way. My dad gets up at three every morning and does the baking. He was depending on my brother to take over, but, well, anyway, Mom works here most of the day and then I come after school on Monday, Wednesday and Friday when I don't have band practice. Do you want the bread sliced?"

"That's okay, we'll do it ourselves," Lily said. "Is your dad or mom here now?"

"No. I'm closing the store today. You should try again tomorrow."

"We will," Chance said and then as though an afterthought had occurred, added, "Forgive me if this is a difficult question, but are you related to the man who was so senselessly killed last year down in Boise?"

Her eyes immediately filled with tears. "How did you know about Wallace?"

"I read about it in the paper. Are you his sister?"

"Yes," she said and flicked away a tear with shaky fingers.

"I'm sorry I brought it up," Chance said. "It must be terrible for you."

"That's an understatement," she said. "It just about destroyed my whole family."

"I know he had a girlfriend—" Lily began, but Betsy cut her off.

"Don't call her that! Tabitha Stevens is awful. Wallace was five years older than her and way out of her league but when Tabitha wants something, she's relentless and Wallace was as stupid as the next guy when it came to girls like her."

She took a deep breath as though winded and shook her head. Her face had turned red and blotchy. "She killed him, not that hitchhiker. Oh, I mean that Fallon guy obviously turned Wallace's knife on him and stabbed him, I mean, he confessed and everything, but I just know Tabitha pushed Wallace into taking that stupid trip. And then she walked around town boohooing like she's Juliet and she's lost her Romeo. It made me sick."

"What did the police—"

"The police? Don't make me laugh. That girl can cry like a banshee. They all fell for her lies. Everyone in this town thinks she's a poor little thing because her boyfriend got killed. Wallace was my brother. My family is the one who lost someone they loved, not Tabitha."

Chance glanced down at Lily who was staring in wide-eyed wonder at Betsy. "I'm really sorry we brought it up," Lily said to the girl. "You're obviously still in a lot of pain. But it will get better. I know people always say that but it's because it's true."

"I don't want it to get better," she said. "I want to hate Tabitha forever. If I can ever prove to the town what she really is, that'll be the day I'll finally feel better."

"What do you mean what she really is?" Lily asked.

"She was running around on Wallace."

"With who?"

"I don't know who. I heard rumors. I still hear rumors. And about two weeks ago I was coming home from a band concert and I saw Tabitha sneaking around over by the east side of town. It's dark and dangerous over there and she was alone and it was late. I tell you, she's rotten to the bone." She stopped speaking and took a deep breath as though to center herself. "I know I sound terrible," she added.

"You just sound angry," Lily said gently. "It's how you feel."

"Yeah," she said, slipping the pastries into the bag with the bread. "You owe me eight dollars and fifty-five cents."

"Something else," Lily said as Chance paid for the goods. "Do you have much to do with the people up at White Cliff?"

"Not too much," Betsy said. "They come into town now and again but they make people nervous and don't ever say too much unless you get them started and then they go on and on about politics."

"Do you know any of them, I mean personally?"

"Not really. There was one lady a year or two ago who was nice. I guess she runs a store up there. She and her sons used to come to town now and again and she was kind of friendly. Her oldest boy is cute."

"You're talking about Maria," Lily said.

"Yeah, do you know her?"

"We're staying up that way for a couple of days and she's been like the White Cliff ambassador of sorts."

"Yeah. Well, some of those people have been up there for years and they've gotten kind of standoffish. Maria was different."

"Was?"

Betsy shrugged. "I haven't seen her in a long time but the last time she came in here to buy bread, she was different. Kind of quiet and preoccupied, I guess. She didn't smile and she always used to smile."

"When did she change?"

Betsy narrowed her eyes in concentration. "A while ago. After Christmas sometime." She handed them the bag. Lily reached for it right as the bell on the door announced another customer. A boy about Betsy's age seemed surprised she wasn't alone.

"Hey, Todd," Betsy said.

"Hey," he responded. He ran a finger along the glass case. He reminded Chance of himself about that age, still growing into the man he'd become with time. His shoulders and buzz-cut hair glistened with water. Chance glanced through the window to see the clouds had finally broken.

"Do you want something?" Betsy asked. Her voice had undergone a distinct change from impatient to silky.

"No, just hanging out," he said and flashed her a smile. His voice cracked as he added, "I thought you'd be alone."

Betsy cast Lily and Chance a pleading look.

"We're just leaving," Lily said, and they beat a hasty retreat.

"Whew," Lily said as they stood on the sidewalk under the awning. "That poor girl is a walking, breathing emotional roller coaster."

"She hates Tabitha and apparently has a thing for Todd," Chance agreed. "I can't see how either of those concern us, but the news about Maria changing is interesting."

"It's gotten cold," Lily said, stretching the poor sweater even tighter around her body.

Chance looked at the stores lining the other side of the

street and added, "Follow me," grabbed her hand and led her across two lanes of sparse traffic.

The store they entered wasn't the kind Chance was used to navigating. Mannequins on one wall modeled what he guessed was the latest in fashion while circular racks held dozens of slacks, dresses and sweaters. The saleswoman hastened their way and asked how she could help them. "This lady needs a warm coat and a sweater and whatever else she wants," he said.

"Come this way," the saleswoman coaxed Lily as she moved toward the back of the store.

"We don't have time for this," Lily protested.

"Then don't waste what time we do have arguing," he said.

"I don't want you buying me clothes," she added stubbornly.

"I'm not. I'm using your husband's money. Technically, I guess it's more your money than mine as I lied to get it."

"Money he gave you to find Charlie?"

"More or less."

The furrowing of her brow suggested she would ask him more about this later. "Okay, I'll get a coat, but don't keep calling that man my husband."

He shrugged.

Fifteen hurried minutes later, they left the store four hundred dollars poorer but at least Lily looked warm in her new faux fur lined raincoat. She carried three shopping bags as well, full of everything from warm pajamas to jeans and walking shoes. She hadn't tried on a single garment, just bought them off the rack, so distracted by the clock that Chance wasn't sure she even knew what she'd chosen.

"I asked the saleswoman about Maria and White Cliff," she said as they got back in the truck. "She had no idea who I was talking about. I gather this is her first winter this far north and the rain is already getting to her."

The Connor house was a modest one-story affair built of brick. Nobody's yard looked great this time of year and theirs was no exception. The rain was quickly turning the sparse grass brown with mud, the cracked cement walkway was slippery with moss as though the front entry was seldom used. They made their way carefully to the front door and knocked.

It took a few minutes, but eventually the door opened and a faded-looking woman of about forty faced them. "May I help you?"

"We wondered if we could talk to you and your husband for a few minutes," Chance asked politely.

"What about?" she asked.

"Your son, Wallace."

"What about my son?" she said, her voice shaking now. "He's dead and gone, murdered for a measly two hundred dollars and a ring. They didn't even take his credit cards. What can you possibly want to talk to us about?"

"Darke Fallon."

A man showed up behind the woman. He appeared to be ten or so years older than her, a smallish guy with a lightly freckled round face and graying hair. Light blue eyes peered from behind wire-framed glasses. "Let them in, Carolyn," he said.

The woman opened the door wider and Chance followed Lily over the threshold. The room they entered was sparsely furnished but fastidiously clean. The woman motioned at the sofa and asked if they'd like anything hot to drink. They declined. The house smelled great to Chance, like roast beef, like home. The table in the corner had been set for dinner.

"My name is Otto," he said, "and this is my wife, Carolyn. Now what's this about our Wallace?"

Chance introduced himself and Lily who immediately asked if she could use their restroom. Carolyn pointed out the way and Lily left the room.

"First of all, I should mention that we stopped at your bakery and talked to Betsy," Chance said.

"About Wallace?" Otto said with a quick glance at his wife.

"Yes."

"Did she cry much?" Otto asked.

"A little. She also talked about Wallace's girlfriend, Tabitha."

"Uh-oh," Carolyn said. She'd perched on the edge of a chair and now folded her hands together between her knees. "Betsy gets kind of wound up when it comes to Tabitha."

"There's no love lost between them," Otto agreed.

"What do you think of Tabitha?"

"She's just a kid," Otto said. "Works a shift at the Burger Barn south of town, seems popular. Comes from a dysfunctional family but just about everyone seems to these days. We didn't see too much of her. Wallace lived with a friend across town and seldom brought Tabitha to our house. I think he was kind of embarrassed because she was his little sister's age."

"And the girls didn't like each other," Carolyn added. "But Betsy shouldn't be bad-mouthing her to strangers. By all accounts, Tabitha was in terrible shape after Wallace's funeral. My heart went out to the girl."

Otto cleared his throat. "You said you wanted to talk about the man who killed Wallace. You do realize no one knows much about him?"

"No one knows anything about him," Carolyn said.

"I read a sketchy article about the murder," Chance explained. "I can hardly believe the police couldn't identify Fallon."

"I know," Otto said. "Neither could we. He said he was hitchhiking from Bend, Oregon, where he lived, but there was no evidence a guy by that name ever lived there. Fallon isn't an unusual last name but the Darke part is different. Anyway, when asked about his friends, the only names he gave were first names like Johnny or Dave or Nick. He said he used Wallace's hunting knife to rob him and when Wallace refused to hand over his money, he stabbed him. But the kid was not only younger than Wallace, he was about half his size. And then the police said it appeared he'd been stabbed while lying down, not standing. But then again, the boy did have Wallace's blood on him."

"How did the police explain the stabbing position discrepancy?"

"They really couldn't. One of the officers told us that Fallon must have lied about what happened. It makes more sense that Fallon came into Wallace's room after he was asleep and killed and robbed him and just didn't want to admit it. Wallace had been drinking that night. His blood alcohol numbers were high."

"He could sleep pretty soundly after a six-pack of beer," Carolyn added.

"What about the murder weapon?" Chance asked.

"Wallace's own knife. It was still in the van when they caught Fallon. He'd tried to wipe it clean, but there were traces of blood on the blade. It was a hunting knife Wallace carried with him all the time."

"He wore it where people could see it?"

"Not really, but for all we know, he'd taken it off when he drove and that's when Fallon saw it. Who knows what they talked about in that van? Wallace was a friendly guy."

"You mentioned a ring," Chance said.

"Yeah. It had a nice stone in it but it wasn't worth more than a few hundred dollars and that was because of the gold. Fallon said he lost it in a river when he stopped to wash all the blood off his clothes. He didn't know which river and he didn't get all of it."

"And he left a bloody footprint in Wallace's room," Carolyn added. "The police said he seemed a little slow-witted. He stopped talking when the questions got tricky. Didn't say a word after that first confession, apparently not even to his court-appointed attorney. And why did he drive around all that time in Wallace's truck?"

"Yeah," Otto said. "And why was Wallace down in Boise to begin with?"

"The newspaper said he was there for a job inter-view, didn't they?" Chance asked with a glance toward the hallway Lily had disappeared down several minutes ago. What was taking her so long?

"Bah," Otto said. "He worked at the bakery with me. In a few years it would have been his. They couldn't find a single employer down there who admitted setting up an interview with him. All they had to go on was his room-mate's word that that's where Wallace said he was going."

"And Tabitha called us and the roommate the next morning to ask about Wallace because he hadn't shown up for a date the night before. If he was going on a job interview, wouldn't he have told her?"

Lily appeared just then and sat down next to Chance right as Otto posed another question. "Why are you asking about Fallon? Do you think you know who he was?"

"No," Chance said. "But do you think it's possible he lived at White Cliff?"

Otto looked at Carolyn again. "I doubt it," she finally said. "The boy had no papers on him, no fingerprints matched up anywhere. Nothing. The police talked to everyone here and everyone up there and no one knew a thing about a Darke Fallon. No one from there was missing, just like no one here was unaccounted for. This Fallon must have been a drifter, maybe from another country or something. I don't know."

"Why do you care where he came from?" Otto asked. "And why are you asking so many questions about Wallace's murder?"

Lily answered this time. "I have a five-year-old boy," she said. "His name is Charlie and we have reason to suspect that the Fallon family might have taken him. We want to talk to them. I need to get my son back—"

She stopped speaking as her voice choked. Chance put his arm around her shoulders. "If you guys think of anything that might help, please let us know," he said. "We're actually staying at White Cliff in a guest apartment."

"I didn't know they let outsiders in," Otto said.

"That reminds me," Chance added. "Do you know a woman named Maria Eastern? Your daughter said she used to come into your bakery."

"Don't recognize the name," Otto said. "How about you, Carolyn?"

"No. Betsy is a lot better with names than I am, though. Is she important?"

"Who knows?" Chance said. He gave them his cell number and Lily's, too. "Please call if you think of anything."

"What about the police?" Carolyn asked. "What are they doing about this?"

"There are complicated reasons they haven't been called yet," Lily said.

"Can't say as they got very far in our case, but they tried," Otto commented.

Chance and Lily thanked them for their time. Their last glimpse of the couple was as Carolyn closed the door and switched on the porch light.

LILY SHIVERED INSIDE her new coat as they walked back to the truck.

"What took you so long in the bathroom?" Chance asked her.

"I wasn't in the bathroom, I was searching the house for some sign a small boy was being held there. That's why we went, right? To see if they might be involved in Charlie's abduction?"

"Right. But I'd bet money those people would rather cut off their arms than put another person through what they've endured."

"I get the same feeling," she said. "And besides that, I didn't find anything to suggest Charlie has ever been in that house."

He opened her door and she climbed in. The stress and disappointment of the past hour had caused a horrible headache and she closed her eyes. All she could see was Carolyn's face, the sadness and loss in her eyes.

The woman would never see her son again. Did a similar fate await Lily?

She was determined not to cry, not to make a scene, not to be weak, but her heart felt broken and she didn't know if it would ever mend. As the rain pelted the truck's windshield, she buried her face in her hands and wept.

Chance pulled the truck off to the side of the road and gathered her into his arms. She was crying so hard by then it was difficult to get a breath, impossible to talk and he held her for what seemed an hour, rocking her gently, smoothing her hair, his body big and warm and comforting. She could get used to being treated with such gentleness. She felt small and treasured in his embrace, a feeling she hadn't experienced since her mother died when she was six. Her father had climbed too deep inside a gin bottle to worry much about parenting.

The sobs abated and she took a few deep breaths. Anxious to look anywhere but in his eyes, she glanced out the window. "Where are we?" she asked as she dug a packet of tissues from her purse.

"I was going to go to a place called the Burger Barn," Chance said. "I'll go tomorrow. Right now, it's time to get you back to White Cliff."

"Are you hungry?" she asked as she blew her nose.

"Now that you mention it, yes, but that wasn't why I wanted to hit the place. Otto says that Tabitha Stevens works there. I hoped she might be pulling an evening shift."

"Why bother with her?" Lily said. "What can she possibly tell us that would help find Charlie?"

"I don't know," he said, scooting back across the bench seat to his place behind the wheel. "But she may know something about Darke Fallon or Maria Eastern that she didn't tell the police, or maybe she's since remembered something. I thought it was worth ruling her out."

"Because of what Betsy said about Tabitha having other boyfriends?"

"Partially. I guess I'm a turn-every-stone kind of guy. But I can do this on my own. It's been a tough afternoon and—"

"Let's go now," Lily said. "I want to see if this kid is the trollop Betsy made her out to be. Besides, it's dark and I can't think of anything we can do at White Cliff to get closer to finding Charlie so we might as well check out Tabitha. Do you know where this place is?"

"Not really. I was going to have you check your phone, but you looked terrible after we left the Connors'."

"I'm better now," she said, wiping away the last of the tears. "The look in Carolyn's eyes just got to me."

He smiled at her. "You know, your face is beginning to heal. You're almost pretty again."

She laughed out loud and hit his arm. "I'll look up the Burger Barn."

A few minutes later, they pulled in front of a fast food place that appeared to have been built in the fifties. They went inside and found a seat where they could see the whole restaurant.

The wait staff all wore blue jeans and red checkered shirts and all seemed to be teenagers except for one woman in her forties who had to feel like a babysitter with these kids. The place was crammed, and music blared from a Wurlitzer jukebox. After the emptiness of the town, the bustling activity in the little diner was amazing.

The older waitress brought them ice water and asked

if they wanted a menu. Chance asked what the specialty was and she looked at him like he was nuts. "Burgers."

"What's the best one?" he said.

"Folks seem to really enjoy the bacon cheese burger."

"Then that's what I'll have. Add fries and a chocolate shake. How about you, Lily?"

"The same," she said because it was easier than thinking about it.

The waitress hustled off and they took turns studying the other staff. There looked to be two beefy guys working the kitchen behind the window and four females and two males taking orders and delivering food. The girls all looked about Betsy's age. One had very long red hair she wore in a high ponytail that she whipped around like a horse's tail on a hot fly-infested afternoon. Another girl was a slender blonde who bit her fingernails when she thought no one was watching, and the last two had dark hair, one cut short, another shoulder length, both kind of nondescript. They all moved about the restaurant and back into the kitchen with quick, sure steps. The operation looked efficient, friendly and unremarkable.

Their food arrived a lot faster than Lily had thought it would. The waitress asked what else they wanted. Chance said nothing but Lily lowered her voice. "Is Tabitha Stevens working here tonight?"

"Why do you want to know? Did she sass you or something? If she did, don't tell her grandfather, okay?"

"Her grandfather?"

"Pastor Stevens. At least he used to be a preacher. Anyway, he's real strict. Tabitha is a handful but I hate to see her in trouble and it isn't because I have a kind heart, she just acts out her hostility and the customers complain and then the manager calls her grandfather and things get worse. She's been real moody lately anyway."

"Don't worry," Lily said quickly. "She didn't do anything. I just know her mother and since I was traveling through this way, thought I'd say hello to Tabitha. I heard she worked here."

"Tabitha's mother has been dead three years," the woman said. "Her grandpa raises her now."

"I know," Lily said, scrambling to think of some excuse for wording her comment in the present tense, but she shouldn't have worried. Another table demanded attention and the waitress left to comply.

"You're a lousy liar," Chance said.

"I know."

He took a bite of his hamburger and made a contented sound in his throat. Lily looked down at the food and started to push it away, but took a French fry instead. Eating hadn't exactly been a priority lately but that fry tasted like greasy ambrosia and she ate another. Then she tried the hamburger. By the time she slurped down the last of the milkshake, her headache had disappeared and she felt ready to track down her missing son. She would find Charlie tomorrow, come hell or high water. They were running out of time in White Cliff and for some reason she couldn't pin down, she wasn't anxious to meet Robert Brighton, the man behind the place.

"Nice to see you eat a meal," Chance said.

"I was hungrier than I thought."

He leaned toward her. "I've been meaning to ask you something," he said as he lowered his voice. "Have you seen any sign of McCord in White Cliff?"

"McCord? You mean that guy who works for Jeremy? No, of course not. Why would he be up here?"

He started to answer when the waitress with the red hair showed up at their table. Gone was the ponytail. Her hair now hung loose on her shoulders, completely covering one eye in an old Veronica Lake look that appeared way too sophisticated for a teen in Greenville, Idaho. She'd also undone a couple of buttons, revealing an eyeful of cleavage, and knotted her blouse above the waistband of skintight jeans. The tennis shoes all the waiters wore had been exchanged for pointy red heels and she'd applied makeup with a heavy hand. The expression in her dark-rimmed eyes was calculating, her stance challenging. "I heard you were asking about me," she said, directing her comment to Chance.

So this was Tabitha Stevens. "Yes, we were," Lily said. "Would you like to sit down for a minute?"

"I wouldn't mind," the girl said. "My shift is just about over anyway."

Before Lily could move her coat and purse to make room, the girl claimed the scant twelve inches on Chance's side of the booth. He slid along to make more room for her but she seemed to ooze along with him.

Her behavior with Chance struck Lily as surprisingly brazen. There was no doubt he'd been endowed with his share of the Hastings male charm and good looks and often affected women with a certain rakish gleam in his eye; it just seemed odd this girl would feel so comfortable with a stranger twice her age.

Tabitha tore her gaze from Chance and stared at Lily. "Why were you asking about me? How did you know my mother?"

Lily saw Chance's lips twitch, probably because he was anticipating how she would dig herself out of this hole. "I didn't know your mother," Lily said. "We just wanted to ask you a few questions."

"So, ask."

"We were hoping you could tell us something about Wallace Connor."

Tears seemed to shoot into Tabitha's eyes. "Poor Wally," she lamented. "I don't know if I can bear to talk about him. I was sick for weeks after that maniac stabbed him to death."

"It must have been horrible for you."

"How about Darke Fallon?" Chance ventured.

Tabitha groaned. "Not *him* again. I told the police I never met anyone named Darke Fallon. What kind of name is that, anyway? I'm sick of hearing about him. He murdered Wally. Let him burn in hell."

"We weren't actually planning a rescue party to the underworld," Chance commented.

Tabitha turned to look up at him, the unshed tears making her eyes look huge and innocent. She smiled and said, "That's funny."

"We'd just like to talk to the Fallon family," Lily said.

"You and everyone else. I can't help you. As far as I know, he was just one of those homeless, nameless freaks that ruin other people's lives."

"How about a woman named Maria Eastern?"

Tabitha tilted her head to the side as though thinking. "No," she said. "Who is she?"

"She owns a store right outside White Cliff."

"Those freaks!" she said. "Why would I know someone like that? Hey, wait, are you one of them?"

"No," Chance said. "We've only known Maria for a day or two. We're staying up at White Cliff. I know she has a son about your age, so we just wondered if you'd met her."

"A son? What's his name?"

"Dennis," Chance said.

"There's another son named Jacob," Lily added.

Tabitha shook her head. "Never heard of either of them. Those kids don't go to our schools and we don't go to theirs." She drummed acid-green fingernails on the tabletop. "Is that all you want to know?" When Chance nodded, she slid out of the booth, started to walk away and turned. The tears were gone and the look she cast Lily was concentrated venom. "I think it was cruel of you to even ask me about Wally. You're as bad as Betsy."

"His sister?"

"Betsy the bitch," she said. "She's always coming in here. She sits in my section and glares at me. I'm the only one who loved Wally and she is stupid and ugly and mean." With that she stalked off.

Chance put enough money on the table to cover the bill and a tip, and they got to their feet. Sitting near the door at a table they hadn't noticed before, they found Betsy sipping on a cola. "I told you she was awful," she said as they passed.

Chapter Eight

When they went outside, they found the rain had let up, though the moon did little to penetrate the still hovering clouds. "Time to get back to White Cliff," Chance said with little enthusiasm as he found the place oppressive.

How did little Charlie feel about it?

He helped Lily into the truck and for a few minutes, they just sat there. He could feel the energy drain from Lily and touched her arm to urge her across the seat and closer to him. With his arm around her shoulders, he whispered against her cool, silky hair. "You're exhausted," he said.

She turned and looked up at him. They were parked in a dark corner of the lot so there wasn't much of her to see except the whites of her eyes and the glimmering ivory of her coat. "I'm not so much tired as discouraged," she said. "But I've made a decision. I'm going to show up at the school tomorrow and talk to the kindergarten people, then I'm going to go find Robert Brighton and level with him. If he kicks me out of there, then I'm calling the police. It's been three days now since Charlie was taken and I'm no closer to finding him than I ever was. I don't care what Jeremy says, something has to be done."

"I don't blame you," Chance said, "but I suggest we

start with Maria. She already kind of knows us and maybe as a woman and a mother, she'll be easier for you to reason with."

"I'll think about it," she said. He felt her fingers touch his face, and he sighed.

"I'm sorry I called you a quitter. It's really not true," he said.

"Yes, it is," Lily murmured. "But my reasons for running have always made sense to me. I don't know, I guess I'm just so scared all the time."

"Are you scared now?"

"For Charlie, of course."

"Are you scared of me, Lily?"

She nuzzled his neck. "I'm scared of what you represent to me."

"And what's that?" he asked, kissing her ear and then her cheekbone.

"Security," she said. "Eternity. Big old concepts that seem to unilaterally unhinge men."

"Not all men," he said, bestowing soft kisses on her eyelids.

"I'm afraid of wanting what I won't be able to have," she said, and before he could respond, guided his lips to her own. The kiss lingered, tender and almost shy at first, but gaining momentum as the seconds slipped by. His fingers lay across her throat and he could feel the pounding of her heart. It was intoxicating to taste her, absorb her. If he'd been sixteen, he would have tried to strip off her clothes and make love to her in the front seat, but those days required a recklessness he no longer possessed. Besides, one way or another, he was going to make her his if only for one night and that night was not going to take place in a truck.

Still, when her hands crept up under his shirt, he shivered deep inside. His fingers roamed her body as well, sure she would put him off as he undid the clasp on her front-closing bra but she didn't. Her freed breasts felt gloriously warm and soft, and the tight, excited nubs of her nipples made his hunger for her jump off the charts.

His head kept screaming, *Stop or lose it right here, right now*, until the warning finally fought its way upstream through a tidal wave of hormones. She seemed to have been struggling with the same war of need versus poor planning. The kisses began to taper, grew gentle again, hands avoided decidedly sensitive areas and his erection throbbed with disappointment.

They finally separated and took deep breaths. "Wow, Chance," she said. "That was some kiss. I can see why all the town girls follow you around."

"It's a gift," he said, lowering his head to kiss her neck.

She laughed softly. "I know I'm sending you mixed messages," she whispered.

"Sort of."

He could hear her readjusting her clothes. "I'm sorry about that," she said.

"You don't need to be sorry, Lily."

"You just seem to be the epicenter of my crisscrossed desires."

"I'll take that…for now," he said. "But I'm warning you the next time we take it that far and don't finish it my head is going to explode."

"Okay," she said softly.

"Because it's surely no surprise that I find you irresistible."

"I thought you found me annoying," she whispered.

"I do. That's part of your irresistibility." He leaned

forward and kissed her again, then straightened up.
"Time to go or we're going to get locked out of White
Cliff." He reached for the keys and noticed how thoroughly they'd managed to fog up the windows. He ran
his hand against the cold, wet glass, causing a sparkly
river of condensation to cascade down the glass. Beside
him, Lily breathed in quickly. "Look," she said as she
peered past his head. He turned to see what had caught
her attention.

"Over there, walking down the street."

"Is that Tabitha?"

"Yes. Look at the wobbly way she moves in those
high heels."

"She must be freezing," Chase said as the girl passed
beneath a street lamp. She'd topped her jeans and knotted shirt with a lacy, flimsy shawl that billowed out behind her. "I wonder where she's headed."

"She's on her way to meet someone," Lily said. "Dressed
like that, I'd wager it's a guy." Tabitha left the lamplight
and Chase was about to look away when another figure
passed under the light, this one stealthily.

"That's Betsy," he said softly as though she might hear
him. "She's following Tabitha." He turned to Lily. "Are
you game?"

"Why not?"

They quickly got out of the truck using one door and
locking it behind them. The last thing Chance wanted
was for someone to steal his truck, and with it, his guns.

They walked quietly up the slight incline to the sidewalk on which they'd seen the girls. Chance wasn't sure
why Lily was willing to follow them—he wasn't even
sure why he wanted to. Curiosity? Partially. But it also
had to do with Carolyn and Otto Connor and their loss.

Betsy was their only child now and she was sneaking around following Tabitha on a dark, overcast night.

They could no longer see Tabitha, but they could catch glimpses of Betsy and by the covert way she was moving, it was obvious she was still on Tabitha's trail. Many of the houses along the way had put Halloween decorations out on their lawns so they had to dodge the lights cast across the grass. And then there were the occasional cars whose headlights swept over them as they moved. Chance thought that an aerial picture of Betsy following Tabitha and them following Betsy would be worth a chuckle to an onlooker.

Chance estimated they'd walked a dozen blocks when they lost sight of Betsy. A car came along and illuminated the sidewalk up ahead for a moment but there was no sign of her. After the vehicle passed, they saw the girl emerge from the shelter of a parked car and resume walking. They followed. She crossed the street and they claimed a hiding place behind a large tree. They waited a few seconds before carefully peeking out to see what Betsy was up to.

She stood on the opposite sidewalk staring at a dark building situated on a large, partially overgrown corner lot. A steeple rose into the night sky. Chance realized it was an old church, but judging from the boards across some of the windows and a general feeling of neglect, it wasn't used as such anymore.

Betsy stared for a few more seconds, then she seemed to shake her head. She turned and they realized she was coming back their way. Standing very still, their hopes were simple: that she would stay on that side of the street and that a car wouldn't come by to expose them. She was walking faster now that she wasn't trailing anyone and eventually disappeared from view.

Chance and Lily cautiously crossed the street. "This is the east side of town," Chance said. "Remember Betsy told us she saw Tabitha over this way before?"

"Yes. But why was she following her?"

"Who knows?" Chance said, his gaze on the hulking building in front of them. "Maybe she was as curious as we were."

"I have a flashlight on my key chain," Lily said as she dug it from her handbag. It emitted a tiny little stream of weak light but it was marginally better than nothing. "Let's see if we can figure out where Tabitha went and what she's up to."

They climbed the church stairs but found the door boarded and locked. When they reached ground level again, Lily's flashlight revealed an overgrown path leading around to the back of the church. As it had rained earlier, it was impossible to tell if anyone had used it until Lily pointed at a couple of muddy footprints, each with a corresponding puncture like a high heel would make.

They practically tiptoed along the path that ran behind the church and beside an iron fence. The fence appeared to surround an old graveyard. Most of the tombstones were weathered and tilting. Once past the gate leading into the graveyard, the path came to a circular area that must have once been a garden. Leading off that was another stairway, this time to a back door. Boards stacked beside the door might once have been nailed across the opening to discourage access, but they'd been taken off. The knob turned easily in Chance's hand and when Lily's flashlight picked up traces of mud inside the building, they knew Tabitha was in the church somewhere.

The room they entered was empty. It led into a much larger space where old pews were still lined up in two rows on either side of an open aisle. The pulpit stood at the front, but little else remained. A tiny bit of outside light made it through the cracks between the boards.

One side of this room had several open doors leading from it and they checked out each in turn, disturbing dust at times. Near the front, they found a closed door and listened with ears against the wood for a few seconds to make sure they couldn't hear voices on the other side. At last they opened the door and found themselves at the head of a rickety-looking stairway leading down.

Chance took the flashlight from Lily. "I'll go first."

She rested her hand atop his shoulder and he actually smiled to himself. Unable to resist the temptation, he turned around and kissed her briefly and wondered how and when they'd managed to get to the point where he could do that without her slugging him or running off.

The stairs were sturdier than they looked and descended to a small cement area that held nothing other than what appeared to be a couple of old wooden panels that had been deposited against the wall. Another closed door stood directly in front of them and from the room beyond came the sound of two voices, a male and a female. Chance handed Lily the flashlight so he could investigate the panels. She immediately turned off her light and just in time, because the door suddenly rattled. Chance pulled her under cover of the wooden panels right as the door opened. The tight quarters prevented them from seeing anything, but they could hear every word and it was Tabitha's voice that dominated.

"You creep," she said. She obviously held a better light source as the room was brighter than it had been. "How could you, and with *her* of all people!"

The responding male voice sounded young, too. "Don't be like that, Tabby," he said and his voice cracked. Chance felt Lily jerk as she heard it, too. "Come here, come on, kiss me."

"Don't call me Tabby. I'm not a freaking cat."

"No, you're just a freaking freak!"

The unmistakable sound of a slap was followed by a mumbled oath and then hurried footsteps as one of them ran up the stairs. It must have been Tabitha because the boy swore again and raced after her.

"That was Todd," Lily whispered.

"The plot thickens," Chance responded.

LILY SHONE THE little flashlight around the room they entered. A big furnace that looked as though it hadn't warmed so much as a mouse in decades squatted in one corner. What appeared to be a workbench ran along another wall, its sole adornment an inexpensive-looking CD player and a few empty beer bottles. Tucked in a corner, they found a cot topped with a couple of rumpled blankets and a pillow. Another closed door finished off the decor and Chance opened that to reveal a small stack of used bricks, a broom and a spool of some kind of wire. Shelves on the back wall were surprisingly cluttered with odds and ends.

"This must have been the maintenance room," Chance said.

"Now a teenage love nest," Lily said. "Is that why

Betsy trailed Tabitha, because she either knew or was suspicious about a relationship her boyfriend had with Tabitha?"

"Why else?" Chance said.

"Her brother…"

"Died months and months ago at the hand of a mysterious man who confessed his guilt. Maybe Betsy feels as though Tabitha has already taken too much from her."

Lily nodded as she turned the light back into the room and focused on the cot. On the wall behind it, someone had carved initials. T.S. and W.C. and encircled it with a heart. A black line had been drawn to cross it out. Tabitha Stevens and Wallace Connor? Maybe. Lily hoped Wallace's parents never saw this tawdry place. There was another heart next to it that appeared to have been created using the same black ink as the line that crossed out the first heart. This time the initials T.S. and J.B. were crudely drawn.

Was this like a trophy bed for Tabitha? It seemed strange a girl would do something like this and yet there was no doubting that Tabitha was a young woman with an attitude and an appetite.

A glimpse of pale lace caught Lily's attention and she took a few steps to get closer. What was that crunching sound? As she looked down at the floor, she heard footsteps and instantly turned off the flashlight, grabbed Chance's arm and pushed him into the closet, closing the door quietly behind them,

He apparently hadn't heard the footsteps and started to speak, but she put a finger where she assumed his mouth was to hush him. His lips were soft, his breath warm and she was distracted for a second until a band of light streamed through the gap under the closet door.

Todd swore under his breath. "First she hits me and then she sends me on an errand," he mumbled. "Where is that thing? Oh." The door slammed a second later and the closet once again plunged into darkness.

"Tabitha left her shawl on the bed," Lily whispered. She started to move and tripped on the spool of wire. Afraid a crash would bring Todd running back, she grabbed the shelves for support. To her surprise, the whole wall kind of rocked beneath her hand. "Chance?" she whispered.

"I'm right here."

"The back wall moves."

"You mean the shelves are wobbly?"

"No, the whole thing feels like it could rotate or something." She turned on the flashlight whose beam was visibly weaker than it had been.

Chance put his hands on the shelves and wiggled them. They could both see and feel movement. He took the light from Lily and shined it on the unit. "You know, these shelves don't look as old as the church. And they're screwed in instead of nailed. Someone retrofitted this unit."

Lily tugged on one of the cans. "It's stuck," she said.

Chance gripped another and when it refused to budge, another. "They're all stuck. That's too big a coincidence. They must have been glued in place."

"Chance, maybe these shelves are really a secret door. In the movies there's always a candlestick or a book that acts as a lever."

They both immediately started pulling on various items. Chance hit the jackpot a few moments later when he touched a red vinyl binder with "maintenance schedule" written on the spine. He tilted it toward himself, and they could both see the hinge at the base of the binder that activated a mechanism. The shelving unit twisted silently in the middle creating space on either side.

"Well, I'll be," Chance said.

Lily shined her flashlight around. The floor and walls were all made of dirt reinforced with lumber. Best of all, a lantern hung on a hook to the left. As Chance lifted it free and switched it on, Lily turned off her flashlight.

"It's a tunnel," she said.

"It's a scary-looking thing," Chance added. "That wood looks like it's one day away from collapsing under the weight of all that dirt above it." Ground water had also seeped from the earth. The place had a forbidding, dank appearance and feel.

"Do you think Tabitha or Todd know about this?"

He shined the lantern light on the ground. "I can see a few footprints dried in the mud. Hard to tell when they were made," he said. "There's no way to know for sure, but I'd wager they don't have the slightest idea this is here. Let's take a look." He touched a more obvious lever next to the hook that had held the lantern and the door swung closed without a squeak.

It was only wide enough to walk single file. Chance led the way. Lily followed along, but as the tunnel kept going and going, she began to get anxious. The oppressive smell of the earth along with the occasional previous collapses jarred already frazzled nerves. But more important than that, how was investigating this tunnel helping them find Charlie?

They finally came to a wide spot of sorts. A metal trunk sat against the wooden support and Lily stopped walking. "Look at that," she said. "What's it doing here?"

"Someone had to bring it for some reason," Chance said and then chuckled. "Do I sound like Captain Obvious?"

She smiled. "It's not very big, but I have to sit down for a minute or two and it'll do." The day had held so many levels of stress that it seemed to have lasted forever. The trunk provided an adequate perch. Chance set the lantern on the floor and sat beside her. Lily leaned her head against his shoulder and peered up ahead where the tunnel stretched on into darkness. The silence felt tangible and when she spoke again, her voice sounded too loud. "Tell me about going to see Jeremy. And you still haven't explained why you asked about McCord."

She listened as Chance related how he'd barged into Jeremy's house as though determined to find the woman who'd played him for a chump. He hemmed and hawed for a few minutes as he obviously tried to figure out if he should be candid and she assured him the time for dissembling was way over.

"You're right," he said. He took her hand and rubbed her knuckles with his thumb. "He told me to drug you."

"Drug me? With what?"

"Just a second, I think I still have—" he began as he patted his coat pockets and then added, "Yeah. Here they are. These look familiar?

"My old prescription for barbiturates," she said, recognizing the label.

"The plan was I give you the pills and take Charlie."

"He wanted you to kill me," she said bluntly.

"Yes. If I were you I'd get rid of those."

"No kidding," she said as she shoved the bottle in her own pocket. "Well, Jeremy wanting me out of the way so

I won't talk is nothing new. Why in the world won't he just divorce me? Pride? It doesn't make sense."

"Maybe you're an heiress and don't know it."

She laughed. It wasn't something she'd done a lot of lately and it felt kind of good. "No, that's not it. But he is getting awfully reckless sending a man he just met to do his dirty work."

"That's what's been bothering me," Chance said. "And why I asked about McCord. I'm wondering if he sent McCord up here right after Charlie was taken. Maybe McCord reported back that he'd seen Charlie. I don't know, but that might have caused Block to leap at the chance of sending a hothead like he thinks I am to take care of you. Then McCord takes care of me and whisks Charlie back to Boise. The people at White Cliff can't complain to anyone because they're the kidnappers and Block sends Charlie overseas to boarding school."

"Is that his plan? Did he say that?"

"Yes."

"That jerk."

"For all we know, McCord already found Charlie and we're being set up. I murder you, McCord murders me. But if we live through all of this, I can testify what he wanted me to do to you. You can bring charges and get rid of him for good."

Like it was that easy, Lily thought to herself with little hope she and Charlie would ever be free of Jeremy's manipulations. "If McCord is here somewhere, he has to realize by now that you haven't killed me and maybe he reported that back to Jeremy."

"I suddenly feel like I have a target on my back," Chance said.

"Welcome to my life," Lily murmured.

"You should realize we're undoubtedly locked outside the gate by now," he added.

"I didn't think of that," Lily said as she noticed a brass lock attached to the trunk's hasp. "I wonder what someone is hiding in here," she mused aloud.

"I'll bring my gun next time and shoot off the lock," he said.

"And bring all that ground up above us down here? No thanks." She peered up the tunnel again, then at Chance. The thought of going back to that drab apartment to wait until morning was just too much to bear and that was if they could even get through the gate. "Maybe it's time to call it a night," she murmured.

"I'd like to know where this leads."

"I know, me, too. But how does that help Charlie?"

"I'm not sure, Lily. But how do we know it doesn't?"

She was quiet for a minute or two before adding, "We could come back sometime after Charlie is safe."

"That's true." They sat contemplating their own private thoughts until Chance stood up and pulled Lily to her feet. "If you want to go back, we'll go back."

She wasn't sure what to do. What was right and what was wrong? She looked into the dark and then up at Chance. "Let's give it a little longer," she said.

"Okay."

Twenty minutes later, the floor of the tunnel started an incline and Lily began to hope they were close to the end. When the light finally glinted off a solid surface ahead, she felt like yipping with joy.

The lever was the same as the one at the church end of the tunnel, a simple handle built into the wall beside a hook on which to hang the lantern.

"What if this opens directly into somebody's house?" she asked as she caught Chance's hand.

"That seems unlikely to me," he said. "This tunnel is at least three miles long, maybe more, which means a lot of earth was moved when it was constructed. I'd wager someone used mining tools to build it. But even if it does lead into a house, it's pretty late now and whoever owns it is probably asleep. We'll just get a feel for where we are and leave, okay?"

She nodded and held her breath as the door swung open just as the other had. The space that appeared was cluttered with boxes stacked atop each other. Chance immediately started investigating the boxes and Lily noticed a path existed from the double metal doors at one end to the entrance to the tunnel. The building sported a domed roof and the air felt cold and dank. She could see no windows. The door on this side also consisted of shelves and they held yet more boxes with lettering she couldn't make out as Chance had taken the lantern with him.

She looked back into the tunnel, dreading the return trip underground, and that was when the light from the distant lantern reflected off a metallic surface. She felt around until she found a cylinder of some kind hanging from a hook right inside the door. Pulling it into the light, she found herself looking at a red-and-white soup can that rattled when touched. It turned out to have a false lid that she pried off with her fingernails. She dumped a key tied to a ribbon connected to a small medallion into the palm of her hand. She put the lid back on the can and replaced it.

Chance spoke from over her shoulder. "What's that?"

"A key I found in that phony soup can right inside the

tunnel entrance," she said. "It's kind of small. Suppose it goes to that trunk?"

"It might."

She handed it to him. "You take it. What did you find in the boxes?"

"They all seem to contain the same thing: food, canned or freeze-dried. The shelves are stacked with boxes of MREs."

"Military food?" she asked.

"Yeah. Meals Ready to Eat. Last forever. I think I know where we are. Come with me."

"Let's close this door, first, just in case." They spent several minutes looking for the lever that opened and closed this door from the outside. Chance finally came across it when he tried to lift a heavy box from the shelf. The effort triggered the mechanism and the door closed soundlessly. They left the lantern right outside the tunnel and then carefully picked their way across the pitch-black room. Chance finally slid what sounded like a metal bar. The door opened and night air, moist and fresh, greeted their faces.

Lily could see very little as it was quite dark, but here and there a light glowed through a window in the distance. "Where are we?" she asked.

"White Cliff. I asked Maria about these bunkers earlier today. She said they'd been built way back at the beginning of things and were now used to store stuff." He took Lily's hands. "I'm going to see that you get to your place safely, then I'm coming back here. I'll take the tunnel to Greenville and tomorrow I'll drive the truck up here. By then you'll have had a chance to make sure Charlie isn't at the school. Together we can go see Maria."

"I told them you were staying in my apartment. Won't they think it's odd when you're not there?"

"That can't be helped. I can't leave my truck all night at the diner and risk it gets towed. You'll have to tell them you changed your mind about having me stay with you. Tell them I dropped you off at the gate and you walked home alone."

"Okay, that should work. Where will you sleep?"

"In the truck. Don't worry about me."

They closed the door behind them and Chance took her arm. "Hopefully no one will notice us," he added as they carefully picked their way along the muddy path toward Jefferson Park. They didn't risk so much as Lily's little flashlight.

"Whose house is that?" Lily asked as they passed pretty close to the big white house at the hub of the community's wheel.

"The head honcho, Robert Brighton and I guess his wife, Maria's sister. Maria lives there, too, in the back with her boys." They paused in the shadows near the fountain, avoiding the solar powered spotlight directed on the three figures. "I don't know where your apartment is," he said. There wasn't a soul around.

"It's a block or two from the park, right in the middle of the town where they can keep an eye on me."

Eventually they got to her apartment. He leaned down and kissed her and her heart pounded. She'd been attracted to him since the first time she laid eyes on him. She'd been new to the ranch and standing outside with Charlie when Chance rode his horse into the ranch yard. There'd been snow on the ground and the air was cold so that both man and beast exuded clouds of vapor. Charlie had trembled at the sight—he'd never seen a horse be-

fore. Chance had gotten off his ride, stared into Lily's
eyes and smiled, then he'd swung Charlie into his arms.
She'd been about to protest this stranger manhandling her
boy, but Charlie had grinned ear to ear and when, after
Charlie agreed, they rode off with Charlie sitting in the
saddle in front of Chance, her quiet, cautious child had
actually squealed with delight.

Chance had captured her attention at that moment and
she'd had to struggle with herself to keep from jumping
out of the Jeremy Block frying pan and into the Chance
Hastings spa ever since. Neither place offered protection or safety. One was just a hell of a lot nicer place to
spend your time.

Her head seemed to spin and for one blinding moment
she glimpsed herself as an outsider might. A slightly built
woman kissing a tall man, comforted by his strength and
power, trusting his plans.

What was she doing? Indulging him in some pointless
quest while her son was held prisoner, while her husband
plotted to kill her and banish their boy to a nameless,
faceless school? Charlie would wither and die off by himself like that. He had one person to champion for him and
somehow she'd allowed herself to do it so poorly that now
she was as good as bound and gagged.

So much of life had been terrifying for so long. She
had to fight the weakness that coaxed her back for an en-
core performance of the old Lily. The meek her, the one
who leaned on broader shoulders.

"This is our first date," he whispered against her
cheek.

She took a step back. She felt shaky as though waking from a nightmare. But she hadn't woken up yet, the
nightmare was in full swing. It wouldn't be over until

Charlie and she were racing off to anonymity and this time she would not goof it up.

"You look unconvinced," Chance said. "Well, think about it. We moseyed about, we went shopping, we ate dinner, we made out in a parked vehicle and then we had an exhilarating stroll through a tunnel. Now I'm kissing you good-night on your doorstep. In my book, that's a date."

She'd been dating while Charlie was in the hands of kidnappers? Is that how Chance saw this night? Is that how she saw it? "It's been an…odd…day," she said.

"But tomorrow we're going to find Charlie," he assured her.

That's what I told myself this morning and I'm no closer than I was! It's not Chance's fault—it's my own. She murmured good-night as she quickly slipped inside her apartment and closed the door.

She emptied her pockets onto the counter, wincing when she saw the barbiturate bottle. Damn Jeremy to hell.

A rap on the door drew her attention and she sighed. She did not want to see or talk to Chance without some time apart to think. She opened the door intending to tell him to go away, but it wasn't him standing on her doorstep.

"May I come in?" the man asked and proceeded over the threshold before she could utter a word.

Chapter Nine

After five minutes of preoccupied walking, Chance turned around and retraced his steps to Lily's door. He raised his hand to knock and then dropped it. Once again he left only this time he kept going.

Of all the women, he had to be stuck on her. What in the hell was wrong with him? Okay, okay, it wasn't really him, it was her. Prickly and sensitive and utterly infuriating. For two cents, he'd…

He'd nothing. But there'd been a change in her before she closed the door. It was like she'd pulled the shades, turned off the light, retreated inside herself, shutting him away.

Apart from her now, he reviewed his behavior in light of the fact that her son was missing. Had he come across as a shallow beast interested only in his own pursuits? Damn it, didn't she know or trust him more than that?

The answer was so obvious it hurt. The answer was no. She'd proven it over and over again and she'd tried to warn him that was how she felt. Well, he wouldn't walk out on her or Charlie, but he had to get his mind out of the bedroom and fix this situation so he could go home where he wasn't constantly being second-guessed.

He entered the bunker and picked his way back to

the tunnel entrance, feeling around in the dark until he found the right box and the door swung open. A second later, entrance once more concealed, he jogged toward the church, his movement causing light from the lantern to dart over the dirt and boards. He kept up that pace until he got to the wide spot where he remembered the key Lily had found. Sure enough, it opened the lock on the trunk.

He lifted the lid with the sense of discovery almost everyone feels when unlocking a potential secret, but it was anticlimactic without Lily there to share it. Was that what he could look forward to from now on? Was this why his father kept getting married? Was being alone so terrible?

Hell no.

He hadn't known what to expect he would find in the trunk but it wasn't a half-dozen colorful spiral-bound notebooks, the kind kids take to school. He opened one of them and found it crammed with small irregular handwriting that was really tricky to read. At first he thought it was written in code, but then he decided that it was just borderline illegible. Here and there he could make out a word. He thumbed through the book looking for some clue to the writer's identity, disappointed it hadn't been more revealing.

And then a name popped out from the writing: Darke Fallon.

At last!

Interested now, he looked through each of the books and discovered the name reoccurred in each of them several times, always buried in the text. He squeezed his eyes closed for a moment to ease the burning sensation and tried reading again. Eventually he deciphered a whole page and realized Darke Fallon was the hero in what appeared to be a poorly written and sexually explicit series of adventure stories. In the passage Chance read, the Fallon character risks certain death to kill a man threatening his beloved.

A beloved named *Tabitha*.

"Damn," Chance said to himself. That girl gets around! So did she come here or did someone from here go to the church? Judging from the bed on one end and the small trunk in the middle, someone from White Cliff went to Greenville. Unless someone from Greenville knew about this tunnel and used it as a hiding place for his or her work.

Okay, so Darke Fallon wasn't a real person, was that what this meant? He was a character created by someone with a good imagination and exceptionally poor writing skills? If that was true, it would explain why the police hadn't been able to track him down. Chance rubbed his eyes again. He was tired deep down inside and it was getting hard to think.

Maria had teenage boys, one of whom Betsy Connor said was cute. He'd met Dennis, a nice enough looking kid, but he seemed kind of unworldly when it came to relationships, and it was hard merging the image of a guy who spent his off time planning which new assault weapon he was going to buy with the lothario in the stories.

Had the person who created Darke Fallon been the same person who later killed Wallace Connor? Regardless of this fictional character, a real-life human had confessed and then killed himself and it was that man, no matter what name he gave, they had been unable to trace. Yet virtually on the eve of his competency trial, he'd chosen to die rather than come clean. Why? What, if anything, did these notebooks mean? Chance checked each again, looking for another name, but the only ones he could see were Darke Fallon and Tabitha. There wasn't a single thing Chance could see in any of the notebooks that identified who might have written them.

As he stacked the binders back in the trunk, he found a sealed envelope and an unopened packet of sunflower seeds. If the seeds were a clue, they seemed as generic as one could get.

But hadn't Dennis said something about his cousin liking sunflower seeds? Not step-cousin, either. Hadn't he mentioned smuggling bags of them out of his mother's store?

He opened the envelope and shook out a few photos with an old fashioned look to them. One was of an older woman with a long blond braid but the rest appeared to be trophies of hunts. A buck, a string of fish, quail.

He put everything back and relocked the trunk then continued on through the tunnel, debating whether or not he should call Lily and tell her what he'd found. If Fallon was a character written by someone who lived in White Cliff, then that could mean the family lived there just as they'd all assumed—and that would mean Charlie was close and maybe even safe. But if the notebooks belonged to someone from the Greenville end of the tunnel, everything got rearranged and without a name and an even larger population to deal with, where did that leave them?

It was beginning to appear they were going to have to bite the bullet and call the police and hope to God that Charlie wasn't caught in the middle. Lily had suggested that was just what she would do if this wasn't resolved soon and he didn't blame her.

Back at the church, he was relieved to find the maintenance room empty of randy teenagers. He moved quickly but almost entirely in the dark as Lily had the tiny flash-light with her and he didn't dare take the lantern in case someone missed it. The building looming above him seemed very large and heavy with the past. It was ex-tremely quiet as though it held its breath, so quiet he could hear his feet crunch on something as he crossed the maintenance room. His imagination supplied the image of scattering cockroaches and he quickened his pace.

He received another surprise that night when he dis-covered the back door of the church was now locked and couldn't be opened, even from the inside. He stood there a second, trying to figure out if Tabitha or Todd had locked it, and then decided it didn't matter. What was important was to get out of there without becoming entangled in some legal issue.

Another question sprang to mind as he searched for a glimmer of light that would indicate a window facing the back of the property instead of the street. The wait-ress at the diner had said Tabitha's grandfather used to be a preacher. Had this been his church? If it had, was he the one responsible for the tunnel? Who owned the church now?

And what about those memorial grassy mounds built by Thomas Brighton, Robert Brighton's father. The tun-nel was old, the church was old, the mounds were old. Was that where all the dirt that came out of the tunnel had gone to: those mounds? If so, it would mean the White Cliff end of things had originated the tunnel.

So what? That had to be decades ago, long before Lily was born, to say nothing of her son.

His hand finally touched the cool smooth surface of glass. He would have to break the window, he knew that, and it worried him that if someone noticed, they would find the glass outside instead of inside and know someone had been in here. He couldn't wait forever, though, so with the quick decision-making prowess a man working with unpredictable animals his whole life learns to hone, he wrapped his fist in his bandana and smashed it through the glass.

The noise it made seemed way out of proportion to the small hole he'd created. Using the bandana, he quickly took out enough shards to get a hold of the boards nailed to the outside. Eventually, he managed to loosen a couple of those and that resulted in additional broken glass. It was a tight fit and a nine-foot fall to the ground once he got through, but he got up quickly. There was no way to replace the boards so they'd look exactly as they had, but he propped them as well as he could and took the time to sweep the broken glass on the ground beneath the branches of the bush that had helped break his fall.

The good news was that the window not only did not face the street, it didn't even face the back of the church. Instead it was one of the windows on the wooded side of the property. No one would notice it had been broken unless they looked for it. He walked around to the street and buried his hands in his pockets as he finally noticed he'd cut himself in a few places. The walk back to the diner and his truck was longer than he remembered and he arrived there beginning to feel the effects of the miles he'd put in that night.

Once in the truck, he took out his cell phone and saw that it was three-fifteen in the morning. He wanted to call Lily in the worst possible way, but she'd be asleep by now and he wasn't sure she wanted to talk to him anyway. Instead he drove outside of Greenville where he'd noticed a frontage road, found a spot under some trees and leaned back in the uncomfortable seat. Twenty seconds later, he was out like a light.

HE AWOKE AT the crack of dawn with a stiff neck. It was very early, but he figured the bulk of White Cliff was already up and going. There was no better way to conserve power like electricity and gas than by adopting nature's light patterns as your own. Life was like that on the ranch quite often, as well, especially in the winter when frequent power outages were more likely.

He was anxious to see Lily and knew he couldn't wait until after she came back from the school. He wasn't sure if she intended on teaching her class today or just investigating. Last night it had sounded to him as though she'd lost all patience with playing this the White Cliff way, or his way, either, for that matter. As much as she feared he would muck things up by becoming a loose cannon, he feared she would do the same. Patience wasn't exactly the woman's middle name.

The guard let him in the gate and Chance drove directly to Lily's apartment. Her car wasn't parked where it had been the night before. Maybe school started early and maybe she'd driven to it. He wasn't sure exactly where the school was, but the community area wasn't that crowded—he should be able to find it. To be on the safe side, he knocked on her door in case there was another explanation about the car. He saw a note taped to the wood and read it. *Come see me*, it said. *I know about you.* It was signed *Maria.*

No one answered the door and as an afterthought, he twisted the knob in his hand and just about fell over when the door actually opened. The room was as impersonal as a generic motel room with the exception of a poster that showed the image of an automatic assault weapon being held aloft and the words *Get yours while it's still legal*. The bed was made and the dishes were done. There were no personal effects to be seen. Lily wasn't here and it didn't appear she was coming back.

"Don't jump to conclusions," he murmured. "Try the school." He hopped back in his truck. Happily, the town signposts were pretty clear about where things were. If he turned right, he'd apparently find an alternate route to Lake Freedom which he recalled seeing a sign for out on the road approaching White Cliff. Left would take him to Jefferson Park and the school was straight ahead. He wasn't foolish enough to think anyone would let him waltz into a classroom, but he could search the parking lot for Lily's car.

It wasn't there.

It hadn't been at Maria's store when he drove past. Was it possible Lily had somehow found Charlie last night and taken off without saying a word to him?

Hell yes, it was possible.

But it was also possible something else had happened to her. And if something had, the possible suspects included Jeremy Block, McCord, Charlie's kidnappers and maybe someone else he wasn't aware of. Where did he start looking?

A van drove up and stopped behind him. A fully armed man he'd never seen before hopped ably from the van and approached the truck on foot. Chance rolled down his window.

"Mr. Reed," the man said but it didn't sound like much of a greeting.

"Morning," Chance responded as amiably as he could. A movement in his mirror caught his eye and he saw two more men dressed in military fatigues and carrying weapons get out of the sliding door of the van. "Something I can do for you?" Chance added.

The man lifted his gun and pointed it at Chance's heart. "Come with us," he said.

Had he and Lily been seen coming and going from the bunker? "What's going on?" he asked.

"Robert Brighton has decided you are not White Cliff material."

"Okay, sure. If that's his decision, but I never met the guy so it seems unfair."

"It's the way it is," the man said.

"My wife is around somewhere," Chance added. "Just let me find her…"

"She has already left."

"Wait a second. Just—"

The other two men advanced. The one he'd been speaking to walked around and got into Chance's passenger seat.

"Drive to the main road, please," he said. His weapon was at ease, but Chance knew the guy would use it with little hesitation.

"Do you know what this is about?" Chance asked his passenger. He got no reply. They drove past the gate and then past Maria's little store. The store's neon open sign was dark. The other vehicle stayed glued to his bumper until they got to the misspelled sign about trespassing. Following barked directions, Chance stopped the truck and the man got out. "Keep driving and don't come back," the man said. Chance pulled onto the road. When he glanced in his rearview mirror, the gunman was still standing there, watching him.

He drove a mile or two and pulled off to the side. He tried Lily's cell phone, but she didn't respond.

As he figured it, these were the possibilities: she had taken off on her own and disappeared into the ether or she was still at White Cliff. If she was gone for good, she was gone. No way could he trace her again. In fact, he wouldn't chase her even if he knew where to go. The next time she left him, she left him for good.

But that was if she left willingly. He just couldn't believe she had, not without Charlie. And if she had Charlie, he could not believe she wouldn't have left him a message telling him so, especially after he'd accused her of being capable of such a thing.

If she was still at White Cliff, she needed help. Those folks had not been kidding around.

He got back on the road and took off for Greenville. Once in town he made a diversion to a department store where he bought fatigues and big clunky black boots. While he waited for change, he looked on the internet for a pastor Stevens, Greenville, Idaho, and found his first name was Roger. He searched for Stevens in Greenville and came up with one: Roger. The address given was a few blocks from the old church. He picked up a stepladder at the hardware store, ate the pastries out of the sack that he and Lily had bought the day before, then parked in front of a tidy redbrick house.

A knock was eventually answered by an old man in a severe black suit. A fringe of white hair surrounded his bald head and two very black eyes seemed to absorb everything in a single glance. It was almost impossible to believe this austere old guy was Tabitha's grandfather.

There was no time for pleasantries or subtle lead-ins to his questions, and Chance paused for a second, trying to figure out how to find out what he wanted. Too late he realized he should have just gone to city hall and looked it up.

"Yes?" the old guy said. He moved his hand and Chance saw that the book he held clutched to his chest was a frayed copy of the bible. "I don't have all day."

Chance offered his hand and introduced himself. His gesture was met with a stern frown and nothing else. "I came to ask you about your church," he finally said as he lowered his unshaken hand.

"I don't have a church anymore." Stevens started to close the door.

Chance hurried to say something that would stop him. "I mean your old church, Pastor. Or do you not keep that title after you stop preaching?"

"I keep the honorific, yes. And the answer to your question is that the good people of Greenville turned the building into a museum a few years back."

"The one a couple of blocks from here?"

"Not that one. That place was sold years and years ago. The buyer was very anxious to purchase it. Heard he paid a good penny and then just let it sit there and rot. The devil's handiwork, if you ask me."

"Do you know who bought it?"

"If I ever did, I've forgotten. Is that all? I have a full day of meditation planned."

"Your granddaughter," Chance began in order to confirm Tabitha still attended school, but the former pastor's demeanor immediately changed. His face turned red as he pointed a finger at Chance.

"You stay away from her, do you understand me?" he growled.

"Sir, no, no, you have this wrong—"

"I'm praying for her salvation. If I see you near her I will use my gun. Now get out of here." With that he almost slammed the door.

Chance stood there a second, the man's anger still vibrating in his head. Obviously he was aware of his granddaughter's exploits with the opposite sex, but did he really think Chance would be interested in a sixteen-year-old kid in that way? Man, he missed home at that moment. Gerard, Pike and Frankie would laugh their boots off if they'd witnessed this. He kind of shook himself free of the nasty feeling such an accusation can create in even an innocent man, and left. He wasn't going to take time to find the actual owners of the church. This had been another long shot that didn't pay off and he was antsy about Lily.

Carrying his new purchases, Chance parked around the corner from the old church, took his rifle out of the locked box in the back and hiked through the wooded property until he almost ran into the building. The stepladder gave him an easy climb to the broken window. Once inside, he hurried downstairs to the maintenance room. Pretty sure he'd come across the squished cockroaches he'd stepped on in the dark the night before, he found something else entirely. Sunflower seed shells. Not a lot, just a few…

Had they been there earlier in the evening when he'd come with Lily? They could have been. The little flashlight hadn't picked up many details, especially on the floor, and last night he'd been moving around in the dark. He wasn't sure what the shells told him. That the writer who stored his books in the tunnel had also come into this room? It was possible, of course, and if he had, maybe it had been to meet with the object of his desire: Tabitha Stevens. Chance had to talk to Tabitha.

He changed out of his jeans and boots and stuffed them into the empty bag from which he took the camouflage fatigues and boots. A few minutes later, he was dressed more or less like the men who had shown him out of White Cliff. He opened the closet and then the tunnel, stored all his stuff inside, closed everything up and slung the rifle over his shoulder.

It wasn't long before he wished he'd waited to change his shoes until he'd gotten to the far end. The tunnel was remarkably straight but he fervently hoped he'd never have to come this way again.

It took a little more nerve to open the door this time. If Lily had told Maria or anyone else about this passage, who knew who or what might be waiting for him? He turned off the lantern and hung it on the hook, activated the lever and opened the door into the twilight of the daytime bunker which was lit by a small skylight he hadn't noticed the night before. He made his way to the door and slid open the bar. Big sigh of relief. Now what? He straightened up, lowered the cap over his forehead to shade his eyes and started walking toward Jefferson Park, anxious not to be off on his own where he might draw attention.

Okay. Lily was not at her apartment, she was not at the school. Maria was not at work. Maria had left a note sometime in the past few hours saying she wanted Lily to meet with her but giving no details. Best bet? Lily was either visiting with or had been sequestered by Maria. And he knew where Maria lived.

He couldn't afford to wait until he figured out an escape plan. Technically, they had potential access to the tunnel, the unfinished wall and Lily's car. He would have to stay fluid and take whatever opportunity came along.

Nodding at but not making eye contact with a man dressed much as he was, Chance walked quickly to the big white house by the park. He took a sidewalk running parallel to the house and then one that took off at a right angle. In this way he was able to see the perimeter of the property. The house itself was easily as big as his father's place on the Hastings Ranch. The backyard was filled with large play-yard equipment, all of which appeared rusty and unused as though the children who had once played on them had outgrown the need to climb and swing. The exception was a single yellow toy tractor that someone had left near a sandbox. It looked brand-new, the paint bright, the color of the sun, the color of happy. It provided a jarring note in the forgotten play yard.

He found the addition on the back where he assumed Maria's family lived. Lily's car wasn't in evidence. He kept walking and found a detached garage. Next to that was a garden area where dozens of withered, dying sunflowers spilled their seeds onto the earth. He peered into the garage found a van and a truck and an equal weight of canned supplies piled on shelves. But he also discovered Lily's red coupe hidden under a tarp and his feeling of foreboding escalated.

Wishing he'd thought to bring the handgun, he spent a moment studying the house from the cover of the garage. The back door was directly in front of him, but you had to let yourself into the play area to access it. Most likely, the kitchen window was at the back of the house as well where a parent could keep an eye on playing children and garden alike. Early on a weekday morning, the chances of someone being in the kitchen seemed pretty high. Better to try the front.

He made his way as quickly as possible to the front of the house, once more passing that bright yellow tractor. He walked up the path, keeping his head down. Once on the porch, he sidled up to the plate-glass window and chanced a quick glance inside.

Lily sat on the sofa. There didn't seem to be anyone else in the room with her. She had her eyes closed and a shot of alarm blasted through him. He moved back to the door, tried the knob. The door opened soundlessly but some sixth sense or change in temperature must have alerted Lily she was no longer alone because her eyes flew open.

The first expression in her eyes was one of profound relief. The second was anxiety. "Chance? Get out of here!" she whispered. He finally saw that her hands and ankles were tied. "It's a trap!"

He crossed the room quickly, knelt to untie her feet.

"Go," she said.

"Not without you. Is Charlie here?"

"I was told that he was, but I haven't seen him."

"Why did they tie you up?" Her feet were free and he started on her hands.

"McCord is here," she said.

He pulled her to her feet. "Come on—"

"I can't leave," she protested. "Charlie might be here. I'm not going anywhere without him."

"Neither one of you is going anywhere," a man's voice said, and Chance turned to see McCord standing nearby. Chance had been so distracted he hadn't heard the man's approach. McCord held a gun pointed at Lily. "Lay your weapon on the floor and back up," he told Chance.

Chance looked back down at Lily, then settled the

rifle on the sofa and the two of them stepped away. A younger man showed up at the front door. "Everything okay, Dad?" he asked.

"Fine, Seth. Come inside and close the door. Take the gentleman's rifle with you. You might start a pot of coffee and wait until I call you, okay?"

"Sure." Seth closed the front door and walked past Chance and Lily. He grabbed the rifle off the sofa and left the room.

"What have you done with Robert Brighton?" Chance asked, but even as he posed the question, he thought he knew the answer. The McCord who stood ten feet away now did not appear much like the old boxer Chance had seen smoking a cigarette after Charlie's abduction. He must have worn lifts in his shoes at Block's house because he was at least two inches shorter than he'd been. His voice didn't sound as gravelly, either, and there was no trace of a limp as he moved. "You're Robert Brighton, aren't you?"

"Yes."

"What were you doing working for Jeremy Block?"

"I was undercover, just like you are now. You aren't really Pete Reed and this lady is not your wife, Dorrie Reed. She's Block's wife, Lily, or at least that's who you think she is."

Chance glanced at Lily. What did that last comment mean? She apparently wondered the same thing. "I have no idea what he's talking about," she said.

"Has he hurt you?"

"No."

He met Brighton's gaze head-on. "What's going on here? Where is Charlie?"

"All in good time. First tell me your real name."

"Chance Hastings. Why did you bring Lily here?"

"To lure you. I recognized your face from the night Charlie disappeared. I saw you out by the grape arbor. And then you show up here telling lies."

"You let me escape that night," Chance said.

"Yes. I assumed you'd come with Lily. I hoped you might even prove to be a good diversion, but Jeremy Block never guessed anyone helped Lily escape, just as he didn't guess that I drugged the nanny so she'd sleep through Seth and his brother climbing into Charlie's room and taking him."

"You took him!" Lily said.

"I arranged it, yes."

"Where is he?"

"First things first," Brighton mumbled. "You'll see him soon."

Lily's gaze was bouncing around the room as though her maternal instincts enabled her to see through walls to find her child. "He's been here all this time? Nearby?"

"Yes."

She glanced at Chance and his heart ached for her. "Maria left a note on your door," he said, hoping to ground her. "Apparently she came to see you sometime after you were brought here. Have you spoken with her?"

"No. This man was waiting for me last night when I returned to my apartment. He brought me here and locked me in a bedroom, then this morning he set this trap because he wanted to catch you off-guard."

"At about the same time he was setting this trap," Chance said, "someone sent a van full of armed men to escort me off White Cliff property. They said you had already left." He looked at Brighton and added, "Was that you?"

"No. What has Maria got to do with any of this?"

"Quite a bit," someone said from yet another door that had opened off a hallway. A woman entered with the aid of a four-prong metal cane to prop herself up. McCord immediately went to help her. With his aid, she made it to an overstuffed recliner and sat down, her ankles and legs red and swollen where they peeked from beneath the hem of her robe. Chance and Lily might have been able to make it to the door to try to escape, but Chance knew he wasn't going anywhere until some basic questions received answers. This was as close to Charlie as they'd come, he was sure of it, he could feel it deep in his bones. And from the way Lily had tilted her chin, he was pretty sure she wasn't going anywhere, either.

The newcomer looked nothing like Maria, though she did look faintly familiar to Chance. Of course. It was her picture in the trunk in the tunnel. Younger in the photo by a couple of years, healthier for sure, but the same woman.

She obviously had some kind of circulation issues and breathing difficulties. Her long hair was faded blond and caught in a braid down her back. Her face was unlined, her skin almost translucent. Her breathing was labored. Two little hoses fed oxygen into her nose via a portable machine she carried in a sling near her body. She looked as if she'd been battling an illness or chronic condition for a long time and it was getting the best of her. It was hard not to feel for her and for the man who stood fussing over her.

"This is my wife, Elizabeth," McCord finally said as he straightened up after tucking a blanket around her lap. "Honey, you shouldn't have gotten up without someone to help. Perhaps you should go back to bed."

"I heard voices," she said. "I was hoping Maria had

come back. I told her about…everything…and she came unglued."

Brighton looked fondly at Elizabeth but there was also contrition in his eyes. "My dear, this young woman is Lily."

His comment was met with stunned silence and then finally a gasp. "*This* is Lily Block?"

"I prefer my maiden name," Lily said. "Kirk."

"You're different," Elizabeth said in awe, then looked up at McCord. "Robert, you said she was a heavy drinker, a druggie."

"She was strung up on something the night she came to Block's house."

Lily laughed with no humor. "I was strung up on nerves. I was scared and worried sick about my son."

He studied his hands for a moment then murmured, "Yes, I can see that now."

Elizabeth wasn't finished. "You said she couldn't be trusted. Then Maria found those pills so I told her what I knew…but this girl isn't like that. She's different than you said. Different from what Maria thinks!"

"Yes," Robert Brighton mumbled and shook his head. "I can see that. I don't know how—"

"Please," Lily said, looking from one person to the next. "Please, everyone, just stop talking. Where is my son? Do you know?"

"Why don't you sit down," McCord suggested.

Lily walked over to Elizabeth's chair and knelt down beside it. "Can you tell me where Charlie is? What does Maria have to do with any of this? Who is Darke Fallon?"

"So many questions," Elizabeth said.

"Then just answer one," Lily pleaded. The hope mingled with fear in her voice made Chance's heart clench. "Do you have my son?"

Elizabeth touched Lily's hair in an almost maternal gesture. "I did have him," she whispered, "but I don't anymore."

Chapter Ten

"We don't have him?" Robert Brighton said, and to Lily's ears he sounded surprised and upset by the news. "What the hell happened?"

Chance put his arm around Lily as he helped her stand. "Hang in there," he said. "We'll get to the bottom of this."

She looked up at him and took a breath, then she spun around and looked at the older woman. "What did you do with my boy?"

Elizabeth's lips trembled. "My sister took him."

"Maria? Where did she take him?"

"I don't know. She just said he couldn't stay here."

"But there's nowhere else for him to go," Lily protested. "The only person left is Jeremy." She gasped. "She wouldn't take him there, would she?" When Elizabeth didn't respond, Lily's voice climbed. "Would she?"

"No, no she hates him as much as I do. But maybe if she felt there wasn't an option."

Lily turned to Robert. "Give me my phone. I have to try to intercept her. I have to talk some reason into her."

"Maria doesn't have a cell phone," Elizabeth said. "Please, another few minutes isn't going to make any difference. Everything is so messed up. Let us explain."

Chance took Lily's hands in his. "We have to listen.

Maybe there's something that will help us get Charlie back. Please, Lily, trust me one more time and give these people fifteen minutes, then we'll figure out what to do next."

"Fifteen minutes," she said.

Chance sat down, pulling Lily to sit beside him. She was too upset for this inactivity. All she wanted to do was run out that door and keep running until she found Charlie.

But which direction did she run? Maria could have gone anywhere. And if she did do the unthinkable and returned Charlie to his father, then what? Jeremy would immediately secret Charlie away.

It didn't matter, she decided. She was ready to stand her ground and press charges and win her son once and for all. She had nothing to lose now, nothing.

"What Lily heard of the note you left after abducting Charlie seemed to indicate White Cliff and retribution for a lost son, an eye for an eye thing," Chance said.

"That's right," McCord agreed. "We aren't heartless. We figured if Jeremy knew we had Charlie that he wouldn't really worry about the child being harmed."

"How did you know he wouldn't call the FBI?" Lily asked.

"Because I know him," Elizabeth said. "I know what a coward he is. I knew he wouldn't risk public knowledge of his link to White Cliff and what he thinks is a nest of crazy people and I knew he wouldn't shed too many tears over his son. With him it's all pride."

"What about me?" Lily couldn't stop from saying. "I've been in hell. What about Charlie?"

"We had a mistaken opinion of you," Elizabeth said with a note of regret in her voice. Or maybe apology.

"We'd heard you abused drugs. Then you got here and told us a phony story but you acted pretty reasonable until your supposed husband came and then you and he just disappeared. Maria went to your apartment to see you this morning, but you didn't answer the bell. She taped a note to your door and then saw that the door was unlocked so she tried it. She found the barbiturates. She packed up your things, and came to me. After I told her about you, she was desperate to get you out of White Cliff. She didn't know Robert had already brought you here."

"I don't do drugs," Lily said. "Jeremy created that story to discredit me. He gave those drugs to Chance to kill me. And I was anxious because someone took my five-year-old child," she added. "*You* took him."

"After we got away from Block," Chance added, "we decided to look for a family who had lost a son. We kept coming up with the name Fallon. Lots of Fallons around, but none with a family member named Darke, not even one with a missing family member. It seemed this guy didn't exist. As far as I know, the police are still searching for his past. What we deduced brought us to you people. We didn't announce our true identities because Block had warned us that to do so would threaten Charlie's life. Was the man claiming to be Darke Fallon actually your son, Elizabeth?"

"I don't have a son," she said bitterly.

"But you did, didn't you? That's why the note you left when you took him said a son for a son. When Maria pointed out this house, she said Brighton lived here with her sister and his kids. But she originally phrased it 'their' kids. I think you had a son and I think he killed himself in a jail cell."

Chance turned to Lily. "There's something you don't know. I investigated the trunk in the tunnel."

"What tunnel?" Elizabeth asked.

"The one in the food storage bunker?" Robert Brighton asked.

"Yes."

"It leads to an old church my father bought three decades ago," Brighton explained. "He constructed the tunnel as another way out of White Cliff if authorities ever tried to take us over. I haven't thought about it in years."

"I'm betting your son knew about it," Chance said. "The trunk is full of stories with one central hero named Darke Fallon. There are also sunflower seeds."

"Darke Fallon," Lily whispered.

"Jimmy loved sunflower seeds," Elizabeth said with a choked sob. "I planted them this year just as I do every year." As Chance withdrew the key complete with its ribbon and small brass medallion from his pocket, she all but gasped. "Let me see that," she demanded. "That's my father's war medal. This is the key to his old trunk. We keep it in the basement."

"I doubt it's in the basement anymore," Chance said. "You said the trunk was full of stories?"

"Yes."

"Why would Jimmy hide his stories?"

"Perhaps because they were blatantly explicit."

"In what way?"

"Sexually. He apparently had a relationship or wanted one with a local girl named Tabitha Stevens."

"Tabitha?" Lily said, looking at Chance. "I saw initials in a heart by that cot in the church: J.B. plus T.S. It seems if that was Jimmy, he didn't tell Tabitha about the stories or his alter ego. Did Jimmy run across Tabitha in the church's maintenance room?"

"It seems likely," Chance said. "I found remnants of sunflower seeds on the floor. Plus, Tabitha's grandfather preached there at one time, perhaps she heard stories, I don't know." He looked at Elizabeth and added, "By the way, Tabitha was also Wallace Connor's girlfriend."

"Are you suggesting Jimmy killed Wallace Connor out of jealousy? We had proof Jimmy was here in White Cliff that day. That damn Block destroyed it."

"I'm not suggesting anything," Chance said. "But why didn't your son's fingerprints show up when the police checked files? Why no birth certificate, no social security card? Why did he lie about himself and why did this whole community never mention one of theirs died at the same time as the man everyone was asking them about? Didn't anyone put two and two together?"

"The first part is easy," Elizabeth said. "I had Jimmy after a very short and violent first marriage. I was so gullible. I left before I even knew I was pregnant and almost immediately met Robert. His father was in the midst of creating this alternate world. He'd been in prison because of a couple of scams he committed earlier in his life so he was keeping this place under wraps, knowing he'd be investigated when the police found out he was collecting money from investors.

"All that aside, White Cliff seemed like utopia to me. Robert already had several children by his first wife who died before we met. It seemed like I'd turned my life around and found my own little slice of heaven. Jimmy was born up here at White Cliff." She wiped at her eyes. "It seems like only yesterday. He was my only child.

And to answer your question, no, I didn't register Jimmy's birth."

"The government of this country is into every aspect of every life," Robert Brighton chimed in. "It doesn't matter what so-called party they belong to, they're all the same. They amass numbers and data and make records so they can control us. They conspire with foreign agents to undermine any expression of independence. Freedom is a concept to them and not one they particularly even like. We *live* freedom."

"That's why I didn't get him a social security number or anything else. As far as the world outside of White Cliff knew, he didn't exist and it seemed like the most pure form of freedom I could gift him with. As time passed, it became clear that we'd made a good choice because Jimmy was different than other kids. He loved to hunt and fish but he was poor in school and awkward around people. Other kids made fun of him at times. I can't tell you how many fights we broke up. I knew he was roaming around at night but I also knew he couldn't get through the gate and the unfinished part of the fence is guarded… I didn't know he wrote stories and I would have sworn girls were the last thing in the world he would concern himself with."

"Boys will be boys," Robert said. "I should have known that. I just had no idea he'd found the tunnel. But how do you know for sure it was Jimmy who wrote those stories?"

"It stretches the imagination to think someone else created those stories and the character Darke Fallon and then got your son to confess to murders using that same name," Chance said. "Plus, there's a photograph of you in the trunk, Elizabeth. We need to verify everything, though.

Perhaps you'll recognize his handwriting. It's very hard to read."

"Like a scribble?" Elizabeth asked.

"Yes. But I still don't get it," Chance added. "Someone here must have seen Jimmy's picture in the newspaper when police were attempting to track Darke Fallon down."

"It was a terrible picture," Elizabeth said. "Most of the people here probably didn't even see it. Most of us believe the government runs the media. Some did, but didn't recognize Jimmy, they just assumed the police had a man in custody named Darke Fallon, and no one had ever heard of that person before. A few people did recognize Jimmy's photo and asked us about it. We told them it was a conspiracy by the police to undermine White Cliff's legitimacy, an attempt to gain access to our community assets and records. We said Jimmy was a victim just as much as the Connor boy and nothing would be gained by admitting he came from here. Anyway, what business was it to the police that our boy had sacrificed himself for some reason we'll never know?"

"Dead is dead," Robert Brighton said. "If the police invade White Cliff, there will be more violence. I have to believe that Jimmy would not want his brothers and sisters dying because of a decision he made."

Lily stared at the Brightons and realized they were on a different planet than she was, not only politically, but in other ways, as well. Charlie's welfare was all that mattered and if anything happened to him, she'd move heaven and earth to avenge him. "What was your evidence that Jimmy wasn't in Boise?" she asked.

"A dated photograph."

"Don't you have the negative or a copy of it on your computer?"

"No, it was one of those old Polaroids," Elizabeth said. "Jimmy found a camera and a whole box of film down in the basement, left there by Robert's father decades ago. He liked to fool around with it. Anyway, Jimmy was ice fishing that day over at Freedom Lake with his stepbrother."

"Then you have a witness," Chance said.

"Yes, but it's doubtful a relative, even a step relative and especially someone from White Cliff, would be believed in America's skewed justice system. What we had was that photograph."

"Of him fishing?"

"Of him with his catch, yes. We ate his fish for dinner that night. He seemed right as rain. The next morning he was gone like he'd been teleported off the face of the earth. A day after that, he confessed to a murder that happened while he was up at Freedom Lake. Maria drove down there with the picture a day later. Jeremy assured her he would use it to help solve the case. She also told him something he didn't know that we hoped might motivate him to work harder on Jimmy's behalf. By the weekend, Jimmy was dead."

"He must have left during the night via that blasted tunnel," Brighton said. "I should have thought of that. It's just been years since anyone talked about it."

"All of this is interesting," Lily said. "But it's been over fifteen minutes. I'm sorry about your son, but it's my son we have to think of now."

Robert had been sitting on the edge of a chair and he got to his feet as though he couldn't sit anymore. "You have to understand…Elizabeth hasn't been the same since Jimmy died. And now she's sick… I thought if I could bring her Jeremy's boy it would give her a reason to keep fighting."

"But why Charlie in particular?"

Robert looked at Elizabeth. "She has to know, honey."

"Know what?" Lily said.

"I never divorced my first husband, Lily, so I'm not really Robert's wife," Elizabeth said. "There's no easy way to tell you this." She took a deep breath and kept going. "I married Jeremy Block right out of high school and left him less than a month later. That's what Maria told Jeremy the day she gave him the photo, hoping it would make a difference to him. But…it didn't."

"Wait a second," Lily said. "Your son Jimmy is my Charlie's half brother?"

"Yes."

"After Jimmy's death, I got a job working for Jeremy," Robert said. "We knew he had a son—we didn't know his mother had taken him when she left. And then, lo and behold, the son is returned, rescued from his hard-drinking, drug-taking, carousing mother down in Reno…"

"None of that is true except that I lived in Reno," Lily said.

"We know that now," Elizabeth murmured. "I should never have trusted a word that man said. But that's why Robert and the boys took Charlie as soon as Jeremy got him back. To protect him from his parents."

"I thought it only fair that Jimmy's half brother have a better life," Robert said.

Chance sprang to his feet. "Jeremy Block is a bigamist?"

Elizabeth nodded.

"That's why he wouldn't divorce me—we weren't actually married," Lily said. "He couldn't go to court and have that come out. Didn't he know all he had to do was tell me that? I would have danced in the streets."

"He didn't want you to dance in the streets," Chance said.

"But what good does this do us?" Elizabeth said.

"Don't you see?" Lily demanded, staring right into her eyes. "Jeremy can no longer deny his past and his current behavior. With two of us to tell the world—"

She stopped talking because Elizabeth was shaking her head. "The only reason I'm alive is that Jeremy can't get to me in here. We allowed you entrance to White Cliff because Robert had met you at Jeremy's house and we were curious to see what you wanted, especially when you lied about yourself. We let Mr. Hastings in because Robert recognized his face on our surveillance camera from that night we took Charlie. No one else gets in here."

"Elizabeth," Lily pleaded, "listen to me. When you decided that your son's death was something to be privately mourned and laid to rest, you were robbing society of finding the true murderer of a young man. That murderer is still out there after having gotten away with a heinous crime. Maybe they'll strike again and someone else will die. And for your son to have taken the blame—it had to be someone he trusted and cared for deeply."

"Someone like Tabitha Stevens," Chance said, meeting Lily's gaze.

"Yes. Or her boyfriend Todd or even Betsy. How do we know who Jimmy met and what he got himself into?" She turned back to Elizabeth. "You've let hiding become a way of life for you. I understand, I did the same thing. But it's time to make Jeremy pay for his past, time to protect innocent people from his manipulations, time to stand up." All this sounded righteous enough but it rang hollow. Charlie was halfway back to Boise by now.

"Why did you let Maria take the boy?" Robert asked Elizabeth.

"I didn't *let* her," Elizabeth said, looking up at him. "She panicked when she found the drugs in Lily's room and then when she heard you had abducted her and brought her to this house, she went nuts. She grabbed the boy and said she had to find somewhere else to take him, that he would ruin everything for everyone if he stayed here. I heard him beg to see his mommy. Why didn't I listen to him?"

Lily knew why. Elizabeth hadn't listened to Charlie or her own common sense because she hated Jeremy with an unabated passion. Her desire to hurt him overrode her ethics and morals and who got to pay for it? Charlie, that's who.

Lily had steeled herself not to break down, but it was a struggle to hold back the anger. How could Maria have done this? But there was another unavoidable consideration. What would have happened if Lily had been honest with everyone from the get-go? It had seemed like such a horrible risk, one she'd been unable to take, and now look where it had all ended up.

They stood or sat in an informal circle, staring at their hands or their feet, no one willing to meet anyone else's gaze. Lily took Chance's hand. It was time for them to return to Boise and the authorities, time for Lily to face the warrant and then press charges, time to fight for her child before he disappeared out of the country.

He looked down at her and seemed to understand what

she was thinking. He put his face next to hers but just then the door banged open and they all turned in shock.

Maria stood on the threshold. For once, she did not look calm and controlled. Her eyes grew huge as she looked at Lily, and Lily's heart sank.

"Where is he?" Lily demanded, stepping toward Maria. "Where is Charlie?"

Maria finally tore her gaze from Lily and looked at her sister. "I didn't know where to take him," she said. "He started sobbing when I mentioned his daddy. I couldn't take him there."

"Thank goodness," Elizabeth said. "We've been all wrong about Lily."

"I found a whole bottle of pills in her room just this morning," Maria said, suspicion and judgment harsh in her voice.

"I know you did, but there's a reason for that and it's not what you think. Where is the boy? He needs to be with his mother."

Maria looked from Elizabeth to Robert. "Just like that? You two put this whole community in jeopardy and now you're just going to let her take him?"

"Yes," Robert Brighton said. "That's what we're going to do."

Maria glanced over her shoulder at her car. That was enough for Lily who ran past her. Charlie was curled up on the backseat. She opened the door and sat beside him, just taking a second to catch her breath so she wouldn't add to his fear. Dark circles ringed his eyes, dried tears clung to his lashes. She ran her hand along his arm. He opened his eyes with a start and began to withdraw and then he saw who it was. Relief swept away the trepidation.

Holding him and rocking him, Lily kissed his cheeks

and peered into his eyes. His precious freckled face looked wan and tired but otherwise okay. Knowing she had been locked in a bedroom last night while Charlie had slept in another one in the same house stung deep, but in this instant of reunion, the pain subsided and Lily's heart seemed to burst in her chest. She buried her head against his warm little neck and uttered soothing words. "You're okay now, baby, you're safe, Mommy is here."

She was suddenly aware that Chance's hands were on her shoulders and he was leaning down. "Hey there, buddy," Chance said and Charlie tore himself from his mother's embrace and threw himself at Chance. As Lily got out of the car, she watched Chance lift her son in the air above his head. Charlie laughed and squealed and she was reminded of the first time Charlie met Chance. But now she also recalled the other sensation she'd had that day. This was how a relationship between a man and a small child was supposed to be: fun, exciting, liberating, not fraught with worry and tension. With Jeremy, Charlie had always known he wasn't quite good enough, he didn't measure up. Even if he couldn't articulate the concept, he felt it at the core of his being.

If she ended up in jail until things got straightened out, would the courts allow Charlie to stay with Chance and the others at the Hastings Ranch? With Gerard's Kinsey in residence and Chance's stepmother, Grace, around, there would be two women to nurture him and five men to teach him how to be a man.

Or would the courts hand him over to Jeremy? She had decided that if she ever got Charlie back, she would act responsibly and legally and strike to win in the courts no matter what the odds. But now that she had him, the temptation to run was so tantalizing it was scary.

Chance finally handed Charlie back to her. As she took him into her arms, Chance leaned down and kissed her briefly, then winked. "You're not married," he said.

"I know," she said as Charlie wiggled down to stand beside her.

"How fantastic is that?"

"Pretty darn fantastic." It didn't really solve any of the more pressing issues, but it felt great to know she wouldn't have to go through a divorce. In fact, between what Chance could tell authorities about Jeremy trying to pay him to kill Lily and what she knew about Jeremy's past now, especially in regards to bigamy and destroying evidence, it began to look hopeful there might be a light at the end of the tunnel. She would stay and fight.

They started to walk back to the house but Charlie grabbed his mother's hand and tried to hold her back. "I want to go home," he said.

"Did those people hurt you, honey?"

"No," he admitted with a trembling lower lip. "Seth is my friend. I just want to go home. I want to see Grandpa Harry."

Chance smiled. Harry Hastings was Chance's dad. He and Charlie had bonded during the summer.

"I know you do," Lily said wishing he hadn't named the Hastings ranch as his home. But what other options had she given him? A big, cold mansion with an uncaring father or the sublet in Reno? Neither held a candle to the Hastings ranch and she knew it. "We're not staying here," she assured him. "We just have to clear up a couple of things."

Chance leaned down and picked the boy up. "I'll hold on to you," he said. "No one is going to take you without your permission ever again, okay?"

"Promise?"

"Promise."

He wrapped his arms around Chance's neck and Chance smiled at Lily. He took her hand and they walked back inside the house.

Robert Brighton now sat on the sofa, Maria beside him, deep in conversation. Elizabeth looked up as the three of them entered and smiled. "You make a lovely family," she said.

"We're not actually a family," Chance said quickly.

Lily figuratively shook her head. Elizabeth's words must be terrifying to a confirmed bachelor like him. Between Charlie's innocent comment a moment before and now this bombshell, the poor guy was probably trying to figure out an exit plan. And hadn't she entertained a momentary fantasy outside when Chance lifted Charlie above his head?

"I've been thinking about what you said," Elizabeth added. "You're right. I need to clear Jimmy's name. I need to help find the true murderer. We need to see those journals and make sure they're Jimmy's."

Lily nodded. "I've been thinking, too. I took a bunch of stuff from Jeremy when I left him. It's locked in the trunk of my car. I know more now than I did when I went through it all before. Maybe if I look again, something will jump out at me."

"It's worth a shot," Elizabeth said.

Maria stood up and approached Lily. "I owe you an apology. With Robert gone for weeks at a time and Elizabeth struggling with grief and illness…it was terrible after Jimmy died. He and Dennis were pretty close. We were all shaken up and then not to even have his body to bury, to have to pretend…well, I almost left White Cliff.

I thought if that's the level of commitment required to live here, was it worth it?"

"A girl at the bakery mentioned that you withdrew after Christmas. That was after Jimmy died, wasn't it?"

"You're referring to Betsy. Nice girl. I didn't know she noticed. I just looked at my own sons and wondered... well, here we are nine months later and I was willing to do almost anything to protect this...this place. I'm getting paranoid."

That ought to make her fit right in at White Cliff, Lily thought. The whole place was paranoid.

"Now, I'd like to help," Maria declared.

"Then get the envelopes of data and things out of my car," Lily said, "and help Elizabeth and I look for something I can show the police. I'll do everything I can to downplay your community's involvement. Jeremy has to be discredited for all our sakes."

Chance looked at Brighton. "Why don't you and I go get that trunk and bring it back here? And then I need to find Tabitha Stevens and see what she knows about Jimmy. It's suddenly occurred to me that the moment this goes public, she might be in danger from Wallace Connor's murderer."

Chapter Eleven

Two hours later and Elizabeth, tears still streaming down her face from finding her photo in with her son's things, confirmed the notebooks were filled with Jimmy's handwriting. They'd each thumbed through the almost illegible raucous events of Jimmy's rich fantasy life looking for clues as to the identities of any other people Jimmy might have met. Even Seth had offered to help and though he had to be in his early twenties, he blushed more than once as he waded through his dead stepbrother's words.

When Maria's son, Dennis, showed up, greeted Chance and offered to help read, his mother sent him to the kitchen to make sandwiches. "He's too young to read this stuff," Maria said, glancing at the open notebook on Elizabeth's lap. "Heck, I think I'm too young."

"You could knock me over with a feather," Elizabeth said as Maria left to help Dennis. "I had no idea my boy had such an imagination."

Chance looked at Lily and a kind of communication raced between them. The events were way too graphic for a kid without experience to be able to make it all up. It sure seemed to Chance as though Tabitha and Jimmy had had a torrid affair. How many other people knew about it? Was Wallace Connor killed because he found out and tried to put a stop to it? But why down in Boise? And if it was true Jimmy couldn't have murdered him, then who?

"I don't understand what Jimmy was doing in the Connor van all the way down in Boise," he said aloud.

"No one does," Brighton said.

Chance checked his watch. He'd tried calling Tabitha's grandfather an hour ago to urge him to pick her up from school and keep her under his watchful gaze, but the phone had gone unanswered and truthfully, Chance had almost been glad. He wasn't looking forward to the old guy's supposition that Chance was lusting after his granddaughter.

After the sandwiches, Charlie fell asleep on the sofa between Lily and Seth with his tractor clutched in his small hands. Lily sorted the papers she must have looked at a dozen times already. "Any luck?" Chance asked her.

"No." She picked up a stack of photos and flipped through them. "Pretty girls, fast-looking boats, dead fish…wait a second. Elizabeth, describe the photo you sent with Maria. Better yet, I'll describe it to you. A young man's profile, three pretty large fish displayed on a newspaper, a hole in the ice and the left half of a sign that says Freed La. I take it that's the sign on Freedom Lake?"

"You have the photo?" Elizabeth cried. "Let me see it."

Chance took it from Lily so she wouldn't have to disrupt the sleeping child and handed it to Elizabeth. There wasn't a doubt in his mind that it was a Polaroid.

"This is it! Robert, this is it! If you get a magnifying glass, you can see that the paper is dated the same day the Connor boy was killed in Boise."

It was on the tip of Chance's tongue to point out the police might claim the photo could have been staged and taken at a later date using an old newspaper and then he realized that was impossible. Jimmy had turned himself in the day after this newspaper was printed and had not come back to White Cliff ever again. It wasn't the kind of photo that could be doctored, either. The technology in the old Polaroid instant camera was ancient by today's standards.

Brighton looked concerned. "The police will show up in White Cliff," he said. "My father would roll over in his grave if he knew."

"Then I suggest you preempt some of the trouble by going to see them yourselves," Chance said. "Be open and up-front, don't hide the truth. This will eventually be figured out. Jimmy will be exonerated and the true culprit will be caught."

"You really believe that, don't you?" Brighton said.

"Yes."

"I was not raised to trust our government or any of its agencies."

"I was," Chance said, smiling to himself when he thought of his father's very firm opinions on the matter of authority. He was also thinking to himself that a lot of people he knew personally were uptight about the police getting into the middle of their lives until someone robbed, cheated or bashed them over the head, something no one here would think of doing. The White Cliff people seemed to live what they preached.

He took out his cell phone and snapped a picture of the photograph. Now he would have something to show the police in Greenville, something tangible to show Tabitha and hopefully elicit her grandfather's understanding.

"I've got to drive into town," he said as he stood.

Charlie woke up just then and upon hearing Chance's

words, rubbed the sleep from his eyes with his fists. "Don't go, Uncle Chance," he said.

Lily hushed him. "How about we come along with you?" she asked, looking up at Chance.

"Sure," he said, glad for the company. He didn't look forward to talking to Pastor Stevens again.

"Will you come back here after you've done what you need to do?" Brighton asked.

"Yes."

"Considering everything we've put you through, I consider that a leap of faith."

"So do I," Chance said. "Don't forget it."

IN THE END, Seth rode along with them in Lily's car, Chance at the wheel. He was very pleased to have Lily beside him though there was an undercurrent between them now. Charlie had been the pivotal force before, his safety and welfare triumphing over any other concern. But now that he was safe, there was a whole lot to figure out.

They'd brought along a book or two so Seth offered to stay in the car and read to Charlie while Chance and Lily went to speak to the old pastor.

This time the tidy house had an abandoned feel to it as they approached. The front door stood ajar. Considering the heavy skies and dropping temperature it seemed an odd thing. Chance knocked on it while holding the knob. "I should warn you the good pastor believes I'm a pervert," he told Lily, who looked up at him with wide eyes.

"How did he figure that out about you so fast?"

"Ha, ha, very funny." He knocked again and then rang the bell.

"Maybe he's hard of hearing," Lily said.

"I don't think so. Anyway, it's late enough that his granddaughter is probably out of school." He stepped inside the house. "Pastor Stevens? Are you here? Tabitha?"

They heard the mewing of a cat coming from behind a closed door. Chance crossed the small, austere room, rapped on a connecting door with his knuckles, then opened it. A small gray cat darted between his feet and headed for the still open front door.

Chance barely noticed this because his gaze had returned to the room and what he saw there riveted him in place. Before he could warn her not to, Lily reached his side and looked past him into the room.

"Oh, no," she said with a gasp as her hands flew up to cover her mouth.

The pastor had been shot right through his heart while he sat at his desk with a half a dozen books lying open in front of him. The expression on his face telegraphed surprise, not horror. There was a lot of blood on the chair and the wall behind him. His open death stare told Chance that checking for a pulse was unnecessary, but he did it anyway and shook his head when he faced Lily.

"Where's Tabitha?" she asked.

"Good question. Look upstairs, I'll search down here. Try not to touch anything you don't have to touch."

"What about the police?"

"I'll call them."

He dialed 911 as he searched for Tabitha. There wasn't a single sign of her except for a backpack sitting by the door in the kitchen as though dropped there minutes before. Tabitha's initials were written on the shoulder strap. Lily showed up with an ashen face. "Someone who apparently knew the combination opened a gun safe in the pastor's bedroom. It looks like a handgun is missing. Did you get the police yet?"

"I'm trying. The signal is really weak. How about your phone?"

"I forgot to get it back from Robert Brighton."

"Wait, it's ringing," he said. As soon as he heard a voice, he reported the address and that there had been a shooting but he had no chance to deliver any details because the signal suddenly died.

"Let's use the pastor's phone," Lily suggested.

"I haven't seen one. Maybe he had a cell but I'm not checking his body to find it. Let's wait outside," he told Lily and took her hand.

They found Seth and Charlie standing on the sidewalk. Lily looked up at Chance and paused midstep. "I really don't want Charlie to see a dead body removed from this house. Frankly, I would rather he not even see the police. He's been through enough and this has nothing to do with him."

"Or Seth. Let's send them both back to White Cliff in your car. We can take my truck when we're finished here. It's parked over by the church."

"I can't believe I'm sending Charlie away with one of the people who kidnapped him," she murmured.

"Life is strange," Chance agreed. "You can leave yourself if you want to. I'll explain it to the cops."

"No. If I'm going to be the mother Charlie deserves, it better start here. I don't want anyone saying I ran out when my fingerprints are undoubtedly inside that house."

They explained things to Seth who was delighted to leave before the police arrived. Lily handed over her keys while Chance handed him a five and told him to buy ice cream on their way out of town. There were no arguments from Charlie as they drove away; Lily was the one near tears. Chance looped an arm around her shoulders and hugged her. "He'll be okay."

"I know he will. But I just got him back." She sighed deeply. "Chance, who killed the pastor, do you have any idea?"

"Suspicions," he said, "but nothing concrete enough to mention. What I really don't get is why." They stood there another ten minutes without hearing a siren. In that time, the clouds overhead grew increasingly ominous as though Pastor Stevens's wrath gathered in the heavens. "I'm wondering if my message got through to the police after all," Chance said at last.

"Should we go look harder for the pastor's phone?"

"Do you want to go back in that house?"

"No."

"Me neither. Wait here." He jogged up the path to the house and closed the door, then walked back to Lily. "The church is only two blocks that way," he said pointing. "Let's go get the truck and drive to the police station."

"Anything is better than standing here," she said and they fell into step. The clouds broke a few minutes into their walk, and they picked up their pace but there was no way to escape the downpour. Lily had her hooded coat, but Chance had stopped wearing his Stetson a couple of days before in an effort to blend in. The little fatigue cap wasn't enough to offer any protection, but he didn't really need any. How many cattle drives had included unexpected weather? Almost every single one. You just kept going.

He was digging in his pocket for his truck keys when Lily grabbed his arm and pulled him behind the same tree they'd hidden behind the night before.

"What's wrong?" he asked.

"I just saw Betsy Connor walk around to the back of the church."

"Uh-oh. That can't be good. I wish we knew for sure where Tabitha was."

"My money is on the maintenance room."

"Maybe. Okay, I'm going to get to my truck and take the gun out of the back. We've got to make sure Betsy isn't in trouble. Do you want to wait in the truck?"

She flashed him a wry smile. "What do you think?"

"I think you want to come with me but I also think you'd better consider what's good for Charlie. He needs his mom."

"Point taken," she conceded. They ran to the truck and Lily slid inside.

Chance took his revolver out of the locked case and handed her the truck keys. "If anything goes wrong, get yourself out of here, okay, Lily?"

"Chance, I—"

"Not now, sweetheart," he said. "I'm in a hurry. Lock the doors. I'll be back." He leaned inside and kissed her. Her lips were cool and wet and perfectly delicious. He tore himself away and ran toward the back of the church.

The back door stood open this time. He entered as quietly as possible, almost tiptoeing in the big black combat boots so his footsteps wouldn't be heard downstairs. Wet marks on the floor possibly belonged to Betsy. If so, she apparently hadn't known where to look first. The marks seemed to wander room to room as though she searched much the way he and Lily had the night before. Had it really been less than twenty-four hours ago?

The floor joists were solid and he heard no giveaway creaks or groans as he moved directly to the head of the stairs where he paused to listen for voices. What came next was a bloodcurdling scream and then a shot. All bets off now, he thundered down the stairs, cursing his earlier caution.

The maintenance room door stood open. Sounds of sobbing came from inside. He paused at the threshold, gun drawn, took a hasty glance inside and felt a chill race through his bones.

The glimpse into the room was a glimpse into hell. Betsy lay on the floor, unconscious and bleeding. Todd, who Chance had only seen once when he came into the bakery to visit Betsy, lay on the bed, half-dressed, bound and gagged and obviously dead. Tabitha stood by the furnace, a gun in her hand, her eyes dark and foreboding as she stared at Betsy's still form. She seemed oblivious to Chance's presence, her gaze only leaving Betsy when she darted a glance at what was left of Todd.

With his heart in his throat, Chance knelt down to check on Betsy and found the bullet had lodged in her shoulder. She opened her eyes as he touched her. It was obvious she recognized him. "Help me," she whispered.

"Stay still," he murmured and stood again. This time, Tabitha's gaze met his and he flinched. The girl's eyes were wild, her bloodred hair an obscene punctuation in this unholy mess. Mascara bled down her cheeks in black streaks.

"Give me the gun, Tabitha," he said gently.

"Why should I?" she demanded.

"You don't want to hurt anyone else."

She looked at the dead boy on the cot. "You mean him? He was two-timing me with that cow," she said, nodding toward Betsy. "He thought he was going to get some bondage sex. I fooled him, didn't I?"

"Yeah, you did. What about your grandfather?" Chance said, and took a small step forward, his goal to put himself between Tabitha and Betsy. Trouble was, the room wasn't that big and even worse, he was pretty sure he heard footsteps on the stairs. If Lily had responded to the sound of gunfire…if she came into this room…he couldn't let that happen.

"Stop right there," she said.

He did as she asked and raised his voice when he spoke to cover any noise Lily might make. "Your grandfather is dead. You killed him just like you did Todd."

"My grandfather was going to send me away. He knew about…things. He said I was a demon and had to be locked up. Me? Do I look like a demon to you?"

As a matter of fact, she did. Chance shook his head. "You look like a young woman in very deep trouble. Let me help you. Give me the gun."

"No," she said, crying now. "It's too late. It's been too late for a long time."

"I know about Jimmy Brighton," Chance said. "I know he didn't kill Wallace. I think you know who did."

"Jimmy," she said and for a second, there was a note of longing in her voice. "Why did he give the police that stupid, phony name?"

Probably to protect his family and White Cliff, Chance thought. But it was possible there was another reason as well. "Maybe it's how he thought of himself in relation to you—larger than life. He would have done anything for you."

"I know."

"How did you meet him?"

"One night after Wally left, the closet door suddenly opened and Jimmy was just here. I'd never seen him

before. He said he'd hidden away and listened to us have
sex many times and fantasized what I must be like but
I was even more beautiful than he imagined. He was so
strange but he was fascinated with me. He admitted he
was a virgin but wow, you could have fooled me."

"Is that why you asked him to cover for you after you
killed Wally?"

She shook her head violently as tears trickled down
her cheeks.

"Tell me about it, Tabitha. What were you and Wally
doing down in Boise?"

"I wasn't in Boise," she protested.

"I think you were. I think you went there with Wally.
Why?"

It took her a few seconds until she resumed speaking
through trembling lips. "I…got…pregnant," she mumbled.

"Was it Wally's baby?"

For a minute, it didn't look as though she would respond and then finally, she gave an almost imperceptible nod. "He said he would marry me. That's what I
wanted. I wanted out of this town. Wally was older, he
could stand up to my grandfather. It was perfect. Wally
said we would run away to Mexico. But when we got to
Boise, he bought a lot of beer and stopped at a motel. He
snuck me into his room. He said it was to protect me because I was underage… We had some beer. He got stink-
ing drunk and finally admitted he was really taking me
down to Nevada because he knew someone there who
would give me an abortion, no questions asked. I said no
way. How could he lie to me like that? And then he told
me to grow up and stop whining. He was going to dump
me, I could see it written all over his face."

"You got in a fight," Chance said.

"Yeah. Eventually he passed out. I saw his knife and I picked it up and stared at it and then I stared at him... I don't know, he snorted in his sleep and something just... snapped. I went nuts. The next thing I knew, he was dead. I took his ring so it would look like he was robbed. I wasn't thinking real straight. I got in his van and drove home. There was a lot of blood on the steering wheel and the upholstery. It smelled like death in there. I smelled like death. I came here to see Jimmy. I told him... I told him the baby was his. He insisted on driving the van back to Boise and confessing...it just all got out of control. And then he killed himself!"

"And you lost your baby."

"Grandpa knew that's why I was sick. I told everyone it was because of Wally, but he just somehow knew I was lying. The truth was I hated Wally by then, I was glad he was dead, I would have killed him all over again if I had the chance."

Goaded by the rage that must have overcome her as she heard this description of her brother's death, Betsy suddenly pushed her way past Chance and screamed at Tabitha. Lily appeared in the doorway. Tabitha aimed the gun at Betsy, then apparently saw Lily as a larger threat and aimed at her. Chance didn't think twice. He fired his weapon. Tabitha screeched and dropped her gun as Betsy suddenly ground to a stop, one arm supporting the other, head bent forward, back heaving as her heavy sobs bounced off the walls.

Chance kicked Tabitha's weapon across the floor. He'd aimed for and hit her gun hand but she seemed impervious to everything, even pain, and stared right through him. He yanked what appeared to be Todd's shirt off the bed and wrapped it around her hand to stem blood loss. Then he put an arm around Betsy and led her to the door where Lily stood, eyes wide, gaze riveted to Todd's body on the cot.

"Lily," he said softly. "Lily?"

She tore her gaze from the cot and looked up at him. "It's so terrible," she whispered. "It's such a waste."

"I know." He'd never in his life wanted to hold someone the way he wanted to hold her right that moment. Close to his heart, protected by his arms. "We need the police and an ambulance," he said gently.

She nodded woodenly and turned away.

LILY WALKED BACK into the police interrogation room and slipped her phone into her purse. "Gerard and Kinsey will be here tomorrow to take Charlie back to the ranch."

"I think Seth will actually be sad to see him leave," Chance said.

The police detective returned to the room, as well. "This is what's happening, folks," he said as he sat down opposite them. "First of all, Boise police knew all along that the man who confessed and subsequently killed himself wasn't the murderer. They say they were close on the heels of the truth and they appreciate the information you'll be able to share. Secondly, since you aren't pressing kidnapping charges against the Brightons and seeing as Betsy Connor confirms your story of what happened in the basement, you can go. However, there's a federal prosecutor bringing Jimmy's remains up here tomorrow and he wants to talk to you about your evidence against DA Block. We'd appreciate it if you stuck around Greenville for a couple more days."

"Of course," replied Chance. "We're at the inn down the street."

"I guess burying Jimmy at White Cliff is as close to a happy ending as Elizabeth is going to get," Lily said.

Chance reached for her hand. "I think so. There are a lot of victims here because of Tabitha and Jeremy. I'm just thankful you and Charlie aren't two of them."

She squeezed his hand and nodded. "Or you," she whispered.

Kinsey and Gerard met them the next day at the inn. The White Cliff/Greenville tragedies were still headlining news stories, not just in Greenville, but all across the country. The mixture of teenage sex, violence and survivalist upbringing made for juicy tabloid reporting that Lily did her best to shield Charlie from seeing. Buried in the back pages was the story that interested her more: the disappearance of what appeared to be the corrupt DA of Boise, Jeremy Block.

"I can't believe he's just disappeared," Kinsey commented as she packed Charlie's gear into the back of Gerard's car.

"I just wish they'd caught him," Lily said as she buckled her son into the car seat she'd bought for his journey back to Hastings Ridge.

"I bet you'd give anything to visit him behind bars," Kinsey added.

Lily did her best to return Kinsey's smile, but the worry of not knowing exactly where Jeremy was wouldn't go away. She'd heard he'd crossed into Canada and fervently hoped he just kept going.

Kinsey spontaneously hugged her as though she could tell what Lily was thinking. Maybe she could. They'd become close the summer before and that friendship now promised to grow even stronger.

"Thanks for taking Charlie back with you to the ranch," Lily said. "We'll be there as soon as we can."

By the time Chance drove the old truck over the cattle guard onto Hastings Ridge land, they were ready to enjoy a reprieve from media attention. Days of law offices and police stations had exhausted them both. Officials had agreed to give them a couple of days to settle things at the ranch before coming back to Boise where the ongoing investigation into the DA office and Jeremy Block's corruption needed information only Lily could provide.

That meant they'd be back in the thick of things very soon, but for now they were home.

"I placed you and your family in jeopardy when I was here last summer," Lily murmured as they drove down the gravel road. The first snow of the season had flown but it was only a light dusting. The black cattle in the fields stood out against the newly white earth and Chance felt a part of himself kind of thaw.

He put his hand over hers. "Don't think of it that way. There isn't a person here who doesn't love you both."

"We should have called and told them we were coming home a day early," she said.

"You wanted to surprise Charlie, remember?"

"Yes, but now it seems silly. I should have at least warned Grace or Kinsey that we'd be here at dinnertime."

"You're forgetting, Lily. There's always enough food on that table to feed everyone for about three days. Stop worrying."

"I'm trying," she said. "It just seems impossible we're finally nearing the end of this ordeal. I'll feel better when

Jeremy is caught but I bet you a million dollars he's on the other side of the world by now. The man is a survivor. Kind of like a cockroach."

"You're a survivor, too," Chance assured her. "Look, we're almost there," he added as they crested the hill and caught a glimpse of the ranch house below.

The main house and a few outbuildings were nestled on a large promontory created by a U-bend in the river that snaked through Hastings land. Wooded acreage rose up the slope north of the house, land that eventually reached a huge plateau complete with splendid examples of spreading oak trees that had been standing for decades. Past the plateau, an old mining ghost town quietly crumbled to the earth. The town had seen its share of tragedy, both in the past and more recently when Gerard's former family met untimely deaths by falling through a floor.

South of the house, the road followed the river, ending at last at Gerard's house which he now shared with his fiancée, Kinsey. They had passed Chance's own A-frame cabin a mile or two back while Pike was in the middle of constructing a home for himself north of the ranch house. Frankie, the youngest brother, still bunked at the main house. Well, he did when he was home, which wasn't a whole lot.

Daylight this late in the year disappeared comparatively early and so now, at twilight, the house was brightly lit and a curl of gray smoke rose into the sky. Chance drove down the road and circled back next to the house, parking in the area set aside for that purpose. The headlamps swept the porch as he turned and they saw the back door burst open and a small figure dash outside accompanied by three smaller shapes—the dogs.

As soon as the truck stopped, Lily opened her door

and jumped to the ground. Chance got out of the truck, but stopped short of advancing, wanting to give Lily the space he instinctively felt she needed. Charlie flew into his mother's arms. She twirled him around while the dogs barked and ran after their own tails.

Lily finally stopped spinning and just hugged Charlie until he slipped back to the ground and ran back into the house. She looked across the yard and apparently saw him leaning against the truck. Stretching out her hand, she smiled and he went to join her.

Chapter Twelve

Phone calls were made and people started to gather. By the time Grace set a roast on the large trestle table, everyone had heard the latest news and welcomed Lily and Charlie "home." They all acted like she belonged there with them and it was hard not to buy into all this goodwill. Did Chance find their acceptance of her threatening? She couldn't tell for sure. He was sensitive enough to her feelings by now that she knew he wouldn't go out of his way to hurt her, but she wasn't interested in trapping him, either.

She looked across the table and met Kinsey's gaze.

"I'm riding out to the ghost town tomorrow," Kinsey said. "I want to sketch. Do you want to come with me?"

"I'd love to watch you draw," Lily said. "Call me in the morning. It'll kind of depend on how Charlie does."

Chance had obviously overheard this conversation. "I'd be happy to take Charlie on an easier ride tomorrow to check out the cattle Gerard and Pike brought down from the hills."

"Do you think he's capable of that?" Lily asked.

"With help, sure."

Frankie had actually joined them for dinner and he sat down next to Kinsey and smiled at Lily. Since all of the

Hastings brothers had individual mothers, there were differences in their appearances and to a large extent, their temperaments. Chance could be a mischief-maker and a flirt, but Frankie had something else going on, as well. There was a darker side to him. He'd spent most of his youth in and out of trouble with the law, chosen friends poorly and tried everyone's patience. Lily didn't know him as well as she knew the others, but the one and only time they'd had a private conversation, he'd admitted he knew he'd been labeled the black sheep of the family and that was fine with him.

As far as looks went, he carried his share of the Hastings gene pool very well. He'd be thirty next year and while he looked friendly enough most of the time, there was also an experienced, tested quality to his eyes. His hair was lighter than Chance's or Gerard's, almost blond in the summer, darker now that fall had arrived with winter nipping at its heels. He sat next to Charlie who adored Frankie.

At the head of the table, Harry Hastings, the patriarch of the family, held rule, but he looked a lot more relaxed than he had the last time Lily had seen him. Then he'd just returned from his honeymoon and summer was in full swing. He'd had a lot on his mind. Tonight he looked almost cheerful, and he smiled often.

When dinner was over, Chance announced that Lily and Charlie would be staying with him at the A-frame. Lily had made this decision when Chance revealed his house was off the main road and few people knew about it. It seemed like a nice refuge and that's what she wanted right now—refuge.

And, to be honest, time with Chance. There were issues to settle.

"But Mommy, I don't want to go," Charlie said.

Frankie ruffled Charlie's hair. "We'll do it next week, sport, don't worry."

"Do what?" Lily asked.

Pike explained. "Frankie and Charlie and me had planned to spend tonight in a tent."

"But it's cold outside," Lily said.

"Inside the house, Mommy," Charlie said with a grin. "We're going to roast marshmallows and sing campfire songs and Uncle Frankie is going to tell me a scary story about the hanging tree."

The hanging tree was called that for a reason. Four bank robbers had made off with the town's payroll decades before. Three had been caught and hung while the money and the fourth man had disappeared forever. The story went that the dead men were left to rot at the end of their ropes because no one cut them down. Lily cocked an eyebrow at Frankie and said, "You're telling him what exactly?"

"A watered-down version," he whispered.

"The campfire is the fireplace," Pike added. "Sorry about getting the little guy's hopes up, we just didn't expect you home until tomorrow."

"Grandpa Harry said the dogs could sleep in the tent with us," Charlie whined. "Please, Mommy!"

"It must be a pretty big tent," Lily said.

"Not big enough," Pike said as an aside. "I've got my sights fixed on the sofa." He took off his glasses. There was a new look in his eyes, one Lily hadn't seen before. She touched his arm. "Is everything all right, Pike?"

"Just fine," he said quickly.

"Please, Mommy," Charlie said as he tugged on Lily's hand. "Can't I sleep in the tent? Just for tonight. Please?"

Lily looked at Chance who shrugged those impossibly broad shoulders. She looked at Pike and Frankie, two men she knew would protect Charlie no matter what the cost. Besides, he'd been here with them for two days already. "Sure," she finally said. "Of course."

"Okay, sport," Frankie said. "Let's set up the tent."

Lily looked from one man to the other. "Good luck, you guys. You know where I am if you need me."

She watched Charlie trot off with the two men, smiling to herself. It was going to be gut-wrenching taking him away from here, though she knew eventually that was going to happen. But maybe she could find a job in town and a little place for them to live where Charlie could still visit occasionally.

"Ready?" Chance called.

"I want to help Grace and Kinsey with the dishes..."

"Not tonight," Grace said as she walked past with a stack of plates. "Tonight, Gerard and Harry are washing, Kinsey and I are drying. Shoo."

After climbing back into the truck, Chance sat there for a second and stared at her. "What?" she asked. "Is something wrong?"

"I'm just surprised," he said.

"At what?"

"At you. I'm surprised you've agreed to come spend the night at my place without Charlie or anyone else to ride shotgun."

"Do I need someone to ride shotgun?" she asked sweetly.

"Yes, as a matter of fact, you do," he said, and started the truck.

She was quiet for a few moments as he drove out of the yard and back up the road. "I thought it would give us a chance to talk," she finally said as he turned off on the winding road that she surmised would lead to his A-frame.

"It's funny," he mused. "We've had time since everything happened but we haven't mentioned what's between us even once."

"I couldn't handle it," she said.

"But you're ready to figure it out now?"

"Yep. Oh, is that your place? It's charming."

"Thanks to the automatic lights you can actually see it," he said. "Come on inside."

The house had the typical highly peaked roofs of an A-frame. She was surprised at how spacious it was inside. "There's a loft bedroom upstairs that I use," he said. "There are two more bedrooms on the main floor, but they aren't furnished yet."

She raised her eyebrows and he laughed. "I'm sleeping on the couch tonight. You get the loft. Would you like a brandy?"

"Sure," she said.

"I'll take your satchel upstairs first," he said. "Make yourself at home."

The kitchen was small but efficient, lacking only the homey touches that would come with time. The dining room consisted of a card table and two chairs. The living room was the most pulled together space with a white shag area carpet anchored by a dark leather sofa and two huge chairs. Two tall windows flanked a rock fireplace where wood was stacked in preparation for a fire. Lily wandered over to one of the windows. The automatic outdoor lights had switched off, and as she stood in front of the black glass, backlit by the room behind her, she was suddenly aware of how visible a target she must make and backed away from the window, shivering now. She ran into Chance who lifted the snifters up high to avoid spilling their contents.

"Something spook you?" he asked.

"No," she said. She took the brandy he offered, clinked glasses, and took a sip. The fire burning down her throat helped clear her mind and chase away the boogie-man.

"Sit down," he said, patting the sofa seat next to him. Lily set her glass down on a small table.

"This is a comfortable house."

"Do you want me to start a fire?"

"That would be nice," she said, and scrunched back on the sofa while he fussed with paper and matches. For a second, she imagined Charlie back at the main house, toasting marshmallows and sleeping with the ranch dogs. A smile just got broader when Chance returned to the sofa. There was no denying the magnetism between them.

"Your face is back to normal," he said, raising a hand to lay his fingers against her cheek. "How come you've never been in my house before?"

"You never asked me."

"That's not true," he said. "The night we kissed, remember that night?"

"I remember."

"I asked you before the fateful kiss. You said you didn't think it would be a good idea."

"I did. Hmm," she said, and sipped more brandy.

"I have another theory," he added. "I think you didn't want to take the chance you might find a place you didn't want to leave."

"Your ego is one of your more endearing characteristics," she said with a soft chuckle. "That's why I thought you were like Jeremy when I first met you. You were just so sure of yourself, so positive a woman would be willing to settle for whatever you cared to offer."

"Comparing me to that psychopath is hitting beneath the belt," he grumbled.

She set aside her glass again. "But then I got to know you."

"And you discovered how dashing I am," he said.

"No, the dashing part was easy to see. What I found out is that you are a very good man."

"Don't go spreading that around," he said. "I have a reputation to protect."

She pretended to zip her lips, and they just both kind of mutually sank lower on the cushions, legs stretched out in front of them on an ottoman, the fire crackling and throwing wild shapes about the room.

"There's something I've been asking myself for a long time now," he said at last. She turned her head to find him looking right at her. He was so close she could feel his breath warm her skin. "I've been wondering and wondering what it is about you. Why do I crave you? Sure, you're gorgeous and interesting and sexy as hell, but frankly, lots of people are those things, right?"

She laughed internally. He sounded as though he was really struggling with this concept. She murmured, "Yes, right, lots of people."

He took her hand in his and squeezed it. "But I can't get past wanting you."

"And that's a problem for you?"

"Yes. You're not easy."

This time the laugh escaped her lips. "I know I'm not." She scooted even closer and his arm slipped around her back. She laid her head against his chest and sighed. "If it makes you feel any less alone in this endeavor, I find you just as hard to resist."

"And yet you do," he said softly.

"I've been running and hiding for so many years, first from myself, then Jeremy… I've just forgotten how to trust people. I'm trying, but I keep feeling any moment now, I'm going to have to grab Charlie and head for the hills."

"I know you do."

She raised her chin and looked up at him, stretched a little more and touched his lips with hers. "But there's this thing between us," she whispered. "Maybe it is just lust. Maybe what we have is supposed to be like a storm, you know, crazy and wild and then over." She looked up into his eyes. "It would be easier if I left and you forgot I ever existed."

"Maybe," he said. "But that's not going to happen and you know it. I've been thinking about no one else but you since the moment I saw you standing in the yard with your wild chopped blond hair and dangling earrings catching the light like sparklers. I admit it, I rushed you, I was crazy to have you. I would have said or done almost anything to get through to you."

"What makes you think you didn't get through to me?"

"You ran off when I kissed you."

"That wasn't just a kiss and you know it," she said. "With you it's never just a kiss." She was about to expound on this theory when he pulled her against him and proved what she'd just said. He kissed her so deeply that it was like the warm mouth of heaven opened to claim her. He teased her tongue with his and she held onto him tighter, pressing against him, the simmering heat off his skin musky and corporeal. His kisses went deep, lasted long, the storm she'd predicted hovering on the horizon about to shake the earth with thunder.

He stood up abruptly and pulled her to her feet. Then he leaned down and lifted her into his arms.

"What are you doing?" she asked breathlessly.

"I'm taking you to bed."

"Just like that?"

"Just like what? I'm been thinking of doing nothing else since last February. However, we're in no rush, and contrary to what you think of me, I'm not going to simply have my way with you." He carried her up the stairs to the bedroom and deposited her on the bed. Then he stared down at her. "You look disappointed," he said as he pulled off his shirt. "Did you just assume I was going to run amok on your naked body?"

She gazed at his bare chest and bit her lip. "I guess I did. However, if that's not your plan, why are you undressing? I thought you were going to sleep on the couch."

"Can't you stop thinking about sex for thirty seconds?" he teased. "I'm getting ready for bed is all. This is my room, after all." He sat down beside her. "You know what you are, Lily Kirk?"

She lowered her head and kissed his chest, then ran a hand downward. He picked up her hand and held it.

"No, what am I?"

"Spoiled. You've gotten so used to me wanting you—"

She put her finger across his lips. "Just shut up and kiss me, will you please?"

"Not so fast," he said. He took off his boots and socks, then stood. "You might want to stop gawking at me," he said. "The jeans are coming off next."

"I'll gawk, thanks," she said and admired the muscles rippling under the skin in his back and shoulders as he unbuttoned his jeans and took them off. Then he spread his arms. "Like what you see?"

She rotated her finger in the air and he did a 360, a silly grin plastered on his face. She could see what this bantering was doing to his anatomy—a guy had a hard time hiding certain things about himself—and it thrilled her.

"Your turn," he said and sat down again. She stood up and unbuttoned her sweater, then pulled off her shirt. He produced a wolf whistle and she bowed from the waist.

"Thank you," she said.

His expression softened as he crooked a finger. "Come here. That bra looks tricky. You may need help getting it off." She stepped closer to him, trembling as he ran his fingers across the bra, feeling his quickening breath clear down in her groin as her breasts escaped the delicate lingerie. She slipped off her jeans, leaned forward and kissed him then put her knee between his legs and pushed him back on the bed, climbing up to join him, straddling him.

His gentle caresses grew more intense as his warm mouth seemed to devour her. He pulled her hips against his. His engorgement between her legs drove her mad and she lay down on top of him, anxious for her bare breasts to touch his chest. He kissed her again and again until there was no definition, until he rolled her over onto her back and stared down into her eyes. His gaze seemed to burn through her skin.

He slowly lowered his head and kissed her, sucking gently on her lower lip. Everything changed. There was no stopping, no going back, no second thoughts. This is what they had both wanted since laying eyes on each other, an abandoned romp where thoughts were as unnecessary as clothes, where bare skin and hot moistness met urgency, where need, exhilarated by desire, pushed them to the breaking point.

There was nothing shy about Lily's investigation of Chance's magnificent physique. The skin on his butt was amazingly smooth and soft, and to possess even temporary power to arouse him to the point he could no longer delay plunging himself into her body was a mystifying feeling.

For an hour or more, they loved each other with abandon. He was a generous lover, rough when it aroused her, gentle when she asked for it, tireless in pleasing her just as she pleased him. Lily had only slept with one other man in her life and he'd boasted he felt about sex the same way he felt about almost every aspect of life: he was in it to win it. Sex hadn't been about desire followed by tenderness. For Jeremy, it had been about conquest, about planting a flag and moving on, not raining tender kisses over a lover's breasts and belly and beyond.

Chance erased that past. And later, when he held her in his arms and drifted off to sleep, she comforted herself that even if she never slept with him again, or more likely, they slept together often until their differences drove them apart, well, even if that happened, she had this moment.

It would be foolish to put too much meaning into what had happened that night. She just had to try to go with the flow and keep her head and give him the room to bolt when the time came.

CHANCE AWOKE WITH a start. He opened his eyes and found Lily sound asleep beside him. She was still here! His lips curved. There was a time not so long ago that last night's sex would have sated his hunger for her and maybe in the back of his mind, he was hoping that was still a possibility. He could tell himself that sex wouldn't change the nature of their relationship; experience had told him that wasn't true. What usually happened was a moment of bliss followed by trepidation as he pondered how to slip away into the night.

For the first time in his life he didn't want to slip away. He wanted the silken bonds he could feel entwining his body and heart to grow stronger. Last night, the more she'd responded to him, the more he'd wanted to give her. The feeling persisted even now. He wanted her here, in this bed, in this house, on this ranch. The thought she and Charlie could disappear again terrified him.

He kissed her cheek and her lashes fluttered. Damn if he didn't find it sexy. "Time to face the day," he whispered. Her phone rang and she groaned. He found her jeans on the floor and tugged the phone out of the pocket. "Looks like it's Kinsey," he said, adding, "Your phone is almost dead. There's a hookup over there on the desk."

Lily sat up straight and smiled at him as the sheet fell around her waist. Naked and tousled, she looked good enough to coax under the sheets for another hour or two. He handed her the phone, sighed, and went to take a shower.

THINGS GOT OFF to a slower start than they'd anticipated when they found the horses had somehow escaped their pasture and wandered off here and there across the fields. Chance finally cornered Jangles, his gorgeous bay gelding, and helped Lily saddle him. That had taken a while as it had been peppered with longing looks between Lily and Chance and excited babble from Charlie detailing the events of the living room campout.

An hour later, she and Kinsey rode past the hanging tree on their way to the ghost town. The October morning was cold and crisp and the snowy ice that had fallen the day before crackled beneath the horses' feet.

"Do you have any idea what you want to draw?" Lily asked Kinsey as they rode abreast.

"Not really. I like to stay open to inspiration. I won't do anything with the building where Gerard lost his family," she said. "I just want to take a look and see what attracts my attention. I hope it won't be boring for you."

"It won't. I've been wanting to investigate the place myself before it's nothing but a heap of wood."

"Just be careful," Kinsey warned.

"I will."

Kinsey studied her for a second and smiled. "You're different today."

"I am?"

"Yeah. You didn't snap at Chance once this morning."

Lily shrugged. "He's not so bad." She slid Kinsey a sidelong glance and added, "As a matter of fact, he's pretty spectacular."

"I knew it!" Kinsey said. She wore a bright yellow baseball hat that had once belonged to Gerard. That and the backpack strapped to her coat made her look like a college student riding to a class. "Finally," she added with an exaggerated sigh.

"Finally. Speaking of Hastings men, what's going on with Pike? He seemed a little distant last night. Chance said he's worried about his sister?"

"Tess isn't really his sister," Kinsey said. "Pike's mom and Tess's dad got together about twelve years ago which in that neck of the woods make theirs a long standing relationship. Heck, I guess it does almost anywhere anymore. Anyway, he was the star of that television show that only aired one season, the one about a private eye married to a belly dancer."

"I'm not big on TV," Lily admitted.

"It was on a long time ago. Rumor has it he got booted when he went into rehab. Tess was born about then and eventually came to live with him. I guess he cleaned himself up. He does television ads and voiceovers now and someone said he bought a restaurant or something. Anyway, Pike has never lived in the same house with Tess but he seems very protective of her. She left when Mona kicked her dad out of the mansion, but no one has heard a word from her since."

"There's always someone or something to worry about," Lily mused.

"Are you worried about Jeremy?"

Lily thought back to the shiver she'd experienced when she stood framed in Chance's window the night before. But Jeremy was in Canada or beyond, it was just the last of her overburdened nervous system working out the kinks. "Not really," she said, and squeezing her knees, urged her horse into a trot. "Last one there is a rotten egg," she called over her shoulder.

They slowed down when the first building rose to their left. The main street stretched out ahead, overgrown with weeds, flanked with buildings slowly sagging to the earth. Lily soon became distracted by an old saloon complete with a decayed-looking balcony. They dismounted and draped the reins over the remains of a hitching post. Kinsey untied a roll from the back of the saddle and produced a folding stool where she perched to open her backpack and withdraw the sketch pad and charcoal pencils. Lily looked over her shoulder for a while, amazed at how adroit her friend was at capturing the nuances of light and shadow. Eventually, she wandered down the street alone, quickly caught in the mystery of the past, wishing Chance was by her side, holding her hand.

GERARD RODE OUT with Chance and Charlie to look at the last herd of cattle brought down from the mountains. With Charlie riding in front of him in the saddle, he took it slow. Charlie, meanwhile, played with the palomino's mane and hummed a tune Chance recognized. Undoubtedly, Frankie had been whistling it the night before around the "campfire." The tune was catchy but the lyrics were borderline obscene and Chance hoped his brother hadn't shared those.

This group of Angus cattle would give birth for the first time this spring. For now it was important they grazed good fields. The cattle milled around the fence, looking for handouts, curious about the people staring at them while Charlie babbled on and on about dressing up as a cowboy for Halloween.

"Can I carry a gun?" he asked Chance.

"A real gun?"

"Yes."

"No."

"Please?"

"No, but we can make a pretend gun out of wood in the shop this afternoon. Would that do?"

"Yes!" Charlie cried and ran to the fence to tell the cows his big plan.

"He's a great kid," Gerard said.

"You bet he is," Chance agreed. "He's been through

a lot but he seems hardwired for happiness, especially when he's here."

"And you and Lily seem to have reached a new level in your relationship," Gerard added.

"You can tell?"

"Duh," Gerard said. "There's still tension between you two, but the nature of it is different. You, little brother, actually seem to be in love. I never thought I'd live to see the day."

Chance shook his head. "Too early to call it that," he grumbled but wasn't positive Gerard hadn't hit the nail on the head.

How did he feel about that? Scared, worried, trapped? Excited? Anxious?

Anxious was as good a word as any, he decided.

His cell phone rang and he was glad for the interruption from his head games. The area code was the one for Greenville but he didn't recognize the number. It was probably the police asking another question as they fought to build their case against Tabitha Stevens.

"Hello," he said, hoping this wouldn't take too long. Then he paused and listened. Meeting Gerard's glance, he finally spoke again into the phone. "Yes," he said. "I understand. Thanks."

"What—" Gerard started to say, but Chance shook his head.

"Lily's phone is at my house charging," he said. "Try calling Kinsey. Now."

Chapter Thirteen

Lily wandered the empty street, pausing to peer into some of the more intact-looking buildings. She didn't actually go into any of them as they were well posted with warning signs. The place could never be reclaimed. It was just a matter of time before the Hastings family would have to demolish it or risk further accidents.

Eventually she ended up at the end of town where the old mining site had existed a long, long time ago. A few pieces of rusted equipment and boards barring entry into the cave itself were all that was left of a human presence. The cave reminded her of the tunnel back at White Cliff and she stared at it for a few minutes, lost in thought, reliving that long hike through the earthy darkness and the accompanying horror of not knowing where Charlie was.

But she knew where he was now. Chance would take care of him, Chance wouldn't let anything or anyone harm him. Charlie was safe, she was safe.

So why was she shivering?

Well, it was cold outside. The coat Chance had bought her was warm, but her cheeks stung from the breeze. She plunged her hands into her pockets and turned to retrace her steps, although she paused at the bank where the robbery signaled the beginning of the end of Falls Ridge.

It was difficult not to speculate about the man who got away with the money. Where did he go? Was he able to enjoy his ill-gotten goods or did the ghosts of his former colleagues haunt him to the end?

And who was he? As far as she knew, the other three men had been locals, but the fourth man was a mystery.

A mystery. Like Chance. What was he thinking? Was he ready to bolt? How could she ever bear seeing him lose interest in her, sensing his needs had been filled and he was ready to move on to a new adventure, a new lover?

Was he the reason she shivered inside? Was this haunting fear one of rejection?

She checked her watch and saw that it was time they started home. A few more minutes and she rounded a slight curve. Jangles and Kinsey's mount should be visible now, but they weren't. Had the horses wandered off? She picked up her pace to ask Kinsey what was going on. But Kinsey wasn't where Lily had left her. The stool rested on its side while the sketch pad lay on the ground, the top sheet fluttering in the biting wind. Charcoal pencils had scattered across the half-frozen earth. The small bag that held the rest of the art supplies sat exactly where it had when Lily last saw it. There were no footprints on the cold, hard-packed earth.

So, had the horses run off and had Kinsey left to get them back? Had the wind caught the sketch pad and blown it to the ground? Was that what pushed over the stool?

"Kinsey?" she called, and though her voice didn't echo, it did sound hollow and forlorn. She kept walking, looking into dark, open doorways as she passed, calling Kinsey's name as she went. Despite there being no evidence of foul play, it was hard to shake a growing feeling of foreboding and she quickened her pace.

She finally caught a glimpse of yellow coming from inside a heavily shadowed building. Was that Kinsey's hat? Lily knew Kinsey would never willingly go inside one of these old deathtraps. Lily stepped up onto the wooden sidewalk, avoided a cave-in and entered the building. She plucked the yellow cap from the floor and scanned the empty room.

The only standing fixture was a counter along one wall. She leaned over it and found Kinsey on the floor. After rushing to her side, she knelt by her friend's body and felt for a pulse in her throat. When Kinsey's heartbeat leapt to greet her touch, Lily swallowed a sob of relief.

A red mark on Kinsey's head suggested she'd been hit. Who had done this to her and why?

How could it be Jeremy but how could it not? Her mind refused to leap farther than him, but it didn't make sense. He was in Canada. She searched Kinsey's pockets for her cell phone but couldn't find it. She had to get help. She had to know what happened. Maybe the phone was in the backpack with the art supplies still resting by the stool. She lifted Kinsey's shoulders, determined to drag her out of this building, but that wasn't as easy as it sounded.

Kinsey's eyes opened. "Gerard?" she mumbled.

"No, sweetie, it's me, Lily. Thank goodness you're awake. Can you stand up? We have to get you out of here."

"Gerard," Kinsey repeated. "Gerard…"

Lily relaxed her hold on the other woman's shoulders. "It's okay," she said, smoothing her hair. "I'll get help."

"…baby," Kinsey whispered as her eyes closed again.

Was she talking about Gerard or was it possible Kinsey was pregnant? Oh, God, if she died in this town carrying Gerard's baby the poor guy would never recover. Lily took off her coat and tucked it around Kinsey's still form, then she leaned over her and listened to the sound of her breathing. It seemed steady enough.

One way or another, she had to summon aid and the best bet for that was to find Kinsey's cell phone. She ran outside and started back toward the saloon, her gaze darting everywhere. Someone had hurt Kinsey. That someone was probably still around and there were so many places to hide…

Suddenly a man detached himself from the shadows of a covered sidewalk and stepped onto the street about a hundred feet away. "Lily," he said in a voice that still struck terror in her heart.

She turned around and took off, the sound of his laughter ringing out behind her. "Run if you want. Where are you going to go?"

Good question, but for now all she wanted was distance and her feet hit the ground with only that in mind. She looked back over her shoulder and saw that Jeremy had started running after her. She passed the building where Kinsey lay, her only thought to get this monster away from her friend and to escape herself.

Of course it was Jeremy. Who else would it be? His stride was longer than hers and he jogged every day of his life. She knew she could not outrun him forever. She also knew she would leave the relative safety of the town very soon and be out in the open. Glimpsing an alley between two buildings, she sprinted to her right. This would take her back toward the saloon and the promise of the phone, but the alley was a dangerous place as it was too narrow to offer protection. Doors opened off it, doors

that led into ramshackle structures, one more treacher-
ous than the next. A blast from behind kicked up a puff
of dirt to her left as Jeremy fired a gun at her, and she
realized nothing inside those buildings could be more
terrifying than what pursued her from behind.

She had to get that phone. She darted into a nondescript building and saw the door onto the street ahead of
her. Sure enough, she exited a few feet from the over-
turned stool. She grabbed the backpack and ran into the
saloon. There was no visible exit, in fact, most of the
back wall had crumpled inside. Footsteps sounded outside and she took the only route open to her and that was
the stairs. She stopped at the top and flattened herself
against a wall as she heard the thud of Jeremy's footsteps
grind to a halt below her.

"Lily!" he yelled.

She tried to quiet her breathing as she felt around the
heavy pack stuffed with Kinsey's art supplies. Momentary joy turned to despair when what she thought was
the phone turned out to be only a metal case for a small
package of tissues. The phone wasn't in the backpack.

"I know you're here," he said. He wasn't even breathing hard. "We can do this easy or we can do this hard."
She heard his footsteps as he approached the stairs.

She was terrified he would go back for Kinsey and
try to use her as a hostage. She couldn't think of a single
thing she could do to stop him. He was stronger, meaner,
and he had a gun. But he also had something else, something she understood the power of: he had nothing to lose.

"You didn't think I'd stay in Canada without a fitting
farewell to my lovely bride, did you?" he said. She could
hear him moving around. What was he doing down there?

She looked around the darkened area in which she

stood. It appeared to be a hallway with doors spaced along it like the rooms of a small hotel. One door stood open and light from it spilled into the dark hall. She inched along the wall. The creaks her footsteps created seemed to jump through the building.

"Might as well come down here," he called.

She wanted to tell him to shut up, but maybe she should engage him in dialogue. The sound of their voices might mask her movement. "I'm not your bride," she hollered.

He laughed. "My first wife is dead now, Lily. That kind of makes you my one and only."

"Elizabeth's not dead," Lily yelled.

"Au contraire," he said. Lily heard something splinter or break downstairs. "I took her out yesterday morning. One shot, right between the eyes. Damn good aim if I do say so myself. I could have done the same exact thing to you. I mean, I had you in my sights last night and this morning, too. But you've really been a pain in the ass. I want to put my hands around your lovely little neck. I want you to look at me when I kill you. I want you to know your lying lover is next. I've already done his family, I just need to find him. But I will. He'll die after you and so will anyone else who gets between me and my kid."

She swallowed what felt like an iceberg. "What did you do to Chance's family?"

"Never you mind. You have your own troubles."

"Please, please, just leave. Don't hurt anyone else, don't take Charlie, you don't love him," she said, coming to a halt across the hall from the open door. "He'll slow you down. You're on the run now."

"I am not on the run," he said. "People like you run, Lily. People like me triumph."

She stopped moving when she got across from the illuminated room. For a second, she struggled with her emotions, tears perilously close to blurring her vision. But that was what Jeremy wanted and she would never again give him the satisfaction of breaking her. People she loved were depending on her. She would not let them down.

She focused on the room. Half the outer wall had disintegrated, showing nothing through the opening but gray skies. What kind of structure was next door? She inched her way toward the light.

Maybe she could use Jeremy's emotions against him. He had to have a raw nerve somewhere. "What about your other son?" she called out.

He didn't respond.

"You must have freaked out when Maria reported that you and Elizabeth had a son and that very son was sitting downtown in your jail, a confessed murderer. How would that look to the people you kiss up to? They would have distanced themselves from you. Your career would be over. I'm surprised you didn't kill the boy yourself."

"Who said I didn't?" he said.

She stopped short. "You murdered Jimmy? How? He hung himself. Besides, I saw you that night, you came home and took out your anger on me."

"That wasn't anger, dear-heart, that was a celebration. I gave him the rope," he added, "in a figurative way, that is. I told him I knew he was covering for someone. I promised him I would find out who it was and I would prosecute them and then pull the switch on the electric chair myself. I swore I would then go after his mother and every whacko in White Cliff. The kid almost wet himself he was so scared. He asked what he could do to fix things and I told him what I once told you."

"You told him it would be better off all around if he

was dead," she said, reliving for an instant the moment he'd said the same thing to her. No wonder the boy killed himself. She had never met Jimmy but her gut clenched as she imagined the pain he must have felt when his long-lost father told him to sacrifice his own life to save the lives of the people he loved. Jimmy had been Charlie's half brother and he was dead and now this jerk wanted to take Charlie. "You are a bastard," she yelled.

"Sticks and stones," he said. "Take a deep breath, Lily. Do you smell something?"

She had inched her way into the room and now approached the crumbled wall. She couldn't allow Jeremy to take Charlie. She had to do something. The roof of the building next door was six feet away with a drop of about the same. The roof had caved in in one place. She might possibly survive a jump but would her weight and momentum send her crashing down through layers of rotting wood?

And then Jeremy's last comment finally sank into her brain. She crept back toward the hall and sniffed the air—smoke!

"The flames are almost touching the stairs," Jeremy called. "Unless you want to burn to death, you better come on down and take your chances with me. I wouldn't wait too long to make up your mind."

Smoke was seeping through the boards by her feet, drawn to the open wall behind her. If she went down-stairs he would shoot or strangle her. If she jumped out that window, she chanced injury or death.

She turned around, gripped Kinsey's backpack in front of her to provide some cushion between her bones and the roof, ran toward the opening and jumped. She hit the neighboring building with a crash and lay very still for a few seconds, not sure if she was just winded from the fall or hurt more badly, taking shallow breaths to control the pain and afraid to move lest the roof give in. Her leg throbbed and her hands burned.

The smell of smoke was more pronounced. A fire in this dead town would move quickly, leaping from roof to roof until there was nothing left but ashes. Kinsey was unconscious less than a block away and no one knew she was there but Lily. Somehow she had to recover enough to get off this roof, evade Jeremy and drag Kinsey out of that building.

Sensing movement, she struggled into a sitting position in time to witness Jeremy launch himself from the opening through which smoke now billowed. He landed a few feet away from her and immediately started to stand, but the stress of his impact following hers was too much for the old roof and it groaned like a tortured ghost. As Jeremy pulled the gun from his waistband, the roof cracked one last time and gave way. Lily fell downward with the wreckage, gripping the raw wood beneath her to keep from sliding into free fall.

Her sitting position helped her maintain some balance and she landed on top of a heap of rubble, jarred to the bone. Debris rained down on her head and the smell of smoke was already creeping into the building. She glanced upward and saw ragged beams torn from the walls and roof, some swinging precariously.

She turned to look for Jeremy. Caught in motion when the roof gave way, he hadn't fared as well as she had and had landed farther down the pile of rubble. He lay face-down, his left arm twisted at a terrible angle. Even as she stared, he somehow got to his feet and lifted the gun with his right hand. The barrel pointed straight at her chest.

Lily realized she still clutched the backpack. She heaved it forward as hard as she could, her strength and aim sharpened by desperation. At the same moment the pack hit the top of his head, the gun exploded, deafening her. She fell onto her bottom and slid downward, grasping for something to stop her descent, finally coming to a halt when a jutting board caught her in the chest. For a second she sat there winded again, eyes closed, trying to breathe, waiting for searing pain to announce where Jeremy's bullet had struck her. Pain didn't come.

She opened her eyes. There was no sign of the backpack but Jeremy lay nearby, on his back, staring upward at flames licking the edges of what was left of the roof. She didn't see his gun anywhere but she fully expected him to rally yet again.

And then she saw the blood spurting from his neck where a nail-studded board had apparently fallen from the rafters, pinning him down and puncturing his carotid artery. She scrambled toward him on stinging hands and skinned knees. The glancing impact of the backpack must have knocked him off his feet. Maybe a reflex action of his trigger finger fired the gun and maybe the bullet dislodged the rafter that subsequently fell, impaling him.

He blinked and she realized he was still alive. Half afraid the geyser of blood was really a trick of some kind, she moved even closer. Thoughts of smoke and mirrors vanished as she watched the color drain from his skin, shrinking him before her eyes. She knelt beside him. The edge of a handkerchief stuck out of his pocket and she grabbed it. Kinsey's phone tumbled out with the cloth. Lily held the handkerchief against his neck without touching the horrid board, without hearing the fire overhead or feeling the warmth of his blood splattering against her arm. The contact of the cloth seemed to signal his dying brain that he wasn't alone. His focus shifted to her face for the briefest of seconds, recognition dawned in his eyes and then he looked straight through her into oblivion.

"Lily!"

She jerked. The action slid her against Jeremy. Repulsed, she stood on wobbly legs as Chance and Gerard ran into the building. Both men stopped suddenly as their gazes traveled from the dead man, up to her face and then to the roof.

"Look out!" Gerard yelled.

Lily glanced upward and saw a burning board teetering over her head. Caught in some kind of limbo, she saw sparks fly across the sky. The next thing she knew, Chance was beside her. He threw her over his shoulder and scrambled down the pile before shifting her weight into his arms and handing her down to Gerard who asked if she could stand. She nodded. Chance jumped to the ground and grabbed one of her arms. Gerard took the other. It felt to Lily like she flew out of there on the wings of two guardian angels. A crash from behind announced the rest of the ceiling had tumbled into the building.

Her feet finally hit the dirt of Main Street. Chance grabbed her arms and searched her face. "Are you okay? You're covered with blood. Where are you hurt?"

"It's Jeremy's blood," she said breathlessly. "You have to find Kinsey. She's in a nearby building. It's on the right side of the street as you come into town, the store with a long counter running along the back wall. You have to go save her."

"Sounds like the old mercantile," Chance said, glancing at Gerard who was already running down the street.

Lily looked back at Chance to find him studying her hands, which she was surprised to see were torn and bleeding from abrasions and imbedded splinters. No wonder they hurt. Pain was good, though. Pain meant she'd survived despite all the odds, despite Jeremy's pathological desire to erase her from the earth, despite her own misjudgments.

Chance kissed her wrist. "Oh, my darling, darling girl," he whispered, and met her gaze. There were tears in his eyes. She'd never been so happy to see anyone as she was him but that wasn't true, she'd felt this same way when she found Charlie in Maria's car. "Where's my child?" she asked.

"He's with my father."

"I'm so relieved to hear that. Jeremy insinuated he killed your family before he hit Kinsey and shooed away our horses."

"He was playing head games with you," Chance said.

"It might have worked if it hadn't been for Charlie and Kinsey…and you."

"You need to see a doctor," he said.

"I need you," she responded. "And Charlie and a pair of tweezers and some bandages."

"What happened to Block?"

"I'll tell you the long story later. The short version is he did his best to kill me but caused his own death instead. I might have contributed to that conclusion."

"That's my girl," he said, and raising her chin, kissed her lips.

She'd been fighting loving him for over nine months, leery of caring more than he did, of being hurt, of losing him because she gave herself to him, not just with her body, but with her heart. And all that meant was that she'd been running, yet again, but from herself this time…from the truth.

And she was done. The truth was she loved him. The truth was she needed him. He could accept those truths or not, his response couldn't change the way she felt, the way she would always feel about him.

Chance's and Gerard's horses were skittish because of the increasing smoke and danced around as Chance led them down the street. Lily took her first real breath of relief as Gerard helped Kinsey walk out of the mercantile. The fact she was on her feet was amazing to Lily, and she felt tears of thankfulness sting behind her nose. Kinsey held out Lily's coat and Chance took it, draping it around Lily's shoulders.

Kinsey leaned close to Lily. "Thank you," she said.

Lily produced a wry smile. "For almost getting you killed? Twice?"

"For helping me," she said. "For sending Gerard."

"Your baby," Lily whispered.

Kinsey smiled and touched her stomach area. "Don't tell Gerard, though. Not yet."

"That's your news to share," Lily said as her gaze traveled down the street to the flames tearing through the old wood. In a triumph of poetic justice, Jeremy's body burned in the inferno he'd created.

Chance called his dad who said he would err on the side of safety by topping off the tank in the water-hauling truck and driving the alternate route up to the plateau and across to the ghost town, just in case the winds shifted. He also said he would call the police and all four of them groaned as they anticipated the rash of questions to come.

There was no sign of the two horses Jeremy had released, but they did find a big roan tethered outside of town. "That's one of our mares," Gerard said, pausing to help Kinsey climb into the saddle.

"Block must have let the horses out of the field when he stole her," Chance said. "I never thought to check the tack and see if any of that was missing."

Gerard climbed onto his horse and Chance lifted Lily into the saddle and climbed behind her. There was no way she could handle reins with her injured hands but his arms provided all the stability she needed.

"I have to tell you some bad news," Chance said as they rode along. "Elizabeth was killed yesterday."

"I know about that. Jeremy bragged about shooting her through the forehead. But how did you know?"

"Seth Brighton called. His father had been trying to reach you since realizing the only one in the world who would shoot Elizabeth as she stood at the sink inside her own house staring out at all those dead sunflower plants was Jeremy Block. When he couldn't get ahold of you, he asked Seth to call me. Then Gerard tried to call Kinsey but she didn't answer."

"Jeremy took her phone," Lily said. "She was out cold in the mercantile."

"I died a thousand times between hearing that Block was on a murdering rampage and the moment I found you," Chance added.

"I know the feeling," she said, leaning her head against his chest. "When he told me he was going after you next, it was as if he nailed spikes into my heart."

Chance kissed the top of her head. "Just so you know, I'm not letting you out of my sight again."

She turned to look into his dark eyes. "You're not?"

"No. I'll marry you if I have to."

She frowned. "Don't do me any favors."

"I didn't mean it that way—"

"Then how did you mean it? I took care of myself pretty darn good back there."

"Sure you did. One more minute and you would have been buried under a ton of burning roof."

"Now just a minute. You act like I go around getting into trouble just so you have to rescue me."

"I wouldn't put it past you."

"There's that ego again—"

He put a finger against her lips. "Just shut up and kiss me, will you please?"

"Oh, what the hell," she said, and touched her lips to his.

* * * * *

Look for more books in Alice Sharpe's
THE BROTHERS OF HASTINGS RIDGE RANCH
in 2016!

'The perfect Christmas read!' - Julia Williams

Jewellery designer Skylar loves living London, but
when a surprise proposal goes wrong, she finds
herself fleeing home to remote Puffin Island.

Burned by a terrible divorce, TV historian Alec is
dazzled by Sky's beauty and so cynical that he
assumes that's a bad thing! Luckily she's on the
verge of getting engaged to someone else, so she
won't be a constant source of temptation... but this
Christmas, can Alec and Sky realise that they are
what each other was looking for all along?

Order yours today at
www.millsandboon.co.uk